OLD GUNS

J.N. CHANEY

AND

NICHOLAS SANSBURY SMITH

Podium

ISBN: 979-8-3470-0164-4

Published in 2026 by Podium Publishing
www.podiumentertainment.com

Podium

To Jeff Chaney and the incredible teams at Variant and Podium,

Thank you for believing in this story and for the support.

I can't wait for readers to meet Frank and Martin;

two washed-up old guns who still have plenty of fight and laughs left in them.

OLD GUNS

PROLOGUE

2173

Giving scientists weapons has to be the dumbest idea in the history of the Marine Corps," Frank Cage muttered. The gunnery sergeant adjusted his position on the ridge overlooking the mining colony. The afternoon sun beat down on his Aegis armor, or Lucky as he referred to her, making the inside of the suit feel like an oven.

"Hell, I'm not sure I disagree with you," said Master Sergeant Martin Kelvin. He shook his head and whistled low as a new group of scientists in full hazard suits walked out of a prefab structure, pistols on their hips.

Below the two Marines stretched the Cretin-4 research outpost, a collection of prefabricated structures arranged in concentric rings around the central science facility. This was just one potential mining location of thousands being targeted by the Colonial Shield Federation. CSF comprised all governmental entities overseeing the colonies established and being established among the dozen planets of the Lort System—humanity's new home in the stars.

The red-tinged landscape of this world gave the whole scene an otherworldly glow as a team of twenty researchers in environmental suits collected samples from the mineral formations that jutted from the dusty plains like broken teeth. From this distance, they looked like children playing in a red sandbox. They were actually searching for deposits of quantum-stabilized xenorite—essential for advanced navigation systems. The scientific mission was to determine if the planet could support large-scale mining operations without causing atmospheric destabilization.

That was why their squad and all of Terminator Platoon had been assigned as security detail. Most of their platoon had lucked out and were with Lieutenant Payton back at the spaceport five miles from here, but Frank and Martin were stuck with their squad here at the field labs.

Shield Command wasn't taking chances after the last science expedition had encountered the native fauna that the scientists had affectionately named "tunnel crawlers" and Frank had less affectionately named "death worms." Those rhino-skinned creatures the length of anacondas were the reason that command had authorized issuing the scientists sidearms, a terrible idea in Frank's opinion, but he didn't have a PhD.

"Dr. Big Head Little Body has his sidearm out again," Frank said. "I got a round of drinks he shoots himself before the day is up."

Between the two Marines, they had given each of the scientists working down there nicknames out of pure boredom. Big Head Little Body seemed to have a real problem leaving his gun alone.

The scientist drew his sidearm and looked straight down the barrel.

"Oh shit!" Martin wailed.

Big Head Little Body fiddled with the weapon and aimed it at the ground.

"Jesus," Frank said, letting out a breath he had held in.

"I thought we were about to see what a million-dollar brain looks like as mush."

"Yeah, me too."

"Hey, Doctor, uh . . ."

"Payton," Frank said.

"Don't point the gun at yourself or anyone else!" Martin shouted down.

The scientist looked up at them on the ridgeline, then pointed at something in the ground and yelled out an indistinct reply.

"Probably saw a bug and got scared," Frank muttered.

"You'd think people with PhDs would understand 'don't point the shooty end at your face.'"

"You'd think, but maybe they believe they can just grow new faces if they blow theirs off?" Frank said with a shrug. He pulled out his water bottle and took a slug that probably looked more like he was downing a shot of vodka. It wouldn't be the first time, and he would have brought some along if they had any on this backwater base.

"Three more days of this shithole, then we're back to real work." He grunted.

"Back to changing diapers?" Martin countered.

"Brother, Lily is nine now, she is house-trained."

"House-trained? What is she, a dog?"

"Funny." Frank laughed. "I guess I forgot you were in diapers until you were six."

"Oh ha ha, that's a good one," Martin mocked, holding his stomach. "You really got me, Cage. You seem to forget I have two kids of my own."

Frank shrugged again. "You telling me you actually changed diapers back then?"

"No, Lucia did everything," Martin said, regret in his voice. "Wasn't around much back then."

"Yeah, I remember."

They had both been in the Marines for twenty-one years, and Martin's daughter, Terecia, and son, Thomas, were at university now. Growing up with Martin being deployed so often was hard on them, but even harder on his now ex-wife, Lucia. Frank had hoped they would work out their problems, but they had recently decided to divorce. It was understandable; hell, Frank had his own marital issues being a married Marine. Sarah was the love of Frank's life, but marriage was hard. Especially with a young child.

Still, thinking of them made Frank a little homesick. Sarah was waiting for him back at Titan Station with their daughter, Lily.

"You remember how little kids ask so many questions?" Frank asked.

"Oh yeah. One day I counted Thomas asking me 'why' over fifty times." Martin chuckled.

"Lily is so damn smart she can answer a lot of her own questions."

"Takes after her mom."

"Smarts and looks, thank God." Frank laughed again in his deep voice. "Straight up beauty and the beast. Not denying it."

"Since when were you humble?"

"Since I got this detail of babysitting science jockeys that get paid ten times what we do."

"Well the shit they're searching for is like gold, brother."

"Yeah, and looks like one of the teams found something," Frank said. He raised his own binoculars to the eastern valley. Working in the shadows of the canyons, four scientists had crowded around to examine something in the red soil. "Ripke and Natalia are in position over that area, right?"

Martin checked his tactical display. "Yeah. Ripke is at the south ridge with the heavy weapons. Natalia's running patrol on the east side. Will's still inside fiddling with the sensor grid."

"Of course he is," Frank muttered. Corporal Will Popovich was brilliant with tech, but getting him out from behind his screens was like trying to separate a hungry Marine from his rations.

"Hello!" someone called out.

A lanky scientist in pristine expedition gear picked his way up the ridge, waving enthusiastically. Frank and Martin exchanged a look of resignation.

Frank sighed. "If he wants us to wipe his ass, you're gonna have to do it."

"Like hell," Martin scoffed.

"Sergeants!" The man was breathless by the time he reached them. "Dr. Lowell. Xenobiology. I was hoping to discuss the weaponry requirements for our expedition tomorrow. The southeastern quadrant shows promising—"

"Doc," Frank interrupted, "these aren't research toys. They're for keeping you alive when you poke things that might want to eat you."

Dr. Lowell pushed his glasses up his nose. "Actually, that's precisely my concern. Last week's incident with the native fauna suggests—"

"You mean when Dr. Marcus nearly got his arm torn off because he ignored our perimeter markers?" Martin stood, towering over the scientist. "How about we make a deal? You stay within the safe zone, we don't have to shoot anything."

Frank grimaced at the memory. Dr. Marcus had ventured beyond the established security perimeter to collect samples from a mineral outcropping. By the time Ripke reached him, the tunnel crawler had already punctured his environmental suit and was working on his arm. The doctor was lucky to be alive.

"The data we could gather just six kilometers beyond your arbitrary boundaries—" Lowell started to say.

"Those boundaries exist because that's how far we can guarantee your safety," Frank cut in. "We've got one squad of Marines to cover twenty scientists on a planet we've barely mapped. Those 'arbitrary boundaries' are all that's keeping you from ending up like Marcus."

"My research requires it, sir."

"Don't call me sir," Frank said.

"My apologies, but you must be aware that the lack of intelligent alien life in the Lort System has long been a mystery to us," he said. "There are five habitable planets, and twelve total planets, yet no advanced intelligence has developed in the Lort System. Why? My work, especially here, will help determine—"

"Your work won't do shit if the nonintelligent life-forms eat your head and big brain," Frank said.

He resisted the urge to tell this guy he was an idiot, that there were intelligent life-forms out there—the Hollow—but Frank and Martin were two of only a handful of people that knew the alien race existed. They had the unfortunate experience of first contact with them eight years ago on a mission in the Gauntlet, a wormhole that brought humanity to this very system. On that mission, their squad was assigned to locate a missing research vessel named *Squanto*, which was searching for a way through the Gauntlet. The Hollow had found the ship first, leaving all but one of the crew torn to pieces in what looked like a science experiment. Frank and Martin had lost two good Marines when they arrived, not realizing they were up against alien creatures that could move through solid hatches and hulls and were almost impossible to kill.

Frank and Martin escaped with their lives and the coordinates that finally allowed humanity a path through the Gauntlet to the Lort System and habitable worlds like this. But for some reason, there were no Hollow on any of the twelve worlds. Not even a trace of them. They had become nothing more than bogeymen.

The frustrated scientist seemed ready to argue further with Frank when the simultaneous blare of emergency alerts from both Marines' comms cut through the conversation.

"PRIORITY ALPHA. TITAN STATION UNDER ATTACK. UNKNOWN HOSTILES. ALL AVAILABLE PERSONNEL RESPOND."

"Titan?" Frank's blood ran cold. His wife and daughter were on Titan.

"Has to be a mistake," Martin said. "Who would attack . . ."

Frank was already accessing additional channels, face grim as fragmented reports came through. Lowell backed away, sensing the sudden shift in atmosphere.

". . . multiple breaches in sectors three through seven . . . security teams ineffective . . ."

Frank's heart hammered against his ribs. "Sarah and Lily . . ."

Martin gripped his shoulder. "I'm sure they are being evacuated."

Their comms crackled again as a new transmission broke through, the voice panicked. ". . . unknown entities . . . conventional weapons having no effect . . ."

Frank and Martin exchanged a horrified look. That sounded eerily familiar to what they had encountered on *Squanto*. It was as if the galaxy had been listening to them, and this was some glitch.

"You think it's the—" Martin began.

"The Hollow," Frank said. He clenched his jaw at a flashback to first contact. "Fuck if it is . . ."

He was already moving before the words left his mouth.

Ripke jogged up with Natalia and Popovich. "We heard the alert," Ripke said.

Natalia's face was drawn tight, her dark eyes scanning the tactical readouts on her pad. "Multiple penetrations of the station's outer sectors are being recorded, but I don't have any other intel," she said. "Shield Command is already encrypting transmissions. They want this locked down."

"We have to call in a shuttle," Frank said. He looked down at the facilities below where the shuttle pads were located.

Popovich looked up from his pad with genuine fear. "Shield Command's denying all transport requests," he reported. "I already tried."

"Then we take the colony's shuttle," Frank said. "On me, move your asses."

The five members of the squad moved as one, their years of combat experience evident in the seamless coordination.

"Where are they going?" one of the researchers asked, shielding his eyes from the red sun.

"Something's happening at Titan Station," another replied, checking her comm unit. "Looks serious."

Frank reached the command center first and practically shoulder-checked the door open. Inside, six staff members looked up in surprise—the colony administrator, a communications officer, and four technical specialists. Displays around the room showed fragmentary footage from Titan Station, the images flickering with static.

"We need your transport shuttle," Frank announced, cutting straight to the point.

The administrator, a thin man with a perpetually worried expression, looked up from his console. "Absolutely not. All vessels are grounded by direct order from—"

Frank slammed his fist against a support column. "My wife and daughter are on that station."

"Wait," the administrator said, taking a step back. "Are you—are you leaving us?"

"Yeah," Frank said flatly. "Give me the launch codes."

"What?" The administrator looked horrified but then seemed to find his backbone. "I will not, sir."

"I'm not a sir," Frank said. He pulled his sidearm from its holster. "Give me the launch codes."

"Easy, Frank," Martin said, placing a hand on his friend's shoulder. But he didn't try to lower the weapon.

The administrator's eyes widened at the gun. "This is madness! You're threatening CSF personnel!"

Ripke stepped up beside Frank, his imposing frame adding weight to the demand. "We need to get in the air. Give us the damn codes, sir."

The administrator looked at Ripke.

"I can't authorize—"

"You don't need to authorize anything," Natalia cut in, sliding past them to the communications console. "Just give us the codes, and we'll be out of your hair."

The administrator hesitated, his eyes darting between the armed Marines. Finally, with shaking hands, he reached for his terminal.

"Access code Alpha-Seven-Nine-Echo-Delta," he said. "But this is under extreme duress. I want that noted."

"Noted," Frank said, holstering his weapon. "Will, get to the shuttle and start the preflight. Ripke, grab whatever weapons and supplies you can. Five minutes."

The technicians watched in stunned silence as the Marines prepared to leave.

"The tunnel crawlers," one of them said suddenly. "What happens if they attack while you're gone?"

Frank paused at the door. "Stay inside the perimeter. Keep your weapons close." He glanced at the administrator. "And don't point them at those big brains of yours."

Within minutes, the squad reached the shuttle bay. The craft wasn't much: an atmospheric transport modified for short orbital jumps, not designed for this long of a jump, but it would get the job done. Hopefully, maybe . . .

Popovich was already at the controls, bypassing security protocols to prep the ship for launch, while Ripke loaded what weapons they had on hand. Natalia established communication channels, trying to piece together more information from the fragmented reports.

"Lieutenant Payton is going to have our nuts," Martin said.

"I could give two shits," Frank said. "That's my family on board."

"I know—"

"Then you know I will do anything to get to them. You would do the same for your kids and Lucia."

Martin nodded.

As the squad boarded, Frank received a direct transmission from Shield Command: "All CSF personnel are ordered to maintain position. Titan Station is under quarantine. No transports are authorized in or out."

"What the hell?" Ripke whispered. "They're not even trying to evacuate?"

Frank didn't respond. His mind was fixated on reaching Sarah and Lily.

The shuttle broke atmosphere, straining its engines beyond safety limits and preparing for jump. Behind them, the rest of the squad checked weapons and prepared for whatever they might find.

"ETA?" Natalia asked, strapping herself into the copilot's chair.

"Ninety minutes with standard propulsion," Frank answered. "But we don't have that kind of time."

"Engaging CAT drive," Martin announced. "Coordinates locked for Titan Station."

Popovich was running calculations on his pad. "The engines weren't designed for sustained acceleration at this level," he said. "We're going to burn them out."

"Then we burn them out," Frank replied. "As long as they get us there."

"We'll make it," Martin assured him. "Quantum jump in 3 . . . 2 . . . 1 . . ."

The shuttle shuddered as the Compactified Access Tunnel drive kicked in and reality seemed to fold around them. The viewport filled with swirling energy—ribbons of blue and violet light stretching into infinity. The quantum corridor was both beautiful and terrifying, a twisted path through the fabric of space-time that could shave hours off their journey . . . or tear them apart if the calculations were wrong.

Inside the corridor, time lost meaning. The hull creaked under the massive strain. It was designed to withstand this type of pressure but still felt like it was about to come apart at the seams. Displays flickered with warning signals that Popovich hurriedly overrode.

"Power fluctuations in the aft stabilizers," he reported, sweat beading on his forehead. "We're redlining everything."

"Keep it together," Martin muttered, as much to the ship as to the crew.

The journey passed in tense silence, broken only by fragmentary reports and static-filled screams coming through on emergency channels. Frank tried repeatedly to contact Sarah, getting nothing but dead air.

With a final, violent shudder, the shuttle burst from the quantum corridor, the swirling energy patterns giving way to the familiar blackness of space. Saturn loomed massive in the viewport, its rings stretching like a celestial highway across the darkness. And there, orbiting the gas giant's largest moon, was Titan Station.

Even from a distance, they could see it was badly damaged—sections torn open, emergency lights flickering across its surface like dying fireflies. Three CSF naval destroyers maintained position nearby, their sleek hulls gleaming in the distant sunlight, weapons systems visibly charged and ready.

"Oh god," Popovich whispered, staring at the scene before them. His fingers flew across his console. "I'm picking up an encrypted military channel. High-level command codes."

"Can you break it?" Martin asked, already bringing the shuttle in on a stealth approach vector.

"Working on it . . ."

As they drew closer, the true extent of the damage became clear. Entire sections of the station had been breached, atmosphere venting into space in crystalline clouds. And something else—strange patterns of light shifting across the hull where the damage was worst.

Popovich's face went pale as he decoded the transmission. "They're going to terminate the station," he said, looking up from his console with wide eyes. "Complete purge. No survivors."

"What?" Frank's voice was deadly quiet.

Frank hailed the station. "Titan Control, this is Marine transport SV-227 requesting emergency docking. I have family aboard."

The only response was static, until a military channel cut through: "Unidentified vessel, you are entering a restricted zone. Turn back immediately or you will be fired upon."

Frank grabbed the comm. "This is Gunnery Sergeant Frank Cage, CSF Marines. My wife and daughter are on that station! Request permission to attempt rescue!"

"Negative, Gunnery Sergeant. Shield Command has declared Titan Station compromised. Stand down and reverse course."

One of the destroyers was turning toward them now, weapons locking on.

"They'll shoot us down," Ripke said.

Martin's jaw set in a hard line. "No, they won't." He opened a channel directly to the destroyer. "This is Master Sergeant Martin Kelvin. I served with Captain Harding. He knows me. Put him on."

Seconds stretched into an eternity before a new voice came through: "Martin? What the hell are you doing?"

"James, Frank's family is on that station. We just want a chance to get them out."

A long pause. "The station has been overrun with unknown contacts."

"Hollow," Frank said.

This can't be happening . . . not again.

"We need thirty minutes," Martin pressed. "Just thirty minutes to get in and out."

Another pause. "You have thirty minutes before I'm ordered to open fire. After that, I can't help you."

The channel went dead.

"Thirty minutes," Frank said. It wasn't much, but it was something—a chance.

Assuming his family was even still alive.

CHAPTER ONE

2188

The damned weeds would be the death of him.

They resisted the assault of fifty-four-year-old Master Gunnery Sergeant (retired) Martin Kelvin like no other enemy had in his entire career as a CSF Marine, refusing to be rooted out and constantly returning in the face of fire, chemical weapons, and sheer brute force.

I could have done this better when I was one-hundred-percent flesh and blood, he told himself, though he knew it was a lie. The bionic prosthetics were just as agile as his old leg and arm, and he was probably stronger than he would have been without them. Not stronger than he'd been in his prime, of course, but his prime had been over twenty years ago. How *much* over, he constantly debated with himself . . . and with Cosmo. Cosmo's opinion was the only other one that mattered to him.

Martin wiped the sweat out of his eyes with the eagle, globe, and anchor tattoo on the back of his right arm and cast an accusatory look at Cosmo.

"Why the hell am I the only one working here?" Martin grumbled. "You just gonna sit there and watch the whole time?"

"Woof," Cosmo replied earnestly, regarding him with the same big brown eyes that had forced Martin to pick him out of all the other pups in the shelter.

He was probably purebred German shepherd, or at least close enough that Martin had never bothered to get him DNA-tested. Not that it mattered. Whether Cosmo had genes that took him all the way back to Max von Stephanitz in 1899 or had a few mutts in the closet mattered not to the dog's primary job . . . keeping one Martin Kelvin sane and, barely, stable.

It would be easy for him to go off the deep end out here, in the middle of nowhere, BFE, with no one for company except the trees and open fields and some pretty mountains in the background. Someone had named the planet

Eden, which it looked like now, in summer, but which seemed very ironic in the dead of winter when Martin was snowed in for days at a time, stuck in the house with old movies and older memories.

The dog had been a condition of his retirement, forced on him by the psychological therapists at the Veteran's Administration. He'd fought tooth and nail right up until the minute he'd seen a ten-week-old Cosmo. How long ago had that been?

Around a decade now, maybe a bit longer, maybe not.

Martin could have looked up the exact date on his link, but that would have involved breaking his concentration on the battle with the weeds. It seemed inconsequential compared to his former job, defending the colonies, but it was just as important to his survival. He needed the output of the garden to make it through the winter. Not that he'd starve to death, being honest. The local CSF office would loan him the money to buy food, but going into debt would mean he couldn't live off his retirement, and he was bound and determined *not* to be forced into the ultimate humiliation of getting a real job.

No, he was content picking weeds on his little homestead and avoiding the bottle, unlike Frank Cage, his best friend.

Former, best friend.

Forget that shit. Pull weeds.

Pulling weeds was easy. Just physical work. He could turn off his brain and let the memories stream away from him. But thinking about Frank had short-circuited the process, and even the rhythmic motion couldn't put the memories to sleep. He didn't need to look up when the last time he saw Frank was, almost five years to this day when they bumped into each other in town with their dogs. It wasn't even noon and Frank was already well on his way to being shit-faced.

They had made eye-contact, and instantly the anger in Frank's gaze ignited like a wildfire. "What right did you have, you bald motherfucker!" he had shout-slurred.

Cosmo and Rex had growled, but not at each other. They had prevented Frank and Martin from getting into a brawl right in the middle of the street.

That memory transported Martin back farther, to images of war; screaming faces, frozen in their death masks, horror and fear. The faces of the Marines were bad, but the faces of the civilians, the *children*, those were the worst.

"Dammit," he murmured.

Cosmo sensed it, as always, and rubbed against his prosthetic leg, whining for attention. Martin sighed and gave it to him, as always. Cosmo loved to have his ears scratched, and his anxiety at his master's stress evaporated into bliss, his tongue hanging out in a goofy smile that put the lie to his fierce appearance. Martin smiled. He couldn't help it. The memories faded as he concentrated on making the one creature he could always count on happy.

But the past wouldn't give up. It always wormed its way back in, and this time, it chose something less subtle than a memory. He had a history of losing people. Not just Marines, but his family. Married twice, the first mostly just a fling, but the second lasting just twenty years.

Thinking of Lucia stirred up a host of emotions. The first was loss—truth was, Martin missed her, even though they couldn't live with each other. Living without her brought its own pain. Then there were their two adult children, Thomas and Terecia. Thomas had followed Martin's career path by joining the Marines, but later decided not to reenlist after his first tour of duty. In fairness, the young man had seen some horrible shit on that tour. Martin understood all too well and didn't judge his son for that. But it was Thomas's next gig that caused their falling out.

When Martin learned Thomas had joined a mercenary crew, it had caused a hell of a fight. "There is no honor in that," Martin had said.

"Honor," Thomas had snorted back. "Is honor what happened at Titan Station, Dad?"

They hadn't spoken since that visit over three years ago.

His daughter, Terecia, called every now and then, but she had moved to a colony on Dorn, the farthest habitable planet at the edge of the system, where she sought a quiet life with her husband, a farmer. Last time Martin heard from Terecia, she was having her third child. All three of which he had never seen. Not that he had been invited to visit. Maybe she thought he would screw up their childhoods like he had screwed up her own.

Martin let out a depressed sigh. His career had taken so much from him.

The link at his belt beeped for attention, and for a fleeting moment, he hoped maybe it was his one of his kids. But the beeping wasn't the tone of an incoming call or message, though that would have been surprising enough since the only people he heard from on a regular basis were the doctors at the VA and the bank that owned the loan on his property. No, this was something else, something less conventional and much less legal.

"Once a Marine, always a Marine" was the saying, and despite the urgings of his psych counselors, Martin just couldn't tear himself away from the political and military current events in the Republic beyond Eden. He'd bought the monitoring app software from a vendor at one of the outdoor markets in town, the kind who always had the best illegal drugs, guns, and apps. This one tapped into the Military Communications Net, decrypting what should have been secure communications, and its notifications occurred with even less frequency than the unwanted calls and messages.

Mostly, they were local alerts about security drills or the occasional ship in distress, commonplace things that still allowed him the luxury of amusement at the poor saps who'd have to deal with the sort of BS he'd endured for decades.

This was not one of those.

"Attention all CSF outposts," the recorded message announced. "This is a broadband alert. This is not a drill. Raxima Mining Corp at Taurus Four-Three has reported multiple attacks on their station by the 'Free Miners Coalition.' First casualty reports indicate civilian targets. Shield Command is ordering immediate deployment of available Marine units to the sector. Outposts in the vicinity are instructed to prepare reserve forces for possible activation. All vessels are advised to avoid the sector until further notice. More information to follow when it becomes available."

Martin whistled low. He'd heard about the unrest in several of the mining colonies. Corporate exploitation pushing the workers past their breaking point. But attacking civilian targets? That crossed a line. The Free Miners had been gaining sympathy in the outer colonies until now.

Still better than the Hollow.

His thoughts drifted to Frank again. Was his old friend still drowning his memories in the bottom of a bottle? The last time Martin had tried to call, Frank's words had been slurred, bitter, and full of the same accusations he'd been hurling since Titan Station. A memory that Martin buried by kicking at the ground.

He's probably drunk right now, while I'm out here fighting weeds.

Just two washed-up, old, cranky, retired Marines.

Martin's jaw tightened. Fighting weeds was better than fighting ghosts. Better than fighting the living, too. Even rebel miners with delusions of revolution.

Cosmo pawed at his leg, whining softly.

"I know, boy. Enough of the past for today."

Martin limped back to the house, his bionic leg glitching again. He swore as he dragged the metal limb for a step, Cosmo yelping in alarm before Martin righted himself.

"Dammit!" he thundered, slamming the door open. "Dammit, dammit, dammit!"

"Is everything alright, Master Gunnery Sergeant Martin?" his AI home assistant asked with solicitous sympathy. "Have you hurt yourself again?"

"What do you mean 'again,' you mechanical moron?" Martin snapped at the computer system, balancing himself against the doorframe and looking around the house.

The virtual AI didn't respond to his outburst, but the news feed activated automatically on the main screen. Martin froze as the footage played across his vision. The camera panned shakily over what had once been a biodome habitat in the mining colony's civilian sector. Emergency response teams moved through floating debris, retrieving bodies that drifted in the zero-g environment created by the dome's breach.

Some of the bodies were tiny.

Martin clenched his teeth. Children. The Free Miners had hit an area with a school. The camera zoomed in on a cluster of small, still forms, their school uniforms identifiable despite the damage. A stuffed toy floated nearby, spinning slowly in the vacuum—a teddy bear with one arm missing.

"Turn it off," Martin said hoarsely. When the AI didn't respond quickly enough, he bellowed, "TURN IT OFF!"

The screen went dark, but the images remained burned into his retinas. Cosmo pressed hard against his leg, whimpering, sensing the sudden spike in his master's distress. Martin's hand found the dog's head, fingers digging into the fur harder than he intended.

"Sorry, boy," he murmured, loosening his grip.

He stood there, staring at the dark screen, seeing not the blank surface but the faces of other children from another time. Frank's daughter, Lily. She'd been just nine and a half. Sarah, Frank's wife, had sent Martin pictures from the girl's dance graduation party just a week before Titan Station. Martin had been planning to send a gift but never got around to it. One of a thousand small regrets that somehow loomed larger than the big ones.

His artificial leg groaned as he crossed the room to the small cabinet in the corner. The green pills were for pain management, but Martin knew that was a lie the VA doctors told themselves so they could prescribe it. It was for days like this, when the memories circled like hungry wolves.

He grabbed a bottle of whiskey instead, poured a finger, then another. For a long moment, he stared at the amber liquid. Frank would be drinking today too, if the news had reached him. Drowning his memories of Sarah and Lily in the same way, but with less success. Frank's ghosts never seemed to let go, no matter how much he drank.

Martin raised the glass, then set it down untouched. No. Not today. Not this path. He had given it up after Titan Station. Given it up a few years too late. After his marriage to Lucia had shattered beyond repair.

Ironically, Frank had become the heavier drinker. Much heavier. Far heavier than Martin had ever been. A full-blown alcoholic. And nothing Martin had said back then to Frank worked. Most of the words only antagonized him more. For the past, for mistakes, for the things they had lost.

Cosmo watched Martin with concern.

"Don't worry, I'm not going back to those days, boy," Martin told the dog. "Been down that road. It doesn't help."

He limped to the door and paused to look at his old armor hanging on the wall. The Marines had stripped out the weapons and computer systems, of course, but it was still his, right down to the blast scars across the hip and shoulder. Reminders of how he'd gotten these prosthetics.

For a moment, he could almost feel the weight of it again. The reassuring hum of the servos, the tick of the targeting system in his helmet display, the solid presence of a new MR-110 phased plasma rifle in his hands. The certainty of purpose.

But those days were gone. Those certainties stripped away like the weapons from his armor.

"Come on, Cosmo," he muttered. Having changed his mind on the drink, he grabbed his hoe from where it leaned against the wall. "Those weeds aren't going to pull themselves."

As he stepped back into the harsh sunlight, Martin squinted up at the clear blue sky. Somewhere out there, Marines were loading into dropships, checking weapons, preparing to face whatever awaited them at the mining colony on Raxima. Young men and women who still believed in something.

He thought of Frank again. What would his old friend say if he could see Martin now? Probably call him a coward for running from his memories. For hiding out here while others fought the battles. Maybe Frank would be right.

Martin attacked a particularly stubborn weed with renewed vigor and tore it from the ground with a vicious yank. He straightened, his back protesting the movement. He almost laughed at the irony of his current situation. From fighting pirates, insurgents, and aliens, to hurting his back from a damn weed.

After breathing in the fresh air, he exhaled. His garden stretched before him, neat rows threatened by invasive intruders. A battle he could win, unlike so many others. A fight with clear enemies and achievable victory.

"Back to work," he muttered, more to himself than to Cosmo.

As he limped back out to his garden, the ghosts followed him, as they always did. But at least out here, under the Eden sun, they couldn't get too close. Not with Cosmo keeping watch, and not with enemies he could actually defeat—one stubborn weed at a time.

CHAPTER TWO

The dim pot lights in the ceiling lent a bit of anonymity to the patrons inside the dive bar, their weak glow failing to reach the faux wood wall panels that amplified the song on the jukebox. It reminded Master Gunnery Sergeant (retired) Frank Cage of Titan Station. Most things did these days. Living in Hephaestus on Eden, so near to the CSF Marine base, meant constant reminders: Marines in uniform, training platoons in powered armor clomping along dirt roads. Each one dragged up memories he'd rather keep buried in the bottom of a bottle.

Like the memory of dancing with Sarah to the very song playing on the jukebox now, something by a guy named Moby.

Who the f names their kid Moby? Frank wondered.

Whoever did, it was a long ass time ago. Ancient history. Like his life. Some days he forgot how old he was.

"Old as dirt," he muttered as he took a slug of warm beer.

You're going to be fifty-five this year, Frank thought. *Or is that next year?*

"Next year, dummy."

He'd stopped celebrating or even acknowledging his birthdays other than his twenty-eight years of service with the Marines. There was no reason to remember anything else, without anyone to celebrate with besides his dog, who had no damn clue what a birthday even was. It was better to forget.

You got a head start on that today, bub.

He downed his ninth beer, and it wasn't even noon.

Going to set a record today, Frank, he thought.

The alcohol served its purpose, keeping most of the bad memories at bay. He'd learned to maintain a careful balance—enough to numb the pain but not so much that the nightmares took over. Memories of Sarah and Lily could remain happy thoughts with the right amount of beer coursing through his system. Without it, the horrific images of what happened at Titan Station invariably surfaced.

His ritual was precise, almost sacred in its consistency. Wake up sweating from whatever nightmare had followed him from the previous night. Take the first shot of whatever was closest—usually the half-empty whiskey bottle by his bed—to quiet the shadows in his mind. Feed his dog, Rex. Then throw on one of five different T-shirts with self-made lines to help him afford the day's expenses. Today, it was "*Drinking-Powered Story Machine: Insert Beer to Activate.*"

Then he would hit a bar by midmorning and nurse free and paid-for beers at a slow but steady pace, just enough to keep the tremors from starting while maintaining the protective fog that blunted memory's razor edge.

Some days were harder than others. Anniversaries were the worst—Lily's birthday, his and Sarah's wedding day. Those required tactical planning, a full arsenal of liquor prepared in advance because he knew from experience that bars wouldn't serve him once he got to a certain point. Those mornings inevitably led to those nights, with Rex whining softly beside him as he sobbed into the dog's fur, the alcohol no longer strong enough to hold back the flood.

Today wasn't an anniversary, just a regular Wednesday, but something about the dumb song by the dumb guy named Moby had conjured Sarah's face more vividly than usual. He grimaced as he sipped the India pale ale. It wasn't his brand, wasn't even his preferred type of beer. He liked them dark and strong enough to stand up to the demons in his head. But since he hadn't paid for this one, he couldn't complain. He just made a face and took another pull, needing to finish it before Heather, the bartender, noticed him drinking a beer he hadn't paid for. The regular bartender, Fedor, would have found it amusing, but Heather had absolutely no sense of humor.

Frank chugged the rest of the beer, then pushed the empty mug away from him.

Ten down.

Heather looked back sharply at the movement, but his hands were already folded innocently around the soda he'd purchased an hour before to have an excuse to sit at the bar. He whistled softly, eyes wandering everywhere except to meet hers.

The Jukebox—the bar's name and not just a feature—sparkled in holographic letters above an empty dance floor. Frank hadn't danced since . . . He squeezed his eyes shut against the thought, more difficult than it had once been since one of them was cybernetic now. He hadn't danced since Sarah. He never would again.

The doctors at the VA had tried to get him into support groups after Titan Station. Grief counseling. Addiction management. PTSD therapy. He'd attended exactly one session of each before deciding that alcohol was a far more reliable therapist. The counselors couldn't understand what he'd experienced there or in the Gauntlet eight years before Titan Station. None of them had witnessed the silver-liquid nightmares phasing through solid matter on the missing recon ship, *Squanto*, when they'd taken Torres and turned him into something that chose a bullet over continuing to exist. They hadn't lost everything that mattered in a single moment of military incompetence.

The VA's solution had been medication—pills that left him feeling hollow and numb in a different way than the alcohol did. At least with drinking, there were moments of warmth, brief interludes where he could remember Sarah's smile without seeing her dead body floating in vacuum. The pills just flattened everything, turned the world gray. The alcohol let him feel something, even if that something was often just a prelude to pain.

He needed another beer.

A burly sergeant entered with his entourage, laughing too loudly and posturing like he owned the place. "Hey there, Heather!" the man boomed. "How about you bring five drafts of stout around for me and my squad? Actually, make it six . . . I'm feeling extra thirsty after killing that PT test today."

Frank's ears perked up. A good stout would be perfect right now.

"I'm gonna hit the head first," the loudmouth announced. "Jimmy, Carl, you two stay here and wait for the beers. And if you even touch mine, I'll beat the piss out of the both of you."

Frank sized them up as the sergeant and his E-5 toadies headed for the bathroom. Jimmy and Carl were lance corporals, looking young and impressionable. Perfect marks. He slid over to them.

"Are you two fine young Marines in the armored infantry?" Frank asked, his casual banter practiced and paternal.

"Hell yeah, we are," the older one said, acne scars dotting his face. His gaze went to Frank's shirt. "That's funny," he said with a youthful grin. "We're both right out of advanced training. Got our own Aegis suits and everything."

"They made me a plasma gunner," the younger one enthused. "That thing kicks ass! Ain't nothing can stand up against a plasma gun!"

"I said that my entire career," Frank said, voice smooth as aged whiskey. "There are distinct advantages to having a plasma gun in a fight. For instance, our old friends the Hollow. Plasma's about the only thing that'll touch them. At least, in my experience."

Both young men froze, staring open-mouthed, and Frank knew he'd struck gold.

"You fought against the Hollow?" asked Jimmy, the youngest of the bunch.

"The Hollow were real?" Carl shook his head, drawing attention to his cauliflower ears. "I always thought they were like a bogeyman story."

The mere mention of them sent a chill through Frank that even ten beers couldn't fully suppress. His hand twitched involuntarily, seeking another drink like a drowning man grasping for air. The Hollow weren't just enemies he'd fought; they were the nightmares that lived in the shadows of his consciousness, waiting for sobriety to give them form and voice.

Heather arrived with the beers just then. After Jimmy paid, Frank lowered his gaze toward the faded text on his sweaty T-shirt. Then he cleared his throat, like a bellman asking for a tip without actually asking.

"Oh right," Jimmy said. "Here . . ."

He passed him a free beer, and Frank happily continued his story, casually helping himself to one of the stouts as the young Marines hung on his every word.

"Like I was telling you," he said, voice unsteady but not entirely from acting, "the Hollow are like ghosts. They don't really exist in space and time the way everything else does."

Frank took a long drink, feeling the rich stout wash down his throat, momentarily silencing the screams that lived in his memory. The alcohol was a welcome anesthetic, numbing the places in his mind he didn't dare touch sober.

"But plasma will hurt them?" Carl asked hopefully.

"Depends." Frank shook his head and took another long pull of beer.

His hand trembled slightly as he set the glass down. The tremors subsided as the alcohol took hold, blurring the edges of memories that otherwise cut like knives.

"Those things shift, and change, like living ghosts." Frank's voice dropped. "The Hollow, if they touch you, they kind of . . . inject you somehow. Phase through you and leave something behind. You start to . . . change."

He patted his chest with his cybernetic hand. The two recruits noticed it for the first time, their eyes widening at the plasticky, VA-issue prosthetic.

"In here. You change into one of them." Frank downed the rest of the mug. "I never saw that though. Everyone who started to . . . they killed themselves first."

A memory of his squad's first contact with the Hollow on *Squanto* pushed through the alcohol barrier. In it, he saw his squad mate Corporal Torres with his brains splattered across the bulkhead after one of those things had gotten to him. The images came in disconnected flashes now: Torres screaming as silvery lines spread beneath his skin. The way his eyes had changed, becoming pools of quicksilver. The sound of the pistol as he raised it to his temple, preferring death to whatever was happening inside him.

Frank had seen it all. Had nearly been next. Sometimes, in his darkest moments of drunken introspection, he wondered if maybe he had been infected too—if something of the Hollow had been left inside him, something that had killed the man he used to be, leaving this barren shell that needed to be perpetually filled with alcohol to function.

The empty stout glass was behind him now as he eyed another. Just one more drink to keep the memories at bay, to maintain the delicate balance between remembering and reliving.

"Hey, what the hell are you doing, old man?"

The sergeant had returned, his face flushed with anger. Frank's hand slipped, knocking over a full glass of stout.

"Oh, sorry about that," Frank said, flexing his artificial fingers. "It's a prosthetic. Sometimes it glitches."

"You're paying for that, you crippled old bastard," the sergeant bellowed. "Don't think just because you were stupid enough to get yourself messed up that I won't kick your ass!"

Frank should have been angry at being called old and crippled, but the beer had given him enough clarity to recognize the truth in it. He was old, he was crippled, and everyone could see it. The booze couldn't hide that reality, just make it easier to bear.

"Let's not get off on the wrong foot," he said, offering his hand. "I'm Frank Cage. Master Gunnery Sergeant Cage, retired."

"I'm Sergeant Johansen," the big guy snapped back. "Not retired, which means I work for a living and can't throw money away because you're clumsy!"

"Well, Sergeant Johansen," Frank said, "you didn't exactly pay for those drinks, did you? You intimidated Jimmy into buying them, which breaks regulations. Should I tell your First Shirt? Or maybe you'd like to pay Jimmy back, and then you'd have a legitimate complaint about me spilling your drink."

Johansen's expression soured as he pulled out his link. "Jimmy, hold out your goddamned link!"

After transferring the funds, Johansen turned back to Frank. "Now about those beers you stole . . ." His fists clenched as he stepped closer.

"Hey! Shitheads!" The bartender's voice cut through the tension, accompanied by the distinctive sound of a shotgun being racked. "No fighting in my bar. Take it outside."

Johansen jabbed a finger into Frank's chest. "I'll be waiting for you outside."

Frank sighed in resignation as they left. "You wouldn't happen to have a back door?"

"I ain't your friend, Frank," Heather said, the shotgun still pointed in his general direction. "Get your ass out of my bar and don't come back this time."

Frank had heard that line before. He sighed and fake-limped toward the front entrance.

Outside, the sun was too bright, forcing Frank to close his natural eye. Jimmy and Carl had disappeared, but Johansen and his two E-5s remained. The skinny male looked like he was riding Johansen's coattails for protection, while the female stood by loyally.

Frank considered making a run for his bike where Rex waited, but that was the coward way. Better to face it head-on. What the hell? It was just pain. The real pain was inside his head anyway, the kind no amount of physical punishment could match.

Johansen peeled off his uniform jacket and tossed it to the female. "Just you and me, old man," he taunted, cracking his knuckles.

"You'll have to come to me," Frank replied, digging his boot into the hard-packed dirt. "I don't get around so good anymore."

When Johansen charged, Frank moved with muscle memory that alcohol couldn't erase. He sidestepped, dragging his bionic leg behind as bait. Johansen's shin connected with the metal prosthetic with a sickening crack while Frank's cybernetic arm delivered a backhand to his shoulder blade.

Fight physics was the only physics Frank knew. Johansen plowed face-first into the dirt and flipped over to land flat on his back. Blood welled from a cut at his hairline. Frank moved faster than he had any right to, smashing his prosthetic fist into Johansen's jaw, dropping him instantly.

Frank knelt to check on him when he heard, "Get away from him, you bastard!"

He never saw the knife before the female sergeant buried it in his side.

"Bitch!" Frank grabbed her arm and slammed his forehead into her nose. She toppled backward as Frank yanked the blade out with his bionic hand, feeling strangely detached from the pain. The wound bled but didn't spurt—nothing vital hit.

As Johansen stirred, Frank's attention was drawn to a holographic news display above the bar entrance. It showed a teddy bear tumbling through space near what looked like the remains of a habitat.

Frank froze, not even feeling the wound in his side anymore. His mind flashed back to Titan Station. To his family. To the Hollow . . .

"What are you staring at, old man? We're not done!" Johansen shouted.

Frank turned, a feral rage transforming his face. He snarled like a wild animal, swiping out with the knife. Johansen and his toadies scrambled back, suddenly realizing they'd picked a fight with someone who had nothing to lose. Someone who'd already lost everything that mattered.

Frank let them go, not concerned with the fight. Not with this fight.

He wanted to be out there, on the station where someone had killed innocent children, rearranging *that someone's* face with his old, bruised fists.

Neither God nor the Devil could stop him from that if he was there. But he wasn't, he was in this shithole, half drunk and bleeding.

Holding his side, he stumbled away to look for the one being that still mattered to him. The dog wasn't far, just around two corners, still leashed to Frank's motorcycle.

"Hey there, Rex," he said.

The massive rottweiler trotted over, tail up at first.

Immediately, Rex whined, sniffing at the wound in his side, and Frank finally realized that it hurt. He also noticed that it had ruined his T-shirt.

"Aw, goddammit, this was my favorite shirt." He sighed, ruffling the big dog's neck. "Don't worry about it, boy. It's not fatal. No such luck. I'll sew it up when we get home."

Frank unfastened the dog's leash from the motorcycle. The vehicle was an old design, fabricated on the cheap, one part at a time with whatever access to the machines he could beg, borrow, or steal from Paddy Finn down at the plant. Once upon a time, hundreds of years ago, the original had run on distilled gasoline, but this one had been engineered for alcohol. Alcohol was simple to manufacture with just a fire, a boiler, and some copper coils, and it had the added benefit of being drinkable, sort of. He only hit up the white lightning if he was desperate because it tasted the same as it made him feel afterward—like hammered shit.

Getting Rex loaded into the sidecar was almost as difficult as getting the old piece of shit started, and every stomp on the starter made his side hurt more. But the dog was eventually belted in, and the bike rumbled to life. The trip back to his homestead was blissfully short. He wasn't even that drunk, not after the fight, and there was no one on the dirt road.

He didn't look forward to the precision needlework on his flesh and on his shirt, and he had no idea how he was going to get the blood out. Frank had started on a deep sulk when he heard the roar of the Black Tigers.

Military space fighters. Nothing else sounded like their growl, and even after so many years as a civilian, there was no mistaking them. As the fighters tore into the horizon, a transport came into view overhead, but not by much, barely clearing the trees.

Frank uttered a string of vile curses when he saw where it was going.

The big, ugly craft set down directly across the path to his house, blocking out the hovel with its metallic bulk and sending up a wave of grit and dust.

"What the fuck!" Frank shouted.

He braked the cycle to a skidding halt and coughed from the storm of dust. By the time it cleared, the hatch of the transport opened. A ramp extended down to the smoking grass, still smoldering from the landing jets. The engines whined down to a halt, and only the groans and pings of cooling metal fought with the clamor of the motorcycle's idle for attention as a Marine walked down the ramp.

This one bore no resemblance to Johansen and his bumbling circus-clown retinue. This was an officer, all serious and all business, a sidearm holstered at his hip.

"Who's this asshole?" Frank asked Rex.

Rex growled as the Marine approached.

"Are you Master Gunnery Sergeant Frank James Cage?" he asked, looking from Frank, then to the dog.

"I heard he's retired," Frank said. "Rex, ever heard of a Master Gunnery Sergeant Cage?"

Rex growled lower.

"He says no," Frank said.

The Marine captain looked back at Frank. "You sure about that?"

"Depends on what this is about," Frank said. "I mean, I got a good idea. But that bitch stabbed me."

"Bitch?" The Captain raised a brow.

"This isn't about what happened at the Jukebox?"

"No, it's not."

Frank considered his options, feeling the last of his beer buzz evaporating. Without the alcohol, the ghosts were already starting to press in at the edges of his vision. "Yeah, I'm Frank," he admitted. "But I'm not in a great mood right now, unless you got some beer. Preferably cold."

"That sounds good, Master Guns, but I'm fresh out." He handed over the tablet. "I do have this for you though."

Frank took it, blinking several times to get his vision to focus while trying to read what looked like a reactivation order.

Frank almost laughed. The universe had a sick sense of humor. Just when he thought he'd drunk enough to forget, it found a new way to make him remember.

"Must be a joke," he said. "Who put you up to this—Martin? That stupid old son of a gun—"

"This is no joke, Master Guns. You'll have to come with me now."

CHAPTER THREE

Martin knew he was dreaming. It was the same dream he'd had almost every night for the past fifteen years.

The shuttle crashed through the breach in Titan Station's hull and skidded across the deck of a cargo bay before slamming into a stack of supply crates. Martin braced against the impact, his combat reflexes keeping him steady while the shuttle's metal frame groaned in protest. Through his suit's sensors, he could feel the vibrations of failing systems: the deep bass rumble of stress on multiple decks, and the high-pitched whine of pressure valves failing throughout the structure.

"Atmosphere critical in sectors three through seven," announced the station's automated system, its calm voice at odds with the chaos around them. "All personnel evacuate immediately."

Martin checked the HUD in his helmet. It displayed environmental readings, team vitals, and threat indicators. Those were flashing with warnings. Low oxygen, radiation, fires.

"We still have gravity, but not sure for how long," he said. "Seal up."

The Aegis combat suit hummed to life around him and sealed with a series of clicks and hisses. Their armor was the best the CSF Marines had to offer: vacuum-rated, radiation-shielded, and built to withstand both conventional weapons and hostile environments.

Ripke and Frank did the same, their faceplates reflecting the emergency lighting that bathed the cargo bay in crimson. Through his visor, Martin could see Frank's eyes scanning rapidly across his own HUD, searching for any signal.

"Comms are scrambled," Frank said, his voice tight. "Can't get a clear signal to Sarah."

Martin pulled up the station schematic on his wrist display, years of combat experience kicking in. "Section C is four levels up. Fastest route is through central maintenance."

"Natalia, Popovich—secure the shuttle for evac," Frank ordered. "Ripke, you're with us. We've got less than thirty minutes before those destroyers turn this place to flotsam."

Martin knew the risk, but he remembered what Frank had said before the shuttle. "You would do the same for your kids and Lucia."

Frank was right. Martin would do anything to save Terecia, Thomas, and his wife if he had the chance. And Martin would also do the same for Frank's family.

Shouldering their MR-110 plasma rifles, the team hurried over to the hatch. It opened to a darkened corridor. Martin went first, his helmet illuminating an empty passage with powerful beams. The station was eerily quiet, the usual hum of life support systems replaced by the intermittent wail of emergency alarms. Their boots echoed on the metal decking, the sound amplified by their suit audio.

"Radiation levels rising," Ripke noted, checking his environmental scanner. "Something's leaking into this section."

"Suits will handle it," Martin replied. "Keep moving."

They passed through a security checkpoint, the doors forced open slightly with a pry bar that lay wedged between. Beyond, they found the first bodies, three members of a security team caught unprepared without their vacuum suits. They were crumpled against the hatch, no visible wounds but their faces frozen in expressions of terror from their final moments gasping for air.

"A damn shitty way to die," Ripke said.

Martin knelt beside one of the bodies, his scanner showing no atmospheric contaminants.

Frank stood at the doorway, impatient. "We need to keep moving."

With a nod, Martin got up and continued on. They pressed through a maze of corridors, the station's layout becoming increasingly disorienting as emergency bulkheads forced detours. Martin's tactical training kept them oriented, but each redirect cost precious minutes.

The team came upon what had been the mess hall. The far hull was completely gone, the void of space visible beyond. Bodies, food, and silverware floated in the zero-*g* environment, preserved by the vacuum.

"Explosive decompression," Martin observed. "Hull breach, not an attack."

Frank backed away and hurried toward the next junction. Just as he edged around the corner, his motion sensor pinged.

"Movement," he cautioned.

The team pulled up behind Frank with their rifles raised. Martin signaled he would take point. Frank gave a nod, and Ripke acknowledged.

Holding in a breath, Martin moved around the junction to the right, where the motion was being detected. For a moment, he saw nothing in the shadows of the strobing emergency light. He took a step forward and froze when he noticed something rippling down the corridor, like heat waves over hot asphalt. It started small, then expanded, coalescing into a silvery, fluid form that seemed to absorb and reflect light simultaneously. It hovered over a dead crew member, its surface shifting and changing constantly.

A Hollow . . .

Frank and Ripke moved up behind him, but he held up a fist to hold fire.

The entity seemed to be examining the dead crewman, its mercury-like form extending tendrils that passed through the corpse without disturbing it. The tendrils retracted, and the Hollow's surface rippled with patterns of light that shifted too quickly for the human eye to follow.

"What's it doing?" Ripke asked.

"Studying the dead," Martin replied. "Just like on *Squanto*."

Only this time, it wasn't dissecting. It was observing, almost respectfully.

Frank's breathing had become audibly faster. "Fuck it, I'm going to blast it to hell."

"Wait," Martin said, raising a hand.

The Hollow suddenly paused, as if sensing their presence. It turned—though *turned* wasn't quite the right word, its form simply rearranged itself to face them. For a long moment, it hovered in place, observing them. Its surface displayed complex shifting patterns, like a language they couldn't understand.

Then, with no aggressive movement, it flowed through the nearest hull and disappeared.

"Holy shit," Ripke breathed.

There was no time to consider what had happened, or how different this experience had been with their first contact.

"Come on already," Frank said. "We need to reach Section C. Now."

With Martin back on point, they continued through the station. In each corridor, he noted the absence of the carnage they'd witnessed on *Squanto*. There were bodies, yes, station personnel who hadn't made it to evacuation points, but they hadn't been dissected or examined as specimens. They'd simply been caught in the chaos.

On approach to another junction, Martin's scanner went wild. "Multiple contacts ahead. Moving fast."

They pressed themselves against the wall, weapons ready. Martin peered around the corner carefully, then quickly pulled back.

"What is it?" Frank demanded.

"A group of them," Martin said quietly. "At least five. They're . . . doing something to the computer terminals."

Frank risked a quick look, then rejoined them. "They're at the command relay. Interfacing with it somehow."

Martin's comm crackled suddenly, Will's voice breaking through the interference.

"Master Guns, I'm tracking the Hollow movements with the shuttle's sensors. They're concentrated around command and communications arrays. Almost all of them. They're ignoring residential sections entirely."

"What are they doing there?" Martin asked.

"Unknown, but they're interfacing with the systems somehow. It's like . . . they're trying to broadcast something."

Frank and Martin exchanged a look. "Not an attack," Martin said quietly. "See if you can get through to Shield Command and let them know."

"Copy that," Will replied.

Martin looked at the digital map on his HUD. "Let's find another way around," he said. "We don't have time for a confrontation."

They backtracked and found an access tunnel that would bypass the junction. The narrow space forced them to move single file, their armor scraping against the walls. The tunnel was pitch-black, their helmet lights cutting thin beams through the darkness.

Halfway through, the station shuddered violently. Debris rained down on them from overhead. Tendrils of wiring, pieces of panels, all of it dumping to the deck as the structure groaned under stress. A moment of vertigo came and went as the artificial gravity suite struggled to maintain functionality.

"Station is losing integrity," Ripke said. "We've got maybe fifteen minutes before those destroyers open fire."

"We're close," Frank replied, his pace quickening.

They emerged into a residential corridor, emergency lighting bathing everything in crimson. The corridor stretched before them. Apartment doors lined both sides. Many hung open, residents evacuated in the station's initial response.

"Which one?" Martin asked.

"C-42," Frank replied, already moving. "End of the hall."

They were halfway there when the station's superstructure groaned. Through a viewport, Martin saw one of the destroyers repositioning, its main weapon charging.

"It's targeting this section," he realized with horror.

Frank broke into a sprint. Martin and Ripke struggled to keep up as Frank raced past doors—C-38 . . . C-40 . . .

The weapon fired.

Martin's honed reflexes saved both of them. He lunged forward and tackled Frank as the energy beam cut through space toward them. Through the viewport, they watched as the section of the station forward of their position erupted in a blinding flash. The blast wave traveled through the structure, bulkheads buckling, atmosphere venting explosively into space.

Emergency bulkheads slammed down, separating them from the destruction beyond. Martin knew then there was nothing they could do.

Frank slammed against one and pounded. "NO! Open up!" He turned to Martin, who tried to pull him back. "NO! They're right there! SARAH! LILY!"

"We can't get through, Frank, I'm sorry," Martin said, his voice breaking as he held his friend.

Frank pulled free and fisted the sealed bulkhead, his armor's enhanced strength denting the metal. "I can get through! I can still—"

"Frank, there's no time!" Martin wrestled him back.

Ripke was already checking his scanner. "We've got multiple contacts converging. The Hollow are coming this way."

Martin held on to Frank, who squirmed and fought to get free in front of the bulkhead. Suddenly, the hull beside them cascaded like a waterfall. Three Hollow entities emerged, their mercury-like bodies flowing through solid metal. Up close, they were even more alien: constantly shifting forms with no fixed shape, surfaces reflecting impossible colors and patterns.

Frank went slack in Martin's grip. His entire body seemed to collapse inward for a brief moment, like someone had cut the strings holding him up. His knees buckled, and a sound escaped him; not quite a scream, not quite a sob, something primal that Martin had never heard from his friend in all their years of combat.

Slowly, Martin let go and backed up.

Ripke raised his weapon, but Martin signaled him to hold fire. The Hollow didn't approach aggressively. Instead, they formed a semicircle, their surfaces displaying rapid patterns that seemed almost like a language of light and form.

One of the entities flowed forward, extending what might have been a limb toward Frank. Before it could make contact, the station rocked with another explosion, more violent than before. The entity paused, its surface pattern shifting rapidly.

For a fleeting moment, it seemed to resolve into a clear communication. Angular lines formed a cipher that rippled across its surface in shifting sequences as it reached out again, not attacking, but . . . pointing.

Pointing away from the station. Into deep space.

It's trying to tell us something, Martin thought, the realization hitting him. These didn't seem like invaders. They seemed like messengers.

"Get out of my way, you alien bastards!" Frank shouted.

The chatter of his plasma rifle echoed through the corridor, flashing light slamming into the creature.

"Frank, stop!" Martin shouted.

But it was too late. The enraged Marine fired on all three of the creatures, pounding their translucent bodies with shots that seemed to connect in some areas, and phase right through in others.

Another blast rocked the station, pushing Frank to the deck. More bulkheads began to seal automatically as integrity failures cascaded through the section.

Martin lost his balance and crashed down. When he glanced up, all three Hollow had vanished.

"We're out of time!" Ripke shouted over the wail of alarms.

Martin grabbed Frank, who was aiming into nothingness. "I'll kill you all," he screamed. "All of you motherfuckers!"

"Frank! We have to go NOW!"

Frank punched Martin when he tried to pull him away. The blow sent Martin crashing into a bulkhead. With a deep breath, he did the only thing he could think of to save his friend. He reached to his rifle, flipped the safety selector switch to stun, aimed at Frank, and fired.

Still screaming, Frank jolted and convulsed. He spun partially toward Martin, and for a second Martin thought Frank was going to shoot him with his MR-110. But Frank finally collapsed, jerking on the deck.

"Help me with him!" Martin yelled.

Ripke reached down, and together, they hauled Frank's unconscious body to an emergency shaft. Moving as fast as possible, they raced back toward the shuttle as the station began to break apart around them.

Popovich met them halfway, his face pale. "They're all at the comms array now. Every single one we can track. They're broadcasting something on frequencies I've never seen."

"Broadcasting what?" Martin demanded.

"I don't know. But whatever it is, Shield Command is determined to stop it."

They reached the cargo bay to find Natalia with the engines prepped. "Did you find . . ."

She went silent when she saw them hauling Frank inside. Martin strapped him into a crash seat, locked him in, and removed his sidearm.

"Get us clear," Martin ordered, taking the controls. "Full thrust."

The shuttle shot out of the breach as Titan Station began to disintegrate under the destroyers' coordinated fire. From the viewport, Martin watched as the station that had housed thousands of innocent people—including Frank's family—broke into pieces and scattered like a new set of rings around an exploding planet.

It had been too late for Sarah. Too late for Lily. Too late for them all.

As they set their course away from the devastation, Martin glanced at his unconscious friend. The man strapped to that seat might look like Frank Cage, but Martin knew the person he'd known for years had died back there with his family. Whoever woke up from that stun blast would be someone else entirely; someone shaped by loss in ways Martin could only begin to imagine.

Martin jolted awake, sweat beading across his forehead despite the cool afternoon air. Cosmo, sensing his distress, padded over from his bed in the corner and nuzzled Martin's hand.

"Just a bad dream, boy," Martin muttered, scratching behind the German shepherd's ears. "Nothing new under the sun."

The hammock swayed gently on his porch as he remembered the dream. It wasn't just Frank who had lost his family that day. It was the official end of Martin's marriage too. He started hitting the bottle harder when he got home. Lucia finally threw in the towel, and Martin hadn't seen her since. Hadn't seen much of his kids either.

This was all he had now.

He sighed in his hammock, looking out over his modest homestead spread out before him: rows of carefully tended vegetables, a small orchard of fruit trees, and herbs planted in concentric circles according to their water needs. The garden was Martin's pride, his therapy, the only thing that had kept him sane during these years of sobriety and retirement.

He was just about to swing his legs over and start his morning routine when the distant rumble of engines cut through the dawn chorus. Cosmo's ears perked up, his posture stiffening.

"What the hell?" Martin squinted at the horizon.

The military transport appeared suddenly, descending far too quickly, its landing jets already firing as it approached. Martin stumbled out of the hammock, his cybernetic leg locking momentarily.

"No, no, NO!" he shouted, waving his arms frantically. "Not the garden, you idiots!"

But the pilot either couldn't see him or, more likely, didn't care. The massive green transport dropped directly onto Martin's prized vegetable patch, its landing struts crushing tomato plants and bean poles. The backwash from its engines scorched neat rows of carrots and obliterated months of careful cultivation.

Martin stood frozen, his jaw slack as the transport settled with a final mechanical sigh, crushing the last of his summer squash beneath its bulk.

"SON OF A BITCH!" he bellowed, snatching up the walking stick he kept by the porch steps. Cosmo barked fiercely beside him, hackles raised. "Five months of work! FIVE MONTHS!"

The transport's side hatch opened with a pneumatic hiss, a ramp extending down into what remained of Martin's herb spiral. A Marine captain descended, his uniform crisp, his posture ramrod straight. He looked around at the devastation with clinical detachment before focusing on Martin.

"Master Gunnery Sergeant Martin Kelvin?" the captain asked, consulting a tablet.

"What's left of him," Martin growled, leaning on his stick. His cybernetic leg was acting up again, probably from the sudden movement. "And you owe me a new garden, you jackass."

The captain glanced at the flattened vegetation beneath the transport, then back at Martin. His expression remained neutral, though Martin thought he detected a flicker of genuine regret.

"Apologies for the landing site, Master Guns. It was the only suitable clearing within range of your homestead."

"Suitable?" Martin gestured wildly at the crushed plants. "That was six varieties of heirloom tomatoes! Beans I've been crossbreeding for three seasons! And those herbs"—he jabbed his stick toward the crushed spiral—"included medicinal plants you can't even get on this planet anymore!"

Cosmo growled, moving closer to the captain, who took a cautious step back.

"Sir, I understand your frustration, but I'm going to need you to come with me."

Martin crossed his arms. "Why? What is this about?"

"That's classified, sir."

"Classified?" Martin barked out a laugh. "That's rich. You destroy my livelihood and then tell me it's classified? I'm retired, Captain. Done. Finished. Got my papers and everything."

The captain remained impassive. "This comes directly from Shield Command."

Martin's eyes narrowed. "What the fuck is going on?"

"That information is classified until we reach headquarters."

Martin turned away, his hand instinctively reaching for Cosmo, who pressed against his leg, grounding him. Whatever this was about, it had to be serious. The CSF Marines didn't reactivate retired personnel with cybernetic replacements for routine operations.

"Okay, but I'm bringing Cosmo," Martin said, nodding toward the German shepherd.

The captain frowned. "That's not standard protocol—"

"Neither is flattening a retired Marine's garden. Cosmo comes, or I don't."

The captain sighed, clearly calculating whether it was worth the fight. "Fine. The dog can come. But you're responsible for him."

Martin nodded, turning toward his cabin. "Give me ten minutes to grab my gear."

"Your gear? No, that's not necessary, we're here just for you. Any gear will be provided—"

Martin turned, ignoring the officer and heading into his house as the captain sighed again.

Inside, Martin moved quickly, packing essentials into a duffel bag. The powered armor he took off the wall was outdated by current standards, but he'd maintained it meticulously. Each dent and scorch mark told a story: old battles, close calls, moments when technology and training had made the difference between life and death.

As he sifted through the contents of his footlocker, his fingers brushed against his old service pistol. He hesitated only a moment before adding it to the bag. Better to have it and not need it.

Outside, the captain was checking his timepiece when Martin emerged, Cosmo at his heels, duffel bag over one shoulder, and powered armor components secured in a cargo net.

"This everything?" the captain asked.

"Everything worth taking," Martin confirmed, casting a final glance at his ruined garden. "You're still paying for those tomatoes, by the way."

"I'll submit the paperwork for compensation," the captain replied dryly.

"Compensation won't bring them back from their horrible death. I was going to make some epic BLTs out of those."

The captain shook his head and muttered something under his breath.

As they boarded the transport, Martin settled into a jump seat, Cosmo lying obediently at his feet. His mind raced with possibilities. What could be so urgent that they'd recall retired personnel? Some new insurrection? Another Chitin outbreak? Something worse . . . something that only came to him in his nightmares.

No, the Hollow are gone, he thought. *Shield Command assured us of that.*

Whatever it was, it couldn't be good.

The hatch sealed with a pressurized hiss, and the vessel lifted off, leaving behind a perfect circle of destruction in Martin's garden. The only trace that he'd ever tried to build something permanent in this world.

"Where are we headed?" Martin asked as the transport gained altitude.

"Hephaestus Base, sir. You'll be briefed there."

Martin nodded, settling back against the cold metal of the bulkhead. He'd find out soon enough what fresh hell awaited him. For now, he closed his eyes, one hand resting on Cosmo's head, and tried not to think about what—or who—might be waiting for him.

CHAPTER FOUR

Hephaestus Base writhed and scuttled like an insect hive all around Frank Cage; thousands of Marines, Navy, and Fighter troops scurrying from one task to another, while cargo trucks and forklifts weaved their way through the currents of humanity. The pilot who'd brought him in had simply dumped him off at the main gate with instructions to find Colonel Shafter's office, leaving Frank to navigate the chaos with Rex and his battered Aegis battlesuit loaded on a cargo sled.

"Some welcome party," Frank muttered to Rex, who panted in response, seemingly unconcerned by the base's frantic activity.

The command center loomed ahead—a harsh wedge-shaped building that rose four stories among blocky military-standard boxes. Troops passed in and out of the doors, while others clustered in the parking lots, waiting with their gear at their feet. They all shared the same look of nervous boredom—the cognitive dissonance between the desire to get to the fighting and the terror of what that would entail.

Frank noticed several squads running drills in the nearby parade ground, their instructors barking orders that carried across the tarmac. Young faces, most of them barely old enough to shave properly. They reminded him of himself once: eager, stupid, and convinced they were invincible. Before places like the Gauntlet taught them otherwise.

As Frank approached the entrance, his eyes locked on a figure who didn't belong among the younger Marines. The man wore a military uniform of an older design that stood out by its different camouflage pattern. The shaved head and beard threw Frank off a bit. So did the civilian gut on this man. The only reason Frank recognized him was the old Aegis armor resting on the pavement and the German shepherd standing alert at his feet.

Martin Kelvin.

Frank's stomach clenched. Five years since they had seen each other, and fifteen years since that tragic day that broke their brotherly bond on Titan Station, when Martin had made the choice that saved Frank's life and condemned him to live with the memories. Fifteen years of drowning those memories in whatever bottle was closest. Fifteen years of bar fights and knife wounds and waking up in places he didn't remember going. All after twenty-eight years of decorated service in the Marines, the only time of his life that he had felt like he was worth a damn.

Frank considered simply turning around, but Rex had already caught Cosmo's scent. The rottweiler leapt from the cargo sled and bounded toward the other dog. Frank swore and hobbled after him, the smart bandage on his side pulling tight against the knife wound.

To his surprise, the dogs didn't fight. They circled and sniffed each other, tails wagging, obviously unaware that their handlers hated one another.

Martin looked up, his eyes hardening when they landed on Frank.

"Jesus, Cage, you look like hell," Martin said flatly.

"Yup, and you look fat as hell," Frank countered, eyeing Martin's middle-aged paunch. "Only one of those things is inevitable, the last time I checked."

Martin's eyes traveled to the bloodstain on Frank's shirt. "Is that blood?"

"Yeah, it's nothing." Frank waved dismissively. "Some self-important E-6 needed his ass kicked, and his E-5 girlfriend didn't take kindly to it."

Martin shook his head. "I don't know what bothers me more—the fact that it doesn't bother you, or that there are enough to make a collection."

"Well, how many do you really need to call it a collection?" Frank's face twisted into a bitter grin. "And not all of them actually stabbed me."

An uncomfortable silence fell between them, heavy after five long years of stewing about the past and what-ifs.

"Did you ever lose any fights these past five years, Frank?" Martin finally asked.

"If I'd lost a fight, I wouldn't be standing here, would I?"

Martin's face darkened. "That's not what I meant, and you know it."

Frank looked away. He knew exactly what Martin meant. The real fight—the one against the bottle, against the memories, against the void Sarah and Lily had left behind.

"You had no right," Frank said, his voice dangerously quiet.

"No right to what?" Martin's tone matched his, low and tense. Even though he knew.

"No right to make that choice for me. On Titan."

Martin stepped closer. "You were going to get yourself killed, man."

"It was still my choice!" Frank's voice rose. "My family. My life."

"You were my brother." Martin raised a hand in an attempt to de-escalate the rising tensions that the dogs both clearly sensed, their tails down and ears up.

"What was I supposed to do?" Martin added. "Watch you die?"

Frank's face flushed with anger. "You should have let me decide!"

"Decide what? To go out in some bullshit blaze of glory that wouldn't have helped anyone?"

"It would have helped me! You took that from me! You stunned me and dragged me off that station! You don't get to decide how I die!"

The dogs both got agitated, whining.

"I saved your life!" Martin said.

That only made Frank madder. He shoved Martin. "I never asked you to save me, you old fucker, or did you forget that?"

The dogs both started growling, but that didn't stop either of their handlers.

"Did you think maybe Sarah wanted me to?" Martin asked.

"Don't fucking speak her name!" Frank said. In a blind rage, he threw a right hook at Martin's jaw before he could reply.

Martin blocked the blow, combat reflexes still sharp despite his age. He countered with a jab that caught Frank in the ribs on the opposite side of his wound. Frank gasped but didn't back down and launched into Martin with a tackle that sent them both crashing against the wall.

"STAND DOWN! NOW, YOU SHITHEADS!"

The command voice cut through their rage. Both men froze, years of military conditioning taking over. They turned to find Colonel Shafter standing in the doorway, his face a thundercloud of disapproval. Behind him, two Military Police officers moved into flanking positions, hands on their stun batons.

"This is how CSF Marines conduct themselves on my base?" Shafter's voice was cold steel. "Two decorated warriors brawling like privates on their first leave?"

Neither man answered, but Martin did stiffen to attention.

Not Frank. He simply wiped blood from his lip, snarling like an animal, wanting nothing more than to pound Martin's dumb, bald head.

"Inside my office. Both of you." Shafter turned sharply on his heel. "Leave the dogs and the armor here. MPs will watch them."

The dogs had settled instantly at the command voice, sitting at attention as if they too recognized military authority. Frank and Martin exchanged one last glare before following the colonel inside.

"Sir, with respect—" Martin began.

"Save it, Gunny," Shafter cut him off. "I didn't drag two broken-down war horses out of retirement to watch them kick each other to death on my doorstep. We got a situation, and like it or not, you two are needed." He looked back at them with narrowed eyes. "So you'd better figure out how to be in the same room, because you're going to be spending a lot of time together."

The colonel disappeared into the room.

"Move it," said one of the MPs.

Frank cursed, unable to shake the feeling that they were both stepping back into the fray, only this time, they'd be facing it as enemies rather than brothers.

* * *

Frank and Martin entered a room dominated by a holographic display showing a familiar sight—the twisted energy patterns of the Gauntlet.

Martin felt his heart thump. His fear of this somehow being about the Hollow wasn't unfounded. Frank must have known it too. His jaw tightened at the sight, and his nose crinkled.

Colonel Shafter stood with his back to them, studying the display before turning.

"Have a seat," Shafter said firmly.

"I'll stand," Frank muttered.

"That wasn't a request," Shafter snarled. "You're here for a reason, a damn important reason."

Martin took a seat and hoped Frank would realize that important reason was the Hollow. With a grunt, Frank finally relented and sat, then began tapping a boot on the deck nervously. Age had only hardened the man, his temples now gray but his eyes still calculating.

"We've detected Hollow signatures on Galean," Shafter said.

"You're sure?" Martin asked.

"Yes, I'm sure. That's why you're here."

Frank chuckled and looked at Martin with a side-eye. "This guy serious?"

"Colonel," Shafter snapped. "You will refer to me as Colonel, or sir, from this moment on, Frank."

"Cage," Frank replied.

Shafter glared at him, and for a second Martin thought he was going to snap and smack the smirk off Frank's face.

"Trust me, if it were up to me, you wouldn't be here," the colonel finally said. "Shield Command wants experienced personnel to train a Marine unit to investigate these signatures."

"Train?" Frank asked.

"Yeah, this isn't adding up," Martin said. "All due respect, but wasn't the military preparing for this? If you need us to train new guns, then my guess is not a whole lot has been done."

Shafter's expression tightened slightly. "There have been plenty of preparations, but intel indicated the Hollow were gone and not coming back after Titan Station."

"Care to share that intel?" Frank asked, straightening from his slouch.

"Classified."

"Of course it is, just like my dick size."

"You better check yourself," Shafter replied, his voice dropping dangerously.

"He's been grieving for the past fifteen years," Martin said. "Drinking for most of that time . . . and getting into fights because Shield Command decided to kill his family."

"And because you decided to 'save' me," Frank mumbled. He suddenly perked up. "While I've been drinking, Master Guns here has been gardening. So, bringing us back into the fray sounds like an absolutely terrible idea."

Shafter alternated his gaze from Frank to Martin.

"You should see his tomatoes, they are super big," Frank said in a mocking voice. "He's gotten great with a garden hoe, but you sure you want to put an MR-110 back in his hand?"

"Still better than giving your drunk ass one," Martin fired back. "You'll be shaking off wild shots."

"I can still outshoot you—always could, always will."

"You can't even shoot—"

"Shut the hell up, goddammit!" Shafter shouted. He walked over and stood in front of them, his breath coming out in hot waves.

He stared at them both like they were nuts and he was wasting his time. Martin had seen that look before. It was the look of a commanding officer who'd drawn the short straw and had to deal with the problem cases.

"Listen to me and don't say another word until I tell you to speak," Shafter continued, visibly reining in his frustration. "We have Marines ready for this. They have trained based off footage, much of it from your own encounters, but someone at Shield Command wants you specifically."

Truth was, Martin knew they were the only two left from the original encounters. Popovich's unit got wiped out in an uprising on some backwater planet—pirates with stolen military hardware, nothing noble about those deaths. Ripke went nuts after too many close calls—ended up in a psych ward talking to walls. And Natalia had gone off the grid. No matter how hard Martin searched, he could find no trace of her.

"Who at Shield Command is asking for us?" Martin wondered out loud. He cursed in his mind. "Sorry, sir, I meant to keep that to myself."

Shafter turned red.

"I don't care if it's the Pope asking," Frank scoffed. "Tell them to fuck a duck. I'm retired now, and I'm heading home."

He faked a smile, offered a haphazard salute, and said, "Sir." Then Frank stormed out of the office, the hatch clanking hard behind him.

Shafter's eyes locked with Martin's, waiting. "That man is a real piece of work."

"He lost everything at Titan," Martin said quietly.

"I know. So did a lot of people." Shafter's voice softened slightly. "But we need him. We need you both."

Martin could tell by the colonel's slight frown that he didn't like the fact he was asking for help. Maybe because Frank and Martin were two washed-up Marines, or maybe because he honestly felt bad for what they had been through.

Either way, Martin knew that the ask would soon become an order, and there was probably little he could do to get out of it.

Maybe you can get something out of this . . . land, weapon upgrades, armor upgrades . . . He grinned in his mind. If Shield Command really needed him, then he had leverage that he never had when he was active duty. It was probably the only reason the colonel had tolerated their colorful remarks up to this point.

"The Hollow are extremely dangerous, not just to this colony, but to all of humanity. I'll say it again—we need you."

"One more time," Martin said.

Shafter gritted his teeth. "We need your help."

Martin stepped forward to study the swirling energy patterns that had haunted his dreams since first contact with the Hollow. He had seen what these aliens were capable of in the Gauntlet. When they had cut up the crew like lab specimens. They were at Titan Station for another reason, perhaps to steal humanity's secrets, or perhaps for something else.

He would never forget the creature forming an appendage and pointing out into the vastness of space, like a warning.

Shafter stood next to him and used a remote to change the data to footage—footage from their encounter on *Squanto.*

"We're facing something we don't understand, and I'd rather have you two cranky old guns on our side than betting on rookies who've only seen training footage," said the colonel. "Lives are at stake, a lot of lives."

Martin sighed. "I'll talk to Frank, but I'm not promising anything."

As he turned to leave, Shafter called after him. "Kelvin." Martin paused at the door. "Whatever's happening . . . it's bigger than Titan. Bigger than all of us."

Martin nodded once, then left to find Frank. The weight of all they'd seen, and all they might yet face, hung heavy on his shoulders as the gravity of the situation set in.

Now he had to find his former best friend. That was going to be the easiest part of his day, as he knew exactly where the salty bastard would be.

CHAPTER FIVE

The Rusty Anchor lived up to its name. The establishment's metal facade had corroded years ago, and no one had bothered to repaint it. Martin pushed through the swinging doors, his cybernetic leg whining as he navigated between crowded tables. Cosmo, his aging German shepherd, padded faithfully beside him, alert despite the gray muzzle that betrayed his years. Friday night meant the place was packed with off-duty personnel from the nearby base—most of them too young to remember Titan Station as anything but a tragedy. Not one of them knew what really happened that day.

It didn't take long to spot Frank. He occupied a corner booth, surrounded by four young Marines in crisp uniforms. Their insignia marked the officers as freshly commissioned, probably on their first posting. Rex lay underneath the table, taking up most of the foot space. The rottweiler's eyes tracked Martin and Cosmo instantly, but he made no move to get up, simply thumping his tail against the floor. Frank's voice carried above the ambient noise.

"—so there I was, pinned down on Ganymede Station with twenty psycho pirates between me and the extraction point." Frank gestured wildly, nearly knocking over his beer. "Comms jammed. Squad scattered. And I realize I'm out of ammo right as an enforcer rounds the corner."

The young officers leaned forward, completely captivated, occasionally glancing nervously at the massive dog under the table.

"So what did you do?" asked the one with lieutenant bars, eyes wide.

"Only thing I could do," Frank said, lowering his voice dramatically. "Tossed the useless rifle at the first bastard's head. Knocked him out cold. But that still left nineteen of them."

"Don't believe a word he says," Martin interjected, approaching the table. Cosmo and Rex exchanged a brief sniff of recognition, the animals having maintained a better relationship than their masters. "He exaggerates everything more than a degenerate poker player."

Frank looked up, his nose crinkling in anger. "You are ruining my story as usual, Kelvin."

"By all means, go on, Cage. I'll sit and keep you honest, since I was there." Martin slid into the booth, Cosmo settling at his feet alongside Rex. The two dogs seemed surprisingly comfortable with each other despite the continued tension between their owners. "Let me guess—the pirate story?"

"Good one for these greenhorns," Frank insisted. "Academy doesn't teach you what to do when all you've got left is a knife and brass knuckles."

One of the officers—the lieutenant with a too-perfect haircut—cleared his throat. "What are brass knuckles?"

Martin laughed. Frank did, too.

"Armor for your fists," Frank said, reaching down to scratch Rex's ears. "I took out nine of those fuckers with broken jaws."

"Seven," Martin corrected. "He took out seven. The rest ran when they realized who they were dealing with."

"Nine," Frank insisted. "You weren't there for the last two in the hangar bay."

"Because they weren't there. You made them up on the transport back."

Frank scoffed. "The blow to your head must've affected your memory. Tell them about the enforcer with the cybernetic arms."

"That part's actually true," Martin admitted. "Biggest pirate I've ever seen. Had aftermarket combat arms. The kind that can punch through hull plating."

"Punched through plenty of Marines before I got to him."

"So how'd you take him down?" the youngest officer asked.

Frank's expression shifted to something between pride and disbelief at his own actions. "Used my brass knuckles to short-circuit the connection points at his shoulders. Had to get in close, though. Too close." He absently rubbed a scar on his forearm. "Worth it to see the look on his face when those fancy arms went dead."

"You've still got the knuckles, I presume," Martin said. "Keeps them polished like trophies, is my guess."

Frank shrugged. "They saved my life."

The lieutenant leaned forward again. "Rumor is you guys were on Titan Station."

"Not discussing that," Frank cut him off sharply, all humor vanishing from his face.

The table went silent. Martin watched as Frank's hand tightened around his glass, knuckles whitening. Beneath the table, Rex sensed the shift in his master's mood and rose to his feet with a soft whine.

"I need something stronger than this bullshit," Frank said.

As he stalked toward the bar, Rex following dutifully at his heels, the officers looked to Martin, clearly sensing they'd stumbled into something well above their clearance level.

"He okay?" one of them asked.

Martin sighed. "Long history. Some missions leave marks you can't see."

After getting up, Martin and Cosmo joined Frank at the bar. "This round's on me." He signaled to the bartender, defusing the tension.

"I don't want your charity," Frank said as Rex settled at his feet.

Martin shrugged. "Fine. Mind if I drink with you?"

Frank didn't say yes, but he didn't say no. As he took his next drink, Martin studied his old friend. The mention of Titan had done what it always did—dragged Frank back to that moment, to the family he couldn't save, and to Martin saving him against his will.

Over the next hour, the bar filled with empty mugs. Frank hunched as he ordered his tenth round. Martin knew that posture well: the weight of memory pressing down, the ghosts that never quite faded. Cosmo and Rex had both settled into a doze beside their masters' stools, occasionally lifting their heads when the bartender approached.

"Vodka, on the rocks," Frank said.

The bartender looked to Martin with concern.

Frank was drunk, but not shit-faced, still plenty sober to discuss the reason they were here.

"The enemy is back, Frank," Martin said.

"Not my problem." Frank stood abruptly. He took a slug of vodka that the bartender slid over to him. "Another."

"The beer that bad here?" a voice asked from behind them.

Both men turned, and Frank let out a low whistle. Both dogs perked up, Rex giving a curious rumble deep in his chest.

A woman stood there—tall, lean, with a bearing that screamed military despite the civilian clothes. Her dark hair was cropped short, a thin scar running along her jawline. Martin recognized her instantly, though it had been ten years since he'd seen her.

"I'll be damned, if it isn't Natalia Ivan," Frank said. "Are you a ghost? Because Colonel Shafter just told us we're the last two surviving Marines from Titan Station."

"Kind of." She smiled, her still perfectly straight teeth now a bit shaded from coffee stains. Her eyes darted momentarily to the dogs before returning to the men, but she said nothing.

"You look good, Natalia . . ." Frank said, eyes narrowing as he took in her appearance.

"Captain," she corrected. "You look . . . drunk."

Frank raised an empty shot glass. "Want in on the fun?"

She looked to the bartender, who stepped back. Then she stepped forward. "The Hollow are back, Frank. We need you."

Martin was still processing her presence. Natalia hadn't gone off-grid—she had become a spook, a member of the intelligence division. The way she carried herself, the subtle tech implants visible at her temple, the calculated alertness in her eyes, it all made sense.

"I guess we know who in Shield Command wants us," Martin said.

"Your guess is right," she replied. "Want to see what we've been doing to prepare all these years? I heard you were curious."

"Not really," Frank said. "I want another drink."

"Drinking can wait. This can't."

"Oh, is that an order?" Frank gave a sloppy salute with his glass still in hand.

"Come on, Frank," Martin said. "Let's hear *Captain* Ivan out."

"Fine, but I want a lifetime supply of the best beer in the galaxy, and wine, and vodka, and an upgrade to Lucky. Maybe a built-in mini fridge."

"You can have whatever you want, within reason." Natalia smiled, but then her expression turned deadly serious. "But we don't have much time if I'm right about what's about to happen."

Something in her tone made both men straighten slightly. Martin had known Natalia long enough to recognize genuine fear, even when she was trying to hide it.

"That bad?" he asked quietly.

She didn't answer directly, just glanced toward the door. "Transport's waiting. Bring your drinks if you want. You might need them after what I'm about to show you."

"Fuck the drinks, we need to get our dogs," Frank said.

Rex was already on his feet, sensing his master's shift in attention. Cosmo followed suit and moved to Martin's side.

Frank and Martin exchanged a look—the silent communication of soldiers who'd faced death together more times than they could count.

"Well"—Frank drained a new beer and slammed the mug down—"retirement was getting boring anyway."

As they followed Natalia out of the bar, Martin couldn't shake the feeling that they were walking back into a nightmare like Titan Station that they'd barely survived fifteen years ago. Only this time, they were going in with eyes wide open, their faithful companions at their sides.

The transport zipped through restricted military corridors, bypassing security checkpoints with Natalia's clearance. Frank's head swam slightly from the vodka, the beer, and the sudden rush of memories he'd spent years drowning. Rex's warm weight against his leg was the only thing keeping him grounded.

"Never thought I'd be back here," Martin said, his cybernetic leg whining as he shifted.

"Makes two of us," Frank muttered, staring straight ahead as the walls blurred past.

For a moment, he was back on *Squanto*, watching silvery entities dissect crewmen like lab specimens, their surfaces rippling with indecipherable patterns. He blinked hard, focusing on Rex's muzzle resting on his knee.

The transport stopped at a security checkpoint with layers of biometric scanners and armed guards bearing a black hexagonal insignia with a glowing cyan eye at its center, the acronym DSIA emblazoned beneath the symbol of the Department of Strategic Intelligence and Analysis.

"DSIA?" Frank asked.

"Yes, a lot's changed since you were active duty," Natalia said. "DSIA was created to study the Hollow."

After several scans and verification protocols, they entered a briefing room that made standard military facilities look primitive. Holographic interfaces lined the walls, and a large table dominated the center, its surface glowing with tactical simulations. Frank squinted against the light, his alcohol-dulled senses struggling to process everything.

Natalia gestured for them to take seats while retrieving two sealed folders marked with the highest level of classification. She placed one in front of each of them with deliberate care.

"Why not just do this from the beginning?" Martin asked, eyeing the folder.

"Because I was busy, and someone jumped the gun," Natalia replied, settling into her chair. Her eyes fell on the two dogs sitting obediently beside their masters. "By the way, did you two really both bring dogs inside?"

"Emotional support animals," Frank replied with a straight face, grateful for Rex's steady presence.

The dog sensed his unease and pressed closer against his leg.

Natalia's expression remained neutral. "To a classified military briefing."

"Not a dog person?" Martin asked, absently scratching Cosmo behind the ears.

"Not really, no," Natalia said.

"Explains why you became a spook," Frank muttered, the alcohol loosening his tongue.

"I'll pretend I didn't hear that." She leaned forward, her voice dropping. "Let's get something straight. I now outrank you, and I won't tolerate disrespect. Get me?"

Frank nodded ruefully. "Sorry, sir." He felt like a scolded recruit, but the vodka had mellowed his usual defiance.

"That's better," she replied, relaxing slightly. "Now open your books."

They flipped open the folders simultaneously. Embedded technology activated, projecting holographic images above the pages—detailed scans of *Squanto*, followed by Titan Station footage. The familiar silvery forms of the Hollow flowed across the display.

There were also sections titled "Xenobiology and the Search for Other Intelligent Species in the Lort System." Frank thought of Dr. Lowell, the scientist at the field lab that Terminator Platoon was babysitting the day of Titan Station.

His vision tunneled, and suddenly he was back at that bulkhead on the station, fists pounding against unyielding metal, knowing Sarah and Lily were just beyond, the station disintegrating around them. Frank closed his eyes, fighting down the wave of nausea.

"This is everything we know about the Hollow," Natalia said. "I . . . Shield Command believes," she corrected, "*Squanto* was a research mission. First contact. They were trying to figure out what humans are and perhaps what we were doing in the Gauntlet."

Frank's jaw tightened as the hologram shifted to Titan Station. "And this?"

"Titan Station was something else," Natalia continued, "but before we could figure it out, we destroyed the station." Her eyes met Frank's briefly. "This new contact, well, that's what we need you to determine, before it's too late. This time, Shield Command wants to be more discreet."

"Without killing twenty thousand people, including my family," Frank said flatly.

A flash of genuine emotion crossed Natalia's face. "I'm sorry, Frank. You know how much I care. I was there and I tried to save them."

"I know, but now you're working with the very same assholes that gave that order."

"Those people are gone," she replied quietly. After pausing a moment, she leaned forward. "You can help ensure more families aren't torn apart like yours."

The room fell silent. Rex nudged his hand, sensing his distress. Frank absently stroked the dog's head, the familiar ritual helping to clear his mind slightly. Maybe the booze was wearing off, or maybe the gravity of the situation was sobering him up. Either way, something from the past was shifting inside him. A sense of purpose he hadn't felt in years.

"Tell me everything you know," he said.

As Natalia activated the table's display and began explaining about the alien signatures, Frank found his tactical mind engaging despite the alcohol fog. The haze of vodka was still there, but beneath it, the old Marine was awakening: analyzing, strategizing, looking for patterns.

"The Hollow energy signatures were detected by a remote orbital sensor array in a mountain valley on Galean before going dark," she explained. "There's an abandoned mining outpost nearby."

"Galean is a rough place in the winter," Martin said.

"Yeah, total frozen hellscape," Frank said. "Isn't winter closing in there?"

Natalia nodded. “In about a month, maybe less.”

“I got a question,” Frank said.

“Shoot.”

“Can’t you just use some fancy tech to see what’s down there?”

“Electrical disturbances and cloud cover make that difficult, and Shield Command wants human eyes on the ground to confirm.”

She activated a map of the location that Frank and Martin both studied.

“Any colonists in that area?” Martin asked.

“Potentially,” she said. “We have evidence of some miners remaining behind after the mines were abandoned, but if they’re smart, they left. No one can survive long-term once the ‘winter’ sets in. Entire planet freezes. All plant life goes dormant. The small life-forms that have been studied are believed to all go underground.”

She indicated to their books. “Page fifty-five, take a look.”

Frank flipped through and found a holographic pattern that projected out.

“The hell is this, a disco?” he asked.

Natalia frowned. “These complex geometric patterns were detected at the Titan incident—”

“The Titan slaughter,” Frank said.

Natalia paused. “The unfortunate destruction of Titan Station,” she corrected.

Frank leaned forward, memories sharpening.

“I believe the Hollow were sending a message at the station,” Natalia said.

“A message?” Martin asked.

“We think so.” Natalia enlarged a section. “Our linguistics team has been working on it around the clock. I also believe it was a warning.”

Frank put his hand on Rex’s head as realization dawned. He’d spent fifteen years blaming the Hollow, blaming Shield Command, blaming Martin—but what if the Hollow hadn’t been there to kill everyone?

Frank felt a strange clarity cutting through the alcohol haze. This wasn’t just about revenge or redemption, this was about the truth.

“What’s the mission?” he finally asked.

“Reconnaissance. Contact, if possible. We want to understand what they’re trying to tell us before Shield Command panics and destroys them again,” Natalia explained. “We don’t want a war with this species if we can avoid it.”

Frank ran a hand through his gray hair.

“You’ll train a Marine Recon Squad to prepare them to fight the Hollow, if needed,” Natalia explained. “And you will accompany them on their mission, but not into the field.”

“Not into the field?” Martin asked. “So we sit back on our asses while they head out to face God knows what?”

“We? I never said I’m going,” Frank protested.

Martin glared at him, the glare of judgment. As if to say, *You're a goddamn Marine, start acting like one.*

Natalia sighed, deeply, like she was genuinely upset about something.

"Truth is, this new squad is not ready at all to face the Hollow. Don't get me wrong, they are good—great Marines with combat experience, but they haven't trained for this." She hesitated, then added, "Actually, some of them don't even have combat experience, but—"

"You've got to be kidding me," Frank said. "Do they even know what the Hollow are?"

"Yes, if you hadn't interrupted me, I was about to get to that." She glanced at her watch with a frown, then looked right back to Frank. "Half of this specialized squad has important scientific backgrounds. One of them is a Xenobiologist."

"Oh shit, please tell me Dr. Lowell didn't join the Marines," Martin said.

"No," Natalia said. "Dr. Lowell is long since retired."

"Honestly surprised he didn't shoot himself on accident in the field . . ."

Natalia smiled but then returned to her serious voice.

"Two of the teams we had trained for something like this were killed in a tragic crash over three months ago," she said. "The third team went MIA on a patrol through the Gauntlet to look for the Hollow."

She opened her folder to page ninety-five.

Frank did the same, seeing documentation of patrols for . . .

"That's right, we've been searching for the Hollow since *Squanto*," Natalia said. "But besides Titan Station, this is the first time we've detected them."

"That makes me feel better," Martin said. "Or worse, I guess."

"We searched for replacements for these specialized squads, but Shield Command dragged their feet, due to failure to find any Hollow all these years," Natalia said. "I feared this would happen, and I was right. Now we're scrambling to put together a new team."

"Fourth time's a charm then?" Frank grunted.

"Sounds like some major red tape," Martin said.

"Tell me about it," Natalia replied with a frown. "Some of my superiors believe we just need bombs and missiles to kill the Hollow, but I disagree. That won't get us closer to understanding them." Natalia looked them both in the eye. "I didn't want to pluck you two out of retirement, trust me on that. I wanted you to enjoy your hard-earned time off from the Corps. But we need you to help train this new squad for what's out there."

Frank sighed internally as he looked down at his classified folder, realizing maybe this was his second chance; not to get his family back, but to prevent other families from suffering the same fate. To make their deaths mean something. To help other Marines face a deadly enemy.

"We would need a month with them. Minimum," Martin said.

"You have a week. We need to know what the Hollow are doing. Right now, a destroyer is parked in orbit, ready to blast them to hell again. I've convinced Shield Command to authorize a week of recon. Fortunately, and sadly, they are busy with the Free Miner terrorist attack, which is more important to brass at this moment. But who knows when that will change."

Martin and Natalia both looked to Frank.

"Well?" she asked after a few beats passed.

"A week," Frank agreed with a grunt. "But we do this our way."

"Good, now that I've got your commitments, take a look at page one hundred. You'll find everything we know about the Hollow, and how to kill them, much of it based off your own experience, but trust me, there's more intel that you haven't seen."

"Damn," Martin muttered. "They've been busy."

The first section showed what they already knew: that modulated plasma could disrupt the Hollow's molecular structure, but only temporarily before they adapted. The following sections revealed new information.

"Temporal disruption fields?" Frank read, his eyebrows rising. "You're telling me these bastards are vulnerable to time distortion?"

"Research teams discovered that the Hollow exist partially out of phase with our timeline," Natalia explained. "They don't just move through solid matter—they move through moments in time. The new TDF grenades create localized temporal bubbles that trap them between seconds. But they'll do the same thing to humans, so make sure if you ever use one, you're far clear of the blast zone."

"Or you'll end up like the protein shakes them young guns love to drink." Frank snorted quietly.

Martin was too concerned to laugh. He studied a simulation showing a liquid-metal form freezing mid-flow when caught in a shimmering field. "So you slow them down enough to what? Run away?"

"Or to hit them with this," Natalia said, advancing to the next display.

The hologram showed a modified plasma rifle.

Frank whistled. "That's a mean-looking rifle, if not a bit nerdy."

"That's the MR-113," Natalia said. "The latest model, designed specifically to terminate the Hollow."

"You've finally figured out how to kill them," Martin said flatly.

"Theoretically," Natalia cautioned. "Lab tests show promise, but we haven't field-tested against an actual specimen."

Frank's eyes narrowed.

"There's one more thing you should know," Natalia said. "Our scientists believe the Hollow may be able to establish temporary symbiotic connections with other species. Your squad member Torres on *Squanto*—his transformation wasn't just an attack. It might have been an attempted communication method."

"You're saying they were trying to talk to us by . . . merging with us?" Martin asked incredulously.

"Their physiology is so fundamentally different from ours that direct neural connection might be the only way they can fully convey complex information," Natalia explained. "Unfortunately, human biology can't sustain the connection without fatal consequences."

"Unless . . ." Frank trailed off, looking meaningfully at his prosthetic arm.

Natalia nodded. "That's why your cybernetic enhancements have been upgraded with quantum shielding. If communication becomes necessary, you might be able to interface with them briefly without the fatal side effects Torres experienced.

"If not hostile," Natalia reminded them. "We don't want to shoot first, if possible."

Frank closed the file, his expression grim. "And if they are?"

Natalia's face hardened. "Then the Marines will use everything in that file to kill anything that moves. And pray it's enough."

"Understood," Martin said.

Frank felt the last of his drunken haze burning away, replaced by a cold certainty. The answers he had been too afraid to search for were out there. Whatever had happened to *Squanto*, whatever the Hollow had been doing at Titan Station—he had the chance to discover it now.

This time, he'd be ready.

"Okay," Frank said. "I've seen enough, let's get this show on the road."

"Good. Next stop, Medical," she said.

"I feel for anyone that has to see this guy naked," Frank said. "Martin's been growing hair everywhere but his head."

"Yeah, and your blood is pure beer at this point. They should be studying you, on how you're still alive."

"Well, I have you to thank for that, old friend. Don't I now?"

He snorted, then turned to leave.

Natalia caught Frank's arm. "I meant what I said. I'm sorry about your family."

He held her gaze, something resolving inside him. Then he nodded. "Thanks, I appreciate you trying to help that day."

Frank glanced back at the holographic data still floating above the table. Then with a deep breath, he walked out with Rex, who sat loyally by his side in the corridor.

"We got a new mission, bub," he said. "Hope you're up for it . . ."

I hope I am, Frank thought.

CHAPTER SIX

"Natalia said Medical next," Martin reminded Frank, struggling to keep up with the cargo sled. It now held two battlesuits and two dogs, which should have slowed it down more, but Martin's leg was glitching again. "I really want to get my leg looked at."

"And you wanna haul Lucky and your damn suit around to Medical and then back to our quarters?" Frank asked, waving the remote for the sled like a laser pointer. "Because we're starting to draw attention. I say we go to armor first. The docs can wait. Hell, I have a hole in my side; don't be such a pussy, Martin."

Martin snickered but refrained from a retort when he saw a second lieutenant coming their way. Both men saluted, and to Martin's surprise, the officer actually acknowledged them. More with a confused glance at their appearance and their rigs.

For some reason, the attention had only gotten more intense since Frank had cleaned up and they'd both put on regulation uniforms. Before, they'd been an oddity, something that didn't belong, with their two deadlined Aegis battlesuits, and the presence of the two dogs. Now that they were very clearly Marines, people were eyeing them and wondering what the hell they were doing here.

If they only knew they pulled us out of retirement because of the Hollow, Martin thought.

He kept waiting for the officer to challenge them, but a master gunny was just a little too high on the NCO food chain for them to mess with, apparently.

They reached the armory a few minutes later. The massive double doors into the secure area of the building spread open invitingly as technicians hauled gear out of lockers for maintenance. The alert, Martin guessed, was responsible for the flurry of activity . . . and more importantly, the flurry of *visible* activity to prove to any senior NCOs or officers passing by that yes, they *were* working.

It always astounded Martin that the person in charge of hundreds of millions of credits' worth of gear, enough to conquer a city, was a staff sergeant, three ranks down from him, yet that was eternally the military way. It didn't take too long to find the chief armorer for the battalion. She was the one bustling from one repair to another, barking corrections at the enlisted as they laid out disassembled weapons on silvery worktables or stripped the outer panels off Aegis suits suspended from maintenance racks.

She shared the universal harried look of someone given more responsibility than one person should have rightly been saddled with, but also the confidence of a woman competent enough to handle the job. The sleeves of her fatigue shirt were rolled down to protect from burns and already covered in grease. A black stain of the same flavor smeared her right cheek despite a couple attempts to wipe it away with an equally stained red shop towel even as the two of them approached.

The armorer didn't notice them at first, not until a few of her technicians looked up, frowning in consternation either at the suits or the dogs. Cosmo and Rex didn't make a sound, seemingly very happy to have found each other again and to be given a ride on the sled for most of the day.

"What th'hell are those two relics doing here?" the armorer blurted.

"I don't know how to take that, Sergeant," Martin said, cocking an eyebrow at the woman, "until I figure out if you mean us or the Aegis suits."

She stared at him for a moment, then seemed to notice his rank and came to attention.

"At ease!" she barked at the other armorers, and they all rose from their tasks, hands folded behind them.

"As you were," Martin said, waving the courtesy off. "We're here on business, Sergeant"—he squinted at her dirty name tape—"Sanchez."

The rest of the team took him at his word and immediately went back to their tasks, the clacking and clanging of tools against metal resuming like an orchestra tuning their instruments. Sanchez tried one more time with the towel but only spread the grease smear farther across her face.

"What can I do for you, Master Guns?" she asked.

"Master Gunny Cage and I are in a sort of unique position, Sanchez," he explained. "I don't know if you know who we are, but we have a very important mission."

"I'm aware, but I can't issue you new armor until you pass Medical, and my files are showing you haven't been there yet."

"That's correct, but you're also wrong on the new armor part," Martin said. "'Cause we don't need *new* armor."

Frank stepped forward. "Instead of waiting for calibration and fitting and all that other happy horseshit that goes along with getting a new Aegis issued, we were hoping to convince you to just reenergize and rearm our personal suits. My girl Lucky here is especially important to me, as she has saved my hide more times than I can count."

Frank grinned, something Martin might have advised against doing until he got his teeth looked at. They needed a nice polish, and maybe a few should be pulled.

"We kinda got attached to them back when we were Armored Infantry," Martin said.

"You're kidding me, right?" Sanchez said. "Those are damn dinosaurs."

Frank's grin vanished. He took another step toward the armorer. "I hope you mean like a T-Rex, or even a raptor, instead of implying they are old as fossils."

Sanchez alternated her gaze from Frank to Martin, who nodded to back up Frank, something he normally hated doing.

"It's just a new power core and weapons installation," Martin explained. "It'll likely save you work in the long run since you won't have to retask two new suits for us and go through that whole rigamarole. And we'd be in your eternal debt."

Sanchez again stared at them in turn before realization set in that they were serious. She sighed, scrubbing at her fingertips with the dirty towel.

"Well, you can leave 'em here, Gunny, and I'll try to get one of my techs to look at them while you two get checked out by the doc. I can't promise anything, but if it's as simple an operation as you said, we might get them back to you in two days."

"We're going to need them faster than that," Frank said.

"Okay, I'll see what I can do."

"Good deal, Sanchez, thanks," Martin said. He offered the woman a hand, not caring about the grease transfer.

"If I ever see you in the NCO club," Frank added, "beers are on Martin."

"Ha!" Sanchez laughed. "I just might take you up on that."

"You always find a way to drink for free, don't you, Cage?" Martin added quietly to Frank.

"Damn right I do, Kelvin."

On the way out, Rex and Cosmo seemed reluctant to give up their ride, but Martin wasn't interested in toting a cargo sled around the base, and he snapped his fingers at the dog. Cosmo whined and jumped down, and Rex followed him with a gentle whoof that might have been the dog equivalent of a sigh. Martin grabbed the shepherd's leash off the dog's harness, and both of them fell into step with their masters.

"That went better than I expected," Frank admitted, grinning.

Martin said nothing even though he would have been willing to argue the point, mostly because this was as focused as he'd seen Frank in . . . shit, he wasn't even sure. The last thing Martin wanted to do was spoil things.

"We should leave the dogs in our quarters," he said instead. "Before we go to Medical, I mean. They're not gonna want to let them in. And if they have to work on us . . . well, it upsets Cosmo when I try to work on my leg. I can't imagine what he'd do if he saw someone else taking it off completely."

"As long as Cosmo is there with him, I think Rex will be okay in the quarters," Frank replied, shrugging. He wagged a finger of his prosthetic hand, his grin broadening. "But hey, I had an idea."

"I don't know that I like the sound of that," Martin admitted, then took a moment to salute a passing captain before turning his attention back to Frank.

"Well, I don't know if you bothered to look at the orders they drafted up to bring us both back into the Corps," Frank went on, not having bothered to look up or salute, "but I read the whole damned thing during the flight here. There's this little section in there about how they're gonna need to upgrade our prosthetics."

"Yeah, no shit." Martin shook his head, then took time to salute another officer. "That's why we're heading to Medical, ain't it?" Another officer. "Dammit, why can't we get some kinda blue force tracker system made up so we can see where all the officers are gonna be walking and avoid them?"

"No," Frank corrected him, ignoring the whining. "We were going there to get our prosthetics repaired and adjusted. This said *upgraded*."

"Yeah? So? What did you have in mind?"

Frank didn't answer, just laughed almost maniacally, and Martin groaned. After so many years, he'd forgotten the talent the man had for getting them both into trouble.

"Is that a *knife* wound, Master Gunny Cage?" the medical technician asked, his eyes going wide as he peeled the smart bandage off Frank's side.

"Why yes, it sure is, Doc," Frank agreed cheerfully. "Thanks for noticing. It's mostly closed up now, though. Those smart bandages are great. If I'd been able to afford to keep them at the house, I probably wouldn't have a few of these scars."

"I'm not a doctor," the tech murmured, making a note on his tablet. "The doctor will be in later to see you, once I finish the initial examination. I'm just a tech."

Frank changed the subject. "Hey, techie, you think you could turn the heat up in here a little if you're gonna keep me sitting around here in my skivvies? This table is damned cold, and it ain't like I can rub my hands together for warmth, since one of 'em ain't got no warmth."

"I'm going to recommend the doctor give you a few hours in the CRC for the wound and"—the younger man grimaced as he looked Frank up and down—"for your general lack of preventative maintenance."

"Yecch," Frank said, shuddering again but this time not from the cold. "You wanna drop me in the damned goo bath? For this little cut?"

"The Cellular Reconstruction Chamber, and not just for that. You've got a worrying infection here where your prosthetic fits with your shoulder joint, not to mention four cavities and"—he squinted at the readout from the MRI Frank had walked through—"what looks like colon cancer. You spend three, maybe four hours in the CRC, you'll be as good as new."

"Colon cancer?" Frank shrugged again. He figured the blood in his shits was from all the beer. "I hate the idea of breathing liquid. Can you knock me out first?"

He gave the man a pleading look.

"Sure, no problem," replied the tech. "I'll go get that set up so we can march you in there right after Dr. Weinstein sees you."

"What about the prosthetics?" he asked, waving the artificial hand. "I was supposed to talk to someone about an upgrade."

"That'll be up to Dr. Weinstein." The tech hurried out the door, letting it close behind him and leaving Frank alone.

He sighed, wishing the man had offered him a hospital gown or something. The exam room was just like every other one he'd seen during decades in the Marines and during his retirement here on Eden before he'd stopped making his VA appointments because the doctors wouldn't stop telling him to quit drinking. Walls painted earth tones because some study or another had said they were soothing, paintings of sylvan woods with deer or elk or other harmless herbivores grazing hanging in whatever spots were free, no feng shui to them at all. Plus a half dozen locked cabinets that probably contained nothing more valuable than tongue depressors.

Sighing, he closed his eyes, determined to at least get a nap out of this if they were going to make him wait around. It was a treasured Marine skill, the ability to grab some shut-eye no matter what the circumstances, whether you were on a bucking, rolling lander running evasive maneuvers through enemy air defenses or sitting on a spaceport landing field waiting four hours for a pickup. Frank hadn't exercised that muscle in a while, counting instead on 180-proof ethanol anesthesia, but he didn't think he'd be able to get away with that here under the watchful eye of the Marine Corps and Martin. Mostly Martin. He'd let his friend down one too many times.

Lying back against the cold metal of the examination gurney, fingers interlaced behind his head, Frank tried to sleep. The eye made it harder than it needed to be. A bionic eye didn't just switch itself off when his eyelid went over it; otherwise, he would never be able to blink without effectively going temporarily blind on that side. No, Frank had to consciously order the eye to turn off, and then when he wanted to be able to see again, he had to do the entire thing in reverse, and the whole situation bothered him. He'd always been a light sleeper, ready to go from sawing logs to combat in a heartbeat, but now, he had to remember to turn his damned eye back on.

Somewhere between gripes, Frank nodded off. He wasn't sure when it had happened, but he knew he was dreaming because he was happy. Back in their apartment on Titan Station, roomy for an NCO because everyone on Titan Station had plenty of room, plenty to eat, plenty of schools and recreational pursuits. It was heaven. But right now, he couldn't see any of the rest of the station, just their quarters. It wasn't *exactly* their quarters, of course. It never was, in dreams. His subconscious had mixed in elements of the house he'd grown up in, bigger and filled with sunlight, with different furniture, yet somehow everything about the place still seemed right.

Sarah chased Lily through the kitchen and back into the living room, growling like a bear while the little girl squealed in delight, her twin braids flapping around as she ran. Sarah always favored bright colors, and Lily had tried to imitate her style in miniature, though she added unicorns and giraffes to the patterns. Both were equally real to the girl, or perhaps equally fanciful, since she'd never see either of them.

Frank looked up from the scansheet he'd been reading and grinned at the two of them. He waited until they were closer, then dropped the folding tablet and lunged off the couch, growling to match Sarah, and lifted Lily off the ground.

"No fair!" she screeched, legs kicking as if she were still running on the tile floor. "I didn't know there were *two* grizzly bears!"

Frank laughed and pulled her into a hug.

"Well, traditionally for Goldilocks, there are three . . . so maybe you're a bear, too!"

She growled and held up pretend claws, baring her teeth before she broke down into laughter.

"Oh, Daddy, you know they aren't going to let bears live on the station! Who'd clean up all their poop?"

"I believe they told me that they're going to make all the little girls who like to pretend they're bears clean it up," Frank said, raising an eyebrow. "Right after they finish their homework." Frank sat Lily down and gave her a gentle push toward her room. "Before dinner!"

"Aw," Lily whined but trudged off dutifully.

"And make sure you wash your hands for dinner," Frank called after her. "Bear poop is really dirty!"

She giggled as she closed her door, then Sarah slid into his arms and kissed him.

"Did you send her off for homework because you have a little aperitif in mind, husband-o'-mine?" she whispered in his ear, following it up by nibbling playfully on his earlobe.

"Roar," he replied with a grin, pulling her to him. She was so warm, so soft. Holding her felt so good it almost hurt.

"Daddy . . ."

He broke the embrace with Sarah, looking up at the plaintive, scared voice of his daughter. She stepped out of the doorway of her room, surrounded by a faint glow, a color Frank couldn't have described. Silvery lines spread beneath her skin, like frost creeping across a windowpane, and the veins in her neck and face bulged, taking on a metallic sheen.

"Daddy, help me!" The voice, once familiar, was now a cacophony of distorted harmonics, an alien chorus replacing human tones. "It's taking me!" Her arms went out to him. "Don't let it take me!"

No. It hadn't happened this way. This was just a nightmare. She was only six years old in this memory. She was nine and a half when the Hollow hit Titan Station. And the classified briefing revealed to Frank afterward it was an explosion that killed his family—an explosion from the barrage of missiles fired by the Shield Command. His family felt nothing. At least, that's what he wanted to believe. But this dream—nightmare, was always so goddamn realistic.

"Lily . . ." He tried to pull away from Sarah, to run to his daughter, but Sarah had a hold of his arm and wouldn't let go.

Frank looked down at the hand holding him and saw those silvery veins beneath glowing skin before he looked up at her face. Sarah's irises had dissolved into liquid silver, mercury tears running down her cheeks.

"You can't go," the chorus of alien voices coming out of her mouth announced. "You brought us here, Frank. You have to stay with us. We should all die together."

She was right. This was the place he *should* have died. But Martin had taken that choice away from him.

Searing pain ran up his shoulder, so real, so damn real.

In the nightmare, the thing Sarah had become still held on to most of his left arm . . . she'd pulled it off at the shoulder.

"No!" he screamed, hand going up . . .

. . . and finding the firm fakeness of his prosthetic. He sat bolt upright on the gurney, panting and sweating like he'd just run a marathon. Blinking, he focused on a dumpy, thick-jowled older man who stared at him from the open door of the exam room.

"Are you alright, Master Gunny Cage?" the man asked him.

"Uh, yeah," he replied, rubbing at his eyes. There were tears in his natural eye that he didn't remember crying. "You must be the doc."

"Yes, I'm Dr. Weinstein." The older man laughed sharply, shutting the door behind him. "Technically, *Lieutenant Colonel* Weinstein, but that's an honorific that strictly shows in my monthly pay."

Yeah, there was the silver oak leaf on the front of his uniform jacket, under his lab coat. He seemed too paunchy to be wearing a uniform, but then, so was Martin.

"So, whatcha find out in there, sir?" Frank asked, nodding to the tablet Weinstein held. "Am I worth salvaging?"

"That's not for me to say, Sergeant," Weinstein told him with an utter lack of bedside manner. "You're *going* to be salvaged, no matter my opinion on the subject, and the first step, as my technician told you, is going to be three point six hours in the CRC. That should clear up some of the liver problems you've developed over what I can only imagine has been several years of heavy drinking and poor nutrition. We'll give you something to keep your involuntary shaking at bay for a month as well. Then there's the matter of servicing your prosthetics."

"No, sir," Frank interrupted, sharply enough for Weinstein to look up in surprise. "My orders specify that my prosthetics—and those of my bald, elderly friend, Master Gunnery Sergeant Martin—are to be *upgraded*, not just serviced. According to Colonel Shafter, we're both to get the very latest in combat-enhanced bionics. Skeletal reinforcement to handle the extra strain, isotope power packs, the works. *And* they need to be covered in synthskin with artificial nerves hooked up to our brains via an implant neurolink."

At the doctor's look of disbelief, Frank shrugged.

"We're here to fight the Hollow, Doc. This ain't no time to be skimping. We're gonna need every advantage we can get."

Weinstein sighed heavily and began tapping commands into the tablet.

"Well, then, forget the four-hour dip in the goo tank," he said. "I have orders to get you both to active duty ASAP, so we'll do the upgrades first, then it'll be *twelve* hours in the tank for recovery."

"Shit," Frank said with a scowl. "I'm gonna have to call someone to go take care of the dogs . . ."

He pulled out his link. "What was the name of that armorer again?" he wondered. "Oh yeah . . . Sanchez."

Frank chuckled, wondering how she'd respond to them asking her for yet another favor. No way to find out except trying, he decided. She could only say no.

CHAPTER SEVEN

She said yes," Frank mumbled, still half in a stupor.

Martin glowered at the man from the next recovery bed over, shaking his head. The smell of antiseptic and the faint metallic tang of the cellular reconstruction fluid still clung to both of them.

"Are you gonna keep repeating that until the anesthetic wears off?" Martin asked.

Frank's eyes blinked rapidly as he emerged from the post-goo-tank stupor. One eye—his natural one—was bloodshot and bleary, while the cybernetic one adjusted its aperture with a barely audible whir, focusing on Martin's face, or head.

"You wouldn't believe what these lights are doing to that bald crown of yours," Frank said. "Shining like a polished stone." Martin was too sore to come up with a retort. He winced when he tried to sit up, the movement sending jolts of pain through his newly upgraded nervous system.

"Thanks so much for insisting we get the upgrades," he said.

"Welcome," Frank replied, wincing from his own pain.

Martin flexed his arm, waggling the new fingers, which gleamed with a subtle metallic sheen beneath synthetic skin that was still too smooth, too perfect compared to his weathered flesh. "It *could* have just been a couple hours of normal maintenance and some downtime in the goo tank, but no . . . you wanted the supersoldier treatment. Now my shoulders, my back, my hips . . . *everything* is sore. The docs said they had to reinforce the connection points all through the skeletal system to handle the extra load. Did they at least give you some new teeth?"

Frank looked up, his eyes drifting over Martin's eyes to study his forehead with exaggerated interest. "Damn, looks like they forgot your hair transplant."

Martin self-consciously ran a hand over his bald head. The skin there was smooth and soft after hours in the reconstruction tank, unusually sensitive to touch. "Give it up, Cage. I happen to like this smooth look."

"The egg look?" Frank dipped his new shoulder joint in a shrug that was almost natural, then grimaced at the unfamiliar sensation. "To each his own."

"My head does not look like an egg," Martin protested, his voice rising slightly.

"No, it has eyebrows. They definitely wasted a good opportunity to plant some grass and fix things up there."

"Too bad they didn't fix your brain."

A nurse passing by the recovery room paused at their bickering, gave them both a disapproving look that probably worked wonders on young recruits, then pulled the curtains around their beds and dimmed the lights to allow them to readjust after the cellular reconstruction.

Frank groaned as he sat up fully and swung his legs off the bed. The hospital gown rode up his thighs, and he tugged it down with his new hand, pausing as he did. He ran a bionic finger over the sheets and laughed, a sound of genuine surprise and delight. "Son of a bitch, I can *feel* things now. Not just pressure, but texture. Temperature. Do you know how long it's been since I actually felt something with this hand?"

"I believe I do," Martin replied dryly, holding up his own prosthetic and examining the way light played across the articulated joints. "And yeah, it's nice being able to touch things again. The VA-issued models were crap—all function, no sensation. But when they give you shit like this"—he made a fist, watching the synthetic muscles bunch beneath the skin, the knuckles whitening just like real ones—"it's because they expect you to use it all the way to its capacity. Nothing comes for free, Cage. Not in the Corps. You should know that more than any of us."

"Get real, dumbass. You think they were going to expect any less from us just because we had cheap, shitty prosthetics? Besides, this is what's called the *sunk-cost fallacy*."

Martin goggled at him, mouth dropping open. The expression added wrinkles to his face that made him look far older than his years.

"What?" Frank demanded, spreading his arms, then wincing at the pain the motion caused him. His new shoulders were still adjusting to the neural interface, sending occasional misfired signals that felt like someone jabbing him with a hot needle. "You think I made that term up?"

"No, I know what it is. I'm just amazed *you* do."

"Well, in this case, it means that they've already invested however much this shit costs into us, so they won't be so quick to throw us away. Or send us on a suicide mission." His eyebrows shot up. "Did I get it right?"

"Yeah, mostly," Martin admitted. Steeling himself, he pushed upright and tried to stand but had to catch the edge of the bed to keep from falling over. The new prosthetic leg was calibrated for a different stance than he was used to, making him feel like a newborn colt trying to walk. "This shit ain't had time to synch with our nerves all the way, but lying around doing nothing ain't gonna get it done any quicker."

Martin winced as he looked down at his hospital gown and realized how big his belly had gotten over years of doing nothing more strenuous than working in the garden. The fabric stretched tight over the paunch, accentuating rather than hiding it. He sucked in his gut experimentally, but it barely made a difference. Still wasn't as bad as Frank's beer gut, which hung over the edge of the bed like it was melting.

"I think the base gym has gear for individual muscle stimulation," Martin said, trying to steady himself without grabbing the IV stand. The stimulation would hurt like hell, but it would kick-start the atrophied muscles around their prosthetics. "Maybe we should check—"

Frank dismissed the idea with a wave of his hand, then raised it to eye level, fascinated by the way the synthetic skin creased at the knuckles just like the real thing. He splayed his fingers, then curled them one by one, watching the tendons move beneath the surface.

"Master Gunnies," came the familiar voice of Dr. Weinstein. The man's footsteps had been silent on the polished floor, giving them no warning of his approach. He entered the recovery room, his ever-present tablet in hand, his uniform crisp despite the late hour and the general chaos of the medical center. The light gleamed off his silver-rimmed glasses and completely bald head—even balder than Martin's.

"You shouldn't be trying to stand yet, but I applaud your dedication to getting back in shape, particularly since it's a requirement for the upgrades you insisted on." He turned the tablet around and held it between them where they both could see. The screen displayed a complex form filled with medical jargon and military regulations in painfully small print. "In fact, it's in the military regulations, section 34-B. You can either get to below the required body fat percentage in one month, or the combat bionics will be replaced with conventional prosthetics."

"One *month*!" Martin yelped, looking down at his gut in dismay, pinching the flesh through the thin hospital gown. It was more substantial than he'd imagined. "There's no flippin' way, Doc! I'd have to go on a starvation diet!"

"I'm writing you a prescription for an appetite suppressant, Master Gunny Martin," Weinstein assured him, tapping at the tablet again with fingers that moved almost too quickly to follow. "And issuing a medical order for you to be required to eat on base three meals a day at the Special Nutritional Requirements section of the mess hall. After your mission, that is." He gave Martin a pointed look over the rim of his glasses. "The suppressant is effective but has some side effects. Dry mouth, insomnia, occasional hallucinations."

Frank guffawed so hard he nearly toppled over.

"They're putting you at the fat-boy table!" he crowed, grabbing Martin by the shoulder and shaking him hard enough for Martin's gut to wobble visibly beneath the gown. "With all the butter-bars who can't pass their fitness tests!"

Martin cursed and swung backward at Frank, forgetting what arm he was using, and forgetting that his conventional prosthetic had been replaced with something far stronger. Frank ducked out of the way with reflexes faster than either man had ever had, even before their prosthetics, then twisting sideways with a grace that belied his years and bulk. Martin's bionic arm continued its arc and smashed into the storage cabinet between the beds instead, caving the doors in with an earsplitting boom of metal on metal. Medical supplies scattered across the floor—bandages, hyposprays, packages of synthetic skin, all tumbling like leaves in a storm.

Frank's stare went back and forth between Martin and the smashed cabinet.

"You can't be serious," said the doctor.

He stood behind them, glaring like a teacher at two preschoolers that had just thrown their shit at one another. Behind him, an orderly poked his head through the curtains, then quickly retreated upon seeing the doctor's expression.

"I'm sorry, Doc," Martin said, grabbing his bionic arm with his biological one as if to restrain it, like it had a mind of its own. "I just forgot . . ."

"Forgot?" Weinstein snapped, jabbing a finger into Martin's chest. "If you forget, you could kill someone out there."

"We're not out there yet, sir," Frank said. "Try not to worry, we got this—"

"Got this?" Weinstein shook his head. "I heard you two were trouble, but my God, brass must be really desperate if they recalled you two back."

"We're not machines, we're Marines," Martin said.

"Precisely, now start acting like them."

"Touché," Martin said. "Our apologies."

That seemed to calm the doctor down. He shrugged a shoulder. "Your advanced enhancements have limits, but they can still crush bone with minimal effort. What do you think they'd do to a human skull?" He glanced at the ruined cabinet. "Both of you get dressed and get the hell out of here."

The doctor headed for the door but paused and glowered at Martin again. "And that cabinet is coming out of your pay, Master Guns."

"Yes, sir," Martin said softly, then patted his belly again, suddenly all too aware of every extra kilogram.

"Would you settle for a bottle of whiskey?" Frank called out.

"I don't drink," Weinstein said. "Perhaps you should consider doing the same thing."

Frank kept his voice low, but Martin heard it all. "Orders denied, Doc," he said. "You can pry my last beer from my cold, dead hands."

* * *

"Oh, sweet Mother Mary," Frank murmured, running a hand down the side of the battlesuit. His fingers traced the familiar contours with something approaching reverence. "Lucky, you never looked so sexy."

The Aegis A-117B stood in its maintenance cradle, gleaming under the harsh industrial lighting of the armory bay. The suit was a design that had been around since before Frank was born, but there'd obviously been a few upgrades since the last time he'd put it on. Technicians moved around them, calibrating other suits and running diagnostics, the constant hum of activity in the background like a mechanical heartbeat.

Lucky had a fresh matte black coating where her armor had worn silver with age, the surface absorbing light rather than reflecting it. Frank ran his fingers over places where he remembered deep gouges and battle damage, but he couldn't even detect where the scars from field patches had been. And beyond the repairs and the repaint, she just seemed . . . sleeker. Slimmer. The joints were more articulated, the armor plates better contoured to the human form beneath. The backpack that held the power supply was definitely smaller, and he pointed to it, looking a question at Sanchez.

The armory sergeant stood with arms crossed, her dark hair pulled back in a regulation bun, face smudged with the grease and grime that came with her job. Unlike many of the techs who looked at them like museum exhibits, Sanchez seemed to appreciate what the two veterans represented.

"They miniaturized the isotope reactors a couple years ago," she said, chin up as if she was more smug about the job she'd done than she was annoyed at having to do it. "No more of that bulky deuterium crap that needed charging every forty-eight hours. These babies will run for months on a single pellet, and they're shielded against EMP better than your old models, too." She gestured to the smooth lines of the suit. "As well as the targeting systems, lidar, radar and thermal and sonic sensors. All beneath the armor now, where they're less likely to be damaged in a firefight. The whole thing is lighter by about a hundred kilos, too. More maneuverable, faster top speed and jumping ability. I think you fellas'll be very happy with the changes."

Martin already had his chest plate open and pulled himself inside with a grunt of effort, then settled into the padded interior.

Frank quickly hurried to get into his own suit that seemed to embrace him, interior padding conforming to his body as systems began to power up. Status lights flickered across the interior display, running through initialization sequences without any input from him.

"Smells like new," he commented, his voice taking on a slight metallic quality as it resonated through the suit's audio system. Then he offered Sanchez a grin. "I would ask for a cupholder, but I've just been informed that I'm off beer for the foreseeable future, so there'd be no point."

"Don't lie," Martin said. "You aren't quitting."

"Oh I'm not quitting anything." Frank grinned at Sanchez. "I'm still very much in a committed relationship with the mistress of the hops. So the invitation still stands, whenever you want to share a few beers, they're on Martin." He threw his hands up in a gesture of sudden realization. "Hell, what am I thinking? You took the time to let our dogs out and feed them while we were stuck in Medical! Rex can be a handful with strangers. I'll throw in a nice steak dinner for that."

Sanchez regarded Frank with a look of suspicion, but there was amusement beneath it, the corners of her mouth twitching upward. A few of the younger techs had stopped working to eavesdrop, nudging each other and trying not to laugh.

"You sure your wife would be okay with you treating me to a steak dinner?" Sanchez asked.

Frank swallowed, all sense of jocularity draining from him like blood after a shot to his T-section.

"My wife passed," he said quietly.

"I'm sorry, I—" Sanchez said.

"You didn't know." Frank forced a smile. "Don't worry, I'm not hitting on you. I'm practically old enough to be your dad."

"Frank's just a generous guy," Martin said, which was clearly a lie and meant to cut through the awkwardness that Frank had created.

He gave Martin a slight nod as if to say, *thanks*, without going all in on it.

"I agree with him; these upgrades are amazing. Thanks, Sanchez," Martin said.

He clambered out of the armor, grimacing as his paunch got stuck at the lip of the chest cavity for a moment. He had to exhale fully to extricate himself, face reddening with the effort.

Frank scratched his jaw, his mind on his wife again. The memory of Sarah flickered briefly—her laughing face, the way she'd roll her eyes at his bad jokes, how she smelled like vanilla and gunmetal after a day at the shooting range. She had loved weapons almost as much as he did. Could handle a rifle better than half the Marines in his unit. They had been so happy once.

A hand fell on his shoulder, and he turned to see Sanchez grinning at him, her expression softened. Perhaps she saw something in his face that went beyond the practiced charm.

"When you get back from wherever it is you're going with those suits, look me up for some beers. I'd love to hear some stories," she said.

"Will do," Frank said with a nod.

He felt, amazingly enough, good. Not the artificial good that came from alcohol dulling the edges of his grief, but something more authentic. Feeling good was a new thing for him, and he savored the experience, despite the trepidation in his gut, the certainty that it wouldn't last. Nothing good ever did.

"Can we leave our suits with you for now, Sergeant?" Martin asked, patting his own Aegis on the shoulder. The metal clanged beneath his palm. "I imagine our training unit will have their own armory, but we don't report to them until this afternoon, and I doubt the Visiting NCO Quarters is going to want us trying to squeeze the things into our quarters. I mean, the staff almost shit a brick when they found out about the dogs."

"Oh, shit!" Frank said, eyes going wide as reality crashed back in. "The dogs! We have to get over there before they crap on the carpeting!" He checked the time on his wrist display. "They've been alone for hours now."

Sanchez burst out laughing, the sound full and genuine, which did attract attention from even twenty meters away. Several techs turned to look, surprised to see the normally stern armorer so amused.

"Go," she told them, making a shooing gesture. "I'll hold the suits here for you until tomorrow, but you'd better get them out of here by then! Loose ordnance doesn't last long on this base! Some eager lieutenant might requisition them for his own unit if they sit too long."

"You got it," Frank promised as the two of them jogged away.

"Damn," Martin said, looking down at himself as they cleared the armory doors and hit the parade ground at a respectable clip. "I haven't moved this fast in years!" The new leg responded fluidly, the gait almost natural, none of the stuttering and dragging of his old model.

"Neither have I," Frank said.

Another familiar voice called out, stopping them in their tracks.

Both men turned to find Natalia standing behind them, her uniform immaculate, her posture rigid. She had approached silently despite the graveled surface of the parade ground, a testament to the training she'd received since they last saw her.

"Captain," Martin said, straightening unconsciously.

Frank saluted, the gesture coming back to him like muscle memory.

"You look . . . better," she said, eyes scanning Frank's face for signs of the haunted, drunk mess he'd been just days ago.

"Thank you," Frank said. "I feel better." He flexed his new hand, still marveling at the sensation of air against the synthetic skin.

"Good, let's get some food in you two. Healthy food," she corrected with emphasis. "Then you get to meet your new squad."

CHAPTER EIGHT

"That was the worst damned lunch I ever had," Martin moaned, running his tongue over his teeth as if trying to scrape off an offensive coating. "I can't get the taste of that horrible no-calorie food out of my mouth! Synthetic protein that tastes like recycled air filters. I almost dipped into Cosmo's food!"

Cosmo looked back at him, his large brown eyes holding what might have been sympathy beneath his dignified German shepherd features. *Or maybe,* Martin thought ruefully, *the dog just resented being on a leash.* He was trained for it, but they'd almost never used one out at his homestead where Cosmo could roam freely across acres of wilderness. Now the animal kept testing the restraint, clearly understanding this tether was the new normal.

"Yeah, well, nobody forced you to eat like a damned pig the last five years," Frank said, squinting up at the afternoon sun that beat down mercilessly. His new cybernetic eye adjusted automatically while his natural one watered in the glare. "Jeez, I forgot how hot it gets here wearing uniform fatigues in the summer. This place is permanently set to 'broil.'"

"You want to talk about heat?" Martin scoffed. "Try working a garden in direct sunlight for six hours straight. At least you were busy getting drunk in air-conditioned bars."

"True. One of alcohol's many medicinal qualities, environmental temperature control. I miss it already."

They turned the corner, and Martin looked up at the looming monolith that was the headquarters building. Twelve stories of reinforced concrete and armored glass, designed to withstand orbital bombardment rather than please the eye.

"Game time," he said quietly.

The enlisted clerk just inside the door, a young corporal with immaculate hair and a uniform so crisp it could cut paper, stared first at the dogs. Then she glanced at the middle-aged men leading them, and finally at Martin's gut, which made him sigh. But once she registered the rank insignia on their collars, she stiffened and stammered something about how she could help them.

"We're looking for Captain Broadhurst," Martin told her. "Fifth Battalion Chief Training Officer."

"Yes, Master Guns. His office is down at the end of this hallway and on the right . . ."

Martin started to move past the desk, but the corporal raised a hand, then quickly transformed it into a more respectful gesture. ". . . but he's not there right now. He has the new training platoon out in the parade ground behind the building. He did say something about if Master Gunnies Martin and Frank arrive, to send them out there. Is that you?"

"Thanks," Martin said, already heading toward the back exit.

"Parade ground," Frank commented, nodding politely to a captain who was staring at Rex with obvious concern. "What the hell use is a parade ground for combat training? Do they think the Hollow will be marching in formation?"

"Just let me do the talking," Martin warned. "We're already late reporting in. Natalia said this Captain Broadhurst is some kind of training specialist, accelerated combat readiness programs for special ops. Not the type who appreciates being kept waiting."

"We were in the hospital," Frank protested. "Getting upgraded for their mission. What were we supposed to do? Break out with our nerve endings still hanging loose?"

"When was the last time you ran into an officer who cared about excuses? Hell, when was the last time *you* did when you were in charge? 'The effective range of an excuse is zero point zero meters.' That was your line, remember?"

"I would've given privates hell about missing formation, but I wouldn't have meant it. It's just what you do to keep them in line."

"Oh, well that makes all the difference." Martin snorted. "Just keep your mouth shut for five minutes. We need to make a good impression. Apparently, Broadhurst handpicked this replacement squad after what happened to the original team."

"Yeah, about that. Natalia mentioned two teams were killed in a transport crash recently, and the other team went missing in the Gauntlet searching for the Hollow. Convenient timing, don't you think?"

Martin halted. "What are you suggesting?"

"I don't know yet. But when was the last time not one, or two, but three specialized combat units died in a 'training accident' or went missing?"

Martin had no answer for that. It was unusual, to say the least. The Corps had safety protocols upon safety protocols for a reason.

They emerged from the shadowed halls into blazing sunlight. Three flagpoles rose from the center of the courtyard: Federation, planetary, and Marine Corps.

The CSF Marine Corps flag, red with its golden eagle clutching arrows, stiffened Martin's spine automatically, an ingrained reaction that retirement hadn't erased.

The Corps was home. Perhaps that explained why Frank had seemed to recover so quickly once back in uniform—there was something about it that straightened your spine and cleared your head.

"Getting misty-eyed, Kelvin?" Frank murmured.

"Shut up," Martin replied without heat. "You're doing the same thing."

Past the courtyard, beyond the sergeant-major's sacred turf with its DO NOT WALK signs, stretched the parade ground. The open space hosted an unusual formation—not a company or platoon, but a reinforced squad of twelve Marines. They stood at parade rest while a tall, broad-shouldered man in field utilities paced before them, his close-cropped hair gleaming in the sun, his uniform impossibly crisp despite the heat.

Before trying to make sense of his speech, Martin studied the squad. This was no ordinary unit. Half were officers—lieutenants, mostly—and half were NCOs. No privates or lance corporals. A specialized task force, then, but hastily assembled. Not standard operating procedure for any mission he'd ever been on.

". . . counting on you," Broadhurst was saying, his voice carrying with practiced authority. He paced back and forth, addressing them in a tone that said he wanted to be a general. "If you can't accomplish this, there may not be time for anyone else. I don't want to hear any reports of malingering, of wasting time, of anyone not training their hardest. I expect each and every one of you to make your families, your trainers, the Corps, and the Federation proud. Am I clear?"

"Yes, sir!" the group replied in unison, though Martin noted some of the lieutenants looked uncomfortable being addressed like recruits.

Broadhurst turned, spotting them immediately. His expression hardened, steely eyes narrowing at the sight of both older Marines, and particularly at the dogs.

"I blame you," Martin whispered to Frank, then snapped to attention and saluted. "Captain Broadhurst, Master Gunnery Sergeants Kelvin and Cage reporting for duty, sir."

Frank saluted too, remarkably sharp for a man who'd been drunk mere hours ago.

"You're both late," Broadhurst snapped, loud enough for the squad to hear. "I do not appreciate being forced to change a vital training schedule at the last moment. Every hour counts with this mission."

"Medical necessity, sir," Martin replied evenly. "We were undergoing cybernetic upgrades per Colonel Shafter's direct orders. The procedures required a mandatory recovery period in cellular reconstruction."

"Both our internal systems needed complete overhauls," Frank added, flexing his new prosthetic hand. "Can't fight the Hollow with outdated equipment. And the doctors were not negotiable about the recovery time."

Broadhurst's stern expression flickered at the mention of the Hollow. Something akin to concern crossed his features before he regained his composure.

"I see Colonel Shafter briefed you on the mission parameters," he said, his tone softening fractionally. "At least that saves us some preliminary work."

Martin nodded, noting the subtle shift. So Broadhurst wasn't fully in the command loop—Shafter was running things from above, and this guy was implementing the training under his direction. No wonder he seemed tense.

"Actually, Captain Ivan briefed us," Martin clarified, watching his reaction. "She's the one who recruited us for this operation."

A flash of irritation crossed Broadhurst's face. "Intelligence," he muttered, almost to himself. "Always running their own agenda." He straightened, clearly deciding to move forward rather than dwell on interservice politics.

"Well, you're here now, and we'll have to make the best of it," he said briskly. "I'm your training CO. I've been running specialized combat readiness programs for the past four years, usually with more time to prepare than I've been given for this mission."

He gestured toward the assembled squad. "This team is the best I could assemble after what happened to our original unit."

"The transport crash," Martin said, watching him carefully. "Captain Ivan mentioned it."

Broadhurst's jaw tightened. "Three months ago. An atmospheric insertion exercise went catastrophically wrong. The official report calls it mechanical failure, but . . ." He shook his head. "That was the best team I've ever trained. Specifically prepared for Hollow encounters based on all available data from your previous contacts."

"And now you've been ordered to prepare a replacement squad in a fraction of the time," Frank said, his earlier flippancy gone.

"Exactly." Broadhurst met his eyes with newfound respect. "Shield Command insists we accelerate the timetable. They want boots on the ground at the identified site within seventy-two hours."

"Captain Ivan said we would have a week."

"She may have recruited you, but she isn't in charge."

"Three days to prepare for Hollow contact?" Martin couldn't keep the disbelief from his voice. "That's not just accelerated, that's suicide."

"Hence, why you're here," Broadhurst replied. "You've actually survived encounters with these things. That makes you more valuable than a year's worth of simulations."

He lowered his voice, speaking just to them now. "I'll be direct with you both. This is a hastily assembled unit. They're good Marines, the best I could find on short notice, but they're not what I would have chosen given more time. Half of them have never seen real combat outside simulations."

"Then why are they coming? Oh right, because they are scientists or some shit," Frank said. "Last time I babysat some scientists, Martin and I were taking bets on which one of them would blow their foot off first."

"These aren't your typical scientists," Broadhurst grumbled. "They are Marines, but with specialized backgrounds."

Martin exchanged a look with Frank. Broadhurst wasn't the obstacle here; he was trapped in an impossible situation, trying to prepare Marines for a threat they couldn't possibly understand in a timeframe that was criminally short.

"We understand, Captain," Martin said with new respect. "We'll work with what we've got."

"Good." He nodded, the brief moment of candor passing. "Come on, I'll introduce you to the new squad, Wolverine-9. They've been briefed on the basic threat profile, but they need your firsthand experience."

Broadhurst started walking toward the squad, waving them to a hangar.

"Something stinks about all of this," Frank whispered as he followed.

"Later," Martin cautioned, though he agreed.

The hangar doors opened to a bay where the dozen men and women filed inside leisurely, some in conversation, others beginning to check equipment. The casual atmosphere spoke volumes.

"FORM UP, MARINES!" Broadhurst shouted.

Martin watched with growing dread as the group scrambled into formation, some moving with practiced precision, others clearly unaccustomed to the drill.

Three days, he thought grimly. Three days to prepare them for something that had taken the lives of so many others.

It wasn't going to be enough.

The training bay reeked of gun oil, sweat, and that particular brand of cockiness that came with youth and inexperience. Frank stood at the front of the room beside Martin, surveying the twelve Marines now arranged in perfect formation before Broadhurst, who was busy evaluating them and their gear one by one.

It was abundantly clear to both Frank and Martin, and probably their four-legged friends, that these Marines weren't your average grunts. Wolverine-9 was a hastily assembled mix of combat veterans and scientific specialists. Some wore combat badges and service ribbons that told stories of cartel takedowns, pirate raids, and insurgent suppressions, while others displayed the distinctive patches of xenobiology, archaeology, and advanced engineering divisions—academic achievements that looked impressive on paper but meant absolutely nothing against the Hollow.

The physical contrast was striking: twelve specimens of varying military fitness and bright minds facing two worn-down veterans, one of them a full-blown alcoholic, and the other a recovering one. The Marines stood ramrod straight in pressed uniforms, while Frank's worn fatigues hung loosely on his frame, his prosthetic hand glinting dully under the lights. Martin's upgraded cybernetic leg made a soft click each time he shifted weight, the sound barely perceptible but a constant reminder of what combat with real enemies cost.

The assembled Marines watched their approach with expressions ranging from curiosity to concealed skepticism. One lieutenant, a tall, athletic-looking man with dark skin and sharp features, didn't bother hiding his disdain as his eyes traveled from their aging faces to their dogs.

Frank scratched his stubbled chin, acutely aware of their stares.

"Why are they looking at me like I'm a grandpa?" he muttered.

"Cause you look like a bum that broke out of an old person's home," Martin chuckled. "Maybe try combing your hair once this decade."

"At least I have hair," Frank shot back, eyeing Martin's shining scalp.

Rex and Cosmo sat at perfect attention beside their masters, more disciplined than Frank felt capable of being at seven in the morning.

"I really need a stim or something," Frank mumbled. "I'm feeling pukey."

"Just keep your mouth shut and let me do the talking," Martin said quietly.

Broadhurst finally waved them forward.

"Master Gunnery Sergeants Kelvin and Cage, I present Special Operations Task Force Wolverine-9, assembled per CSF DOCA directive 48-A7 for Operation Obsidian Shield. Marines, these NCOs have been assigned as your tactical advisors with full authorization from Battalion Command. They survived both encounters with the Hollow on *Squanto* and at Titan Station."

He turned to Frank and Martin, lowering his voice. "Tactical protocols are in your briefing packets. I'll leave you to make your assessment." After a sharp nod to the formation, he added, "They're all yours, Sergeants. I'll be in Operations if you need me."

Broadhurst halted a few steps away. "Play nice," he said.

Frank couldn't help but crack a half grin. Martin scratched at a scar on his forehead, a nervous tick.

First Lieutenant Aaron Hernandez, the squad leader, cleared his throat within seconds. The young officer, no older than twenty-five, had the intense, sharp-eyed gaze of an Academy grad and dark hair buzzed almost to his scalp. "Master Guns, we were briefed that you'd be providing specialized training on Hollow encounters. We're ready to begin at your convenience."

Frank exchanged a glance with Martin. The lieutenant's tone was polite but couldn't quite hide the skepticism.

"At our convenience?" Frank repeated, stepping forward.

"Frank," Martin whispered warningly.

"Thank you so much for being so goddamn accommodating," Frank continued. "Did you know my bald friend here and I were both happily retired after many long years of service risking our necks for the Federation?" Frank paused, then tilted his head like a curious schoolteacher. "Tell me, Lieutenant, how many Hollow have you killed?"

The squad remained at rigid attention, but Frank could see the slight shift in their postures—the almost imperceptible bristling.

"None, Master Guns. As you know, there haven't been any Hollow encounters since Titan Station. That we're aware of, at least."

"And yet here you all stand"—Frank swept his gaze across the formation—"looking at us like we're relics dragged out of storage rather than the only people alive who've faced these things and survived."

Sergeant Andrew Grommet, with his round, doughy face, bulbous nose, and perpetually surprised wide-set eyes, stepped out with a proud grin. "Master Gunny Cage, I've completed over two hundred hours in the Titan simulation and *Squanto* classified trainings. We've reviewed every record of these encounters."

"Yes, we have studied them extensively," added Sergeant Jennifer Bolesky, a tall and thin Marine with blonde hair and green eyes. She adjusted her glasses, the gesture of an academic rather than a soldier. "I have a doctorate in xenobiology. My dissertation was on theoretical non-carbon-based life-forms and their potential physiology. I've been analyzing the *Squanto* footage for two years."

"Studied?" Martin scoffed. "Doctor, have you ever tried to shoot something that can flow through solid walls? Something that doesn't bleed when you hit it? That doesn't die when you shoot it?"

"Some of us who are Recon Marines have taken down targets that conventional forces couldn't touch," Hernandez cut in. "But as retired Marines, you already know that, don't you?"

Frank snorted. "Humans. You've killed humans. The Hollow aren't human. They don't think like humans, they don't move like humans, and they sure as hell don't die like humans."

Staff Sergeant Jose Contreras shifted his weight. The husky NCO's field utilities were neat but worn, and his boots were shined but had seen better days. It was his long hair that was most obviously pushing regulations. "Maybe the tech's improved since your day, Gunny—"

"*Our* day?" Martin interrupted. "Son, 'our day' is the only reason there still is a 'your day.'"

Sergeant Buck Hallstatt—tall, broad-shouldered, with arms nearly as big as an Aegis suit and the look of a Celtic warrior from a Roman sculpture—patted the sleek gauss rifle he cradled. The redhead's expression remained stoic and unimpressed. "This bad boy can fire two thousand armor-piercing rounds a minute. Nothing moves through that."

Frank stepped forward, unexpectedly quick for a man his age. "Mind if I see that fancy rifle, Sergeant?"

Hallstatt hesitated, then handed over his weapon. Frank examined it with practiced hands.

"Nice toy," Frank said. "Let me show you something."

Frank tapped a command into the room's control panel. Suddenly, the floor between them and the squad appeared to liquefy, swirling with silvery patterns that rose up like octopus limbs reaching for the ceiling.

He aimed the rifle and fired a burst of bullets that went right through the entity, sparking against the range wall behind the projections.

Several of the younger Marines flinched backward. Sergeant Kara Patel—a short, elfin-looking woman—was the only one that seemed not to recoil.

"A hollow projection," Frank explained, shutting it off. "Just light. Not even close to the real thing."

He tossed the rifle back to Hallstatt. "Now imagine that coming at you at triple the speed, passing right through your armor and into your chest while your fancy gun fires straight through it without any effect. That's what Corporal Torres experienced on *Squanto*. Know what his last words were? 'The bullets aren't stopping it!' Then we watched as one of those things reached into him and tore him apart to see how he was put together."

The room fell silent.

First Lieutenant Yanto Phillips raised his hand. Unlike the others, his uniform bore both combat insignia and the distinctive patch of the Xenoarchaeological Corps. "Gunny, I specialized in nonhuman cultural artifacts before joining Recon," he said with a British accent. "From what I've studied of the Hollow's behavior patterns, it appears they were conducting research, not simply attacking. Their methodical dissection suggests—"

"Research?" Frank interrupted with a bitter laugh. "Is that what you call it when they rip apart living people?"

"I'm not justifying it, I'm trying to understand it. There's a difference."

Frank paced in front of the formation, Rex falling in step beside him. "The only thing that worked was a X-15 heavy plasma cannon, but the operator, Rodriguez"—he crossed his chest—"bless her heart, died buying us time to get off *Squanto* while she too was torn inside out."

Martin sighed heavily as if recalling the horrific memory. "There's a reason Shield Command blew up Titan Station," he said. "For fear of this enemy you know nothing about."

Frank winced at the words, his own memories flooding him like a Hollow had shot through his body. For a moment, he was back at that bulkhead, fists bloodied, screaming for his family just beyond as the station crumbled around him.

Martin paused, clearly realizing he had stirred up some old memories.

"Sorry, Frank," he said quietly.

"So what worked against them, just an X-15?" asked Sergeant Phyllis Gillford, a woman built like a bruiser with the wide-shouldered physique of a hockey player and a jaw set to take no one's nonsense.

"Didn't you read the briefing?" Sergeant Emilio D'Agata asked.

The middle-sized man with short dark hair and darker eyes tapped his datapad. "Plasma isn't the only thing that works . . . I spent three years in the Xenobiology Research Division before transferring to Recon. The Hollow seem to exhibit properties consistent with quantum-entangled matter. Theoretically, we could disrupt their molecular cohesion with properly calibrated pulse weapons."

"Don't worry, you're going to get new fancy weapons that will 'probably' work on the Hollow," Frank said.

"Probably, theoretically?" Hernandez asked. "That's a joke, right?"

"Am I laughing?" Frank heaved a breath, smelling the booze still on his breath. "Weapons aren't the only thing to use in a fight. Thinking. Adapting. Making decisions that weren't in any manual because there is no manual for what you're about to face."

"But the simulation seemed pretty accurate when we experimented—" Grommet cut in.

"Fuck the simulation," Frank snapped. "Did your simulation show you what it feels like when they pass through your armor? When they examine you like you're a bug under glass?"

The room fell silent.

"That's right, be scared, that's good," Martin said. "No shame in that."

He glanced at Frank, then continued. "What my eloquent friend here is trying to say is that simulations are based on our experiences. But our experiences were limited. Incomplete. I spent over a decade thinking about what we should have done differently. That's what we're here to teach you."

Sergeant Hassan Ali—a clean-shaven Recon Marine with a hint of piratical recklessness in his dark eyes—stepped up. "I'm assuming then you're going to tell us how to avoid them as well, and not just kill these hostiles?"

Frank laughed, a harsh sound that echoed through the room. "Finally, an intelligent question. The point isn't to kill them. The point is to understand them before Shield Command decides to blow up another station full of civilians."

"And stay alive long enough to report back," Martin added.

Hernandez's professional facade cracked slightly, showing genuine concern. "You're saying our mission isn't to neutralize the hostiles?"

"It's recon, you are a Recon Marine, right?" Frank said, shaking his head. "Shield Command doesn't even understand what they are. What they want. That's your job, and why half of you have degrees in subjects my older friend Martin here can't pronounce."

Martin shook his head. "For now, consider the Hollow unknown entities with unknown intentions. Your mission is reconnaissance and, if possible, communication."

Second Lieutenant Bryan Fielding scoffed with his faintly upturned nose and haughty chin, suggesting either wealth or Academy breeding.

"Communication?" he said. "With aliens?"

"They were trying to communicate at Titan," Martin said quietly. "Nobody listened."

An uncomfortable silence fell over the room.

"Gunny," Sergeant D'Agata said, "based on my xenobiological studies, I've developed some theories about potential communication methods. The Hollow's molecular structure suggests they might perceive reality differently than we do. They might be attempting to understand us through direct interaction with our physical forms."

"You mean by sticking their mercury hands inside our bodies?" Frank asked dryly.

"Essentially, yes," D'Agata replied, unperturbed. "What appears as violence to us might be their equivalent of shaking hands."

"Sounds like you don't really know," said Second Lieutenant Matthew N'joku. The tall man had a voice like gravel and a chest broad enough to give pause in the combatives ring.

Frank stepped back to the center of the room. "First things first—forget everything you think you know. You're not elite. You're not prepared. You're not special. You're just the poor bastards who drew the short straw like we did back when we flew out to find *Squanto*."

"But if you listen," Martin added, "you might survive like we did."

Rex barked once, as if punctuating the statement. Cosmo remained silent but alert beside Martin. In that moment, Frank realized something odd—he was actually working with Martin without wanting to punch him.

Nah, I still want to punch him in his bald head, Frank thought.

Phillips let out a sigh, his initial skepticism replaced by something closer to wary respect as he looked at Frank and Martin in turn.

"We're listening," he said.

"So what's first?" Hernandez asked.

Frank grinned. "First is understanding that everything you've learned in combat will be different. The Hollow don't follow any rules you know. So we're going to teach you new ones."

"Starting with this," Martin said, activating a holographic display. The three-dimensional image of a Hollow entity appeared, its liquid-metal form shifting and flowing in unnatural patterns. "Meet your new dance partner."

The squad stared at the display, and there was a mixture of fascination and unease visible on their young faces.

"Don't worry," Frank said again, his voice dripping with sarcasm. "By the time we're done with you, you'll be too terrified to be cocky anymore."

"And that," Martin concluded, "is when you'll be ready to learn."

CHAPTER NINE

Think they're ready to learn?" Frank asked, leaning against the simulation control panel. His cybernetic hand made a soft metallic sound as he drummed his fingers against the console's edge, the new prosthetic still feeling foreign despite its enhanced sensitivity.

"Not a chance," Martin said, watching the Marines with a mixture of concern and resignation. "Let's see how they handle things without any guidance. Sometimes failure is the best teacher."

The Marines all held their sleek new MR-113 plasma rifles, examining the weapons with varying degrees of confidence. Hernandez moved with practiced ease, clearly familiar with advanced weaponry, while Grommet kept adjusting his grip nervously. N'joku held his rifle with the casual confidence of someone who believed technology would solve all problems.

In front of them, the massive simulation chamber transformed before their eyes. Barren rock formations rose from the floor, and jagged peaks created a treacherous mountain landscape. A holographic mining outpost materialized against the far wall, its structures weathered and abandoned, metal surfaces corroded by years of exposure to Galean's caustic atmosphere. The lighting dimmed to mimic Galean's twilight conditions, casting long shadows across the terrain.

"Pretty impressive tech," Frank admitted grudgingly. "In our day, we trained with cardboard cutouts and imagination."

"And we survived anyway," Martin replied.

He glanced up at the shaded viewport overlooking the chamber. Captain Broadhurst stood watching, arms crossed, his silhouette visible against the glass. Several other officers flanked him, datapads in hand, no doubt recording every moment of the exercise. Frank spotted Colonel Shafter among them, his stocky frame unmistakable even in silhouette.

"Wolverine-9, this is a live-fire simulation," Martin announced over the comms, his voice echoing slightly in the chamber. "Terrain matches your mission zone with 95 percent accuracy based on recent satellite imagery. Objective: locate source of Hollow signatures and gather intel. Rules of engagement: observe and report unless directly threatened." He paused, then added with emphasis, "We're not looking for heroes; we're looking for survivors who can bring back information."

Frank flashed a wolfish grin as he triggered the simulation sequence. "Clock starts now. Try not to die in the first thirty seconds."

The simulation's ambient sounds kicked in, the low moan of wind through rocky crevices, the occasional metallic groan of the abandoned outpost settling. It sounded too much like former combat zones for Frank's comfort, bringing back memories he'd spent years trying to drown.

Rex and Cosmo settled by their feet, eyes alert and tracking the Marines as they moved into the darkened simulation. Unlike their masters, who shifted restlessly, the dogs remained perfectly still, as if conserving energy for what was to come. Frank noticed Cosmo's ears twitching slightly, following sounds inaudible to human ears.

First Lieutenant Hernandez signaled his squad to fan out in textbook formation: a three-point patrol pattern with overlapping fields of fire. On the surface, it looked professional, disciplined. Frank knew better. So did Martin.

"They're moving too fast," he muttered to Frank. "Not taking time to scan each sector before advancing."

"Ten credits says they shoot at the first thing that pops up," Frank muttered, absently patting Rex's head.

"Sucker bet," Martin replied, watching Hallstatt sweep his weapon barrel too widely across his zone. "I'll give them three minutes tops before someone pulls a trigger."

The Marines advanced cautiously through the rocky terrain, their footfalls echoing despite attempts at stealth. Martin watched Second Lieutenant N'joku checking his frequency settings as they moved. At least someone had been paying attention. He'd adjusted his MR-113 to the baseline emission pattern they'd shown them earlier—the right move, but only if the Hollow hadn't already adapted.

Five minutes in, the first holographic Hollow materialized without warning. It flowed like silver water through a rock face twenty meters ahead of Second Lieutenant Fielding's fire team, its surface rippling with complex geometric patterns. Unlike the simple projections they'd shown earlier, this simulation captured the alien grace of the entities. The way they seemed to exist in multiple places simultaneously, their forms never quite solid, shifting between states of matter.

Even knowing it was a simulation, Frank felt his heart rate spike. His body remembered the threat before his mind could process it rationally.

"Contact!" Fielding called out, raising his weapon with textbook precision.

N'joku's voice cut through the comms. "Hold fire! Observe patterns first, remember? Check your pattern analysis before engaging."

But Grommet, positioned on their right flank, had already fired. His shot passed harmlessly through the projection. The holographic Hollow's surface configuration shifted instantly, becoming more chaotic, more aggressive. Swirling lines of light that had been regular and geometric became jagged and rapidly cycling.

"Now you've done it." Frank sighed with a shake of his head.

Three more Hollow projections emerged from different directions, drifting through solid objects like ghosts; one through the outpost wall, one from beneath a boulder, a third seemingly materializing from empty air. Their patterns synchronized, pulsing with what Frank recognized as attack formations he'd seen on *Squanto*.

"They're coordinating," Sergeant Patel said in a strong, firm voice. She calmly adjusted her frequency settings. Her small hands moved across the rifle's configuration panel with practiced ease, but her adjustments were too slow for the rapidly changing threat.

"Damn, these things are fast!" shouted Bolesky. Her tall body moved with surprising nimbleness as she tried to maintain her firing position.

"That's because they're not moving through space the way we do," Martin said quietly, though only Frank could hear him. "They're slipping between moments in time."

"Weapons free!" Hernandez ordered, abandoning protocol as the Hollow closed in. "Shift to formation Delta! Establish a perimeter!"

What followed was chaos. Marines firing in all directions, most shots ineffective as they failed to match frequencies properly. The modified plasma bolts either passed through the Hollow projections or caused minimal disruption before the entities adapted. Shouts and curses filled the comm channel as the squad struggled to establish any kind of coherent defense.

Hallstatt and Gillford managed to disrupt one projection temporarily by combining their fire in a flanking maneuver. But the entity re-formed almost immediately, adapting to their frequency and splitting into two smaller projections that moved with increased speed.

"They're learning!" Gillford called out, her voice tight with tension. "Every time we hit them, they adapt faster!"

From the observation window, Captain Broadhurst's posture had gone rigid with disapproval. Frank could almost feel his frustration radiating through the glass.

"We need to reset," Martin suggested. "At this rate, they'll all be 'killed' in the next sixty seconds."

Frank shook his head. "Enough of this circus." He tapped the control panel, and the simulation froze. The Hollow projections hung suspended in mid-motion, the Marines frozen in their defensive postures, confusion evident as the scenario stopped without warning.

"What the hell was that?" Broadhurst's voice boomed over the facility speakers, his frustration evident. "I handpicked this shitshow? You just got yourselves killed in under seven minutes."

Silence filled the chamber as the Marines lowered their weapons. None of them spoke. Their expressions were a mixture of frustration, embarrassment, and genuine fear.

Frank stepped forward. "Captain, permission to show 'em how it's done," he said, newfound determination in his tone.

"Feel fucking free, Master Guns," Broadhurst replied.

"Gunny, care to join me?" Frank asked.

Martin nodded and grabbed two MR-113s from the rack, then tossed one to Frank. The weapon was lighter than he expected, its balance almost perfect. They had already been through the simulation twice themselves, testing the weapons and using the intel from their classified folder to train.

With confident strides, they entered the simulated terrain, dogs on their heels. The Marines moved aside and formed a semicircle to observe, their expressions ranging from skepticism to genuine curiosity.

"Reset simulation," Martin called out.

The frozen Hollow projections disappeared in a shimmer of light, then re-emerged in their initial positions. The first entity flowed from the rock face, its patterns once again calm and measured.

"Watch and learn," Frank said, raising his MR-113 but not taking aim. Instead, he positioned himself at an angle, presenting a smaller target profile.

The first Hollow materialized fully. Its patterns were serene and exploratory as it drifted toward the center of the mining outpost. Frank made no move to fire, instead watching the entity's movement, studying its surface patterns with the practiced eye of someone who had faced these things for real.

"First rule," he announced, his voice carrying across the chamber, "don't shoot until you know what you're shooting at. These patterns"—he pointed to the rhythmic pulsing across the entity's surface—"indicate investigative behavior. Nonthreatening. It's cataloging, exploring, learning about the environment."

Martin moved to the left, creating distance between them, flanking the entity without directly approaching it. "Second rule: never bunch up. They sense energy signatures, particularly the electrical impulses in your nervous system. Stand too close together and you become one big target that they can't miss."

The Hollow shifted, its form rippling as it detected their presence. Its patterns changed slightly, becoming more complex but still regular, a geometric sequence that repeated with minor variations.

"This looks like it's trying to communicate," Martin explained. "Notice the repeating sequence. When you see this, you've got an opportunity to observe without immediate danger."

Frank adjusted his MR-113 settings deliberately, using the calibration pad with some difficulty but learning fast. "Third rule: match frequencies before you even think about firing. But firing should be your last resort. These aren't conventional enemies. Killing them doesn't always solve the problem."

The Hollow approached Martin, and its liquid metal form extended tendrils in his direction. Several Marines tensed, hands tightening on their weapons, but Martin remained perfectly still, not even blinking as the entity moved to within arm's reach.

"Fourth rule: stillness confuses them. Their perception is based on quantum disturbances. Minimal movement means minimal signature."

The Hollow entity passed Martin and surged within two meters of Frank. At that moment, Frank smoothly deployed a temporal disruption field grenade. The TDF created a shimmering bubble that trapped the entity mid-movement, freezing it in a moment between moments.

"Now you can study it safely," Frank said, approaching the trapped entity. "Learn its patterns, its intentions. Most importantly, determine whether it's an immediate threat or something you can work around."

N'joku stepped forward from the group, curiosity overcoming his pride. His eyes narrowed as he studied the trapped Hollow. "And if those intentions are hostile? What then?"

As if on cue, the Hollow's patterns shifted dramatically, becoming jagged and erratic. The repeating sequences vanished and were replaced by chaotic pulses that Frank recognized from bitter experience.

"Then you do this," he said, raising his MR-113 and adjusting it with three rapid movements to match the entity's new frequency signature. His shot was precise, hitting the center mass. The Hollow fragmented and dispersed in a shower of light particles.

"One shot," Frank emphasized. "Conserve ammunition. These bastards learn from every encounter. The more you shoot, the faster they adapt."

First Lieutenant Hernandez approached the safety line. "And if there are multiple hostiles?" he called out. "We saw how they coordinated their movements."

Frank shrugged, the gesture deceptively casual. "That's when it gets interesting."

He nodded to Martin, who activated the next phase of the simulation. Five Hollow projections materialized simultaneously, surrounding them in a perfect circle, their forms more solid and threatening than the exploratory entity they'd encountered first.

"This is where most squads would die," Frank said calmly. "Pay attention."

What followed was a master class in Hollow combat. Frank and Martin moved with the synchronicity of old partners, positioning themselves back-to-back and deploying TDFs strategically to control the battlefield. They created chokepoints, used the terrain to limit approach vectors, and maintained absolute discipline with their fire. They didn't shoot until absolutely necessary, and when they did, their shots were devastatingly effective.

Throughout, Rex and Cosmo remained perfectly still, only their eyes tracking the action. The dogs seemed to understand the fourth rule, something the Marines hadn't yet grasped, that movement drew attention, that stillness was safety.

When the last projection dissipated, silence fell over the simulation chamber. The Marines stared at Frank and Martin with new eyes, reassessing everything they thought they knew about these aging veterans.

N'joku cleared his throat. "Not bad for a couple of old timers," he said, but the edge had gone from his voice, replaced with something closer to grudging respect.

"Old timers?" Frank scoffed. "We're just getting warmed up, son."

Frank noticed movement in the observation window. Captain Natalia Ivan had joined Broadhurst, watching the proceedings with analytical interest. When she caught Frank's eye, she gave a slight nod of approval.

"Reset the simulation," Martin ordered. "Your turn. Show us what you learned."

The Marines exchanged glances, newfound determination in their eyes. Even Grommet, who had fired prematurely, seemed focused now, his earlier nervousness replaced by concentration. N'joku was the only one whose expression remained carefully neutral, though Martin detected a hint of challenge there.

"This one's going to be trouble," Frank whispered. The slight nod from his old friend confirmed he'd noticed too.

"He reminds me of a younger version of you," Martin replied quietly. "Same chip on his shoulder."

"I was never that bad." Frank snorted.

"No, you were worse."

The simulation reset once more, and Martin leaned close to Frank. "Ten credits says N'joku still screws up," Martin whispered.

Frank grinned, a flash of his old self returning. "Now who's taking sucker bets?"

Martin was right. N'joku had screwed up. So had the entire squad. It took them three times before they did a halfway decent job in the simulation. Frank and Martin were making them pay for those mistakes with a brutal physical training session.

For the past four hours they had put Wolverine-9 through a gauntlet of exercises specifically tailored to the mission parameters: navigating unstable terrain while maintaining situational awareness, moving silently with full gear, and responding to random simulated Hollow attacks and communications.

Now even Martin had to admit they'd earned a break.

"Ten minutes," he announced, watching the Marines collapse against rock formations or simply sprawl on the simulated ground. "Hydrate and recover."

The training facility had been reconfigured to match Galean's challenging topography: steep inclines, loose scree, and narrow passages that required careful maneuvering. Sweat darkened the Marines' uniforms, their breathing heavy in the chamber's thin air.

Frank leaned against the control console, massaging his shoulder where the prosthetic connected to flesh. The strain of demonstrating proper movement techniques seemed to aggravate the old injury. Rex lay at his feet, panting lightly but still alert, eyes tracking every Marine in the room.

"They're improving," Martin admitted, keeping his voice low. "Patel's tracking all projections with almost perfect speed, and Ali has a natural talent for the TDFs."

"Still wouldn't bet on half of them making it back," Frank replied. "Especially not with Lieutenant Perfect leading the charge."

He nodded toward Hernandez, who despite the grueling session, maintained his rigid posture as he conferred with several squad members. Even exhausted, the first lieutenant carried himself with the unmistakable confidence of someone who'd never truly failed at anything.

Martin shrugged. "He's arrogant, but he's sharp. Did you see how quickly he adapted to the ambush scenario?"

"Yeah, right after his tactical brilliance got D'Agata and Grommet 'killed.'" Frank took a swig from his canteen. "Reminds me of that hotshot on Gamma Four Niner. Ralph."

"Rodney, you idiot," Martin corrected automatically.

"I know, I liked to call him Ralph, like the kid from *The Simpsons*."

"I forgot you watch cartoons."

"Helps mellow me out," Frank said with a shrug. "You should try it. Might prevent additional wrinkles on your egg."

The familiar bickering felt oddly comforting, a return to rhythms established decades ago. Cosmo padded over to Martin and nudged his cybernetic leg as if sensing his momentary contentment. Martin scratched behind the shepherd's ears, earning a soft whine of approval.

From across the chamber, the sound of laughter drew their attention. A small group had formed around N'joku—Contreras, Hallstatt, and Fielding. The lieutenant was gesturing expressively, his back to Frank and Martin.

". . . then the old man shuffles in like this," N'joku was saying, adopting an exaggerated limp that unmistakably mocked Martin's gait. "Barking orders like he is General Patton."

More laughter. N'joku continued, encouraged by his audience. "Probably can't even remember what century it is. 'Back in my day,'"—he mimicked Martin's deeper voice—"'we killed Hollow with rocks and sharp sticks.'"

Martin noticed Frank stiffen and narrow his eyes at the performance.

"Take it easy," Martin said, sensing rage building in Frank.

"Then I tried to kill them with my shiny head," N'joku continued.

"Oh, hell no," Frank whispered, setting down his canteen. "I'm the only one who gets to make fun of your dome."

Martin caught his arm. "Let it go, Frank. Kids blow off steam."

"Not like that, they don't." Frank shook off Martin's hand and strode across the chamber as fast as his patched-together body would carry him.

N'joku had moved on to an impression of Frank now, pretending to swig from an invisible bottle while staggering dramatically. "Everyone knows the guy's a drunk . . . and he has the audacity to say—"

"Say what, Lieutenant?" Frank asked, his voice deceptively calm. "Making fun of me is one thing—hell, I'd earned some of that with my drinking and attitude, but joking about a Marine who lost his leg in combat?"

N'joku turned, not quite managing to hide his surprise at Frank's sudden appearance. To his credit, he didn't back down, Martin observed.

"Just discussing training techniques, Sergeant," he replied smoothly.

"Looked more like you were auditioning for a comedy routine." Frank stepped closer. "Not very funny, though. Maybe if your audience were three-year-olds. But you aren't all toddlers, are you now?"

Frank shot the formerly grinning Marines a glare. They weren't grinning now.

"Toddlers could do a better job against the simulation," Frank said. "Shit, I just snuck up on you without you even knowing. How's that for an old drunk ass? If I was a Hollow, your eyes would be bursting with silver metal right now, you goddamn imbecile."

Most of the Marines backed away slightly, sensing the dangerous undercurrent. Across the chamber, Martin watched with resignation, knowing better than to intervene when Frank got that look in his eyes.

"Just messing around, Master Guns," N'joku said.

"Messing around?" Frank nodded thoughtfully. "You think this training is a joke? Do you think where you're going is a joke?"

"No, we're blowing off steam is all."

"Oh, okay, well blowing off steam's healthy. Let's blow some off together."

N'joku's eyebrows rose. "Meaning?"

"Meaning I want to see what they've been teaching at the Academy these days." Frank stepped back, creating space between them. "Old-fashioned boxing. You and me."

A tense silence fell over the chamber. Even the Marines resting on the far side had noticed something was happening and were sitting up, watching with interest.

"With respect, Sergeant, I don't think that would be appropriate," N'joku replied, though the gleam in his eyes suggested otherwise.

"Scared?" Frank prodded.

"Of hurting a senior NCO? Yes, actually."

"Combat simulation," Frank clarified. "Training purposes only. Captain Broadhurst authorized full-contact exercises."

He glanced up at the observation window, where Broadhurst was indeed watching, arms crossed. He made no move to intervene.

N'joku hesitated, then seemed to come to a decision. He squared his shoulders and stepped into the open space Frank had created.

"If you insist, Gunny." He stripped off his tactical vest, revealing a physique that wouldn't have looked out of place in a recruitment ad. "Rules?"

"Boxing rules. No kicking, no grappling." Frank shrugged out of his own gear. "First one to stay down loses."

N'joku raised a brow. "You sure?"

"No, one more thing," Frank said. "No gloves. Just good old bare fists."

The brow dropped and N'joku cracked a shit-eating grin. "Good luck."

"Luck?" Frank scoffed. "I'm too cursed to get lucky in my 'old' age."

The Marines formed a ring around them, an impromptu fighting circle. Martin pushed through to the front, shaking his head but making no move to stop it. He knew Frank too well to try.

"Ten credits on the lieutenant," Contreras muttered to Hallstatt, not quite quietly enough.

"Twenty," Hallstatt replied.

"I've got my money on Cage," said Bolesky.

Frank looked over at the tall blonde. Was this some sort of trick to distract him?

N'joku squared up, hands raised in a textbook boxing stance. He bounced lightly on the balls of his feet, his reach advantage obvious as he squared off against Frank. The physical mismatch was almost painful to watch: N'joku in his prime against a hard-living veteran with a prosthetic hand and decades of wear and tear.

Frank, by contrast, simply stood there, hands loosely raised, looking almost bored.

"Whenever you're ready, Lieutenant," he drawled.

N'joku didn't waste time with words. He launched forward with a precise jab-cross combination that would have dropped most opponents. Frank slipped the jab by millimeters and deflected the cross with his forearm, the impact making a dull thud that seemed to surprise N'joku.

"That all they teach you at the Academy?" Frank taunted.

N'joku's jaw tightened. He pressed forward with a more complex series of strikes—jab, hook, uppercut—his form perfect, his power impressive. Frank weathered the assault, blocking or slipping just enough to take the sting out of each blow, but N'joku's youth and reach were telling. A hook caught Frank on the cheek, snapping his head to the side.

A murmur went through the watching Marines. First blood to N'joku.

Frank spat on the deck, touching his split lip. "Not bad."

He advanced then, for the first time taking the offensive. N'joku braced for the attack, his guard high and tight. But Frank's movements didn't match any conventional boxing style. His rhythm was unpredictable, and his balance constantly shifted. N'joku found himself defending against random swings and blows.

A quick one-two combination slipped through N'joku's guard, and Frank's prosthetic fist connected solidly with his ribs. The lieutenant grunted but maintained his composure, countering with a straight right that Frank barely avoided.

Whatever cocktail the doc had given Frank to keep his shaking at bay was working great. Without it, he probably would have been knocked on his ass by now.

The two Marines circled each other, N'joku's initial confidence eroding as he realized the old man was far more dangerous than he'd appeared. Frank's breathing remained controlled, his movements economical, while N'joku's frustration began to show in increasingly powerful but less precise strikes.

"Getting tired, Lieutenant?" Frank asked calmly.

N'joku responded with a blistering combination that drove Frank back several steps. A left hook connected with Frank's temple, staggering him. N'joku pressed his advantage and launched a haymaker that would have ended the fight.

But Frank wasn't there. He'd ducked under the punch and delivered a savage body blow that left N'joku gasping. Before the lieutenant could recover, Frank followed with a perfectly placed right cross that connected with N'joku's jaw.

A distinctive crack of bone on bone echoed throughout the room.

N'joku dropped to one knee, blood trickling from his split lip, eyes wide with surprise. The circle of Marines went silent.

"Stay down, son," Frank advised. "You've got nothing to prove."

Pride warred with pain on N'joku's face. He spat blood and pushed himself back to his feet, fists raised.

"Not done yet, old man."

Frank shrugged. "Your funeral."

The next exchange was brutal and swift. N'joku launched a desperate flurry, some blows landing, but none with the force needed to stop Frank. In return, Frank delivered a devastating three-punch combination—body, head, jaw—the final blow landing with enough force to lift N'joku momentarily off his feet.

The lieutenant crashed to the deck in an ungraceful heap. This time, he stayed down.

Frank stood over him, breathing hard but still steady. He was bleeding from his lip and a cut above his eye but otherwise seemed remarkably unscathed.

"This grandpa just kicked your ass, and by the fucking way, I'm not a grandpa because I never got that blessing," Frank announced, loud enough for everyone to hear. "My wife and daughter died on Titan Station. I tell you that because the Hollow aren't some Free Miners or pirates, or anything else you have taken down in your careers. They are an advanced alien race far smarter than any of you. So maybe it's time to start listening. Because where you're going, I'll be the least of your concerns."

He offered a hand to N'joku, who, after a moment's hesitation, accepted it. The lieutenant rose unsteadily, respect mingled with disbelief in his eyes.

"How did you—"

"Experience," Frank cut him off. "Not the kind you get in simulations or training exercises. The kind you get surviving when everything goes to hell." He turned to address the entire squad again. "That's what we're trying to teach you. The Hollow don't follow rules. They aren't human. They don't understand fair."

He locked eyes with N'joku again. "Making fun of Martin's leg? You should be fucking ashamed. That leg is a badge of honor. He got it pulling two Marines out of a Chitin nest after they disobeyed orders and got trapped. One of them lived because of him."

N'joku wiped blood from his mouth, genuine contrition crossing his features. "I didn't know."

"Now you do," Frank said. "And now you also know that looking good on paper doesn't mean shit when you're facing something that doesn't care about your Academy records." He gestured to the gathered Marines. "This isn't about humiliation. It's about survival. Remember that when you're out there."

As the Marines dispersed, some shooting impressed glances back at Frank, Martin approached, Cosmo at his heels.

"Was that really necessary?" he asked, though there was no real reproach in his tone.

"Absolutely," Frank replied, wincing as he dabbed at his split lip. "Though I'm going to regret it tomorrow."

"Getting old sucks."

"Yeah, especially without . . ." Frank swallowed, letting his words trail.

"Being drunk?"

"Yeah, but I was actually thinking about Sarah and Lily. I miss them more than ever."

Martin sighed. "Sorry, Frank."

Frank folded his arms across his chest as N'joku gathered his gear, his demeanor noticeably subdued. The lieutenant's eyes kept darting to Martin's cybernetic leg, then away, as if seeing it in a new light.

"Think he learned something?" Martin asked.

Frank shrugged. "Maybe, but I'm not sure how long he will survive the lesson," he said. "Not sure how long any of them will."

Up in the observation window, a figure had joined Captain Broadhurst. Captain Natalia Ivan stood watching the proceedings, her expression unreadable at this distance. She said something to Broadhurst, who nodded in response.

"We've got company," Frank murmured, nodding toward the window.

"I saw. Think they're impressed with your teaching methods?"

"They should be. More effective than those fancy simulations."

Martin snorted. "For what it's worth, that was a good fight. Haven't seen you move that fast in years."

"Don't get used to it," Frank replied, massaging his knuckles. "I'm definitely going to need a drink after this."

"After?" Martin raised an eyebrow. "I figured you already had something in your canteen."

"Nope, maybe I'm finally getting serious about this mission."

"Or maybe you just wanted an excuse to beat up a cocky lieutenant."

"Por qué no los dos?"

For the first time since before Titan Station, they shared a genuine laugh. Cosmo and Rex looked up at their masters, tails wagging slightly as if approving of the momentary truce.

The moment was interrupted by Captain Broadhurst's voice over the facility speakers.

"Sergeants Cage and Kelvin, report to the command center immediately and make sure Lieutenant N'joku reports to the infirmary."

Frank and Martin exchanged looks.

"Ah, fuck. Think I'm in trouble?" Frank asked.

"You may be. Wouldn't be the first time," Martin replied. "Won't be the last."

He noticed N'joku also leaving, but watching them with an expression he couldn't quite read. Maybe it was resentment. Maybe it was newfound respect. Either way, the lieutenant now knew there was more to the "old dogs" than met the eye. Whether that knowledge would keep him alive where they were going remained to be seen.

CHAPTER TEN

Everything will be fine," Martin insisted.

It felt like all eyes were staring at him and Frank on their way from the training bay to Battalion Headquarters. Grunts and officers alike stepped out of their path, conversations halting mid-sentence.

Word of Frank's "training accident" with N'joku had spread through the base like wildfire. "Not like they are going to court-martial you or anything," Martin finished.

"Yeah, they need my old ass," Frank said, ignoring a pair of wide-eyed privates who pressed themselves against the wall to let them pass. "Plus, the lieutenant had it coming. I'm the only one that can make fun of you, egg brows."

"Cut the shit, Frank. I didn't ask for your help. I don't need a big brother. If anything, I just want the old Frank back." Martin's voice dropped lower, an unexpected note of sincerity breaking through his usual gruffness.

Frank halted so abruptly that a corporal nearly collided with him from behind, mumbling apologies as he scurried away. "The old Frank is dead. His heart died at Titan Station, you know that. Should have let my body die with it."

He kept going, leaving Martin to consider the words. Fifteen years had passed since that day, but sometimes it felt like mere hours. Martin sighed, then hurried to catch up, his new cybernetic upgrade not even whining with the effort. The old version would have grumbled like Frank's jerry-rigged motorbike.

They reached Colonel Shafter's office door, and Martin noticed a slight hesitation in Frank's step. It was barely perceptible, a fraction-of-a-second's pause, a slight tightening around the eyes, but after decades fighting alongside each other, Martin could read Frank's micro expressions like large-print text.

"Listen," Martin said quietly, pulling Frank slightly to the side as an aide hurried past with a stack of datapads. "Let me do the talking. This isn't your first rodeo with getting chewed out by brass."

"Don't worry, I'm sober, and I won't embarrass you," Frank replied with a wry grin that didn't quite reach his eyes. His upgraded prosthetic hand flexed at his side.

Martin knocked on the colonel's door with more confidence than he felt. This meeting could either solidify their role in the mission or end it before it began.

"Enter," came the terse response, the single word carrying the weight of command.

They walked into the office where Colonel Shafter sat behind his desk, a weathered face beneath close-cropped silver hair and eyes that had seen too many wars to be impressed by much of anything anymore. Captain Broadhurst stood at his side, spine rigid, uniform still impossibly crisp despite the long day. To Martin's surprise, Captain Ivan was there too, lingering in the background near the viewport. Her presence was unusual for what should have been a simple disciplinary meeting.

"Master Gunnery Sergeants Kelvin and Cage reporting as ordered, sir!" Martin announced, and the two of them snapped to attention with a precision that belied their age and injuries. Old habits died hard, especially those drilled into you through decades of service.

Shafter let them stand at attention for several uncomfortable seconds before responding, a power move they'd seen a thousand times from officers testing the discipline of their subordinates. "At ease."

They shifted to parade rest in unison, feet shoulder-width apart, hands clasped at the small of their backs.

"Would one of you care to explain to me," Shafter began, his voice dangerously controlled, fingers steepled before him on the desk, "why Second Lieutenant N'joku is currently in the infirmary with a mild concussion and facial lacerations?"

"Training accident, sir," Frank said without hesitation, his face the perfect mask of professional concern.

"Training accident," Shafter repeated flatly, one eyebrow rising slightly. "Is that what we're calling unsanctioned fistfights between instructors and trainees now, Master Guns?"

"With respect, Colonel," Martin interjected, keeping his voice measured, "we were demonstrating practical combat techniques—"

Broadhurst scoffed, the sound sharp in the otherwise quiet room. "That's what you call it?" He glared at Frank, arms crossed tightly over his chest. "Cage here just beat the shit out of *Lieutenant* N'joku."

"And you did nothing to stop it," Shafter said, turning to him with a directness that made his posture stiffen even further.

Broadhurst straightened, momentarily thrown off-balance. "I—"

"Probably because you thought N'joku would win," Shafter said, a hint of amusement entering his voice despite his stern expression.

Broadhurst briefly looked to Frank, who grinned. The captain's expression confirmed Shafter's assessment, and Martin could almost see the words *guilty as charged* hovering in the air above his head.

Shafter leaned back in his chair, the faintest smile crossing his face before being quickly suppressed. "I'm glad you didn't, to be honest," he said. "Maybe now your squad knows Frank and Martin aren't two washed-up has-beens. As much as they are a pain in the ass, they have real-life experiences that are unmatched and invaluable."

"Thank you, sir," Martin said, caught off guard by the unexpected support. He exchanged a glance with Frank, who looked equally surprised beneath his carefully maintained expression.

"Don't get cocky," Shafter said, the momentary softness vanishing as he looked at them in turn. "You're still assholes, and I need you to tone that back once you're out there. Lives are at stake. We're not sending you to train these Marines for the fun of it." He tapped a folder on his desk, classified markings visible on its cover. "The Hollow are unlike anything we've faced before, as you both know firsthand."

"Yes, sir," Frank said politely—or as politely as he could, which for Frank meant only a slight undertone of sarcasm.

Martin processed Shafter's words, replaying them in his mind to be sure he'd heard correctly. "Wait, does that mean we're going into the field?"

Frank perked up visibly, like Rex when he got a treat, his eyes suddenly alert and focused where before they'd held the dull sheen of a man going through the motions.

"Yes, it does," Shafter said, nodding to Natalia, who finally moved from her position by the viewport. "Due to moving up the timeline, I need you both to accompany Wolverine-9—and Captain Broadhurst, you're going with them."

"What?" Broadhurst asked.

"You picked this squad, did you not?"

Broadhurst nodded.

"You told me, and I quote, 'these are the best candidates for this unorthodox mission.'"

"Yes, sir, I did."

"I know you did, I am quoting you."

"Sir."

"Due to this unorthodox mission and assembled group of personalities, I need you in the field with them, Captain, do you have a problem with that?"

"No, sir, I do not."

"Good."

Natalia looked at Frank and Martin ruefully but said nothing. Her silence conveyed more than words could. This wasn't the plan, but orders were orders.

Frank didn't look mad, he looked excited, energized in a way Martin hadn't seen since before Titan Station. Martin wasn't sure he shared that sentiment. Field work meant risk, and they'd both seen what the Hollow could do. The memories of *Squanto* still haunted his dreams, the screams of Marines being dissected alive by curious alien entities studying human anatomy.

"How soon can the squad deploy?" Shafter asked, turning back to Broadhurst. His tone made it clear the decision had already been made, with or without his approval.

"Given the accelerated timetable, twelve hours, sir," he replied, professional mask firmly back in place.

"Make it six," Shafter ordered, his voice brooking no argument. "We've received new intel."

He nodded to Natalia, who stepped forward and activated the room's holographic display with a gesture. The familiar terrain map of Galean appeared, but was now dotted with pulsing red markers that sent a cold feeling through Martin's gut.

"The Hollow are on the move," she said, her voice calm but her expression grave. "Our sensors from orbit picked up multiple signatures several hours ago, moving toward the abandoned mining outpost."

Martin's muscles tensed, the familiar precursor to combat that he hadn't experienced in over a decade. Beside him, Frank was leaning forward, his relaxed demeanor instantly replaced by focused intensity, a predator scenting blood.

"These readings match the ones from Titan Station?" Frank asked quietly, his voice steady despite the fear only Martin could sense in him.

"Nearly identical," Natalia confirmed, manipulating the display to show waveform patterns that danced and shifted like the surface of the Hollow themselves. "But there's more. The patterns have changed. They're showing signs of organized movement: purposeful, not random."

"They're searching for something," Shafter added, rising from his chair to study the display more closely. "Or someone."

Frank and Martin exchanged glances, years of partnership allowing them to communicate volumes without words. This wasn't just a recon mission anymore, this was potentially humanity's last chance to understand an alien intelligence.

"We haven't been able to figure out more than that from orbit due to cloud and electromagnetic disturbance, but we have a team working on it," Natalia said. She manipulated the display to show atmospheric conditions that would hamper surveillance.

Shafter nodded and returned to his seat with the deliberate movements of a man feeling every year of his service. "This mission will be completely covert," he continued. "Once you're on the ground, all comms will be off limits unless in absolute emergency. We can't risk alerting the enemy to your presence."

"Understood," Martin said.

Frank nodded, his focus still on the display as he studied the patterns with an intensity that spoke of personal stakes.

"There are elements in Shield Command who would prefer a more . . . permanent solution to the Hollow question," Natalia explained carefully. "They're preparing a strike package as we speak."

"Like Titan Station," Frank said, his artificial hand clenching into a fist.

"You will be given adequate time to evac if it comes to that," Shafter said, his tone suggesting he didn't entirely agree with the approach but was bound by orders.

"Very kind of you, thanks. Too bad my family wasn't given that option."

"Yes, it was a tragedy."

"How long do we have on the ground before the strike?" Martin asked, redirecting the conversation before Frank could say something they'd both regret.

"Thirty-six hours," Shafter said.

"Guess brass is finished with the Freed Miners?" Frank asked.

"Yeah, the Free Miners are no longer a problem," Shafter said, his face hardening. "They were on the wrong end of a different strike package."

"Hopefully without any collateral or civilian deaths."

Shafter didn't respond with more than a slight shuffle of a few fingers, and his silence confirmed what they already suspected. Military solutions were rarely surgical, despite what the propaganda vids claimed.

"The countdown is already on," he said, effectively closing that line of discussion. "So if you don't have further questions, I'd say you should get to it, Gunnies."

Martin exchanged a glance with Frank. Thirty-six hours to unravel an alien mystery that had eluded them for over twenty-three years. It seemed impossible, but then again, their entire careers had been about achieving the impossible.

"One more thing," Natalia added, almost as an afterthought. "Your dogs have been authorized to go, since I figured you would ask."

"The dogs?" Martin blinked in surprise. "Really?"

"They've shown unusual sensitivity to Hollow projections during training," she explained. "Their behavior might provide early warning signs that our technology can't detect."

"Rex will be thrilled," Frank said with a grin. "He's been itching for some action."

"Good," Shafter said, gathering his datapad. "You'll have full tactical authority once you're on the ground. The squad may outrank you, but in Hollow territory, experience trumps rank. I've already made that clear."

Broadhurst looked like he was battling a frown, clearly not entirely comfortable with NCO commanding officers, even under these unusual circumstances.

"Report to Dr. Reese for final cybernetic calibration," Shafter ordered, rising to indicate the meeting was concluded. "Captain Broadhurst will oversee mission prep. Dismissed."

Outside in the corridor, Natalia stopped Martin with a light touch on his arm. "A moment, Gunny?" she asked, her voice low.

"Hey, don't mind me," Frank said, continuing down the hall without looking back, his stride purposeful.

When he was gone, Natalia reached into her pocket. She pulled out a small data chip, and then what looked like a pair of syringes inside a clear case.

"The data chip will upload to your Aegis comms. When activated, it will communicate with the Hollow," she said.

"The lab jockeys figured out how to speak Hollow?"

Natalia paused, just long enough for Martin to doubt the tech would work.

"Lab tested, not field, but we're confident it will work," she said firmly.

"Confident. Good." Martin eyed the syringes. "And those super long ass needles?"

"Experimental. Only have enough serum for two. Lab tests show it should mitigate any contact with the Hollow, to a certain degree. But if one of those things touches you . . ."

"*But* never sounds good."

"There has never been a field test, and—"

"Jesus, there's an 'and,' too?"

"Yes, while this could save you, it could also cause cardiac arrest."

"The old widow-maker. Good thing Lucia left me a long time ago." Martin grinned. "I guess it's still better than turning into a silver alien . . . Then again, you don't really know if that's the case, do you?"

"No. You and Frank are guinea pigs, I'm sorry."

"Appreciate the condolences. So we got needles that might make our hearts blow up and a language that might tell the Hollow we come in peace, or might tell them to go fuck themselves."

Natalia grinned. "Pretty sure you're going to have to make sure Frank doesn't say the latter."

Martin secured both items, wondering when the right moment would come to tell Frank about them, if that moment would come at all.

"Oh, and about Frank . . ." Natalia's voice softened slightly. "Keep an eye on him. Shield Command may have cleared him for duty, but we both know he's never fully recovered from what happened at Titan."

Martin nodded. "I've got him, don't worry. I'm more worried about how much he hates needles. His best-kept secret."

Natalia smiled, but only briefly.

"Good luck," she said. "Come back alive. Both of you."

"We'll do our best."

Martin hurried down the corridor and found Frank leisurely resting his back against a bulkhead, his posture deceptively casual though his eyes remained alert.

"She say anything about that punch I threw?" he asked, a hint of the old Frank showing through.

"No, and cut the shit for one damn minute, Frank." Martin glanced around to ensure they were alone, then lowered his voice. "We've got a bigger problem than we thought."

"What's new?" Frank snorted. "Thirty-six hours until orbital bombardment wasn't enough of a challenge?"

Martin decided to keep the chip and syringes a secret for now. There would be time for that conversation later, when Frank was more settled. "It's not ideal, I know, but we've been in shittier situations."

Frank shrugged, pushing off from the wall. "Well, at least we get to go out and do something instead of playing drill instructor."

"That's the spirit," Martin said dryly. "Just try not to punch any more officers before we leave."

"No promises, but I'll try to save my knuckles for the Hollow."

They headed toward the medical bay, both men walking with renewed purpose. After fifteen years of running from the past, they were finally heading back to face it. Martin just hoped they'd live long enough to finally understand what the Hollow had been trying to tell them all along.

The hangar bay of Hephaestus Base echoed with the frantic final preparations of Wolverine-9. Frank leaned against a supply crate, taking in the controlled chaos as Marines double-checked equipment, loaded supplies, and ran diagnostics on their weapons systems.

The matte black hull of the Comanche dropship dominated the space, and its loading ramp extended like a massive metal tongue.

Rex sat alertly at Frank's feet, wearing a specialized tactical vest with lightweight armor that Frank had insisted on. It had taken some arguing with Requisitions, but Frank had prevailed. If Rex was going into combat, he'd be protected.

"Isn't that cute," Frank muttered as Cosmo trotted up wearing similar gear next to Martin.

"Like it?" Martin said with a grin. "Sanchez hooked us up."

Frank nodded. "She's good people."

"I think she likes you," Martin teased.

"Everybody likes me. I'm very likable."

Martin snorted. "Sure, when you're not being a complete asshole."

"Which is . . . sometimes."

Through the hangar's massive viewport, Frank could see the red glow of dawn spreading across the horizon. Six hours had passed quickly, the squad and their equipment readied in record time. Frank had to admit they were efficient, if nothing else.

Across the bay, Lieutenant Hernandez conferred with Captain Broadhurst, nodding seriously as he pointed to something on his tactical pad. The lieutenant's face was a study in focused concentration, all business now that the mission was imminent.

N'joku stood nearby, the bruises from yesterday's "training accident" still visible despite medical treatment. The lieutenant caught Frank watching him and gave a respectful nod. Frank returned it with a slight tilt of his head. Maybe the lesson had stuck after all.

"You ready for this?" Martin asked Frank quietly.

"As ready as I'll ever be. You?"

Martin glanced around to ensure no one was within earshot, then pulled Frank further behind the stack of supply crates.

"I need to tell you something," Martin whispered. "Natalia gave me classified tech yesterday."

Frank raised an eyebrow. "Is this the part where you tell me you're not actually bald but wearing a skin cap, and now—"

"Be serious." Martin grunted. "This is serious shit."

He reached into his pocket and extracted a small data chip, no larger than his thumbnail. "It's a Hollow communication device. Not proven, but a test."

Frank took the chip and turned it over in his prosthetic fingers, feeling the smooth surface with his newly enhanced tactile sensors. "So we have no idea if it works?"

"No, and I don't think it's been authorized. Natalia gave it to me in confidence."

"Good, we're guinea pigs then." Frank handed the chip back. "How's it supposed to work?"

"It's designed to translate our neural patterns into something the Hollow might understand—and vice versa. Our new cybernetics are supposedly compatible."

"And let me guess, you're planning to be the one to test it?"

Martin nodded. "I'll do it if the time comes."

"Like hell you will," Frank said, taking the chip back. "I've got less to lose if this thing fries my brain."

"Frank—"

"Don't start, Martin. I'm doing it, and that's final."

"How about we both download it and use it if the opportunity presents itself?"

Frank considered it, then nodded. "Fine."

Discreetly, they inserted the chip into the Aegis data ports, downloaded the contents, and uploaded it to their HUDs while no one was paying attention. Then Frank tucked the chip into his pocket, feeling the weight of it despite its negligible mass. Another secret. Another potential sacrifice. Just another day as a Marine.

"There's something else."

"Of course there is."

Martin pulled out a case with two very long needles inside.

"Oh, hell no," Frank said. "You know I fuckin' hate needles. I'd rather be shot or fight a Chitin in hand-to-hand combat than stab myself with one of those."

"Yeah, I know, but it might just save us if the Hollow touch us."

Frank thought of what had happened to Torres. The Marine had ended up turning his gun on himself.

"Just take it," Martin said.

Lieutenant Hernandez's voice cut through the hangar's ambient noise. "Wolverine-9, gather up!"

Frank decided to accept the sword-looking syringe. He placed it in a secure part of his armor and nodded.

The Marines assembled in a semicircle around Broadhurst and Hernandez. Frank and Martin joined them, standing slightly apart with the dogs at their sides. Frank noticed how the squad had begun to unconsciously position themselves in relation to him and Martin—not quite deferring, but ready to take cues from the veterans.

Broadhurst's eyes swept over the Marines, his posture rigid with the formal bearing of an officer about to deliver a final premission briefing. The overhead lights caught the insignia on his uniform, making it gleam like a warning beacon.

"This is it, Marines," he began, his voice carrying across the hangar without need for amplification. "In ten minutes, we'll be wheels up and headed for Galean. The mission parameters are clear: locate the source of the Hollow signatures, gather intel on their activities, and report back."

He paused, straightening to his full height. "I need to clarify the command structure for this operation. While I retain overall command of the mission, Lieutenant Hernandez will handle day-to-day squad operations and tactical decisions. However, Colonel Shafter has authorized Master Gunnery Sergeants Cage and Kelvin to assume tactical command during any Hollow encounters."

Frank watched the faces of the Marines carefully, expecting at least a few grimaces or exchanged glances of disapproval. To his surprise, none came. Instead, he saw what looked like relief flicker across several expressions.

"Not looking at me like I'm a grandpa anymore," Frank muttered to Martin.

"I'll take it," Martin replied under his breath.

"This is not a reflection on your capabilities," Broadhurst continued, "but a recognition of specialized knowledge. Sergeants Cage and Kelvin have firsthand experience with the Hollow that is invaluable. Their insights could mean the difference between mission success and failure; between life and death."

He turned to Frank and Martin directly. "You two will defer to Lieutenant Hernandez on standard military operations and to me on all strategic matters. This is a precise division of authority with clear boundaries. Is that understood?"

"Yes, sir," they replied in unison.

"Good." Broadhurst paced in front of the squad. "Regarding any civilians or miners you might encounter—avoid them if possible. They've chosen to remain on Galean despite evacuation orders and official warnings. This is not a rescue operation. Your priority is gathering intelligence on the Hollow. Do not compromise the mission to assist civilians unless absolutely necessary for operational security."

Frank saw the slight stiffening in some of the Marines' postures; the conflict between their training to protect civilians and these explicit orders. It was a hard balance, one he'd struggled with himself over the years.

"There are additional mission parameters you should be aware of," Broadhurst added. "DSIA has specific scientific objectives for this operation. Some of you have been briefed on these individually." His eyes lingered on Bolesky, D'Agata, and Phillips. "You're to collect environmental samples, document any Hollow behavioral patterns, and—if possible—retrieve intact Hollow tissue or technology."

Frank saw Bolesky straighten slightly at this, her hand unconsciously moving to the collection vials on her belt. D'Agata was already checking his quantum scanner, while Phillips adjusted the xenoarchaeological recording device mounted on his shoulder.

"The science team believes the Galean site may have significance beyond a simple Hollow incursion," Broadhurst continued. "There are indications of unusual mineral deposits that might attract or sustain Hollow presence. Understanding this connection could be crucial."

"Or it could get us killed poking around things we don't understand," Grommet muttered, earning a sharp look from Hernandez.

"Remember," Broadhurst continued, his tone hardening, "once we hit the ground, we have thirty-six hours before Shield Command considers alternative measures."

The unspoken implication hung in the air like a blade. If they failed, orbital bombardment would follow, just like at Titan Station. Frank felt his jaw tighten at the thought.

"Any questions?" Broadhurst asked.

Sergeant Gillford raised her hand, her wide shoulders set in a determined line. "What if civilians have information about the Hollow, sir?"

"Extract the information with minimal engagement," Broadhurst responded tersely. "Then continue your mission."

Frank noticed that N'joku was watching him intently. "Something to add, Lieutenant?" he asked.

N'joku straightened, the bruises on his face catching the light. "Just wondering if you have any final advice before we ship out, Master Guns."

The question seemed genuine, devoid of the earlier cockiness. Frank exchanged a glance with Martin before addressing the squad.

"Remember what we taught you," Frank said. "The Hollow don't fight like anything you've encountered before. They don't think like us. They don't move like us. And they sure as hell don't die like us. Stay flexible, adapt, and for God's sake, when Martin or I tell you to do something, do it without hesitation."

"Communication is key," Martin added. "Standard comms may be compromised near Hollow concentrations, so rely on hand signals and direct visual contact when possible."

Frank looked at each Marine in turn, taking the measure of these young men and women who were about to face humanity's most enigmatic adversary. Despite their training and confidence, he could see the undercurrent of tension in their postures. Not fear exactly, but the coiled readiness of those about to step into the unknown.

"They say the key to survival is knowing which rules you can break," Frank continued. "Out there, you might have to break all of them. Just make sure you're alive to face the court-martial afterward."

That earned a few nervous laughs, breaking the tension momentarily. Even Patel, the short warrior that had taken training more seriously than anyone, cracked a slight smile.

"One more thing," Frank added. "The Hollow . . . they're not just mindless killers. They're intelligent. They want something. Understanding what that is might be the key to all of this."

"Or it might get us killed trying to figure it out," Hallstatt muttered.

"Maybe," Frank acknowledged. "But I'd rather die understanding my enemy than live forever in ignorance."

"Alright, enough with the commentary, Marines," Broadhurst said. "Load up. Launch in five."

The squad dispersed to gather their final equipment, and moved with practiced precision that belied the gravity of their mission. Frank watched them, noting how differently they carried themselves compared to yesterday. The cocky bravado had been replaced by a focused intensity that might just keep them alive.

As the Marines filed toward the Comanche, Frank noticed Contreras performing a last-minute check on his MR-113's frequency calibration, while D'Agata distributed specialized sensor IFF tags to each squad member. Fielding appeared to be running calculations on his datapad, likely plotting optimal insertion routes.

"They remind me of us before *Squanto* a long time ago," Martin said quietly.

"Yeah," Frank admitted. "*Long* ass time ago."

He turned away, not wanting to let any sentiments or empathy cloud his judgment. At least these kids knew what the Hollow were. Frank and Martin had gone into that mission with zero intel before First Contact.

Across the hangar, Frank spotted Natalia standing by a far viewport. She hadn't been there earlier, and she made no move to approach them. The captain simply observed with that analytical expression he remembered from years ago. Two figures in civilian clothes stood near her—scientists, by the look of them, with the pale complexion and slightly hunched posture of people who spent too much time in labs rather than sunlight.

Frank nudged Martin. "Check it out."

Martin followed his gaze. "She's got a lot riding on this mission. And it looks like she brought the brain trust."

"Scientists," Frank muttered. "Probably looking for their Nobel Prize in xenobiology."

As they watched, one of the scientists—a thin man with thick glasses—gestured animatedly at a datapad, pointing to something that made Ivan lean in closer. The other scientist, a woman with short gray hair, seemed to be arguing with him, shaking her head emphatically.

"Wonder what they're debating," Martin said.

"Probably whether we should try to talk to the Hollow or dissect them," Frank replied. "Same thing they did to us, ironically."

"Dr. Bolesky looks pretty excited about this," Martin said.

Frank glanced at the tall sergeant who was making adjustments to her xenobiology field kit.

"Different breed," he said. "Military scientists understand the danger. Civilian ones, they tend to think everything's a controlled experiment."

"Another reminder we're part of an experiment," Martin said.

The boarding call sounded, and the Marines filed up the ramp into the troop hold. Frank and Martin lingered for a moment, the last to board. As Frank turned to ascend the ramp, he saw Natalia raise her hand in a subtle gesture: not quite a wave, not quite a salute. He returned it, adding a two-finger salute that might have looked casual to anyone watching but conveyed his understanding of the unspoken message: come back alive.

Inside the ship, the Marines had already strapped into their crash seats, weapons secured, expressions tense but determined. The dogs settled into specially modified restraints near Frank and Martin's positions.

Frank took a moment to study the interior of the Comanche. Unlike the utilitarian transports he remembered from his active-duty days, this vessel combined functionality with advanced technology. The crash seats were ergonomically designed to minimize impact trauma, the interior walls lined with quantum-dampening materials to reduce the signature of their emissions. Even the lighting had been calibrated for optimal visibility without compromising night vision.

"All personnel secure for launch," the pilot's voice announced over the comms.

Frank settled into his seat beside Martin and secured the harness over his chest. Rex whined softly from his nearby restraint, and Frank reached over to scratch behind the dog's ears.

"Easy, boy," he murmured. "I won't let anything happen to you."

As the ramp sealed with a pneumatic hiss, Frank felt the familiar premission sensation he hadn't experienced in years: the heightened awareness, the clarity of purpose, the push of adrenaline tempering the fear. He glanced at Martin, catching his old friend's eye.

"Just like old times," Frank said.

"God help us," Martin replied, but there was a hint of a smile beneath his concern.

The ship's engines hummed to life, and the deck vibrated beneath them as the Comanche lifted off. Through a small viewport, Frank watched Hephaestus Base fall away, shrinking rapidly as they ascended into the atmosphere.

Across the hold, N'joku sat with his back straight, eyes fixed on some middle distance as if already visualizing the mission ahead. Beside him, Hernandez reviewed mission parameters on his datapad, his expression taut with concentration. The rest of the squad maintained a disciplined silence, each preparing in their own way for what lay ahead.

Frank leaned his head back against the seat and closed his eyes briefly. Five years of trying to drown the memories of Titan Station in alcohol and bar fights, and now here he was, hurtling back toward the very nightmare he'd been running from. There was irony there, he supposed, though not the funny kind.

The Comanche's CAT drive engaged with a subtle shift in gravity that pressed Frank deeper into his seat. Soon they'd be making the jump to Galean, and after that . . .

After that, they'd be facing the Hollow again, the enigmatic enemies that had haunted his nightmares. Only this time, they wouldn't be running. This time, they might finally get answers.

Frank settled back in his seat, one hand resting on Rex's head, and prepared himself for whatever awaited them in the darkness between worlds. For the first time in years, he felt truly alive; not the artificial alertness of adrenaline or combat, but the focused clarity of purpose. Whatever happened on Galean, he would face it head-on.

The ghosts of Titan Station would have to wait a little longer for him to join them.

CHAPTER ELEVEN

"Quantum jump in five, you armored grunts," announced WO-1 Nathan Kirby, not turning from the right seat of the Comanche. "All personnel secure for transition."

Martin gripped the armrest of his crash seat as the ship's engines hummed with increasing intensity. The Comanche was the only reason he found warrant officers tolerable at all. She was a beautiful bird with deadly, curved lines, a seed pod, wrapping the squad in her armored embrace.

The CAT drive was charging, preparing to tear a hole in the fabric of reality. Despite all the technological advances of the past few decades, quantum jumps remained inherently violent affairs: a brief, nauseating transition.

"I hate this part," Contreras muttered.

"Just think of it as the universe throwing up," Frank offered, earning a few uneasy chuckles.

Martin glanced over at him, shaking his head slightly. "That's not helping."

"Three . . . two . . . one . . ." the pilot continued.

The universe blinked.

Martin's stomach lurched as the familiar twisting sensation rippled through him. For a split second, it felt like every atom in his body was being pulled in different directions. Then, with a thunderous crack that wasn't quite sound but something deeper, the Comanche punched through the quantum barrier.

"Transition complete," the pilot announced, sounding professionally disinterested. "Welcome to Galean system. ETA to planetary orbit, seventeen minutes."

Frank unclipped his harness and pushed himself up. Several of the Marines were looking distinctly green, a few with their eyes squeezed shut as they fought the postjump nausea. Cosmo and Rex, secured in their special restraints, seemed completely unfazed.

"Let's get a look at our destination," Frank said, walking to the viewport.

Martin joined him, and gradually the others followed. Through the reinforced glass, they could see Galean growing steadily larger against the backdrop of stars. It was a predominantly blue-green orb, with long swaths of mountain ranges visible even from this distance. Dark patches marked vast forests, covering much of the northern hemisphere.

"Looks like Earth," Patel said. "Before Earth went to shit."

"Trust me, this planet is nothing like Earth," Bolesky replied. "Seismic instability makes it unsuitable for long-term habitation."

"Which is why the mining operations were temporary," Phillips added. "Extract the resources and evacuate before the ground swallows you whole."

"What about the wildlife?" Fielding asked, his voice soft with wonder as he studied the approaching planet. "Seems like there should be plenty down there with the conditions being so ripe."

"Plenty sure, but mostly vegetation and insects," Bolesky explained. "Massive trees that can reach a hundred meters, some fungal growth, and a few hundred mammal-like creatures, but nothing bigger than a rabbit. Galean has a very strange ecosystem that evolved without intelligent life, despite being here for billions of years."

"It's like they were all extinct when we discovered this world," D'Agata added. "Scientific teams found fossil evidence of larger creatures, but something wiped them out millennia ago. Now it's just plants and bugs."

D'Agata activated his quantum resonance detector. "I'm already picking up anomalous readings even from here. The electromagnetic field around Galean is exhibiting quantum fluctuations."

"Could be natural," Phillips suggested, his xenoarchaeology background showing. "Or it could indicate long-term Hollow presence. We've theorized they might leave quantum footprints in the environment after extended visits."

"The storms are the real attraction," N'joku said, surprising everyone with his scientific observation. "Galean has electromagnetic tempests that can knock out electronics from orbit. That's what made the mining challenging, equipment failures were constant."

"And that's also what made it valuable," Phillips said. "The unusual electromagnetic properties created rare mineral formations. Worth the risk, until it wasn't."

As they watched, something else came into view—a massive CSF naval destroyer, hanging in high orbit above the planet. Its angular silhouette was unmistakable, studded with weapon arrays and sensor platforms.

"That's the *CNS Vigilance*," Broadhurst said. "Orion-class heavy destroyer."

"That's our thirty-six-hour countdown timer," Martin said quietly. "If we don't complete the mission, those guns will do the job for us."

Just like Titan Station, Martin thought.

The Comanche banked slightly, bringing the planet into fuller view. The pilot's voice came over the intercom again, but this time with a note of concern. "We're detecting severe electromagnetic activity in the lower atmosphere. Far beyond standard parameters for this region."

"Explain," Broadhurst demanded, moving toward the cockpit.

"Electrical storm system encircling the entire northern hemisphere," the pilot replied. "The mining surveys documented occasional storms, but this is . . . unprecedented."

"Will it affect our landing?" Broadhurst asked.

"We'll get down," Kirby assured him, "but communications with the *Vigilance* will be compromised once we enter the atmosphere. The EM field will severely degrade our signal quality. The portable array is our only chance for reliable contact."

Frank and Martin exchanged a glance. Being cut off from orbital support was never good news, especially with their thirty-six-hour deadline.

"It makes tracking our movements impossible, even with all the fancy tech on that destroyer," Contreras said, gesturing toward the viewport where the *Vigilance* hung like a steel predator. "If we get into trouble, they won't know until it's too late."

"Or they'll assume the worst and jump straight to orbital bombardment," Frank said.

Broadhurst returned from the cockpit, his expression grim. "We've received our approach vector. Prepare for atmospheric entry in seven minutes. The electromagnetic interference means we'll be operating with degraded comms once we're planetside. Deploying the portable array will be our first priority."

"Back to your seats," Hernandez ordered.

As the Marines strapped back in, Martin noticed Broadhurst staring at the destroyer, his expression unreadable behind his visor. He caught Martin's gaze, and there was something in his posture—a rigidity beyond normal military bearing—that told Martin he understood the implications of that warship's presence.

"Here we go," announced the pilot.

The Comanche began its descent, engines adjusting as they hit the outer atmosphere. Metal groaned as the craft fought against sudden crosswinds that seemed to come from multiple directions at once. The lights went dark, casting the troop hold in darkness.

Each Marine was strapped in facing each other, though with the visors down, the only way to tell one from another was their IFF signal. The ship rocked violently as it penetrated the first layer of clouds, a bone-jarring shudder that rattled through the hull.

"Jesus Christ!" Hallstatt exclaimed.

The turbulence intensified as they penetrated deeper. Martin tried to relax at the sight of flames licking at the edges of the narrow viewports in the side of the dropship, adding visual effects to the gut-deep vibration of reentry. Flashes of blue-white lightning crackled around the hull, momentarily blinding even their auto-adjusting visors.

The ship bucked again, this time with enough force to slam Contreras's helmet against the bulkhead with a dull clang. The Marine shook it off, but Martin could see the mounting tension in everyone's posture. By contrast, Rex and Cosmo looked placid and at ease, their harnesses clipped into their seats, unfazed by the heat or vibration.

The vessel dropped suddenly, losing altitude before the engines compensated with a roar.

"I hate this shit," Hallstatt muttered, probably not realizing he'd left his helmet mic hot.

"What?" Gillford teased from across the aisle. "A big guy like you getting nervous at a little turbulence? What's wrong, Buck? You think we'll break up and scatter across the landscape?"

"It wouldn't be the first time. Besides, give me a threat I can shoot at every time. In here, I'm just a passenger."

"This is the easy part." Frank grunted. "No one shooting at us, no responsibility, everything in the hands of an expert. I usually try to sleep on orbital drops, if you children weren't making so much noise."

A deafening crack of thunder shook the Comanche, followed by the unmistakable sound of a warning alarm from the cockpit. Red emergency lights bathed the cabin, casting ominous shadows across the Marines' faces.

"Status report!" Broadhurst demanded.

"Lightning strike to port stabilizer," Kirby called back, his voice tight with concentration. "We're compensating, but we're flying through an electrical storm that makes the Jupiter vortex look like a light breeze. Primary systems taking intermittent failures."

The ship lurched again with stomach-churning suddenness and dropped what felt like a hundred meters before the engines screamed back to life. Martin looked out the viewport in time to see another lightning bolt flash past, close enough that the static discharge crawled across the exterior hull like luminous blue spiders.

"Portable array status?" Broadhurst asked, his voice remarkably steady.

"Intact, but we need to get it on the ground and deployed," the pilot replied. "This level of interference will knock out standard communications within minutes of landing."

Bolesky was monitoring her instruments. "These electromagnetic readings are off the charts. If the Hollow are quantum-based entities as we suspect, this kind of field could be disrupting their ability to maintain coherent form."

"Or enhancing it," D'Agata countered. "My readings suggest the storms might actually be creating favorable conditions for quantum tunneling. The Hollow could find it easier to phase through matter in this environment."

The Comanche banked hard to port, compensating for a violent crosswind that threatened to flip the craft. Through the viewport, Martin caught glimpses of a swirling storm system below them: massive, slate-gray clouds shot through with constant lightning that forked in complex geometric patterns across the sky.

"Look at that son of a bitch!" Ali said, shouting over the roar of the engines and the constant thunder. "Is that normal?"

"Negative," Fielding replied. "Historical data shows nothing close to this intensity."

"Storm cycles on Galean run in seven-year intervals," D'Agata said. "But this looks more like the once-in-a-century superstorms the miners used to talk about."

"Lucky us," Frank muttered.

The Comanche lurched again, this time accompanied by a sharp bang from somewhere in the hull. The emergency lights flickered momentarily, then stabilized.

"We've lost the primary communications array," Kirby announced. "Lightning strike, direct hit. Secondary systems operational but severely degraded. The portable array is now our only option for reliable contact with the *Vigilance*."

"How long to deploy once we land?" Broadhurst demanded.

"Twenty minutes minimum," the pilot replied. "And that's assuming optimal conditions, which this mission sure as hell doesn't have."

"Then we'll have to work fast," Broadhurst said. "We need that link to the *Vigilance*."

As if to punctuate his point, the Comanche dropped suddenly, losing altitude in a sickening plunge before the engines compensated. Through gaps in the storm clouds, Martin caught brief glimpses of the landscape below. Vast forests of towering trees that dwarfed even Earth's ancient redwoods, networks of narrow canyons carved by ancient rivers, and the distant glint of what might be the abandoned mining complex.

"Be advised," Kirby called back from the cockpit, his voice strained but professional. "We got some readings near the LZ here you might be interested in. Energy signatures, high intensity."

"The Hollow signatures?" Broadhurst asked.

"No, this is something else. Looks like heat signatures. Possibly a fire."

"A fire . . ." Martin whispered.

"That doesn't align with previous encounters," Frank said. "The Hollow we encountered on *Squanto* and on Titan Station didn't alter the ambient temperature around them. They created localized cold variations."

"Could be an interaction with the environment," Bolesky said.

"Interaction like setting something on fire," said Gillford.

"What do you make of it, Gunny?" Broadhurst asked.

Martin took a moment to realize he was asking him. "Uncertain without visual confirmation, but in all our previous encounters, they've left thermal signatures. It's one way we've been able to track them. This could be something similar, just . . . larger scale. My recommendation would be to avoid an LZ anywhere close to it."

Broadhurst nodded and turned to the cockpit.

"Can you put us down in the forest clearing east of the complex?" he asked.

"Copy that, Captain," Kirby replied. "I'll put you down there. Silent approach protocol. No running lights."

Phillips looked up from readings on his scanner. "The fire patterns might indicate Hollow attempts at communication. Many Earth cultures used fire as a signaling method. If the Hollow are trying to establish a dialogue—"

"Or one of those billion lightning strikes hit one of those billion trees down there," Frank cut in. "Either way, we need to be ready."

The ship began a controlled descent through the storm layer, the hull groaning under the stress. Through the viewport, Martin watched the lightning intensify around them, striking with increasing frequency as they approached the ground. Each flash illuminated the landscape in stark detail: ancient forests of massive trees, some rising well over a hundred meters, their canopies creating a second sky below the clouds.

"Atmospheric stabilization at forty percent," Kirby announced, his voice tight. "The interference is wreaking havoc with our systems. We're flying partially on visual now."

Another violent jolt rocked the ship, sending loose equipment flying across the cabin. Something struck Grommet's helmet with a loud crack, but the Marine gave a thumbs-up to indicate he was unharmed.

Darkness had fallen on this side of Galean, which would work to their advantage. The night would provide additional cover for their stealth insertion, and their enhanced visors were equipped with thermal and light amplification systems. But the storm system made visibility a challenge even for advanced optics.

"Remember," Broadhurst said, his voice pitched low but carrying through their comms, "this is pure stealth. No unnecessary chatter, minimal equipment noise, and absolute fire discipline. We observe only."

Acknowledgements rang out.

"Okay, you two have tactical command," he said to Frank and Martin.

Martin nodded. It was a good sign that the captain was reinforcing the chain of command again, ensuring everyone understood who would be calling the shots once they landed and the Hollow appeared. Because they would appear—Martin felt it in his bones.

"Listen up," he said. "We drop, we establish a perimeter, deploy the array, then move out. Intel places the Hollow signatures approximately two klicks north of the abandoned mining facility. We go in quiet, we observe, we gather data, and we get out."

"Team assignments," Broadhurst added. "Grommet, Contreras, and Patel on comms array setup. Priority one is establishing contact with the *Vigilance*. The rest will begin recon with Kelvin and Cage."

Martin didn't like splitting their forces, but he understood the necessity. Without communications, they were effectively blind to orbital support or orbital threats.

The descent flattened out as they reached the lower atmosphere, the fiery glow fading from the viewports. Cloud layers whipped past, occasionally giving glimpses of the landscape forests and jagged mountain ranges extending to the horizon.

"Five minutes to LZ," the pilot announced. "Comanche prepped for landing."

Kirby's voice crackled over the intercom. "Be advised, I'm detecting a lot of electromagnetic interference. The portable array is going to face significant challenges."

"Can we establish any comms without it?" Broadhurst asked.

"Brief transmissions only, heavily degraded, and only during breaks in the storm. The portable array is designed to cut through this kind of interference, but even it will be operating at reduced efficiency."

"We'll make it work," Broadhurst said firmly. "We have to."

Martin leaned over to Frank, his voice low. "You good?"

"Peachy," he replied, but Martin noted the tension in his artificial hand, flexing and unflexing unconsciously.

Martin put his hand over the chip he had installed into his suit, hoping the gift from Captain Ivan would work if needed. The syringe in his pocket felt heavy against his thigh, a constant reminder of the experimental countermeasure.

The Comanche banked sharply toward the planet below, and the last of the storm clouds finally gave way to clear night sky. Frank watched through the small viewport as they descended toward their landing zone. The abandoned mining facility was visible as a collection of dark structures in the near distance. Beyond it, the dense forest and mountains waited, concealing whatever had brought them to this hostile world.

Somewhere in those alien forests, the Hollow were waiting. And this time, Martin was determined to learn what they wanted before Shield Command decided to solve the problem with orbital bombardment. Too many innocent lives had already been lost to that solution.

The Comanche's engines shifted to hover mode as they approached the clearing. Kirby rotated from the cockpit. "LZ in sight. No sign of fire or light from here, but the energy signatures are still registering several klicks north. Touchdown in thirty seconds."

"Copy," Broadhurst said.

"One more thing," the pilot added, his voice grave. "That electromagnetic interference? It's intensifying the closer we get to the ground. The portable array will need to be positioned on high ground to have any chance of cutting through this mess."

"Understood," Broadhurst replied, but Martin could see the concern in his posture. Being cut off meant being cut off from their extraction, and from warning the ship if things went sideways.

"Could be geological," Phillips offered. "The mineral composition—"

"Keep telling yourself that, but my guess is this has to do with the Hollow," Frank interrupted.

No one argued with him, which told Martin everything he needed to know about how seriously the squad was taking their situation.

Martin tightened his grip on his MR-113, feeling the familiar calm of pre-mission focus settling over him. Frank also looked steady and resolved. Perhaps so many years of drowning in alcohol and self-loathing had been washed away in the clarity of purpose. This was where they both belonged. In the field, doing what they were trained to do as Marines.

"Ready for deployment," Hernandez announced.

"Remember," Frank called out, "standard perimeter formation once we touch down. Eyes open and stay alert. Science Marines, get your science ready for contact, the rest of you, get your weapons ready, but keep the fingers off the triggers."

"Well said, Frank," Martin commented.

"Thanks."

"I was kidding, you sound like—"

"Someone that didn't pass sixth grade science? You'd be correct." Frank laughed manically during the last few seconds of the flight.

The Comanche touched down with a gentle bump, its landing struts absorbing the impact.

The belly doors slid open silently, revealing a moonlit forest clearing. Unlike a combat drop, there was no rush, no shouting. The Marines moved with deliberate stealth, and established a perimeter around the Comanche without a word.

Martin's boots touched the soft earth, his MR-113 shouldered. Night vision activated and turned the darkness into shades of green. The air was cool, carrying the scent of something like pine but with a metallic odor of Galean's mineral-rich soil even through his filtration systems. In the distance, a mountain range loomed against the starlit sky, its peaks jagged and unwelcoming.

"Outlaw Two, this is Comanche," Kirby's voice came softly through the comms. "We're shutting down and going dark. Radio silence unless emergency. Will remain here for extraction."

"Copy that, Comanche," Broadhurst replied. "Going silent."

Frank joined Martin at the edge of the clearing, and Rex and Cosmo moved like shadows at their sides. Broadhurst came up beside them, his rifle held at the ready.

They all studied the horizon, where tendrils of smoke fingered up against the night sky.

"Something was burning," Frank said.

Martin nodded, uncertain what to make of it. The electromagnetic disturbance was palpable even without instruments: a subtle tingling on exposed skin, a faint buzz in the audio pickups of their helmets. The air felt charged, as if a lightning strike was imminent.

"How do you want to proceed, Gunny?" Broadhurst asked.

"Double wedge formation," Martin replied. "Team Rex on point, Team Cosmo providing rear security. We move slowly, five-meter intervals, communication by hand signals only unless absolutely necessary."

Frank nodded, then turned to the assembled squad. "Remember what I said in training," he said.

Your very short training . . .

"The Hollow don't move like anything you've encountered before. They can pass through solid matter, which means they can be anywhere, anytime. Stay alert, watch your sensors, and for God's sake, don't fire unless Martin or I give the order."

Bolesky checked her xenobiology scanner one more time. "I'm detecting elevated quantum signatures already. Whatever's out there, it's affecting the local quantum field."

"Keep monitoring," Frank said. "Any changes, you signal immediately."

"Fielding," Martin said, "you're on point. Take us in."

The lieutenant moved forward silently, his steps careful and measured as he led them toward the tree line. Rex trotted beside him, the dog's senses far sharper than any technological scanner. Frank and the rest of Team Rex fanned out behind him in perfect formation.

Martin waited for them to establish position, then moved forward with Team Cosmo. The German shepherd padded silently at his side, alert and watchful.

As they entered the forest, the canopy above blocked out most of the moonlight, plunging them into deeper darkness. Their night vision compensated, but the massive trees created a maze of shadows and hidden spaces. Perfect terrain for an enemy that could move through solid objects.

The forest of towering trees rose like cathedral pillars, their trunks wider than a Marine transport. Smaller vegetation clustered at their bases, and occasional chittering sounds revealed the presence of insect life, but nothing larger. The absence of animal calls created an eerie silence broken only by the wind through the canopy above.

Phillips paused to scan a massive tree trunk. "These growth patterns are unusual. The trees show signs of rapid cellular mutation, possibly in response to long-term quantum field exposure."

"Keep the science brief," Martin reminded him. "We need to stay focused."

"Sensors are picking up the energy signatures about two clicks to the north," Hernandez reported.

Martin nodded, his eyes never leaving the forest ahead. The buzz of electromagnetic interference grew stronger with each step, and the heads-up display in his helmet flickered occasionally, struggling against the disruption.

"Then that's where we're headed," he said quietly. "Let's find out what the Hollow want before that destroyer up there decides to remove the question altogether."

He only hoped they could complete their mission and establish communications before the *Vigilance* decided they were lost—or worse, compromised. With the electromagnetic interference growing stronger, they were effectively cut off from orbital support, alone on a hostile planet with an enemy they barely understood.

Just another day as a CSF Marine.

CHAPTER TWELVE

Frank raised his fist, bringing the patrol to a silent halt. Rex's ears perked forward, a low rumble building in his chest. Through the dense forest canopy, something glinted in the fading light—metal, where there should only be ancient trees and undergrowth.

The forest had been unnaturally quiet for the past kilometer, Frank realized. No insect chirps, no rustling in the undergrowth. Just the whisper of wind through branches a hundred meters overhead. Rex's hackles were up now, the dog's body tense with alertness.

Frank motioned for Fielding to move up, then pointed through a gap in the massive tree trunks. He shifted positions with his rifle shouldered.

"Structure," Fielding confirmed quietly. "Man-made. About fifty meters ahead."

Frank turned and signed to Martin, who hurried over.

"Hernandez, bring up the rear guard," Martin ordered. "Possible contact ahead."

Frank studied the terrain. The trees here were ancient, their trunks easily twenty meters in circumference. Twisted roots created natural barriers and defensive positions. Perfect for an ambush, but also excellent cover for their approach.

"Bolesky," he called softly. "What are your sensors showing?"

The xenobiologist checked her scanner. "Electromagnetic interference is spiking, but . . . wait." She frowned at the display. "I'm getting biological readings, but they're . . . strange. Not quite human baseline."

"Hollow?" asked Broadhurst, who had moved up to join them.

"Unknown, sir. The signatures are . . . mixed."

Frank froze. Mixed signatures? He didn't know what that meant, but he had a theory that made his abused stomach drop inside of him.

"Standard approach pattern," Martin ordered. "Two teams. Frank, take Rex, Fielding, Hernandez, Gillford, D'Agata, and Bolesky. Circle left. I'll take the rest around the right flank."

"Copy," Frank acknowledged. He turned to his team. "You know what to do."

They moved through the forest like ghosts, decades of training evident in every silent step. Rex padded ahead, his training keeping him close and quiet despite his obvious agitation. The glint grew clearer as they approached, prefabricated structures from the look of them.

A faint metallic tang drifted on the air, like old pennies left in rain. The temperature seemed to drop several degrees, and their breath began misting in the sudden chill.

Phillips whispered, "Those are CSF supply modules. Standard frontier configuration."

"Part of the mining operation?" Fielding wondered.

"Wrong setup," Frank replied. "Security's too tight for civilian work."

As they drew closer, details emerged. Five modules arranged in a defensive semicircle, blast shields facing outward. Gun ports. Reinforced doors. This wasn't a mining camp—not anymore—it was a fortified position.

"A military-style compound," Fielding confirmed. "Five structures. No movement visible."

Frank held up his hand, studying the scene through his scope. The miners that had stuck around had added some major defenses, but why?

I doubt it's because of the weather . . .

He zoomed in with his rifle optics.

The main entrance of one of the structures stood open—never a good sign. Emergency lighting flickered through the doorway, casting red shadows across the threshold. His enhanced vision picked up heat signatures inside, but they were . . . wrong. Too cool for living bodies, too warm for corpses.

"Gunny," Phillips said quietly, "look at the perimeter."

Frank followed his gaze. Scorch marks on the ground, geometric patterns burned into the earth. He'd seen similar marks before, on *Squanto*. The Hollow had been here.

"D'Agata," Frank said quietly. "Can you get a reading on those burn patterns?"

"Gonna try, Sarge," D'Agata replied.

The Marine scientist's scanner hummed softly. "Quantum displacement residue. Definitely Hollow signatures, but . . . they're recent. Within the last forty-eight hours."

Frank's jaw tightened. Recent meant they could still be in the area—waiting, watching. He glanced at Rex—the dog remained alert but wasn't showing signs of immediate danger. Small comfort.

The rest of Martin's team emerged from the tree line on the opposite side of the compound. His hand signals were clear: no contacts, proceed with caution.

"Fielding, Gillford—cover the flanks," Frank ordered. "Bolesky, Phillips, you're with me. Rex, stay close."

They approached the open door slowly, weapons raised but not quite aimed. The smell hit them first: ozone and copper. Rex whined softly, pressing against Frank's leg.

"Easy, boy," Frank murmured.

Through his visor's filters, Frank could see inside the main module. Bodies. At least three, sprawled where they'd fallen. But their limbs were all at unnatural angles, twisted and mangled. Then Frank saw the metallic sheen on exposed flesh.

"Jesus," Phillips breathed. "Are those—"

"Transformed," Frank finished grimly. "Like Torres, but . . . complete."

Martin's voice crackled through the comm. "We've got bodies in the north module too. Same condition."

"Any survivors?" Broadhurst asked.

"Negative," Martin replied.

Frank stepped carefully through the doorway, and Rex followed reluctantly. The interior was a typical frontier setup: communication gear, tactical displays, supply lockers. But the deceased occupants . . .

"Captain," Frank called, "you need to see this. These aren't miners."

Broadhurst entered behind him, taking in the scene. The bodies wore tactical gear, weapons still in their holsters. Military-grade equipment lined the walls.

"Pirates," Broadhurst concluded. "This was a raider base."

"Explains the location," Martin added, joining them. "Hidden, defensible, perfect for hitting xenorite shipments."

"I thought the mines were abandoned," Bolesky said. "What was there to hit?"

"Maybe they weren't all abandoned," Frank said.

He knelt beside the nearest body, studying the transformation. Unlike Torres's agonizing partial change, these victims seemed almost peaceful. Their features were recognizable beneath the metallic skin, expressions calm despite their inhuman appearance. One pirate's mouth hung open in what might have been a scream, but instead of teeth, thin metal filaments sprouted from his gums like delicate wire grass. His fingernails had elongated into hardened silver structures that had fused with the metal floor beneath him.

"No signs of struggle after initial contact," he reported. "Whatever the Hollow did here, it was quick."

"Or they didn't resist," Gillford suggested, her massive frame filling the doorway. "Maybe they couldn't."

Outside, the sound of someone retching broke the eerie silence. Frank didn't bother finding out who it was. Could have been any of them. Could have been him, thirty years ago. At least Bolesky had kept her shit together. The tall woman fidgeted uncomfortably, shifting her weight from one foot to another as though she'd rather be anywhere but in the module with them, but she hadn't panicked.

"Want me to collect their personal effects, Gunny?" she asked, her voice betraying only the slightest tremor. "There might be data drives, comm logs . . ."

"No," Frank replied. "Don't touch anything you don't have to. We don't know how this spreads."

"The Hollow," Broadhurst said—not a question but a statement as he knelt beside one of the corpses. "They really did this to them?"

Frank nodded. One man's arm had been partially penetrated by the metal surface of the floor; his flesh seemed to merge with it in exactly the way they'd seen with Torres on *Squanto*. But unlike Torres, who had screamed and clawed at his own flesh before putting a pistol to his head, these victims showed no signs of attempting to escape their fate.

Someone had propped the main door open, and on the other side of it, D'Agata wiped his chin dry with a gloved hand before he closed his visor. The scientist had gone pale beneath his helmet but was already activating his quantum scanner, documenting the bodies with clinical precision. Cosmo stared up with concern on his canine features, while Rex tagged along with Fielding, who had moved out to the edge of the compound to make sure no one snuck up behind them.

"D'Agata, give me a report," Broadhurst ordered.

The scientist looked up from his scanner. "The quantum signatures are off the charts, sir. The bodies show cellular reconstruction at the molecular level—consistent with what we know of Hollow interaction, but the rate of change suggests a more controlled process."

Broadhurst turned to Phillips, who was examining the walls. "Phillips, any xenoarchaeological significance to the patterns?"

"These geometric burns"—he traced the marks with a gloved finger—"they're similar to communication glyphs I've seen in theoretical xenolinguistics. It's possible the Hollow were trying to leave a message here."

Broadhurst's command style became evident as he seamlessly balanced the combat veterans' experience with the scientists' expertise. He moved between the modules, checking on both groups—ensuring the Marines maintained security while the scientists gathered critical data.

"What kind of pirates choose a seismically unstable planet as their base?" N'joku asked, sweeping his weapon across the room as if expecting the corpses to suddenly animate.

"Smart ones," Martin replied. "The electromagnetic disturbances make tracking difficult, and the planet's reputation keeps away casual visitors. Perfect for launching raids on shipping lanes and then disappearing. Maybe they just chose a location close to the mines, despite the mines being abandoned."

"Gunny, you need to see this," called Hallstatt from one of the other modules.

Frank moved across the clearing, and Rex padded after him with ears perked. Inside the module marked as ARMORY on the prefab's exterior, Hallstatt stood over a weapons cache that confirmed Frank's suspicions about the outpost's true purpose.

Dozens of spent casings were scattered around, along with the telltale scorch marks of weapons discharge. These weren't your average weapons either.

Military-grade machine guns. Rocket launchers. Even a few shoulder-mounted rail cannons—high-end hardware that could take down small spacecraft. Not civilian equipment by any stretch of the imagination. The stockpile would have been worth a small fortune on the black market.

"Heavy-duty shit. Must have been some advanced pirates," Frank said definitively.

"Well trained," Hallstatt agreed. "The communications array was good enough to track shipping lanes."

"These guys did put up a fight, unlike the others," Martin said.

Frank knelt to examine one of the gauss rifles. Its ammunition counter showed empty, carbon scoring along the barrel proving it had been fired repeatedly. He checked several others, and they were all in similar condition.

"They put up a hell of a fight," he said. "But it didn't help them."

"Check this out," N'joku called from across the room. The lieutenant was examining what looked like a security terminal. "Cam footage still intact."

"Don't touch anything," Martin ordered sharply. "Just document it for now. We can review footage back at base if we get out of here alive."

"Bolesky, can you extract the data without contamination risk?" Broadhurst asked, showing his trust in the scientist's expertise.

"I can use the remote extraction protocols," she replied. "Give me three minutes."

As he stepped back outside, Frank spotted distinct tracks in the soft earth between the modules. Not footprints exactly, more like where something had flowed across the ground, leaving a trail of crystallized soil behind. The patterns matched what he'd seen on *Squanto*, when the Hollow had moved through solid objects, altering the molecular structure of anything they touched.

"See how the soil's changed composition?" he said to Martin, who had followed him out. "It's like they chemically analyze everything they interact with. Transmutation at the molecular level."

Fielding's voice cut across the comms. "Captain, I've got something. Northwest ridge, about two klicks out. More smoke, but not like a campfire. Bigger."

Frank moved to where Fielding stood at the edge of the compound. Through the canopy of trees, he could see a thin plume of dark smoke rising against the late afternoon sky. Broadhurst joined them.

"Gunny, what do you make of that?" he asked Martin.

"Another attack site, potentially," he said. "Hard to say from this vantage."

Broadhurst nodded, then turned to address the mixed squad. "Phillips, Bolesky, D'Agata—finish your scans and data collection. Two minutes. Combat personnel, maintain perimeter security."

Martin stepped over to Frank.

"If the Hollow are attacking again, then maybe Captain Ivan was wrong, maybe they weren't trying to send a message at Titan," he said. "Maybe they're back to declare war."

"After what Shield Command did to Titan Station, I'd declare war too," Frank replied.

The rage Frank had kept buried for fifteen years flared back to life. The memories crashed over him: Sarah and Lily, the station breaking apart, Martin dragging him away. The destroyer's weapons turning an entire habitat into fragments. All those people . . .

Without a word, he turned and stalked away, needing space, needing air that didn't reek of copper and death. He heard Martin's voice behind him: "Give him a minute."

Rex trotted over to Frank, sensing he was off. "I'm good, boy," he said, running his hand over the dog's head. The familiar texture of Rex's fur helped ground him in the present.

But the truth was, seeing these dead bodies had pulled Frank from his newfound confidence. The metallic sheen on their flesh, the twisted bodies—it was too familiar. The forest began to blur at the edges, and reality bled away as his mind dragged him back. The trees became corridor walls, the prefabs morphed into blast doors, and suddenly he was there again, on Titan Station, pounding metal with bloodied fists while Sarah and Lily were trapped beyond his reach. He could taste the recycled air, hear the alarms, feel the station shuddering. He could see the shifting Hollow and feel his vibrating rifle as he fired like a madman, screaming with animalistic rage.

A hand shook him from the trance, just like it had back then. From the same person.

"You good?" Martin asked, concern etched on his weathered face.

"Not as peachy, but I'm fine," Frank said.

Martin hesitated, then nodded and walked away. He motioned for Bolesky. "Get everyone together," Martin ordered. "We're moving out in five mikes."

The Marines hurried out of the prefabs, looking eager to be away from the half-transformed bodies now that they had an excuse. *The dogs were smarter than the people they served,* Frank thought, since neither of them had shown any inclination at all to go into the modules.

He composed himself with effort, moving back to the formation. It was time to keep going, to search for answers that he wasn't sure he still wanted answered.

Broadhurst finished conferring with Patel, who'd been running messages between the patrols and the Comanche. Judging by the captain's expression, the news about the communications array wasn't encouraging. Patel remained nearby, catching her breath while awaiting further orders.

Martin turned his attention to more immediate concerns—specifically, who should take point as they advanced toward the smoke.

The standard formation had Fielding taking lead, but Martin was increasingly concerned about what they might encounter. It made no sense from any standpoint of rank or seniority or leadership. He was a master gunnery sergeant, and if it wasn't usual to have a second lieutenant walking point, it at least made more sense than Martin being there. But he had something none of these kids did: combat experience against the Hollow.

That logic ran headlong into the cold calculus of the battlefield. If Martin was up front, he'd be the first to die, which would end his problems, but it would also mean that the others would be more likely to follow him into an early grave without his guidance. And Frank . . . Frank needed to be where Martin could see him, not trailing behind where old ghosts might get the better of him.

Broadhurst grunted as he walked over to Martin.

"They're still working on that comms array," Broadhurst said. "Grommet and Contreras can't cut through the interference. In the meantime, let's get moving to investigate the smoke."

Martin nodded and made his decision. "Fielding, fall back to center," he said. "I'm taking point."

The lieutenant looked surprised but didn't question the order. "Roger that, Gunny."

Martin moved to the front of the formation, Cosmo walking alongside him. "Cage, you're with me," he called back. "Rest of you maintain intervals and stay alert."

He caught Frank's eye as his old friend moved up to join him. Frank looked steadier now, focused, though the haunted edge hadn't entirely left his expression.

"Don't think I need a babysitter, Kelvin," Frank muttered.

"Good, because I need the old Cage back," Martin replied. "I need someone who can spot Hollow signatures before the rest of these Marines can process what they're seeing. That's you."

Frank seemed to accept the explanation, his posture straightening slightly. The dogs seemed happier with the new arrangement too, able to stay together at the front of the formation.

The hardest part of their trek was avoiding obstacles. As they advanced, signs of destruction became more evident. Massive trees had been knocked flat, their roots clawing at the air in a final, desperate gasp before they'd succumbed. Trunks two meters across blocked the easy paths, forcing Martin to skirt the edge of the thick brush and steeper ground on either side of the draw, often following Rex and Cosmo as they picked out a route lacking in tanglefoot.

For all his original doubts, he was glad to have the animals along. Despite the infrared optics and motion sensors, the Aegis targeting systems couldn't hold a candle to the nose and instincts of a dog. If there was anything in the thick brush around them, the animals would know before the suits. Not that the suits were useless. The course to the smoke source was a steep one, which might not have been as much of an issue for Frank and him, but it would have been for the others. The armor might have been built to protect against bullets and beams, but it came in just as handy against thorns and snags.

Most of all, Martin appreciated the optics of his suit. The night had deepened around them, throwing everything into pitch darkness, yet the enhanced vision of the helmet visor cut through the blackness. Night vision painted the world in ghostly greens and grays, while thermal overlays highlighted heat signatures in the cold mountain air. The effect eliminated the darkness, and with it some of the paranoia, the feeling of a monster in every pool of shadow.

Martin trudged through the last line of trees and halted as the source of the smoke became visible.

"Holy nun from hell," Frank said quietly as he came up beside Martin with his rifle scope raised.

Martin took a look through his own scope and zoomed in to 10x.

Approximately 2,000 meters ahead of them, a massive crater had been gouged into the mountainside, trees flattened outward in a perfect circle of destruction. In the center lay a twisted mass of metal. The material gleamed with an oily black sheen that seemed to shift and twist against the light. Patterns of energy crawled across its surface, geometric shapes that made Martin's eyes hurt to look at directly.

"What in the galaxy is that?" Broadhurst whispered.

Martin knew what it was, or what it had to be, but his mouth wouldn't quite speak the words his brain was thinking.

The craft—if you could call it that—resembled no human vessel Martin had ever seen. It seemed to be constructed of liquid metal frozen mid-flow, its hull flowing and merging with itself in ways that defied conventional engineering. Parts of it still pulsed with energy, while other sections had gone dark and cold.

"That's a Hollow ship." Frank grunted. "Son of a bitch, I didn't realize they had ships."

Rex and Cosmo had both halted, growling low in their throats. The rottweiler's ears were flat against his head, his body rigid with tension. Cosmo was pawing at the ground, as if trying to warn them away.

"Note the battle damage on the hull," Gillford said, pointing to blackened patches across the wreckage. "Small arms fire, rocket impacts. Matches the ordnance we found at the pirate compound."

"Affirmative," N'joku added. "They engaged with everything in their arsenal."

"Well, it worked. They took it down," Martin said, a bit surprised.

"This is unprecedented," Broadhurst said. "First confirmed Hollow vessel on record."

"This is extraordinary," Bolesky said.

"Incredible," D'Agata added. "The technological sophistication suggests an advanced civilization with significant resources."

"The Lort System has intelligent life after all," Phillips said with a chuckle. "I freaking knew it. Everyone that said the Hollow were some primitive creatures can suck it."

"Cut the science bullshit," Broadhurst snapped in a quiet but firm voice. "You're looking at a lethal, advanced craft from unknown origins."

Martin nodded. "Stay alert, we don't know if something's still alive on that vessel."

With his rifle scope, he surveyed the crash site methodically. The ship had carved a deep furrow through the forest before smashing into the mountainside. The impact had shattered trees for hundreds of meters in every direction, and the vessel itself appeared to be partially embedded in the rock face.

"Captain," Martin said, turning to Broadhurst, "we need to secure the area and confirm hostile disposition before advancing."

Broadhurst scoped the area, taking it all in. He clearly didn't like the exposure, but he likely knew Martin was right. Intelligence on Hollow technology was virtually nonexistent. This was a critical intel opportunity.

"Looks like multiple trails bearing north," Phillips said. He pointed to several trails leading away from the crash site where the soil had transformed into metallic patterns they'd seen at the outpost.

"First priority is vessel assessment," Broadhurst said.

"Copy that. Squad, listen up," Martin ordered, steeling himself. "Tighten formation, weapons condition one. Cage, N'joku, maintain overwatch. The rest, on me to the crash site. No one initiates contact with anything without my authorization."

"Gunny," Bolesky interjected, adjusting her scanner. "I'm detecting residual quantum flux patterns. The molecular structure shows signs of controlled phase transition. This could provide critical data on their propulsion systems."

D'Agata nodded, his own instruments active. "Confirmed. The quantum entanglement signatures are incredible. If we can analyze the decay patterns, we might understand how they achieve transdimensional movement."

Broadhurst waited a few moments, probably to digest all the science jargon, before giving the advance signal. The team fanned out, weapons up and ready.

Martin couldn't shake the feeling they were under observation. The strange patterns on the hull seemed to shift and flow even in his peripheral vision, as if the craft itself were somehow still alive despite the damage.

"Maintain your intervals," Frank warned, his voice tight. "These things can play possum."

"I'm not detecting any current signatures," D'Agata said.

Martin moved a few steps closer, leading them to ten meters from the ship. Heart pounding, he stopped, scanning all directions with Cosmo by his side. The dog didn't seem to sense anything in the crash site.

"Clear." Martin waved the rest of the squad up. They advanced cautiously with their weapons and science tech out.

Phillips held up his recorder to capture every detail. "These geometric patterns match theoretical models for advanced communication systems," he said. "This entire vessel might be a massive data storage device."

Martin ducked to look through a section of the hull that had been torn open by the impact. Inside, the structure appeared to be a single continuous piece, with no visible seams or separate components. No crew compartments, no engine room, no control systems—at least none that made sense from a human perspective.

"The entire structure appears to be a unified organism," Bolesky said excitedly. "No discrete systems, it's all one integrated matrix."

"Look at this," Frank called, taking a knee near what might have been the bow. He indicated a rapidly cycling pattern of geometric shapes that appeared to be pulsing with increasing frequency. "Is this thing still hot?"

Martin moved closer and studied the sequence. The geometric shapes seemed to be shifting in a sequence, almost like a language or code.

"Could be an automated distress beacon," he suggested. "Or emergency protocols."

Bolesky hurried over with her scanner. "The quantum decay signatures are degrading—if we don't capture them now, we'll lose critical data."

"Capture what you can, but stay close," Broadhurst said.

"On it, sir."

Frank stood, taking a step back from the craft and joining Martin. "We've got a downed Hollow vessel, Gunny. It might be empty, but Shield Command needs immediate notification of this intel."

Martin nodded. This was beyond their mission parameters.

He signaled to Broadhurst and Hernandez, who were examining another section of the craft. They converged at what seemed a safe distance from the pulsing mosaic.

"Captain," Martin said, "recommend immediate data upload to Shield Command. If the Hollow have vessels of this capability, it changes our entire threat assessment."

"Agreed, I would have already relayed this to the *Vigilance*," Broadhurst said. "Problem is the comm array. Contreras got the array deployed, but the EM interference is worse than projected. They're barely maintaining a carrier wave, and that's with full power output."

Patel nodded, speaking up for the first time. "Grommet said the storm's creating electromagnetic layers they didn't anticipate. They can receive fragments, but outbound transmission is nearly impossible."

"How bad?" Martin said.

"They're working on signal amplification, but it'll take time," Patel continued.

"If there are Hollow survivors from this crash, they'll be defensive, possibly compromised," Hernandez said. "That increases the threat level exponentially."

"You're right, too big of a risk to follow now, and who knows when or if any hostiles will return to this site," Broadhurst said. He turned to Patel. "Sergeant, when you head back to the Comanche, stay there this time. Help Grommet and Contreras boost that signal. Tell them we need comms with the *Vigilance* yesterday. We'll hoof it back as soon as we have intel gathered."

"Understood, Captain," Patel replied.

"D'Agata, Bolesky, Phillips—I need you three on that vessel. Extract every bit of data you can while we hold position."

D'Agata's eyes lit up. "Yes, sir. The quantum signatures alone could revolutionize our understanding of their technology."

"The rest of us, defensive positions at fifty-meter intervals. Three-sixty coverage. Call out anything that moves," Broadhurst ordered. "No pursuit ops until we have solid comms and potential reinforcement."

Martin surveyed the squad. Most looked tense but focused. They'd processed the horror at the pirate outpost, understood the Hollow's lethality. But they hadn't engaged directly yet, hadn't experienced how conventional tactics meant nothing against an enemy that could phase through solid matter.

As the squad dispersed to their assigned positions, Frank moved closer to Martin. "Think we're making the right call?" Frank asked.

Martin watched as Rex and Cosmo circled the crash site, still agitated but no longer actively hostile. The dogs' behavior suggested the immediate threat had passed.

"It beats tracking the enemy out there," Martin replied. "Still, I don't like hanging around, even if it's by the book to gather intel."

"Better by the book than KIA," Frank said. He glanced toward the metallic trails leading deeper into the mountains. "Whatever's out there isn't going anywhere."

Martin nodded, though he couldn't shake the feeling that they were under surveillance. The forest beyond the crash site was unnaturally quiet, as if the entire ecosystem had withdrawn in the presence of something alien.

"You ever consider they might be as concerned about us as we are about them?" he asked quietly.

"After Titan?" Frank replied, his voice hard. "They should be running scared."

Martin unclipped his rangefinder, an old habit from countless missions. "Been ranging those trails. They extend at least two klicks before the terrain blocks line of sight."

"Lot of ground to cover," Frank said.

"Yeah, and perfect for an ambush if they're waiting for us."

"Always the optimist, Kelvin."

"Just stating facts, Cage. We get out of this, I've got a victory cigar with your name on it in my gear."

"Now you're talking. But I'm starting to worry we aren't making it back."

"Cut that shit out, Frank. We've been in worse spots."

"Name one."

"Bomede. The Chitin nest on Arcturias. That clusterfuck on—"

"Okay, okay. Point taken."

The two veterans took up position on a slight rise that offered good sightlines of both the crash site and the surrounding forest. Rex and Cosmo settled beside them, alert but calm.

Martin scanned the tree line through his scope, unable to shake the feeling they were standing at a crossroads. The Hollow weren't just transients anymore, weren't just enigmatic beings passing through human space.

They were here, with ships and technology beyond human comprehension, for purposes still unknown. And one way or another, Martin was determined to get answers.

CHAPTER THIRTEEN

Frank flexed his fists, both real and prosthetic, trying to keep the shakes at bay. They were supposed to be gone after the cocktail of meds he got back at base, but lack of alcohol and raw nerves had brought them back. *Get your shit together, old man, or you and Rex aren't getting off this shithole.*

His dog glanced up at him as Frank regulated his breathing and flexed his muscles until the tremors subsided.

"I'm good," Frank said.

Rex paced restlessly at his side, occasionally stopping to sniff the air, hackles half raised. There was no denying the dog was nervous too. Something was out there, watching them. Frank could feel it.

The night sky flickered with distant lightning, the Hollow vessel's twisted form taking on an even more sinister appearance in the intermittent illumination. They had established a defensive perimeter around the crash site, maintaining fifty-meter intervals as ordered. Behind them, Bolesky, D'Agata, and Phillips huddled around the alien wreckage with their scanners and instruments—the science squad, as Frank couldn't help thinking of them.

The sight stirred an unwelcome memory: those researchers at Cretin-4, fumbling with their sidearms while Frank and Martin had run overwatch. He remembered one scientist—Dr. Yahoo, or something—nearly shooting himself while trying to check if his weapon was loaded. What had seemed darkly amusing then felt like a lifetime ago.

But that wasn't the only thing he remembered. That scientist had boasted about how his work was so important—work to determine why the Lort System was absent of intelligent life. The irony wasn't lost on Frank as he held watch over evidence of not just an intelligent alien species, but a very advanced species.

He pushed the memories aside, focusing on the present. At least these Marines knew which end of a rifle to point downrange.

N'joku had positioned himself on higher ground, his MR-113 propped on a fallen tree trunk, covering the approach from the north. Gillford and Hallstatt guarded the eastern and western approaches respectively, while Fielding had taken up position to the south, facing back toward the mining outpost.

Frank moved to check in with D'Agata, who was examining something near what might have been the propulsion system of the crashed Hollow vessel.

"Finding anything interesting?" Frank asked, keeping his voice low.

D'Agata shook his head. "Nothing I can make sense of. No seams, no welds, no conventional manufacturing signatures. It's as if the entire structure was grown rather than constructed."

"Remarkable, isn't it?" Bolesky asked.

"If you say so," Hernandez said. He patrolled behind the scientists, seemingly uninterested in their work or this find.

Frank took a second to study the twisted metal—if it could even be called metal. The substance had a strange, oily sheen that seemed to shift when viewed from different angles.

Rex suddenly growled, head snapping toward the direction of the LZ. Frank tensed, and his hand automatically moved to his weapon.

"What is it, boy?" he murmured.

The first shots rang out before Rex could respond. Distant plasma fire echoed through the forest, followed by screams that carried clearly in the mountain air. Frank's blood ran cold as he realized the shots were coming from the direction of the Comanche.

"Contact!" Grommet's voice crackled over the comms, breaking the order for radio silence. "Multiple Hollow signatures converging on our position! They're everywhere! Request immediate backup—"

The transmission cut off abruptly and was replaced by a cacophony of voices and static.

Frank was already moving.

Martin emerged from behind the crashed vessel, Cosmo at his side. Broadhurst rushed over, helmet looking at them in turn. "Cage, Kelvin, you have tactical," said the captain. "What's our play?"

Frank could tell Martin was struggling with the decision: hold position or risk everything on a rescue attempt.

Martin gave Frank the nod, confirming they were on the same page. They couldn't abandon the others or their ride out of here.

"Squad, rally on me!" Martin ordered. "We're moving to assist the LZ! Weapons hot, TDF grenades ready!"

The Marines abandoned their positions and converged on them before racing into the forest. Even the science squad fell into line without a complaint of leaving behind the greatest scientific discovery since the Gauntlet wormhole.

Frank took point with Martin, their dogs leading the way.

"Shit, comms are broke dick," Broadhurst said, his voice strained as he kept pace. "I can't get the pilot."

Frank pushed harder, vaulting over fallen logs and crashing through underbrush. The sounds of combat grew louder: plasma fire, inhuman shrieks, and the distinctive pop of TDF grenades detonating.

D'Agata and Hernandez kept pace with Frank and Martin, but were clearly holding back in their Aegis suits. The younger Marines were more agile and in far superior shape. N'joku too closed in, nearly passing the others.

"Martin," Frank started to say.

"I know," Martin huffed back. "D'Agata . . . N'joku, Hernandez, go ahead, but don't . . . engage . . . unless . . . fuck."

Frank looked over at Martin, who was already out of breath. In any other situation, he would be cracking jokes about his gut, but now wasn't the time.

"Come on, Gunny, you got this," Frank said.

"Shut the fuck up, Cage," Martin said.

"I'm just trying to help!"

"Don't!"

Another flurry of gunshots broke out, silencing them both. They were closing in on the clearing where they'd left the Comanche. Frank spotted N'joku behind a tree, aiming his rifle at the clearing about 500 meters through the tree line ahead. Hernandez was close, but Frank didn't see D'Agata.

Nearly a full minute later, Frank caught up with the rest of the Marines bunched up at the edge of the clearing and took position at an adjacent tree with Rex behind him. Martin came next, panting heavily. He signaled to the rest of the squad to spread out and find cover among the terrain around the clearing. They needed to assess the situation before charging in blindly.

"Multiple thermal signatures ahead," N'joku reported.

"Remember your training," Frank said. "Maintain dispersion. Watch for phase-through attacks."

Slowly, the squad moved up and reached the edge of the forest just as another burst of plasma fire illuminated the scene. What Frank saw in the clearing beyond made his stomach drop.

The Comanche sat in the center of the field, its engines cycling erratically, emergency strobes painting everything in alternating red and white. But it was the ground action that seized Frank's attention.

D'Agata had charged right into the field and was dragging Contreras away from a shimmering mass of silver-green light. The two Marines were about fifty meters from the Comanche, D'Agata struggling to support Contreras, who seemed barely able to stand.

"Fight it, Jose!" D'Agata shouted, his voice carrying across the clearing. "Don't let it take you!"

Frank could already see the metallic lines spreading beneath Contreras's skin, tracing neural pathways along his neck and face where his helmet had been compromised. The staff sergeant convulsed, his body contorting unnaturally.

"It's . . . so cold." Contreras gasped, his voice shifting into multilayered harmonics that weren't entirely human. "I can see . . . everything . . ."

"Fall back from him, D'Agata!" Frank shouted, raising his MR-113. "He's already compromised!"

D'Agata turned toward them, desperation etched on his face. "Negative! We can save him!"

Frank reached into his armor's storage compartment, and his fingers closed around one of the syringes Natalia had given them. But looking at Contreras's advanced transformation, he knew it was already too late. The syringe might stop infection, and reverse it, but not at this point.

And the communication chip that they had downloaded?

These things are past listening to anything but plasma, he thought.

But even that window was closing.

Contreras's body went rigid, then impossibly fluid. Silver tendrils erupted from his hands, gripping D'Agata's arms with inhuman strength. The silver-green aura expanded, encompassing them both as D'Agata screamed, trying to pull away.

"Help!" D'Agata's voice broke with terror.

"Everyone back!" Frank ordered, priming a TDF grenade. "Clear the blast radius!"

He watched in horror as Contreras and D'Agata began melding together, their separate forms becoming indistinct as the Hollow entity flowed between and through them. Their armor liquefied at contact points, metal flowing like mercury under the alien presence.

"TDF out!" Frank shouted, hurling the grenade in a perfect arc.

The temporal disruption field grenade detonated with a distinctive warping sound, and reality bent around the blast point. For a moment, Contreras and D'Agata froze mid-transformation, caught between seconds as the field trapped them in a temporal bubble.

"Now!" Frank commanded. "Concentrated fire!"

The squad opened up with their MR-113s, plasma bolts converging on the frozen figures. The temporal field made the Hollow entity vulnerable, unable to phase or adapt while trapped between moments.

The combined plasma fire tore through the suspended forms. When the TDF field collapsed seconds later, all that remained was a smoking crater where two Marines had stood.

A gust of coppery odor and burned flesh rushed through the field in what felt like slow motion.

The moment stretched, Frank frozen in horror at what he had just done. He felt the familiar weight of command decisions—taking his own men's lives to prevent something worse. It never got easier.

"Contact front!" Martin's voice snapped them back to reality.

Frank lifted his gaze to the Comanche. The dropship's engines were spooling up chaotically, the craft beginning to shudder as systems engaged without proper sequencing.

"They're attempting liftoff!" N'joku shouted.

Frank watched the erratic engine patterns. "Something's wrong."

Through the cockpit viewport, silver-green light pulsed and flowed. Not the steady glow of instrumentation, but the same eerie luminescence they'd seen consuming their squadmates.

"The Hollow have breached the cockpit!" he shouted.

The Comanche lurched violently skyward and had barely cleared the ground before listing hard to port. Its stabilizers sparked, venting atmosphere as the craft fought to maintain attitude control.

"Should we engage?" Gillford asked. She tracked the unstable vessel with her rifle.

"No, hold your fire!" Broadhurst ordered. "That's still our only way home."

Frank ducked as their hope for extraction spiraled out of control. The Comanche's port engine suddenly erupted in a cascade of explosions.

The craft corkscrewed wildly, trailing fire and debris as it careened toward the forest. The Comanche punched through the canopy like a missile, shearing massive trees in half. A wing separated and tumbled end over end through the air. The main fuselage impacted a cluster of ancient trees with devastating force.

"Hit the deck!" Martin shouted as the shock wave approached.

Frank tackled Hernandez behind a boulder as debris whistled overhead. The ground bucked from secondary explosions, each detonation painting the night sky orange.

When the barrage subsided, Frank emerged to survey the devastation. Their transport was reduced to burning wreckage scattered across 200 meters of forest. Trees had been flattened in a wide radius, some still ablaze, others reduced to charred stumps.

"Kirby! Warrant Officer Kirby, respond!" Broadhurst shouted, his voice erratic.

"Fuckin-A," N'joku said flatly. "We're so fucked now."

Frank couldn't argue as he watched their last hope burn, but he couldn't let morale slip down the shitter like their ride. The longer the squad had to think about being stranded on a hostile planet with an unknown number of Hollow entities and no way to signal for help, the worse they were going to be.

"Maintain security," Frank ordered. "Remember your training—as long as we're still breathing, we've got a chance to get out of this . . . situation."

"You heard him," Martin barked. "Defensive positions now!"

The Marines scrambled into a somewhat decent formation with weapons angled in all directions. Rex and Cosmo kept close to Frank and Martin while they too scanned the area.

"Where's Patel?" Fielding said. "And Grommet?"

Frank's blood ran cold. In the chaos of the engagement and crash, they had lost two Marines.

"Anyone have eyes on Grommet or Patel?" Broadhurst asked, his voice calming slightly.

"Negative," came the replies.

"Search pattern," Broadhurst ordered. "Five-meter intervals, buddy teams. Nobody goes solo."

They swept the clearing methodically, calling names over comms and checking thermal signatures. Frank kept Rex close, monitoring the dog's behavior for any sign of Hollow presence.

"Got something," Hallstatt reported from near the wood line. "Blood trail, leading north."

Frank and Martin converged on the location. The blood was fresh, drops leading into the forest—human blood, according to their suit diagnostics.

"Could be Patel," Martin said. "She was supposed to be with the comm team."

"Or Grommet," Frank added. "Either way, someone's wounded and mobile."

"Or being dragged," N'joku said darkly.

Broadhurst joined them, his expression grave. "We can't leave them behind if they're alive."

Frank understood the captain's position, but their tactical situation was deteriorating rapidly. No comms, no extraction, unknown number of hostiles, and now missing team members.

"Sir," Frank said carefully. "We need to establish a defensible position before conducting search and rescue. We're too exposed here."

Martin nodded. "Ridge line, one klick east. High ground, good fields of fire, natural barriers."

Broadhurst clearly struggled with the decision—duty to his missing Marines versus the survival of the remaining squad.

"We have a narrow window," Frank pressed. "The Hollow know our position. They'll be back."

Lightning flickered across the sky, briefly illuminating the carnage around them. In that moment of stark clarity, Broadhurst made his choice.

"We move to the ridge," he decided. "Establish a defensive position, then organize search teams for Patel and Grommet."

"Roger that, sir," Frank replied.

He took one last look at the burning Comanche. Their lifeline to orbit, to the *Vigilance*, to home—reduced to twisted metal and flames. Two Marines KIA and two more MIA in less than an hour. Plus the two pilots.

"Move out," Martin ordered. "Combat spacing, noise discipline. We're not losing anyone else tonight."

The squad formed up and slipped into the darkness with stealth precision. Behind them, the wreckage continued to burn, a beacon for any hostiles in the area. The sense of being watched had been replaced. Now Frank felt like they were being played with, like a cat would play with a mouse.

Their mistake, he thought. *I might be old, bitter, and a half cripple, but I still got bite.*

This wasn't the first FUBAR situation Martin had been in throughout his distinguished career as a CSF Marine. But in all those other fucked up beyond all recognition and repair situations, he was in his prime and trusted his squad with his life. Now he was in his midfifties and was in tactical command with Frank, who up until a few days ago had wanted nothing more than to pound Martin's "egg head" into oblivion.

They had been moving for nearly thirty minutes when Martin held up a closed fist, signaling the squad to halt. Something felt wrong. The forest had gone completely silent around them—no nocturnal sounds, no insects, no rustle of small animals in the undergrowth. It was as if all life had suddenly evacuated the area, sensing a predator that humans couldn't detect.

Not even the branches were creaking now. There was no breeze. Nothing. The forest stood frozen, every tree a sentinel watching their passage with hidden eyes. Martin could hear the soft whir of his suit's ventilation system, the sound unnaturally loud in the perfect stillness. Cosmo's breathing beside him, N'joku's careful footsteps as he took up a defensive position—each noise seemed to carry for kilometers in the unnatural quiet. Martin felt the weight of observation, of alien intelligence studying their every move, though his scanners detected nothing.

The dogs, however, did. Both growled simultaneously, oriented west.

"Contact," Frank called out quietly. "Vector two-seven-zero."

Martin turned to see the unmistakable silver-green shimmer of Hollow entities emerging from the forest. Three of them, moving with that unsettling fluidity that defied normal physics.

"Martin . . . we got seconds," Frank said. "Communicate or engage?"

The Hollow entities surged forward, accelerating rapidly. They seemed to phase in and out of reality, sometimes transparent, sometimes solid. This wasn't the time for diplomacy.

"Hostile intent confirmed," Martin decided.

"Copy that," Frank said.

"Hold fire until optimal range." Martin shouldered his rifle. "On my mark. Three . . . two . . . one . . . mark!"

The squad opened fire simultaneously, MR-113s unleashing concentrated plasma into the night. N'joku and Hallstatt's weapons created momentary suns where they impacted, the flash temporarily overloading Martin's visor.

The forms of two entities dissolved into vapor that quickly dissipated. The third phased through the ground itself and re-emerged behind Gillford's position.

"Six o'clock!" Frank shouted.

Gillford spun, but the entity was already striking. Its tendril-like appendage slashed across her armor, leaving a metallic gash. She staggered back, firing on full auto.

"Controlled bursts!" Martin commanded.

Hallstatt stepped forward, deploying a TDF grenade. The temporal field caught the entity mid-phase, freezing it between states. Frank finished it with a precisely calibrated burst.

For a moment, silence reclaimed the forest. Martin scanned the perimeter, waiting for the next wave, but the woods remained still.

"Status report," he ordered. "Any casualties?"

"Armor breach, no penetration," Gillford said, gasping.

Broadhurst kept his distance to inspect the damage.

"I'm good, Captain," Gillford said, like she was trying to convince him and herself. "I'm okay, it didn't get me."

Broadhurst, Hernandez, and Bolesky all moved over to check.

"I think she's fine," Bolesky said after a few scans.

Gillford took a few deeper breaths, then nodded. "Fine, I'm fine," she kept saying.

The others reported in—all combat effective. The psychological toll was harder to assess.

A sudden crashing through the underbrush sent every weapon swinging toward the noise. Phillips fired off a burst into the tree line right as an armored figure stumbled out.

"Hold fire!" Martin barked, recognizing the Aegis suit and IFF. "It's Grommet!"

The sergeant slowly made his way into their perimeter, his visor up, face pale and slick with sweat. His eyes were wild, darting between shadows.

"Jesus, I'm sorry," Phillips said.

Grommet staggered right past Phillips, reaching out with both hands, his firearm gone.

"Sergeant," Broadhurst said. "Get ahold of yourself!"

Grommet shifted toward Broadhurst and grabbed him by a shoulder plate.

"Captain, we have to get the hell out of here," he said. "Those things—they just fucking appeared out of nowhere! Phase-shifting through the trees like ghosts. We didn't have a chance at the comms array. One second Contreras was next to me, the next he was screaming with that thing inside him—"

"What happened to Patel?" Hernandez asked urgently. "Where is she?"

"I don't know." Grommet gasped, doubling over to catch his breath. His voice carried a raw edge of shame. "When those things took Contreras, when I saw what they were doing to him . . . I just ran. I'm fucking sorry, but I just ran."

Broadhurst grabbed Grommet hard and shook him. "It's time to get your shit together, Marine. No more running. You run again, and I'll fucking shoot you myself, got it?"

Grommet hesitated, then nodded. "I'm sorry, I'm sorry—"

"Shut the fuck up. You want those things to find us again?"

"No," Grommet whispered.

Broadhurst let out a grunt and then pushed Grommet away. "We still have one Marine unaccounted for," he said. "Patel could be out there too. We need to find her."

Martin nodded. "Search pattern Delta. Stay in visual contact."

The burning wreckage of the Comanche cast flickering shadows through the trees as they continued to search for a trail. By now, all signs of the blood they had seen back at the field were gone. But Rex and Cosmo still had a scent.

They swept the area methodically, the dogs leading the way with their enhanced senses. Both animals cautiously moved through the underbrush, occasionally pausing to sniff at disturbed ground.

Twenty minutes of searching yielded nothing until Hallstatt said, "Got something over here. Looks like blood."

Martin and Frank converged on Hallstatt's location. Dark droplets spattered across fallen leaves, leading deeper into the forest. The blood pattern suggested someone moving while injured—irregular spacing, occasional smears against tree trunks where they'd steadied themselves.

"Human blood," Phillips confirmed, scanning with his medical sensors. "Fresh. Maybe thirty minutes old. Has to be Patel."

They followed the trail for another fifty meters, and the droplets became more frequent, the smears larger. Cosmo suddenly froze, a low growl building in his throat as he stared upward into the canopy.

"Contact high," Frank whispered.

Martin raised his weapon, tracking upward.

There, partially concealed in the branches, hung a humanoid figure. The armor was unmistakably Marine-issue—Patel's IFF still broadcasting weakly. But the body inside moved with alien articulation, silver tendrils extending from the joints to anchor it to the tree.

"Contact confirmed," Martin reported quietly. "Southwest sector, elevated position."

"Status?" Broadhurst's voice was carefully neutral.

"Subject's been compromised," Martin confirmed, keeping his tone clinical.

The entity that had been Patel tilted its head at an impossible angle, studying them with what might have been curiosity. Silver liquid wept from where its eyes should have been, mercury tears tracing down the helmet.

Martin didn't even consider the syringe Natalia had provided. The neural integration was clearly complete. The countermeasure required a living host, not this hybrid abomination.

The creature emitted a multilayered harmonic that set Martin's teeth on edge. He clenched his jaw and tracked it with his rifle as what had once been Patel began descending from the tree with arachnid grace.

"Hallstatt, take aim," Broadhurst said. This was one tactical situation where the captain exerted command. For that, Martin was glad.

"Wait," Ali interjected. "We might be able to help her still."

"Negative," Phillips said. "She's hostile biomass now."

"Don't say that." The formerly quiet sergeant was clearly friends with Patel or cared for her on some level.

"I lost someone like this too," Martin said. "That's not Patel anymore. Trust me, she would want us to do this."

Hallstatt aimed his plasma rifle, looking to Broadhurst.

"Weapons free," he ordered. "Make it quick."

Ali looked away, his head down.

The crack of plasma fire split the night. The entity's head vaporized in a burst of silver-green mist. The body tumbled from the tree and impacted with a wet thud. Residual nerve impulses resulted in grotesque twitching.

"Christ," N'joku muttered.

Hallstatt fired two more controlled bursts, ensuring termination. The corpse smoldered, finally still.

"Target neutralized," he reported, then added quietly, "I'm sorry, Kara."

Eerie silence reclaimed the forest. Only wind through branches disturbed the quiet. Martin waited a moment before speaking.

"We need to relocate," he said.

Broadhurst nodded. "Options?"

Martin consulted his tactical display. "The mining complex is five klicks southeast. Defensible position, possible supplies, maybe functional comms. We have to find a way to contact *Vigilance*." He checked his mission clock. "T-minus twenty-eight hours, thirty-one minutes until orbital strike authorization. That's our window."

"And if that complex is crawling with hostiles?" N'joku asked.

"Then we adapt," Frank replied. "But we're sitting ducks out here."

Martin assessed their deteriorating tactical situation. The decision was clear, however unpalatable.

"Equipment check," he said. "Verify suit integrity—no compromised seals. Weapons at full charge. We move in sixty seconds."

"We're not recovering her body?" Ali asked quietly. "She deserves a proper burial if you don't want to take her with us."

"Negative," Broadhurst responded firmly. "Contamination risk is too high. I know it goes against everything we've been taught, but we can't help them if we're infected too."

Ali turned away, shoulders rigid with suppressed emotion. The other Marines busied themselves with final preparations.

Frank pulled Martin aside as the squad readied to move.

"Why didn't you attempt the communication protocol?" he asked in a low voice.

Martin's expression was incredulous behind his visor. "You serious? When? Between the ambush and the firefight? Why didn't *you*?"

"Fair point. Everything went sideways too fast."

"That's the understatement of the century," Martin said. "If they're moving this aggressively, we need to move faster."

He felt the weight of his age and of command pressing down on them. A quarter of their force eliminated in the first engagement. Transport destroyed. Mission parameters completely FUBAR. But dwelling on losses wouldn't keep the survivors alive.

"Alright, people, listen up," he addressed the squad. "Tactical column formation. Maintain five-meter intervals. We're not losing anyone else tonight."

The trek through dense forest tested their endurance and nerves. Every shadow potentially concealed death. Every sound triggered weapon sweeps. The dogs proved invaluable, their enhanced senses helping Martin feel like they had an edge over the Hollow.

After an hour of careful navigation through increasingly challenging terrain, they reached a rocky promontory overlooking a deep ravine. Martin signaled a halt, studying the natural barrier.

"That's our route?" Broadhurst asked.

"Affirmative," Martin confirmed. "Ravine bisects our path completely. Detour would add twenty klicks minimum."

"Mother of God." N'joku breathed, calculating the descent. "That's a hundred-meter drop, easy."

The canyon walls plunged nearly vertically to a narrow floor where water had carved through bedrock over geological time. The opposite face appeared equally daunting, sheer rock with minimal handholds.

"Descent's manageable," Martin assessed, his visor overlaying climb routes. "But going around keeps us exposed for hours."

"I'll take the climb," Frank agreed. "Better than waiting for round two with our phase-shifting friends."

Martin nodded. "Suit servos can handle the descent. We'll need to improvise anchors."

"With what?" Gillford asked skeptically. "Nobody packed climbing gear."

Martin turned to N'joku. "Your MR-113 Heavy has the tactical cable launcher attachment, correct?"

"Roger, but it's rated for emergency extraction only," N'joku said. "Not certified for full squad deployment."

"It'll have to suffice. We anchor topside, descend individually. Far side will require free climbing with suit assistance."

"What about the dogs?" Frank asked suddenly. "How do we get them down safely?"

Martin looked at Cosmo and Rex, who both looked back at him with their curious gazes. "Harness them to us," Martin said. "The armor can compensate for additional mass."

"This is beyond improvised," Broadhurst muttered, but his tone held resignation rather than objection.

"Alternative proposals, Captain?" Martin asked evenly. "Dawn's approaching. We need hard cover before daylight, and this is our most direct route."

"He's right," Frank supported. "I'd rather not be caught in the open when those things regroup."

"I could attempt the descent," Ali offered, studying the seam. The sergeant's voice carried none of the cocky bravado they'd heard during training. Losing Patel had tempered his confidence but not broken it. "I've completed technical climbing courses."

"In powered armor?" Gillford asked skeptically.

"Negative, but the tactical principles apply. The suit's enhanced strength should actually facilitate grip maintenance."

"There might be an alternative approach," Phillips interjected. "The mimic circuit."

"Elaborate," Martin said.

"It's a remote-control function." Phillips brought up a schematic on his wrist display that projected a small hologram between them. "Allows one suit to slave to another. Armorers utilize it for maintenance and storage procedures."

"I've heard of it," Frank admitted. "But that's for workshop conditions, not tactical operations."

"Affirmative, but it might be applicable here," Phillips insisted, manipulating the hologram to show the control interface. "I can descend first and then remotely guide each of you down the same path."

"Are you proposing remote-piloting our suits while we're operational?" Hernandez asked, staring at the lieutenant. "That's beyond experimental. If I'm going to die, I want to go down fighting, not falling trapped in my Aegis."

"You got a better tactical solution?" Broadhurst asked. "So far, I've got two options, but I'm happy for more."

"Salvage the wings from the Comanche," Frank said. "We can fly down one at a time."

"Cut the shit, Gunny."

"Sorry, Cage uses humor when he's nervous," Martin said.

"A good laugh never killed a Marine," Frank said. "At least, not that I know of."

A few chuckles, followed by a tense silence fell over the group. The wind whistled through the canyon below, a mournful sound that emphasized their isolation. In the distance, something howled, a native predator or something worse. Frank shifted closer to Rex, his hand instinctively reaching for the rottweiler's head.

Finally, Broadhurst spoke up, his captain's bars catching the last light. "What's your confidence level on this seam, Phillips?"

"High confidence, Captain," the young officer replied, straightening his posture. "With the Aegis's enhanced capability, we can create a friction brake using the seam."

Broadhurst exhaled slowly. "Proceed."

As N'joku secured the tactical cable to a sturdy rock formation for extra support, Martin evaluated their depleted squad. Exhausted, traumatized, but still functional. Still Marines.

The mining complex represented their only viable option for survival.

"I'll take point," Frank volunteered. "Test the anchor, reconnoiter the bottom."

Martin nodded. "I'll bring up the rear."

The squad conducted final equipment checks before the hazardous descent. Above, stars emerged through gaps in the cloud cover of the retreating storm, indifferent witnesses to their struggle. Somewhere up there, *Vigilance* waited like a giant metal sentinel, preparing to rain hellfire down on them.

"Less than twenty-eight hours and some change," Martin reminded the squad for motivation. "That's our operational window."

"Before they turn this entire region into glass," Frank added darkly.

The specter of Titan Station loomed over them as they prepared to descend into the abyss. Martin compartmentalized the memory, focusing on immediate threats.

One obstacle at a time. One hour at a time. That was survival.

CHAPTER FOURTEEN

Martin took a knee at the edge of the canyon rim, trying not to silhouette himself against the darkening sky. Cosmo sidled up beside him, the German shepherd's presence a small comfort against the growing chill of night. Before them stretched a drop of nearly a hundred meters to the canyon floor, with the visible sliver of the mining outpost beyond the opposite wall taunting them with its proximity. If they could get there, they might be able to boost a signal strong enough to reach the *Vigilance*.

Frank crouched next to Martin and let out a grunt.

The unspoken operational challenges hung in the air between them. If they could cross this canyon. If they could evade the Hollow. If they could repair whatever damage the array had suffered. Too many variables.

The rest of the squad had established a descent order, gathering in a tight circle as Broadhurst displayed the plan on a holographic projection. Phillips would go first, then Frank with Rex, followed by the others in sequence. Hallstatt and N'joku would maintain overwatch with Martin until the last moment to secure the position and cover their six.

Phillips approached the edge and ran final diagnostics on his armor systems, the readouts flickering across his HUD. "All systems green," he reported. "Initiating descent."

Martin watched as the lieutenant swung his legs over the edge and found purchase in the narrow seam. For a moment, Phillips's entire weight hung from his armored fingers, the cliff face crumbling slightly under the pressure. Then he found his footing and began to work his way down, inch by methodical inch.

The rest of the squad watched nervously as he disappeared below the rim. Every scrape of metal against stone, every grunt of effort transmitted clearly through their helmets.

"Seam's holding." His voice crackled over the tactical net after several tense minutes. "It narrows approximately forty meters down but remains viable. Lock your joints when I give the command."

The minutes stretched on, each second measured by the steady countdown on their mission clocks. Above them, the stars emerged as full darkness settled over the canyon.

"On the deck," Phillips finally reported, his voice breathless but triumphant. "LZ is clear. No Hollow signatures detected."

A collective exhale passed through the squad. Martin nodded to Frank. "You're up, Cage."

Frank secured Rex to his back using field-expedient strapping.

"Don't worry, boy, I won't let anything happen to you," Frank said.

"This will work," Martin assured him, gripping his old friend's shoulder plate. "Trust the mimic protocol."

"Copy," Frank muttered as he approached the edge. "Still think this is a shit plan."

"Your objection is noted," Martin replied with forced levity.

Frank conducted a final inspection of his harness and Rex's attachment points. Then he transitioned over the cliff edge, movements precise and controlled. For a critical moment, he hung suspended, the combined mass of armor and canine testing his grip. Then he located the seam and wedged himself into position.

"In position for mimic control," he reported.

"Initializing protocol," Phillips replied. "Stand by."

Martin observed as Frank's body suddenly locked, then began executing precise, programmed movements. The sensation must have been profoundly disorienting—surrendering motor control to external command.

Rex whined as they descended, his powerful frame pressed against Frank's back. Martin could see the dog trembling, but to his credit, he maintained position, somehow comprehending the gravity of their situation.

"If I buy it, I'm filing a posthumous complaint," Frank called up. "You hear me, Kelvin?"

"Yeah, I heard you!" Martin shouted down. Then he whispered, "This guy never stops complaining . . . even in death he'll have something to bitch about."

The descent progressed with agonizing slowness. Martin maintained overwatch above, scanning for Hollow activity while monitoring Frank's progress.

"On deck," Frank finally reported, his voice echoing. "That's a hard negative on ever doing that again."

One by one, the Marines executed their descent. Hernandez followed, then Gillford and Broadhurst, each guided by Phillips's precise control. As the bottom team expanded and the top team diminished, Martin's unease intensified. Environmental factors were shifting.

The wind had ceased entirely, leaving an oppressive stillness that triggered every combat instinct. Even the distant fauna had gone silent, as if the ecosystem itself was holding its breath.

Over the next hour, they sent the others down at a cautious but faster pace. Broadhurst, Ali, Grommet, Hernandez, Fielding, Bolesky, and Gillford all reached the bottom with Frank and Phillips.

"Almost done," Martin said.

He turned to the remaining Marines—just N'joku and Hallstatt, plus Cosmo.

"Hallstatt, you're next," Martin ordered. "N'joku and I will follow."

The big Marine acknowledged, securing his plasma rifle. "Copy that, Gunny."

As Hallstatt started the descent, Martin detected Cosmo's behavioral shift. The shepherd's ears rotated forward, muscles tensing as he focused intently on the forest behind them. A subsonic growl rumbled in his throat.

It was too late to stop Hallstatt, who had gone over the edge into the seam.

"N'joku," Martin said quietly, steadying Cosmo with a hand signal. "Possible contact."

The lieutenant acknowledged, raising his plasma weapon and transitioning to thermal imaging. His visor painted the forest in temperature gradients. "Negative thermal signatures."

"Absence of detection doesn't mean absence of threat."

Hallstatt was ten meters below the edge when Martin caught peripheral movement. A distortion of silver-green light, resembling heat shimmer but containing geometric patterns that flowed and shifted within it.

"Contact," Martin called softly, acquiring target lock.

"Visual confirmation," N'joku reported, weapon tracking.

"Hold fire unless engaged," Martin ordered, maintaining his sight picture. To Hallstatt: "Expedite descent. We have company."

"Copy that—Phillips, we need acceleration!" Hallstatt shouted.

The Hollow entity advanced, its form solidifying as it approached. The surface mosaic shifted in complex algorithms, reminiscent of quantum calculations rendered visible.

The entity paused at twenty meters, apparently observing. Its surface rippled with silver-green luminescence, shapes pulsing in rhythms that strained human perception. For a moment, Martin hoped it might maintain distance.

Then it accelerated with inhuman velocity, closing distance in seconds.

"Weapons free!" Martin shouted, engaging his trigger.

N'joku synchronized perfectly, their plasma discharges converging on target. The energy release strobed the clearing in actinic light. The entity's form scattered momentarily, and patterns fragmented like shattered crystal.

But it reconstituted almost instantly, flowing around the energy discharge. Martin adjusted frequency settings, remembering hard-won lessons. The Hollow adapted to energy weapons with terrifying efficiency.

They engaged again, temporarily forcing the entity back. But it was learning, evolving tactically with each exchange. It divided into three components, each maneuvering independently.

Martin and N'joku maintained suppressing fire. Their weapons were approaching thermal limits. Cosmo barked aggressively, sensing threats beyond human perception.

Below, Hallstatt remained partially suspended, caught between Phillips's control and gravitational forces. His descent stuttered as Phillips compensated.

"Get me down! It's coming right at—" Hallstatt began, but his voice cut off in a howl as one silver-green form evaded their fire. The entity flowed over his armor like liquid silver and enveloped his lower body in alien luminescence.

"Get it off!" Hallstatt screamed, his voice gaining inhuman harmonics. His body convulsed, mimic circuit corrupted by the intrusion.

Martin watched in horror as the transformation accelerated. The silver infection spread upward like mercury in his veins, visible through the gaps in Hallstatt's armor. The big Marine's hands clawed at the cliff face, leaving gouges in the stone as his fingers gained unnatural strength. His visor began to crack, and spiderweb fractures spread from where silver liquid pressed against the inside.

"Fight it!" N'joku called desperately. "Concentrate on something human—your name, your family!"

Martin's hand found the experimental syringe—the quantum stabilizer from Natalia. Theoretically, it could disrupt Hollow molecular cohesion at this point. They could save him, if they could get to him. But Hallstatt was too far down, suspended between them and the abyss.

Hallstatt's body jerked erratically as silver veins spread beneath exposed skin. His face contorted behind his visor as the entity merged with him, armor liquefying at contact points. The sound was horrific—metal groaning and reshaping, mixed with Hallstatt's increasingly distorted screams.

"Can't . . ." Hallstatt gasped, voice barely human through alien modulation. His eyes, already metallic, locked with Martin's. In that instant, Martin saw full awareness—comprehension of his fate and the threat to the squad.

Martin aimed his rifle when Hallstatt made his choice. With supreme effort that must have cost him everything, Hallstatt released his grip on the seam. He pushed off the cliff face with both legs, launching himself backward into the air.

"No!" Martin and N'joku shouted simultaneously, reaching futilely as Hallstatt fell.

Hallstatt's form plummeted through the darkness, the silver-green shroud still enveloping him. For a terrible moment, he seemed to hang suspended against the stars. The alien glow made him appear like some twisted constellation. Then gravity reclaimed him.

The impact resonated through the canyon like thunder, the sound carrying up the walls. The alien luminescence flared brilliantly at the moment of impact, then began to fade, silver light bleeding away into the rocks.

"Jesus Christ!" Broadhurst shouted from below. "Engaging! Engaging!"

Martin forced himself to assess. Hallstatt lay motionless below, the alien luminescence dissipating as the squad on the ground engaged with controlled bursts, driving the weakened entity into a crevice. The plasma fire lit up the canyon floor in strobing flashes, each burst revealing Hallstatt's twisted form—no longer entirely human, no longer entirely alien, but something caught horribly between.

"Gunny," N'joku's urgent voice recalled his attention. "Multiple contacts inbound."

Two additional Hollow emerged from the forest, their patterns more sophisticated than the first. They displayed coordination, learning curves accelerating.

"Cosmo, close," Martin ordered, and the dog immediately took position. "N'joku, prepare for tactical engagement."

"What about descent?" he asked, glancing at the cliff.

Martin rapidly calculated options. Hollow advancing from the forest, escape route compromised. The cliff remained their only egress, but descent under fire . . .

"Broadhurst, proceed to objective with the rest of the squad," Martin transmitted. "N'joku, Cosmo, and I will find an alternate route."

"Gunny, come again?" Broadhurst said over the comms.

"You heard me, main element proceeds to the outpost," Martin explained rapidly over squad net. "N'joku and I execute delaying action, then find an alternate route."

"That's suicide," Broadhurst protested, his voice cracking over the comms.

"It's the only option," Martin countered. "We'll draw them off, then reestablish contact."

Frank's voice cut through, surprisingly calm. "He's right. Mission priority is reaching that outpost before *Vigilance* executes."

Martin consulted his mission clock: Twenty-seven hours and nineteen minutes remaining. Time compressed, each second critical.

"Reach the outpost," he ordered. "Establish *Vigilance* contact. Report our findings."

"You'll report them yourself when you link up," Frank replied firmly. "Don't be late to the party."

"I'm always late to the party," Martin responded.

The Hollow entities closed distance, patterns cycling faster. They moved with enhanced coordination. The first had been reconnaissance, Martin realized. These were the hunters.

"Move out!" Martin ordered the team below. "That's a direct order, Captain!"

"Weapons hot," N'joku reported. "On your command."

Martin acquired his targets, calculating engagement probabilities. Odds were suboptimal, but they'd survived worse. He and N'joku needed to create sufficient chaos to draw the Hollow from the canyon, buying Frank's team time.

Cosmo pressed against him, radiating readiness. The shepherd had been his constant through everything—post-Titan trauma, nightmares, recovery. Abandoning him wasn't an option.

"On my mark," he told N'joku, synchronizing their weapons. "Three . . . two . . . one . . . execute!"

Their weapons discharged simultaneously, converting darkness to artificial day. The Hollow scattered under concentrated fire. Patterns fragmented as they withdrew toward the forest.

"Effect on target?" N'joku queried, peering through residual ionization.

"Temporary disruption," Martin assessed, monitoring his tracker. "They'll reconstitute. We displace now."

He glanced over the edge one more time, confirming Frank's team moving out. They faced their own challenge—traversing the wide-open canyon floor and ascending without drawing attention from the enemy. But Frank could navigate them through.

The Hollow were reconstituting, adapting to their plasma frequency. Faster response time, enhanced determination. Evolution in real-time.

"Kel," Frank transmitted. "You make it out, tell Natalia I want my posthumous decorations melted into dog tags for Rex. He's earned them."

Martin chuckled despite the circumstances. "Copy. And if you make it out, contact Thomas. Tell that mercenary to find legitimate employment."

With that exchange complete, Martin turned from the canyon, Cosmo flanking him and N'joku covering their withdrawal. They sprinted toward the forest, drawing the Hollow in pursuit. The entities followed, and their luminescence painted the forest in spectral light.

The trees ahead seemed to part before them, ancient trunks wider than Marine transports creating a maze of shadows and uncertain footing. Martin's enhanced leg servos compensated for the uneven terrain, but he could hear N'joku struggling to keep pace as he fired. The lieutenant's breathing came in controlled bursts over the comm, professional even in extremis.

Behind them, the Hollow entities moved like liquid lightning through the forest canopy. Their forms were sometimes visible, sometimes just suggestions of movement that Cosmo tracked with preternatural awareness. The shepherd's hackles stood rigid, a constant growl rumbling in his throat as he guided them through paths invisible to human eyes.

Martin's hand found the three TDF grenades on his belt. Each one represented precious seconds, perhaps minutes if deployed correctly. He pulled the first and counted down as the Hollow entities gained ground behind them.

"TDF out!" he shouted, hurling the grenade behind them.

The temporal disruption field erupted with its distinctive warping effect, and reality bent in a sphere that caught two of the pursuing entities. They froze midphase, trapped between moments like insects in amber. The shimmering field pulsed, holding them in temporal stasis.

"Nice throw," N'joku commented, adjusting his position to cover their right flank. "How many more?"

"Two," Martin replied, already calculating optimal deployment.

They needed maximum time, maximum distance.

The third Hollow entity flowed around the temporal field, learning, adapting. It surged forward with renewed purpose, closing the gap with frightening speed.

N'joku fired controlled bursts, his plasma rifle cycling through frequencies. "It's not slowing down!"

Martin waited, calculating. The entity was fifteen meters back. Ten. Five—

He pulled and tossed the second TDF grenade, and the sphere caught the entity perfectly. Time distorted around it, the silver-green form freezing in its pursuit, patterns locked in a recursive loop.

Martin kept running, and Cosmo matched his pace perfectly as they navigated the forest terrain. The dog guided them around obstacles invisible in the darkness.

Behind them, the first temporal field was already degrading, the trapped entities beginning to shift within their prison. These weren't the standard thirty-second fields from training—field conditions were affecting duration.

"There." N'joku pointed to a narrow ravine ahead. "Natural chokepoint."

Martin saw the perfect defensive terrain. They could make their stand there and use the last grenade to maximum effect.

They reached the ravine just as the temporal fields began collapsing behind them. The Hollow entities emerged from stasis, their patterns more complex, more aggressive. They'd learned from the experience.

"Last one," Martin said, hefting the final TDF grenade. "Make it count."

The entities flowed toward the ravine entrance, their forms merging and separating in a hypnotic dance of alien geometry. Martin waited until they committed to the narrow passage.

"Now," he whispered, activating the grenade and rolling it precisely into the ravine's mouth.

The temporal field bloomed, catching all three entities in its expanding radius. The ravine amplified the effect, containing the field's energy, extending its duration.

"Run," Martin ordered unnecessarily—N'joku was already moving.

They sprinted into the forest depths, Cosmo leading them through paths only the shepherd could sense. Behind them, the Hollow remained trapped, allowing precious minutes for both escape and Frank's team below.

Twenty-seven hours exactly until the *Vigilance* executed its solution.

The mission had evolved from reconnaissance to survival, and now to something more desperate: preventing their own extermination.

CHAPTER FIFTEEN

They'll make it," Captain Broadhurst said to Frank.

"I fucking know," he replied quietly, though the words tasted like battlefield rations.

Frank especially didn't like splitting up, particularly with Martin, Cosmo, and N'joku being on their own out there. But there was no alternative with the Hollow tracking them. Getting the surviving Marines moving hadn't been nearly as hard as keeping them from bolting randomly in a panicked retreat after losing Hallstatt.

A glance at his mission timer confirmed they had been groundside for nine and had lost four Marines. Not to mention the flight crew. And then there was Grommet, who had just come out of the shock from the attack at the Comanche when Hallstatt splattered on the ground. Now Grommet was back to muttering to himself—a full-blown case of a battlefield panic attack.

Broadhurst knew it too and removed his sidearm, leaving him unable to harm himself or anyone else. He was useless in a fight now.

A KIA every hour was far worse than Frank's operational projections. But it was terminating Contreras and D'Agata that really gnawed at him.

The weight of those deaths pressed down on his shoulders like fallen comrades he'd never stop carrying. At least with Patel, she was gone, but Contreras and D'Agata were very much aware of what was happening to them.

Two good Marines transformed into something alien, and he'd been the one to pull the trigger. Mercy killing—that's what they called it in the manuals. But manuals didn't prepare you for the sound of plasma burning through what used to be your squadmate's face.

Dread hollowed out the center of Frank's chest with each stride, a black hole of despair threatening to consume him, as if he physically diminished inside his armor.

Get it together, he thought when he saw Phillips nearly overtaking Fielding at point.

"Maintain tactical spacing!" Frank barked.

He didn't necessarily blame the Marine. Phillips might not have been trying to simply break formation—maintaining consistent pace over rough terrain in powered armor was challenging. They could have advanced faster, he admitted to himself, if it hadn't been for Rex. The armor didn't fatigue, but the dog did, and the rottweiler's labored breathing drowned out the impact of his own footfalls on the canyon floor. He'd need to hydrate the dog soon, or Rex would collapse.

Frank checked his water reserves—two liters remaining, split between him and Rex. The suits could recycle moisture, but the dogs had no such luxury. Another tactical consideration he hadn't factored into the mission planning. Then again, nobody had planned for this clusterfuck.

Operating in powered armor wasn't the same as standard movement, of course, since the exoskeletons handled the physical load, but his limbs still had to synchronize with the servos, and that took its toll eventually.

"I can't believe we didn't even attempt extraction for Hallstatt," Gillford said in her rough voice. "He deserved better."

"Or Patel," Ali added.

"Hallstatt made his choice, and Patel was gone," Broadhurst said.

"You planning on shooting any of us that get touched by one of those things?" Gillford asked.

It was a legit question, and Frank decided to let the captain handle this one.

"My research indicates the transformation might be reversible in early stages—" Bolesky started to say.

"Your research is based on theory," Hernandez cut in, his normally steady voice sharp. "We saw what happened to Contreras. To D'Agata. To Patel. There's no coming back from that."

Broadhurst agreed with a nod. "If that happens to me, you all have permission to take me out too."

"We did the only thing we could for them at the point of infection," Frank said.

Bolesky fixed her gaze on him.

"Terminating them was mercy, and like the captain said, Hallstatt made his own tactical decision," Frank continued.

"He jumped," Hernandez said. "Rather than let that thing take him completely. That's not suicide—that's sacrifice."

"Affirmative," Broadhurst confirmed. "Now maintain momentum. What's done is done. Keep focused and avoid infection, and no one else dies."

Ali and Gillford seemed to accept the conversation and followed in turn.

The squad pressed forward at maximum sustainable pace. They'd abandoned standard ten-meter intervals because priority one was maintaining clear firing solutions on any Hollow before the entities could compromise another Marine.

"Entry point to the mining complex should be within visual range shortly," Fielding announced.

Frank consulted his tactical display. Initial distance from the ravine was five kilometers, and five klicks passed quickly when Aegis armor could manage three-meter strides at full extension. The terrain had evolved during their advance—the canyon broadening, walls transitioning from sheer rock to vegetated slopes, hills converging on either side. Between those elevations lay a draw, constricting where ancient water had carved through resistant stone.

The geology reminded Frank of combat zones where natural chokepoints had become killing fields. His tactical mind automatically cataloged defensive positions, fields of fire, and potential ambush sites. Old habits that might keep them alive.

Sure enough, centered in the geological formation stood an access portal.

"Is that it?" Grommet asked.

"Yes, finally," Fielding said.

"Save your gratitude," Frank replied.

He joined Fielding on point as they approached the entrance. The portal was dimensioned for vehicle access—wide enough for cargo transport if you could navigate one down here. Frank assessed that was likely the original intent. The canyon provided adequate clearance for all-terrain vehicles, and the pirate facilities they'd discovered would have served as ideal landing zones. They couldn't have inserted here directly—not with the rough terrain and canopy coverage. Not even the Comanche could have achieved touchdown. Not that it mattered now.

The structure itself was a masterpiece of defensive architecture built into the canyon. It certainly didn't look like a mining outpost, but whoever designed it had expected trouble. Angled walls were designed to deflect explosive force, sensor arrays positioned to eliminate blind spots, and what looked like automated defense hardpoints were built into the rock.

"Hold position," Frank ordered.

Fielding had already decelerated from tactical advance to cautious approach.

Rex collapsed into an exhausted stance, head drooping. Frank retrieved his hydration unit and knelt beside the dog. The rottweiler consumed the water stream efficiently, not wasting a drop, continuing until the reservoir depleted.

"Good boy," Frank murmured, running his cybernetic hand through Rex's fur. The synthskin registered temperature and texture with startling clarity—another reminder of how much had changed since his forced upgrades.

"Establish perimeter," Frank commanded as he rose and secured the empty container. "I want three-sixty security centered on the access point."

Decades of training demanded he utilize cover and approach from oblique angles, but those were tactics refined against conventional enemies. The Hollow knew their position and anticipated their vector. As to why they hadn't engaged again . . . Frank had difficulty understanding human motivations, much less extrapolating extradimensional alien psychology. His primary concern was maintaining unobstructed fields of fire so they could engage any hostiles before the entities achieved physical contact with the Marines.

"How do we breach this security system?" Broadhurst said.

Frank stepped up to examine the entrance. Heavy blast doors were sealed at the center with an industrial-grade security mechanism. The main access was integrated into corrugated metal walls partially concealed by accumulated soil and vegetation. Oxidation and corrosion marked the exterior surfaces, a testament to the duration since these doors had cycled and the facility's abandonment. The lock assembly appeared equally degraded. Corrosion had accumulated on the lock surface, collecting a mineralized crust of particulate matter. Frank delivered a percussive strike, and centimeter-thick detritus fragments separated, revealing an interface screen. It flickered, then activated.

"Remarkable," he observed. "Still has power. Must be photovoltaic backup."

"These installations are engineered for autonomous operation spanning years," Broadhurst explained. "Likely has an independent reactor core somewhere internal. Not like they can extract it during decommission."

The interface presented Frank multiple authentication options, but none were immediately accessible. He could utilize personal identification from his link, could access via RFID implant, could input current authorization codes, or alternatively, could provide biometric verification if his credentials existed in the database.

"Damn," Frank muttered, manipulating the interface. It failed to register through his gauntlet's material, and he exhaled, making the decision to compromise the seal.

He selected his cybernetic hand for exposure—the upgraded synthskin should interface properly given the enhancements. It also presented the advantage of superior damage resistance compared to biological tissue, which was critical if something attempted a hostile breach.

"Navigation," he verbalized his process. "Security protocols . . . emergency override . . . there. Military authorization. For emergency military access, input via interface: name, rank, service number, and mission priority designation."

He glanced at Broadhurst. "Database currency is questionable. Should we utilize your credentials?"

"Given this hardware's vintage, I was probably still at the Academy during its last update. But worth attempting." Broadhurst gestured. "You've already broken the seal, so input as I dictate."

He relayed the information while Frank entered it via the interface . . . and corrupted the service number twice, requiring deletion and reentry.

"Never excelled at data entry even with original equipment," he acknowledged, finally achieving accuracy on the third attempt. "Mission priority designation? Was one even assigned to this clusterfuck?"

"Every operation has priority coding. Twenty years of service, and you're unfamiliar with that?"

"Twenty-eight years of service," Frank corrected, resisting the urge to add, "Shithead."

"Got it. Doubtful it'll authenticate regardless, but it's One-Zulu-Three-Alpha . . ."

Despite requiring two attempts, Frank eventually input the correct sequence and waited without optimism as processing indicators cycled.

Emergency military access authorized.

The lock disengaged with mechanical finality, and the barriers separated like biblical waters before Moses's cybernetic descendant.

"Fuck a nun," Frank said with a grin. He resealed his gauntlet and transitioned to ready position with his MR-113 as Broadhurst stepped into the passage beyond.

"Clear," the captain reported.

Not entirely vacant though. The entry corridor extended before them in deteriorating concrete surfaces where illumination penetrated, and arthropods resembling mutant roaches dispersed, seeking darkness that had become their preferred environment. But no personnel, no Hollow, nothing significant beyond a neglected materials handler corroding in an alcove. Not even shipping debris or packing remnants.

The air tasted stale, having been recycled through filters that hadn't seen maintenance in years. Frank's suit diagnostics showed breathable atmosphere—76 percent nitrogen, 21 percent oxygen, traces of xenon and other noble gases. Standard Galean mix, if a bit musty.

"Reconnaissance element," Frank decided. "Four-operator team. Fielding, Broadhurst, Phillips, with me. Remainder secure this access. Nobody operates solo."

The facility's interior complexity increased with penetration depth. Beyond the entry corridor, they discovered laboratory spaces and equipment bays, all stripped of useful materials. Emergency illumination cast crimson ambiance throughout the complex, projecting disturbing shadows across vacant workstations.

"What was the operational mandate here?" Phillips inquired, examining a dust-laden terminal.

"Xenorite extraction logistics, officially," Broadhurst answered. "But this configuration exceeds simple mining support."

Frank concurred. The architecture suggested research applications beyond mining operations. Multiple chambers featured containment protocols, with reinforced barriers and atmospheric locks between sections. Whatever they'd investigated here warranted substantial precautions.

He paused at one containment chamber, noting the scratches on the interior walls—deep gouges that looked almost like claw marks, but too regular, too precise. Something had been kept here—something they'd wanted very much to keep contained.

After twenty minutes' reconnaissance, they'd mapped the primary structure—a central nexus with four radiating wings. Most facilities were subterranean, with a minimum of three levels per emergency evacuation indicators.

"Hell yeah, this location is beyond optimal," Frank said as they reconvened at the entry. "Defensible, multiple egress options, and infrastructure remains operational. If we can restore communications capability, we might establish uplink to Shield Command."

"What about Gunny Martin and Lieutenant N'joku?" Fielding queried. "How will they locate us if they reach the objective?"

The image of Martin disappearing into forest terrain, pursued by Hollow entities, flashed through his consciousness.

"They'll find us," Frank stated with confidence.

Strange how deeply it affected him—the possibility of Martin's potential loss. Fifteen years of anger and resentment suddenly seemed insignificant when confronting the Hollow again. Despite the resentment, their combat bond remained.

"Alright, huddle up," Frank said. He addressed their remaining force: Hernandez, Broadhurst, Bolesky, Fielding, Phillips, Gillford, Grommet, and Ali. Plus Rex, maintaining position despite exhaustion.

The sight of them stirred something unexpected in his chest. Their faces, streaked with dirt and sweat, reminded him of every squad he'd ever led. Young, scared, but still standing. Still looking to him for answers he wasn't sure he had.

"Here's the deal," Frank said, deliberately casual despite the weight pressing on his shoulders. "We're setting up shop in the central hub. Good sight lines, multiple ways to run like hell if things go sideways. Grommet, take a breather and stay where we can see you."

"I'm better," he said with a deep exhale.

"Good to hear, but you aren't getting your service weapon back if that's what you're after," Frank replied. "Fielding, Phillips—you're with me on security. Try not to shoot at shadows."

"What about the rest of us?" Broadhurst asked.

"You get the fun job," Frank said. "Take Ali and Bolesky, see if you can find anything down there that actually works. Priority one is comms—if this place has anything that can phone home, I want it."

Phillips cleared his throat. "These facilities were built to last. The reactor's still running, so there's a chance—"

"There's a chance Martin will admit to being ugly when he gets back, but I'm not holding my breath," Frank cut in. "Just find something that works."

"Copy that," Broadhurst said, suppressing a smile. He motioned to Ali and Bolesky. "Lower levels first. That's where they'd put the hardened communications gear."

"Stay together," Frank added, his tone shifting serious. "And keep comm chatter to a minimum—we don't know who's listening. You see anything that even looks like a Hollow, you haul ass back here. No heroics."

"Understood. We'll check in every fifteen."

Frank directed Hernandez and Grommet to a relatively defensible corner, then took up position on what used to be a security platform. From here he could see all four corridors—not perfect, but better than being blind.

"Clock's ticking," he announced, checking his mission clock. "Twenty-six hours and some change before the *Vigilance* turns this place into the galaxy's biggest glass parking lot."

As Broadhurst's team disappeared into the facility's depths, Rex flopped down beside Frank's feet and was snoring within seconds.

"Must be nice," Frank muttered, settling in for what promised to be a long watch.

The minutes crawled by, broken only by periodic check-ins. "Level two clear," Broadhurst reported. "Moving to comms."

"Roger," Frank replied, trying not to think about what might be hunting them in the darkness.

His mind wandered to Martin, despite his best efforts. The stubborn bastard was out there somewhere, probably complaining about his knees while outrunning alien death machines. The thought almost made him smile.

"Thinking about the Gunny?" Fielding asked, moving up beside him.

Frank grunted. "Someone's got to worry about that chrome dome."

"He'll be okay. Guys like you two don't go down easy."

"You don't know what these things can do," Frank replied, his voice harder than intended.

"I saw enough," Fielding countered quietly. "What happened to our people . . . Between us, you did what had to be done."

Frank didn't respond, but he appreciated the kid's attempt at reassurance.

Fielding moved off to check the perimeter, and Frank returned to watching empty corridors. Rex whimpered in his sleep, legs twitching as he chased something in his dreams. Probably better than their current reality.

"Cage, we've got something." Broadhurst's excited voice crackled over comms. "Comms array looks mostly intact. Bolesky thinks she can get it running."

Hope sparked within Frank's consciousness, but he suppressed it immediately.

"Good work, maintain updates," he responded, grip tightening on his weapon.

Twenty-five hours, forty minutes and counting. Somewhere out there, Martin was facing the same countdown with fewer people and fewer options.

"You better not die on me now, you bald-headed pain in the ass," Frank muttered under his breath. After all these years, he wasn't ready to lose the only friend he had left from the past—even if he'd never admit it out loud.

CHAPTER SIXTEEN

"How, exactly," N'joku asked, "are we going to get down from here?"

It wasn't a bad question, Martin had to admit. The cliff had been intimidating but manageable. There was the ground, there was the wall—the trick had been getting from A to B without falling to their deaths. The situation at the rugged escarpment was more complicated. There didn't seem to be any one right way down, and even from up here at the top, Martin could see plenty of wrong ways.

"Slowly," he finally told N'joku and Cosmo.

The German shepherd appreciated the break from running, not appearing to understand the daunting task ahead. Martin pulled a water bottle from his gear and gave Cosmo a drink as he considered the steep slope stretching out before them.

The biggest problem was that even if they reached the bottom, he wasn't certain the draw below would get them to their rendezvous point. The map only showed one way out, and from the topography, getting there would be harder than descending this damned hill. But one problem at a time.

"Okay, the way I see it, we go down feetfirst, keeping most of the weight in our power packs, weapons, and torso armor leaning into the hill." Martin's combat knife was strapped to his right calf, and he knelt to slide it out of its sheath. "These things won't do shit against the Hollow, so we might as well put them to use. Think of them as ice axes, the kind those crazy rich people use to climb glaciers. One hand searching for handholds," he said, holding his left palm up demonstratively, "the other with the knife. If you start to slide, jam the blade into the dirt, or a tree, or whatever's available and catch yourself. We stop every twenty or thirty meters and check on each other, whenever it's safe. Any questions?"

Their faceplates were up, the better to grab as much fresh air as possible. The Aegis armor had a ventilation system, but the recycled air ended up smelling like your own sweat after hours of continuous operation. N'joku's harsh expression might have been anger or perhaps a mask to hide the trauma of watching Hallstatt and the others die.

"I'll go first," N'joku volunteered, pulling out his combat knife.

"That's not a question, Lieutenant," Martin pointed out, "but I'll allow it. Give me five minutes to prep."

Martin used every one of those five minutes to consider Cosmo. If he let the dog off the lead for the descent, there was a chance Cosmo might tumble off the edge. On the other hand, if he left the German shepherd connected to his armor's harness, the dog might pull him over if he lost his footing, and they'd both die.

It was strange how little that prospect bothered him now, but he had to think about the mission. About what the other Marines had died for already. Without Martin, would N'joku have any chance of survival? Did he have the right to risk both their lives?

The hell with it. He hadn't asked to be recalled to active duty, and Cosmo hadn't asked to be hauled into this nightmare. The discovery of the Hollow and their ship was important enough to risk it all.

"Come on, buddy," he said, pulling the lead out of its retractable housing and clipping it into the dog's reinforced chest harness. "You need to be a good boy and not send us both over the edge, okay?"

If being petted with armored gloves felt strange to the dog, Cosmo didn't show it. His tail wagged like this was just another day on the homestead.

"Alright, N'joku, let's do this."

"Yes, Gunny," the lieutenant said, swinging his legs over the side and beginning the cautious scramble downward.

Martin let N'joku get about ten meters ahead before starting his own descent. He'd considered leaving his faceplate open for better breathing, but after thirty seconds of twisting around trying to see his footholds, he resigned himself to closing the visor. Toggling the controls, he brought up the view from his helmet's rear camera and positioned it in a corner of his HUD. The change gave him the ability to see where to place his feet while maintaining his grip. And to keep an eye on Cosmo.

The dog took a few seconds to understand what they were attempting, but finally figured out he needed to pick his way forward while Martin crawled backward. They fell into a rhythm within minutes—grab a handhold, dig a foot into whatever indent offered purchase, then release and repeat. Just as Martin considered standing up and bounding forward to save time, N'joku disappeared over the edge of a drop about ten meters below.

"Shit!" the young officer blurted, and Martin fought the urge to rush after him. "Don't come this way, Gunny!" N'joku's warning came out strained, like a man holding on for dear life. "Steep drop-off . . . I'm hanging on, but it's tricky. Go around to my right instead."

"Can you pull yourself up?" Martin called.

"Working on it."

Martin shifted direction and moved laterally across the hillside toward safer ground. Cosmo followed cautiously, his nails scraping against loose stones. Suddenly, the shepherd froze, and a low growl rumbled in his chest.

"Cosmo?" Martin turned to see what had caught the dog's attention.

The air about five meters to their right shimmered with the familiar glowing silver-green distortion of a Hollow entity materializing from solid rock. It hovered just above the ground, geometric patterns shifting across its surface in complex, alien rhythms.

"N'joku," Martin said, not daring to make sudden movements. "We've got company."

There was no response from the lieutenant, only the sound of scrabbling as he fought for a better grip.

The Hollow entity drifted closer, its movements fluid and unpredictable. Martin slowly raised his MR-113 but hesitated to fire. In this position, the weapon's recoil could send him tumbling down the hillside.

To his surprise, Cosmo wasn't barking or lunging as he normally did when encountering the Hollow. Instead, the shepherd stood rigid. The entity moved closer still, now only three meters from the dog.

"Cosmo, come," Martin whispered urgently, tugging gently on the lead.

The dog didn't budge. The Hollow paused, its surface patterns shifting more rapidly. It seemed to be studying Cosmo with an almost curious intensity. Martin held his breath, finger hovering over the trigger, waiting for the inevitable attack.

But the attack never came.

Instead, the entity backed away slowly, and its sequence changed to something Martin had never seen before—simpler, less chaotic. Almost like a signal. Cosmo tilted his head, watching the entity with what looked like recognition.

The Hollow retreated further, then vanished in a cascade of geometric light, leaving nothing but a faint shimmer in the air where it had been.

"What the hell . . ." Martin muttered. This was nothing like their previous encounters. The Hollow had always been aggressive or indifferent. Never cautious.

He cursed himself for not trying the communication protocol that Natalia had given him, but in the moment, he had totally forgotten.

"We're clear," Martin said.

N'joku's panicked voice snapped him back to their immediate crisis. "I'm slipping!"

Martin scrambled across the hillside, and Cosmo finally moved with him now that the Hollow was gone. They reached a position about five meters to the right of where N'joku had vanished. Peering over the edge, Martin saw the lieutenant clinging to a twisted root, his feet dangling over a fifteen-meter drop to jagged rocks below.

"Hang on," Martin called, quickly assessing the situation. "I'm going to anchor myself and reach down to you."

"Hurry," N'joku urged. The root was visibly bending under his weight.

Martin drove his combat knife deep into the ground and locked his armor's joints to create a stable anchor point. He unclipped Cosmo's lead and secured it to the knife handle.

"Stay," he ordered the dog, who obediently sat, watching intently.

Martin lowered himself over the edge and reached down with his cybernetic arm. Its enhanced strength would be crucial. "Grab my hand!"

N'joku strained upward, fingertips just brushing Martin's reaching fingers. "I can't quite reach!"

"You have to," Martin insisted. "That root's about to give."

The lieutenant made one final, desperate lunge upward. His fingers scraped past Martin's, failing to catch hold. In that instant, the root gave way with a sickening crack.

Martin scurried farther over the edge, his armor's servos screaming in protest.

His cybernetic hand caught N'joku's wrist just as the lieutenant began to fall.

"I've got you," he assured the younger Marine.

The sudden weight threatened to pull Martin over too, but his anchored position held—barely. With a grunt of effort, enhanced by his upgraded prosthetics, Martin began to haul N'joku up. Once he was safely back on solid ground, they both lay there for a moment, catching their breath.

"Thanks, Gunny, I owe you," N'joku said finally, his voice shaky.

Martin nodded, but his mind was still on the strange encounter with the Hollow. "Did you see that thing? With Cosmo?"

"No, I was a little busy trying not to fall to my death," N'joku replied, managing dark humor despite the tremor in his voice.

"It didn't attack," Martin said, staring at Cosmo, who seemed entirely calm. "It looked at him and then just . . . backed away."

"Maybe they don't like the taste of dog."

Martin shook his head. "No, it was something else. Like it recognized him. Or was . . . communicating somehow."

"Communicating? With a dog?"

"I don't know what it was doing, but it wasn't hostile. And that's completely different from any Hollow encounter I've ever had. Even the ones that were studying us on *Squanto* were aggressive."

They sat in silence for a moment, processing this new development along with everything else that had happened in the past hours.

"We should keep moving," N'joku finally said. "If there's one of those things around, there could be more. And we need to reach the rendezvous before our extraction window closes."

Martin nodded, then retrieved his knife and reattached Cosmo's lead. As they resumed their careful descent, he kept glancing at the German shepherd. What had the Hollow seen in Cosmo that made it retreat? And more importantly, what did it mean for their understanding of these enigmatic beings?

The questions haunted him as they continued their treacherous journey down the escarpment, each step taking them closer to their extraction point—and hopefully, to answers about what the Hollow truly wanted.

Footsteps snapped Frank to attention. He turned to see Broadhurst approaching the central hub alone, his face pale beneath his usual composure.

Rex's head popped up as if he'd been waiting for his master to awaken before abandoning his own quest for slumber, though the impression was an illusion. Rex had been dozing the entire time.

"How's the comm array coming?" Frank asked.

"Bolesky's still working on it," Broadhurst replied, slightly out of breath. "She's the only one with the technical expertise to rebuild those transmission protocols. Ali's providing security. But that's not why I'm here. I found something during a security sweep—something you need to see."

Frank studied the captain's face, noting the tension. Whatever he'd discovered had clearly rattled him.

"What is it?" Frank asked, already reaching for his MR-113.

"A breach in one of the mining tunnels. Sub-level three," Broadhurst said. "It's . . . not natural. I think we should bring Phillips—his xenoarchaeology background might help us understand what we're looking at."

Frank nodded, then turned to the assembled Marines. "Phillips, Fielding—you're with the captain and me. Hernandez, you maintain position here with Grommet and Gillford. Keep our secure area locked down."

"Copy that, Gunny," Hernandez grumbled, clearly not happy about his babysitting duty with the still-shaken Grommet.

Phillips retrieved his scanner. "What kind of breach are we talking about?"

"You'll need to see it," Broadhurst said.

Frank knelt beside Rex and gently roused the dog fully. "Come on, boy. Time to earn your keep."

The rottweiler rose and stretched before falling into position beside Frank.

"Lead the way, Captain," Frank instructed.

They moved deeper into the facility, following Broadhurst through a maze of corridors and down several flights of stairs. The emergency lighting cast everything in an eerie red glow, shadows stretching and distorting with each turn.

"We'll pass the comm station on level two," Broadhurst explained as they walked. "I want to check Bolesky's progress."

Two levels down, they entered a technical area filled with equipment banks. Bolesky was elbow-deep in an open panel, diagnostic tools and fiber-optic cables scattered around her workstation. Ali stood guard, weapon at the ready.

"How's it coming, Sergeant?" Frank asked.

Bolesky looked up and adjusted her glasses with the back of her hand to avoid getting grease on the lenses. "The hardware survived, but the software's completely corrupted. I'm having to rebuild the transmission protocols from base code."

"Why can't someone else handle this?" Frank asked.

"Because I'm the only one here who speaks both xenobiology and quantum communications," she explained. "These aren't standard military comms—they're designed to cut through the EM interference."

"You got an ETA yet?" Broadhurst asked.

"Another hour, maybe two," she estimated. "The EM field's playing havoc with the quantum stabilizers. It's like trying to tune a radio in the middle of a lightning storm."

"Keep at it," Frank said. "We need that link to *Vigilance*."

"What did you find down there, Captain?" Ali asked, maintaining his watch position.

"Find?" Bolesky asked.

"Just focus on the comms," Broadhurst said.

It was obvious, then, the captain was keeping this from Bolesky for a reason, which told Frank whatever the captain had found was likely Hollow—something Bolesky would be far more interested in than the comms.

"Let's move," Broadhurst said.

They continued deeper into the facility, taking another stairwell down a level into the mining operations sector.

"It's in the eastern tunnel," Broadhurst said. "I was checking for alternate routes to the surface when I found it."

They reached a heavy industrial door marked: MINING OPERATIONS—AUTHORIZED PERSONNEL ONLY.

Beyond it stretched a long tunnel bored directly into the bedrock. It was reinforced with metal struts and lined with conveyor systems for ore transport. The equipment was dusty but intact, as if the workers had simply walked away one day and never returned.

After several hundred meters, the tunnel branched. Broadhurst guided them down the eastern fork, where the boring machine still sat, its massive drill head pointed at the rock face. Or what had once been a rock face.

"There," Broadhurst said, pointing to a section of wall beside the boring machine.

Phillips moved forward immediately with his scanner up. "This is extraordinary," he breathed, examining the damage.

Frank approached cautiously. What had initially appeared to be a cave-in was something else entirely. The rock face hadn't collapsed inward—it had been pushed outward, the solid stone bulging as if something impossibly strong had forced its way through from the other side.

"The fracture patterns," Phillips explained, running his hand near but not touching the damaged area. "The geological stress patterns suggest tremendous force applied from within."

Frank examined the damaged section. The rock had splintered in a radial formation, with a roughly circular opening at the center. Beyond the opening was darkness.

"Is it Hollow?" Broadhurst asked, his voice hushed.

"I mean, that would be a damn good guess," Frank replied, playing his light into the opening. "But my combat experience doesn't make me a xenoarchaeological expert."

Phillips was already taking readings with his scanner. "The mineral composition around the breach has been altered at the molecular level. Similar to what we've seen with Hollow interaction, but . . . there's something else."

Frank approached the opening carefully, signaling the others to stay back. Rex remained at his side, alert but not agitated. The dog's behavior was encouraging—he'd shown good instincts for detecting the Hollow before.

The opening led to a tunnel that appeared to have been deliberately created, not naturally formed. The walls were too smooth, too precise. And as Frank moved deeper, he noticed something else—geometric sequences etched into the stone.

"Fielding, with me," Frank ordered. "Phillips, right behind us. Captain, secure the entrance."

Fielding nodded, moving up to join Frank as they ventured deeper into the mysterious passage. Phillips followed closely, his scanner humming as he documented everything. The tunnel sloped downward at a gentle angle, leading them deeper beneath the planet's surface.

"These markings," Phillips whispered, his voice filled with scientific awe. "They're similar to what we've observed on Hollow entities but far more complex. More . . . permanent. This is deliberate communication or . . . or something ritualistic."

"Older," Frank suggested. "More organized."

"Exactly!" Phillips's excitement was palpable. "The quantum resonance in these patterns suggests they're thousands of years old, maybe more."

The implications chilled Frank to his core.

The passage widened suddenly and opened into a chamber that stopped all three men in their tracks. The room was vast, its ceiling lost in darkness above.

But it wasn't the size that rendered them speechless—it was what the chamber contained.

Ships. The exact kind the pirates had shot down. Three of them, resting in cradles of the same silvery metal that lined the walls. Their design was unlike anything human—no clear distinction between hull and propulsion, no obvious cockpit or crew quarters. They appeared to be formed from a single piece of that same silvery material, shaped into elongated, asymmetrical forms that somehow suggested movement even while stationary.

"My God, this discovery might be the most important yet," Phillips breathed, moving forward with reverence. "Look at the quantum resonance imprints in the hull material."

Frank approached the nearest vessel cautiously. Its surface was covered in the same geometric patterns they'd seen throughout the tunnel, but more complex, more densely packed. Parts of the hull appeared damaged—not from weapons fire, but as if something had erupted outward from within.

"We really need to get that line open to *Vigilance*," Frank said, his voice echoing slightly in the cavernous space.

As if in response to his words, a flicker of movement caught his eye—a shimmer of silver-green light reflecting off the hull of the nearest ship.

"Down!" Frank hissed, pulling Fielding behind the vessel's landing gear. Phillips ducked with them.

Rex growled softly, his hackles rising. Frank peered around the edge of their cover, scanning the chamber for the source of the movement.

Another flicker, this time near the far wall. Then another, closer.

"We're not alone," Frank whispered, raising his MR-113.

"Hollow?" Fielding asked, his own weapon at the ready.

"Maybe. Or maybe something else." Frank's grip tightened on his rifle.

The flickering light moved again, dancing across the chamber like a will-o'-the-wisp. It paused near the center of the room and hovered above the floor. Frank adjusted his weapon's frequency, preparing to fire if the entity made any aggressive move.

But the entity didn't attack. Instead, it began to pulse in a regular pattern, the geometric shapes within it shifting and changing in what almost seemed like a sequence.

"It's . . . it's attempting communication," Phillips whispered urgently. "Those patterns—they're mathematical in nature. Prime numbers, then Fibonacci sequences. This is deliberate!"

Frank felt a cold weight in his pocket—the communication device Natalia had given to Martin, now with the added protocol Martin had downloaded into his suit before they were separated. In the chaos of the past few hours, he'd almost forgotten about it. His hand moved to the small chip, and he hesitated only briefly before making a decision.

"Cover me," he whispered to Fielding.

"What are you doing?" Fielding hissed as Frank stepped out from behind cover.

Frank didn't answer. His eyes remained fixed on the pulsing entity as he carefully attached the signal device to his suit's external interface port and triggered the communication protocol. For a moment, nothing happened. Then lights on his armor began to flash in a complex geometric array, and a high-pitched frequency emanated from his suit's external speakers.

The Hollow entity froze, its own patterns stuttering momentarily before shifting to match the sequence projected from Frank's suit.

"Holy shit, it's working," Phillips breathed. "It's actually synchronizing!"

"Lower your weapon," Frank ordered softly, still watching the entity.

"Are you crazy?" Fielding whispered harshly.

"Just do it. Signal the captain too."

Reluctantly, Fielding complied, using hand signals to convey the order to Broadhurst at the tunnel entrance. Frank stood completely still, watching as the Hollow entity drifted closer, its patterns continuing to synchronize with those emanating from his suit.

The entity circled him once, twice, its movement less erratic now, more purposeful. Rex remained at Frank's side, tense but not aggressive—another good sign. After what felt like an eternity, the Hollow entity backed away, its surface geometry shifting once more before it drifted toward one of the ships. It paused at the vessel's hull, then seemed to dissolve into it, leaving the chamber in darkness save for the red emergency lighting.

Frank exhaled slowly, realizing he'd been holding his breath.

"What the hell just happened?" Broadhurst demanded, approaching from the tunnel entrance, his weapon still lowered but clearly ready to raise it at a moment's notice.

"Some sort of communication protocol," Frank replied, disconnecting the chip from his suit. "It works. Or at least, it didn't get us killed."

"No one told me about any communication device," Broadhurst said, his voice tight with controlled anger. "Where did it come from?"

"Captain Ivan provided it," Frank said, deciding honesty was the best approach. "It's experimental—DSIA tech. She said to use our judgment."

"And you decided to test it now?" Broadhurst's tone was sharp.

A chittering sound echoed through the chamber—high-pitched and unnatural, coming from somewhere deeper in the facility. Phillips's scanner began beeping urgently.

"I'm reading multiple quantum signatures," he reported. "Something's coming—fast!"

"Fall back to the entrance," Frank ordered. "Now!"

They retreated quickly but in formation, weapons sweeping for contacts. Frank took rear guard, Rex at his side. They had nearly reached the tunnel when a second Hollow entity emerged from the darkness ahead, its patterns more chaotic, more aggressive than the first.

Frank immediately activated the communication device again, and the lights on his suit blinked in the same array as before. The high-pitched frequency filled the air, but this time the entity didn't pause. If anything, its movements became more erratic, its patterns shifting violently.

"Not working this time," Frank muttered, raising his MR-113. "Weapons hot! Fall back!"

They retreated down the tunnel, the entity pursuing at a distance. Its form flickered and phased, sometimes appearing solid, sometimes transparent, moving through the tunnel walls as easily as the air. Frank continued to try the communication device, cycling through different settings, but nothing seemed to affect this second entity the way it had the first.

"TDF grenade out!" Fielding shouted, deploying one of their last temporal disruption devices.

The grenade detonated, creating a shimmering field that caught the pursuing entity. It froze mid-phase, trapped between moments.

"Move! That won't hold it long!" Frank shouted.

Phillips was still taking readings even as they ran. "Fascinating! The two entities had completely different quantum signatures."

Finally, they reached the heavy door at the tunnel entrance and sealed it behind them. The entity's eerie glow was visible through the crack for only a moment before the TDF field collapsed and it vanished from sight.

"Phillips, what the hell was that place?" Broadhurst demanded once they were safely back in the main corridor. "Did we just stumble into a Hollow nest?"

"The pirates must have broken through while mining," Phillips theorized, still checking his readings. "Released whatever was sealed down there. But Captain, this is extraordinary! Those ships could be thousands of years old. The Hollow might be indigenous to this system!"

Frank pocketed the communication device, his mind racing. "This facility was definitely built on top of something much older."

"Do we evacuate?" Broadhurst asked, glancing nervously back at the sealed door.

"Not yet," Frank said firmly. "We need those comms online. Shield Command needs to know what we've found." He paused, thinking of Martin out there somewhere with Cosmo and N'joku. "And we're not leaving without the rest of our squad."

Broadhurst nodded, though his expression remained troubled. "Phillips, I want you to compile everything you've recorded. Every reading, every observation. Hernandez and I will assist Bolesky with the communications array. But Cage—next time you decide to test experimental alien tech, you tell me first."

"Copy that, Captain," Frank acknowledged.

On the hike back toward the central hub, Phillips couldn't contain his excitement despite the danger. "Did you see how the first entity responded? It recognized the communication protocol! But the second one . . . completely different behavioral patterns."

"Different types?" Frank mused. "Different . . . intentions?"

"Perhaps, or different roles within their society. If they have a society. Oh, the questions this raises! Bolesky is going to shit a brick when I tell her."

Frank lingered at the sealed door for a moment, staring at it while the others moved ahead. Whatever was happening here went deeper than a simple reconnaissance mission. The Hollow weren't just visitors to Galean—they might be its original inhabitants. And if that communication device had worked on one but not another . . .

"You coming, Gunny?" Broadhurst called back.

"Yeah," Frank said, turning away from the door.

With Rex by his side, Frank hurried, hoping that Martin, Cosmo, and N'joku would be back by the time they returned to the central hub. But something told Frank that wasn't going to happen—that something horrible had happened to the other Marines and dog.

CHAPTER SEVENTEEN

The cascade of water tumbled down the cliff face, carving a shallow depression in the stone behind it. It wasn't much of a cave—barely two meters deep—but the curtain of water provided a natural camouflage that had kept them hidden for the past several hours.

Martin sat with his back against the damp rock wall, watching the canyon through the wavering curtain of water. His Aegis armor, now caked with mud and grime, had served them well during their desperate flight through the forest.

Cosmo lay with his chin on his paws, looking up every few minutes.

"You miss Frank and Rex?" Martin asked.

Cosmo wagged his tail.

"Yeah, I kinda miss the asshole and his dog too," Martin said.

"When I first met you guys, I thought you guys hated each other," N'joku said.

"Yeah, well you weren't wrong, but that's a long story."

N'joku nodded and didn't press it. He sat across from Martin, his injured leg stretched out awkwardly before him. He had injured it back on the hill during their last run-in with their silvery friends.

"How's it looking out there?" N'joku asked.

Martin squinted through his visor's enhanced optics. The Hollow signatures were still visible on the canyon wall across from them—eerie patterns of silver-green light that pulsed and shifted in complex geometric sequences. Four distinct entities had been moving back and forth across the rock face for the past hour.

"They're still there," Martin replied quietly.

N'joku shifted his position to ease the pressure on his injured leg. "You think they know we're here."

"If they did, I think they would have come for us," Martin said, though he wasn't entirely convinced. The Hollow's behavior had been erratic and unpredictable throughout this entire mission. "Maybe the water is interfering with whatever they use to detect us."

"We have to get out of here. The clock is ticking, Gunny."

"I know." Martin checked his display. "Twenty-three hours and thirty-five minutes left."

"And we're stuck behind a waterfall, watching aliens play tag on a canyon wall," N'joku said with a bitter laugh that quickly turned into a grimace of pain.

Martin studied the younger Marine. Despite his injury and their dire situation, N'joku had shown impressive resilience. Gone was the cocky, argumentative officer who had mocked Martin's cybernetics just days ago. In his place was a Marine sobered by combat and loss.

"You know," Martin said, breaking the tense silence, "when we first dropped, I pegged you as one of those academy hotshots—all theory, no practical sense." He adjusted his position, feeling the ache in his bionic joints. The damp was never good for the connections. "Thought you'd be the first to crack under pressure."

N'joku snorted. "And I thought you were a washed-up relic who should've been decommissioned years ago." He met Martin's gaze. "Guess we were both wrong."

"Not entirely wrong," Martin conceded with a half smile. "I am old. And you were a bit of a hotshot."

"Were?" N'joku raised an eyebrow. "I prefer to think of it as 'temporarily humbled by circumstances.'"

The small joke drew a genuine chuckle from Martin. It was a bit like Frank's humor, always at its sharpest when things were at their worst.

"You remind me a little of myself at your age," Martin said. "Too smart for your own good, convinced you've got all the answers."

"And now?" N'joku asked, genuine curiosity in his voice.

"Now I know I don't have any of the answers. Just a lot of experience making mistakes and living through them. Sometimes that's enough."

He thought of his ex-wife, Lucia, and their kids. Thomas and Terecia were two of his greatest regrets. Not getting to know them as children, and losing most contact with them as adults. It was hard to think about, but with their demise looking more likely, he found himself thinking often about his family, and what could have been.

"I had this instructor at the Academy," N'joku said. "Commander Blaskie. Veteran of the Delta Fire Campaign. Used to say that experience isn't about what you know—it's about what you've survived long enough to forget, then remember again when it matters."

"Sounds like a smart man."

"She," N'joku corrected. "And yeah, she was. Lost both legs at the Battle of Darian. Refused synthetic replacements, said the scars were a better teacher than the medals they gave her."

Martin nodded in understanding. His own prosthetics were a daily reminder of battles won and lost, of friends saved and those left behind.

"You should try to get some sleep," Martin suggested. "I'll keep watch."

"Yeah, right," N'joku scoffed. "Like I could sleep with those things out there."

Martin understood that too. Even with his decades of combat experience, the presence of the Hollow left him uneasy in a way that human enemies never had. There was something fundamentally different about them that violated the natural order of things.

"This isn't the worst situation I've been in," Martin said, deliberately keeping his voice conversational.

N'joku raised an eyebrow.

"No, really," Martin continued. "At the beginning of our careers, total greenhorns with combat . . . we were on Mars, deployed to this true shithole of a settlement called Kesserton. Frank and I got separated from our unit during an operation against the Moni insurgents."

"The religious extremists?" N'joku asked, showing interest despite himself.

Martin nodded. "The same. We were pinned down with just a lance corporal—kid everyone called Cheese, fresh out of boot. Had about three hundred insurgents hunting us across the Savage Desert."

"Bullshit," N'joku said, but there was a hint of a smile on his face.

"God's honest truth," Martin insisted, warming to his story. "Two hundred klicks on foot, just our suits, no support. Frank got hit in the shoulder early on—that's when he got his first cybernetic, actually. The kid, Cheese, was panicking, sure we were all going to die out there."

"What happened then?"

"We spent the first night hiding in a dried-up well," Martin continued, eyes still scanning the canyon beyond the waterfall. "Frank was bleeding bad, and the kid wouldn't stop talking. Kept saying we should surrender."

"What did Cage say to that?"

Martin chuckled softly. "He told Cheese that the Moni would skin him alive and wear his face as a mask during their next religious ceremony."

"Jesus, I bet that shut him up."

"Oh yeah. But Frank wasn't entirely wrong. The Moni weren't known for their humane treatment of prisoners."

"I read some stories, real brutal fuckers."

"Yeah. Anyway, by dawn, we'd patched Frank up as best we could. I took point, Frank in the middle, with the kid bringing up the rear. We had to move during the day despite the heat—the Moni had better night vision tech than we did back then."

"How'd you navigate? The Savage Desert's like a thousand klicks of nothing but sand."

"Frank had an old-fashioned magnetic compass," Martin replied with a smile. "Real antique, brass case, belonged to his grandfather. Said he never trusted the digital stuff. Ended up saving our asses when our nav systems got fried by an EM pulse."

Cosmo suddenly perked up, ears forward, tail thumping once against the stone floor.

Martin raised his rifle, immediately alert.

The German shepherd tilted his head, listening to something beyond human perception. After a moment, he settled back down, but his ears remained forward, attentive.

"He does that a lot," N'joku observed. "Like he's hearing things we can't."

"Dogs have senses we don't," Martin replied, reaching over to scratch Cosmo's ears. "Been that way since humans first teamed up with wolves thousands of years ago. Might be why the Hollow seemed interested in him back on the hillside."

"Yeah, that was strange. Wish Cosmo could talk, tell us what he thinks of that experience."

Martin chuckled. "Cosmo's always been sensitive, can tell when a storm's coming hours before it hits, knows when I'm having a bad day before I do. Maybe the Hollow operate on frequencies dogs can perceive." He shrugged. "Frank would have a theory. He always does."

"You and Cage. You've been through a lot together."

"Twenty-eight years of fighting battles and then Titan Station."

N'joku was quiet for a moment. "What really happened there? I know the official story, but I know there's more to it."

Martin's jaw tightened. The true story was classified. But something about their current situation—trapped, outnumbered, with death seemingly inevitable—loosened his usual reserve.

"Official story isn't all that wrong," he said flatly. "The Hollow were there, and Shield Command decided to destroy it, but what you didn't hear is that the Hollow weren't killing people. At least, not that I saw. I believe—and some above my pay grade believe—they were trying to communicate. Which is why we're here."

"Yeah . . . but communicate what?"

"Never got the chance to find out. Shield Command panicked, ordered the destroyers to open fire." Martin's voice dropped. "Frank's wife and daughter were on that station. We couldn't save them. We tried, but . . ."

"I'm sorry, Gunny. Not many people can come out of something like that and live a normal life."

"Yeah." Martin nodded. Frank's bitterness, his drinking, his self-destructive behavior—all of it made perfect sense when you knew what he'd lost. "I had to drag him off that station. He wanted to stay with them, even though it meant dying. Never forgave me for saving his life."

N'joku's expression shifted, understanding dawning in his eyes. "That's why you're here, isn't it? On this mission. It's not just about stopping the Hollow."

Martin hadn't thought about it that way, but there was truth in what N'joku said. "Maybe. Or maybe it's about giving both of us a chance to make it right. To understand now what we didn't understand then."

"And if there's nothing to understand? If they're just hostile aliens that want to kill us or use us for experiments?"

Martin shrugged. "Then at least we'll know. Better than spending the rest of our lives wondering."

They sat in silence for a while, the only sound the constant rush of the waterfall. Martin continued monitoring the Hollow through the curtain of water, while Cosmo dozed fitfully.

"You never finished the Kesserton story," N'joku finally said, breaking the silence. "How'd you make it out?"

Martin was grateful for the change of subject. "We made it to an old military spaceport from some previous war," he continued. "Abandoned but structurally intact. Found a working comms array and managed to call for help. Then we just had to hold out for three days waiting for extraction."

"The Moni must have been pissed when they found out where you were."

"Oh, they were. Hit us with everything they had—mortars, rocket launchers, even tried to tunnel under the perimeter walls." Martin chuckled at the memory. "Frank caught them digging—heard them through a drainage pipe. We flooded the tunnel with fuel from the depot and threw in a flare."

"Damn, bet that was messy."

"Messier than I like to remember, but effective. After that, they kept their distance. By the time the dropships arrived, the Moni had pulled back to regroup. Cheese rigged the remaining fuel depot to blow as we took off—created enough chaos that all three ships got away clean."

"Good old Cheese for the win. Did he get a medal for that?"

"Yeah, Bronze Star." Martin nodded. "Though it was Frank's plan. He didn't care about the recognition by that point. Just wanted to finish the job and go home."

Cosmo suddenly stood up, a low growl rumbling in his throat. Martin immediately went silent. The German shepherd's growl deepened, his focus entirely on the solid rock wall behind them. N'joku shifted uncomfortably and winced as he too raised his rifle.

Martin did the same, but before he could bring it to full ready position, the rock face began to shimmer, solid stone becoming translucent as a familiar silver-green glow emanated from within. Geometric patterns started forming, the unmistakable signature of a Hollow entity passing through solid matter.

"Well, shit," Martin said calmly.

"Any brilliant plans, Gunny?"

Martin assessed their options quickly. The tiny cave offered no escape route except through the waterfall and a steep drop beyond. Fighting was futile at this range if it attacked, but there was the communication device.

Good as any time to try it, he thought.

N'joku slid back and propped himself up next to Martin while Martin activated the device. His suit began to flash light.

"The hell are you doing?" N'joku asked.

"Experimental communication protocol from the science jockeys," Martin said.

"Oh great, we're lab rats."

The Hollow was now halfway through the wall, and shifting rapidly, trying to break through. The geometric mosaic flashed different colors, from yellow to white, and then to green.

"Doesn't look like it's working," N'joku said.

"Yeah, I'm getting that feeling too."

Which left only one choice.

"New plan," Martin said, back edging closer to the waterfall. He patted his leg for Cosmo to follow.

"Why do I get the feeling I'm not going to like it?" N'joku asked, watching as the Hollow entity pushed further through the rock wall, its patterns becoming more defined.

"Remember how I said we escaped the Moni? Sometimes the only way out is straight through the worst possible option."

N'joku glanced between Martin and the waterfall. "You can't be serious."

"Dead serious," Martin confirmed. "It's either jump or become the next Hollow science experiment."

"That's a hell of a choice. What are the odds we survive that drop?"

"Better than the odds of surviving contact with that silver asshole."

The Hollow entity emerged fully from the wall now, its surface array shifting from exploratory to something more aggressive. Cosmo barked viciously.

"Look at it this way," Martin said, grabbing N'joku's arm to support him. "If we die in the fall, at least it'll be quick. Not like whatever that thing has planned for us."

"That's your idea of a pep talk?" N'joku asked incredulously.

Martin shrugged. "Never claimed to be inspirational."

The Hollow began advancing toward them, its patterns pulsing rapidly.

"So we jump on three?" N'joku asked, tensing for the leap.

"Nah, Frank always said counting just gives you time to reconsider." Martin tightened his grip on N'joku's arm. "Cosmo, come!"

Without further warning, Martin pulled N'joku through the curtain of water and into open air. N'joku let out a surprised yell that quickly transformed into a stream of creative profanity. Cosmo leaped after them without hesitation, his loyalty overriding any canine survival instincts.

"Geronimo!" Martin shouted. It was an old habit picked up from his early days of combat drops.

The fall seemed to last both an eternity and no time at all—that peculiar distortion of time that comes with plummeting through open space. Wind rushed past Martin's helmet, the roar of the waterfall momentarily drowned out by the sound of his own heartbeat thundering in his ears. The world around them became a blur of mist and stone, and the canyon walls streaked past in his peripheral vision.

Martin caught glimpses of N'joku tumbling beside him. The lieutenant's arms windmilled as he tried to stabilize his descent. Cosmo was a dark blur slightly above them, the shepherd's body stretched out in a surprisingly graceful diving position. Under different circumstances, it might have been comical.

Martin's combat training kicked in, overriding his body's natural panic response. He pulled his limbs in tight, positioning himself feetfirst toward the churning pool below. His Aegis armor would absorb some of the impact, but hitting the water wrong could still snap his spine or shatter his remaining organic limbs.

He felt a moment of clarity, a crystalline awareness of every sensory input—the dazzling rainbow created by sunlight hitting the waterfall's spray, the weight of his armor around him like a metal coffin. He caught a fleeting glimpse of the Hollow entity at the cave entrance. Its silvery form seemed almost perplexed as it watched them plummet.

The roar of the waterfall grew louder as they approached its base, the mist thickening around them. The surface of the pool below came rushing up to meet them like a dark mirror that would either break their fall or break their bodies.

They hit the surface with bone-jarring force, and the shock reverberated through Martin's armor despite its absorption systems. The impact drove the air from his lungs in an explosive grunt. Water closed over his head, cold and disorienting, plunging him into temporary darkness. His suit's emergency systems activated, the helmet sealing automatically to provide him with recycled oxygen.

The current immediately seized him in its powerful grip, tumbling him like a leaf in a tornado. Martin fought against the disorientation, struggling to determine which way was up as his armor's systems recalibrated. The weight of the suit dragged him deeper, and for a terrifying moment, he thought he might sink to the bottom and drown.

Then his training asserted itself again. He activated his armor's emergency buoyancy system. The suit stiffened momentarily, then began to rise toward the surface, carrying him with it.

His head broke the water, and he gulped in air as his helmet unsealed. The current was carrying him rapidly downstream, away from the waterfall's impact zone. He twisted in the water, searching frantically for N'joku and Cosmo.

He spotted N'joku a few meters away, struggling against the current, his face contorted in pain as his injured leg slammed into submerged rocks. The lieutenant was barely keeping his head above water, his suit offering none of the buoyancy advantages of Martin's armor.

"N'joku!" Martin called out, trying to swim toward him, but the current was too strong, pulling them farther apart.

Cosmo appeared suddenly, paddling strongly toward N'joku with powerful, determined strokes. The German shepherd reached the struggling Marine and circled him, offering something to grab onto. Martin watched in amazement as N'joku managed to grasp Cosmo's tactical vest, and the dog helped to keep him afloat.

The river carried them swiftly downstream, a violent roller coaster of white water and sudden drops. Martin tried to navigate toward the shore, but every attempt was thwarted by the current's unpredictable surges. His armor, while offering protection from impacts, now worked against him, its weight threatening to pull him under with each turbulent eddy.

Jagged rocks jutted from the water like the teeth of some primordial monster, ready to shred flesh and armor alike. Martin felt a moment of panic as he was swept directly toward one such formation, barely managing to twist his body so that his shoulder plate took the brunt of the impact rather than his helmet. The collision sent him spinning through the water, momentarily submerging him again.

When he surfaced, gasping, he realized they were approaching a bend in the canyon. The river widened briefly, offering a moment of relatively calmer water. N'joku and Cosmo had somehow stayed together, the dog still helping to keep the injured Marine's head above water.

"Head for the right bank!" Martin shouted, spotting what appeared to be a gentler slope on that side.

N'joku gave a weak acknowledgment and tried to angle himself and Cosmo toward the shore. Martin kicked hard, fighting against the current to join them. The shore was getting closer, the current slightly less powerful.

For a brief, hopeful moment, it seemed they might make it.

Then the canyon curved, opening into a wider space, and Martin felt his stomach drop as he heard the distinctive roar ahead—a sound no swimmer ever wants to hear. The river was about to drop again, over another waterfall far larger than the one they'd just jumped from.

Martin spotted N'joku ahead of him, already approaching the precipice.

"Hurry, get to the shore!" Martin shouted. He fought desperately against the current, trying to reach N'joku, who was clearly exhausting the last of his strength. Cosmo paddled frantically nearby, somehow keeping pace despite the rushing water. The roar grew deafening as they neared the edge and the mist rose from below obscuring whatever awaited them.

"Gunny!" N'joku called out. "I can't—"

As the edge loomed closer, Martin made one final lunge toward N'joku, arm outstretched. Their fingers brushed briefly, almost connecting, and then they were falling once more, plunging over the edge into misty darkness below.

The second fall was different—longer, more terrifying for being unexpected. Martin had no time to position himself, no chance to prepare for impact. He tumbled through the mist, catching fragmented glimpses of the massive waterfall, of N'joku's flailing form, of Cosmo's silhouette against the spray.

The last thing Martin saw before darkness claimed him was Cosmo's form silhouetted against the water, the loyal shepherd following them into the abyss.

CHAPTER EIGHTEEN

Frank paced the central hub, his boots echoing on the concrete floor. The ancient mining facility hummed with the faint vibration of machinery that had somehow remained operational after decades of abandonment. Rex lay near the main corridor entrance, ears perked up, alert for any sign of danger. Occasionally, the rottweiler would look toward the main entrance, as if expecting someone.

Frank knew exactly who Rex was looking for—Cosmo and Martin. The knot in his stomach had been growing for hours. Something was wrong. Martin and N'joku should have been back by now. Cosmo was too smart to let them get lost.

"Come on, you bald bastard," Frank muttered. "Where the hell are you?"

He checked his mission clock again: twenty-three hours until orbital bombardment. Martin and N'joku had been out of contact for too long. The thought of Martin being lost, killed, or worse—turned by the Hollow—was something Frank refused to contemplate fully. After all their years of fighting, all their years of distance, he wasn't ready to lose that connection, that history. Not like this.

Across the hub, Broadhurst, Gillford, and Hernandez stood around a makeshift planning table they'd assembled from empty storage crates. Grommet sat in the corner, still visibly shaken from their earlier encounters, while Ali and Bolseky worked feverishly at the communications array they'd transferred here after their last run-in with the Hollow.

"Any progress?" Frank asked.

Broadhurst looked up from the crude maps they'd found of the facility.

"Need another hour, maybe a bit more," Bolesky said. "Ali is helping. He knows more than he let on."

Frank nodded and looked back toward the entrance. "Still no sign of Martin, Cosmo, or N'joku."

"They'll make it, they had a long ways to go," Broadhurst said.

Frank nodded, though the gnawing worry wouldn't subside. He'd always believed Martin was indestructible—right up until the moment the idiot had decided to lead a Hollow hunting party away from their position. N'joku was tough but inexperienced, and if they'd run into serious trouble . . .

"So let me get this straight," Bolesky said. "You found three alien ships in an underground hangar, and some kind of Hollow entity that didn't immediately try to kill you? I want to know everything."

"That's the gist of it," Frank confirmed, tapping the communication device in his pocket. "This thing worked . . . at least temporarily. It established some kind of connection."

"The miners must have broken through into something ancient during their excavation," Phillips said. "The symbols on the walls, the architecture—none of it matches human design principles."

"We need more intel," Bolesky said. "This discovery is beyond all of us, more important than all of us—our lives, even."

"I agree," Phillips said.

"Captain, requesting permission to leave final comms work with Ali," Bolesky said. "There are other tunnels we didn't explore. We need to know what else is hidden down here."

"Gotta say I agree," Frank said. "I don't care about the science part; I care about the military implications. If they have more weapons, we need to know so we can fight back if the time comes."

Broadhurst considered this, running a hand through his close-cropped hair. "Ali, you can finish this?"

"Yes, sir," Ali replied.

"Okay, Cage. Bolesky's expertise would be better utilized examining those Hollow artifacts. Take her, Phillips, and Fielding with you. The rest of us will stay here to secure the hub and complete the communications array."

Frank glanced toward the main entrance again, still hoping to see Martin and Cosmo emerge from the shadows. "If you get the comms online, try to reach Martin."

"He's our first priority after contacting the *Vigilance*," Broadhurst assured him.

Frank knelt beside Rex, checking the rottweiler's tactical vest. "You up for another adventure, pal?"

The dog's tail wagged vigorously.

Thirty minutes later, Frank, Bolesky, Phillips, Fielding, and Rex were descending into the lower levels of the facility. They avoided the tunnel that led to the hangar, instead taking a passage they hadn't explored yet.

"This section doesn't match the rest of the facility," Phillips observed, running his hand along the wall. "Different construction material, different architectural style."

Frank had noticed that. The tunnel walls were lined with a metallic substance that resembled the material of the Hollow ships. Geometric patterns were etched into the surface, glowing faintly with a bluish light that seemed to pulse in slow, rhythmic sequences.

"These aren't random," Bolesky said, studying the patterns. "They look almost like circuit diagrams but far more complex."

"Phillips, any thoughts on how old these markings might be?" Frank asked, trying to distract himself from thoughts of Martin.

"Based on the mineral accretion at the junctions with the human-built sections, I'd estimate thousands of years, at minimum," Phillips replied. "These structures obviously predate human presence in this system by eons."

The tunnel forked ahead, splitting into three separate corridors that descended deeper beneath the planet's surface.

"This place is massive," Frank said in awe. "Far bigger than any mining operation would need."

"Which way?" Fielding asked.

Rex answered for them, trotting confidently down the leftmost corridor, his nose to the ground. Frank followed, trusting the dog's instincts. The passage sloped gently downward, and the glowing patterns on the walls grew brighter as they descended.

After several hundred meters, the corridor opened into a chamber that left them all speechless.

"My God," Bolesky whispered.

The space was enormous—the size of a small city—with a ceiling so high it vanished into darkness above them. The chamber was filled with structures that resembled buildings, arranged in concentric circles around a central platform. But unlike human architecture, these structures flowed and curved, as if they had been grown rather than built, all formed from the same silvery metal they'd seen in the ships.

"What do you think this place is?" Fielding asked.

"A city, maybe," Bolesky said.

Frank moved forward cautiously, Rex at his side. "Or some kind of alien base," he added.

As they explored further, he began to reconsider. The "buildings" had no doors, no windows, no features that would suggest habitation. Instead, they seemed to be housing for something else.

In the central area, they discovered a series of tubelike structures arranged in rows, each about three meters long and one meter in diameter. The tubes were made of a transparent material, allowing them to see what lay inside.

"Holy shit," Fielding breathed.

Each tube contained what appeared to be a living organism—though many unlike any life-form Frank had ever encountered. Some resembled scaly fishlike creatures with no eyes, tails, or fins, just blobs or discs for bodies. Others were more structured, with limbs and features that reminded Frank vaguely of terrestrial creatures—sensory organs, body symmetry—but with alien proportions and functions.

"These aren't all Hollow," Phillips said, moving between the tubes, scientific curiosity overriding caution. "Look at the physiological diversity."

Frank joined him, peering into a tube containing a creature with multiple limbs and an exoskeleton that resembled a cross between an insect and a reptile. Its surface was covered in iridescent scales that caught the light. Next to it was something that looked almost plantlike, with appendages and a central mass that pulsed faintly.

"Different species," Frank said, realization dawning. "They're collecting different alien species."

Then they found a section that stopped Frank cold.

"Humans," he said, moving closer to a row of tubes that contained unmistakably human forms—men and women, all suspended in a clear fluid, apparently in some form of stasis.

"Are they . . . alive?" Bolesky asked, her voice trembling slightly.

Frank studied the nearest tube. Inside was a man in his forties, wearing what appeared to be a miner's uniform. A monitoring panel beside the tube displayed vital signs in those same geometric arrays they'd seen throughout the facility.

"I think so," Frank replied. "These must be some of the miners."

"That's not a mining uniform," Phillips said suddenly, examining the next tube. "Look at the insignia."

Frank moved closer and wiped condensation from the transparent surface. Inside was a woman in her mid-thirties, wearing not the utilitarian garb of a miner, but a tailored uniform with distinct patches and markings.

"CSF Science Division," Bolesky identified, her voice rising with surprise. "That's a Phase 9 clearance badge. Xenobiological Research Department."

"How the fuck is that possible?" Frank asked.

"Good question."

Phillips examined the control panel next to the woman's tube. "These preservation systems are more sophisticated than the ones for the miners. Different settings, more monitoring equipment."

"They're being preserved differently," Bolesky said. "But why?"

Phillips held up his scanner. "I know who this is," he said, glancing up. "Dr. Hiraru Kitano, disappeared during an expedition to catalog flora in the Cydon Sector."

"Look at this one." Fielding pointed to another tube. "This insignia is from Titan Station."

Ice flooded Frank's veins at the mention of Titan Station. "They must have somehow extracted them from the station before . . ." A horrifying thought occurred. What if his wife or daughter were here?

He rushed down the rows of tubes, his heart pounding against his ribs. There were only a few more, and he stopped at each, frantically wiping away the condensation with his palm, dreading what he might find. Each unfamiliar face brought both relief and renewed grief—relief that Sarah and Lily weren't suspended here like specimens, grief that crashed over him anew as he remembered they were truly gone, beyond even the Hollow's reach.

"This is deliberate collection," Phillips said. "The Hollow are gathering specific people and depositing them here."

"Scientists," Bolesky said, scanning another tube. "People who study alien life."

"And those who fight it," Phillips said.

Frank turned to find the xenoarchaeologist outside a tube containing a soldier in combat armor.

"Not just any soldier—a Marine," Phillips said, wiping away condensation from the tube's surface.

Frank felt his stomach tighten. The Marine's armor was a newer model than their own, with markings he recognized from the tactical briefings Natalia had given them.

"Bolesky, can you pull up any information on this guy?" Frank asked, examining the control panel beside the tube.

Bolesky ran her scanner over the panel, attempting to interface with the alien technology. "I'm getting something . . . looks like this specimen was collected more recently than the others."

She studied the readout. "There's a human-designed medical tag embedded in his armor. Lieutenant Isaiah Reynolds, CSF Marine Corps, Special Operations. Assigned to Operation Obsidian Shield."

"That's our operation," Frank said.

"How is that possible?" Fielding asked.

"Captain Ivan told me three teams prior to ours had been trained for Hollow encounters. Two died in a crash, and the third vanished in the Gauntlet."

"So Reynolds here must have been abducted by Hollow in the Gauntlet," Bolesky said.

Frank nodded. "Only thing that makes sense."

The Marine in the tube looked to be in his early thirties, his face locked in an expression of pain or strain. Unlike the other specimens, silver lines ran beneath his skin, pulsing faintly with the same rhythm as the patterns on the walls.

"He's infected," Frank said.

"Yeah, but it looks . . . contained somehow," Phillips said. "Perhaps the stasis field is suppressing it."

Frank noticed something else—slight fluctuations in the tube's energy field, areas where the transparent material appeared damaged. "This unit's failing. Not like the others."

"Should we . . . ?" Fielding began, gesturing at the control panel.

Frank hesitated. Opening the tube could be dangerous, but if the Marine was conscious, if he had information . . . plus, Frank had the special syringe that Natalia had given Martin. This was as good a time as any to try it.

"Get him out of there," he decided. "But be ready for anything."

Bolesky tapped the panel as she attempted to decipher the alien interface. "I think I've got it," she said after a moment. "Emergency release protocol."

The tube's front panel slid aside with a hiss of escaping pressure, and stasis fluid drained from outlets at the bottom. The Marine slumped forward, caught by Frank and Fielding as they rushed to support him.

"Reynolds," Frank said urgently, lowering the man to the floor. "Lieutenant Reynolds, can you hear me?"

The Marine's eyes fluttered open, unfocused at first, then settled on Frank's face. He gasped, trying to speak, but only managed a wet cough as fluid drained from his lungs.

"Easy," Frank said, supporting the man's head. "You're safe now."

"Not . . . safe," Reynolds managed, his voice barely audible. "Never . . . safe . . ."

The silver lines beneath his skin pulsed more rapidly, spreading visibly across his face. His body seized suddenly, back arching in pain.

"He's deteriorating," Bolesky said, scanning him. "The infection's accelerating now that he's out of stasis."

Frank reached for the syringe and removed it from the case.

"Hold him steady," he ordered.

"What the hell is that?" Bolesky asked.

"Something that might help him."

Phillips raised a brow as Frank prepared the syringe but said nothing.

"Hold him," Frank said again.

Fielding gripped Reynolds's shoulders as Frank pressed the needle against the Marine's neck, just below where the silver lines were spreading. The injection hissed as it delivered its payload, and the blue-green liquid disappeared beneath Reynolds's skin.

The silver lines retreated, their pulsing rhythm disrupted. Reynolds grasped Frank's arm with surprising strength. A long gasp exploded from his mouth, and his eyes widened. He screamed, a howling bellow of fear and rage combined.

"It's okay, we're Marines," Frank said. "Take a breath, then another, then a third. We got you, brother."

Reynolds looked at all three of them in turn, but their presence didn't seem to calm him down. "I have . . . I have to get . . . out . . . of here."

"We're going to get you out, don't worry," Bolesky said.

He tried to push up, but Frank held him down. "Relax, take some air, Marine," he said. "We got you."

Reynolds shook his head weakly. "You . . . you don't understand. They took us in the mountain . . ."

"What?" Frank looked back to Phillips.

"As soon as we landed . . . they were waiting." Reynolds shook hard but then focused on Frank and gripped his arm. "They ambushed my team, turned them all . . . took . . . me."

His body convulsed, and the liquid metal lines surged back with renewed intensity despite the injection. Frank watched the silver retreating in some places, advancing in others, like a battle was being fought in the man's bloodstream.

In the back of his mind, all Frank could think of was what the Marine had just said. About how he had landed . . . was that right? Or was he hallucinating?

"His heart rate is nearing critical levels," Bolesky said as she leaned down. "We have to lower it, or he is going to go into cardiac arrest."

"Reynolds, listen to me," Frank said. "You have to try and breathe."

"This place, they knew it was here, they used—"

Before Reynolds could finish, he shook violently from a seizure. Frank held his head, trying to keep him from banging it on the ground. The implications of what the young Marine said banged around in Frank's own head as he gripped the squirming man.

If Reynolds's team had been sent here *deliberately*, not lost in the Gauntlet as Natalia had claimed, then Frank's team wasn't the first sent to this location.

Why would Natalia lie about that? he wondered silently.

Unless DSIA suspected what was waiting in these rocks all along and needed someone to confirm it.

"They're collecting us," Reynolds continued, his voice growing weaker as the silver spread across his face. "Studying us . . . like we . . . study them . . ."

Reynolds's eyes locked with Frank's one last time, a moment of clarity amid the spreading silver. Then his body went rigid as a final convulsion shook him before he went still, eyes staring sightlessly at the ceiling.

Bolesky put a finger to his neck and then shook her head.

"He's gone," she said, slowly closing the dead Marine's eyes.

"At peace now," Phillips said quietly.

Frank stood slowly, mind racing as he went over what Reynolds had told them. If his team had been sent directly to this planet, not lost in the Gauntlet . . . If Natalia had known . . . And if the Hollow were targeting specific humans . . .

"We need to get this information back to Broadhurst," Frank said. "If what Reynolds said is true, our entire mission might be compromised."

Rex suddenly growled, hackles rising. Bolesky and Fielding both backed away. Frank turned and flinched when he saw Reynolds jerking on the ground again—but not with the random spasms of a corpse. The movements were controlled from within. The silver lines beneath the dead Marine's skin began to move independently, flowing together like mercury seeking its own level, pulsing with increasing intensity.

"Back up," Frank ordered, raising his weapon. "Now!"

They retreated as Reynolds's body began to convulse again, though no life remained in it. Reynolds's chest bulged upward, the skin stretching unnaturally before splitting with a wet, tearing sound. Silver fluid poured from the wound—not spilling to the floor but rising, taking form as it left its human vessel behind.

"Fire!" Frank shouted, unleashing a burst from his MR-113.

The plasma charge struck the forming entity, disrupting it momentarily, but it quickly re-formed, flowing away from Reynolds's body and toward them. Worse, other silvery forms began to emerge from cracks in the floor and walls, drawn by the disturbance.

"We need to move," Fielding said, laying down covering fire as they retreated toward the entrance. "There are too many of them."

Frank nodded, backing away as he continued to fire controlled bursts at the approaching entities. "Phillips, try to reach Broadhurst. Tell him what we found."

Phillips activated his comm, speaking urgently as they retreated. "Broadhurst, this is Phillips, do you copy?"

Static was the only response.

"Comms aren't working down here," he said. "Too much rock."

The Hollow entities advanced steadily, forcing them back toward the chamber entrance. Unlike previous encounters, these entities didn't attack directly—they seemed to be herding them, blocking certain routes while leaving others clear.

"Hold fire," Frank said. "They're driving us somewhere. Not trying to kill us."

"Yet," Fielding added.

They reached the chamber entrance, but the corridor they'd used to enter was now blocked by a wall of shifting silver forms. The only clear path was a different passage on the far side of the chamber.

"They want us to go deeper," Bolesky said, her scientific curiosity warring with evident fear.

Frank looked at his HUD. Twenty-two hours and thirty minutes remained before bombardment. "We don't have a choice. Keep moving, stay together. We'll find another way out."

With Rex leading, they entered the new corridor, which sloped steeply downward. The patterns on the walls were different here—more complex, more densely packed.

"It's like a different dialect," Phillips observed. "Same language, different style."

As they descended deeper, the corridor widened into another chamber, smaller than the first but filled with what appeared to be data terminals or control stations—panels covered in the same geometric sequencing but arranged in grid-like formations. The air here felt different—charged, almost alive with an electric quality that made the hairs on Frank's arms stand up. The surfaces seemed to respond to their presence, subtle pulses of light following their movements like ripples in a pond.

"It's a library," Bolesky whispered. "Or an archive."

Frank tried his comm again. "Broadhurst, this is Cage. Do you copy?" Only static answered him. "Son of a bitch."

Bolesky approached one of the panels. The glowing geometry shifted, responding to her presence. The panel illuminated, and patterns flowed across its surface like liquid light.

"Don't touch anything," Frank said, holding up a hand. "Seriously, not a fucking thing, okay?"

"Then how are we going to find answers?" Phillips asked.

"Something tells me we're about to get more answers than we bargained for," Frank muttered. His thoughts turned to Martin again—wherever his old friend was, Frank hoped he was faring better than they were.

CHAPTER NINETEEN

Martin's first conscious thought was of Cosmo.

His second was wonder that he was still alive, which seemed improbable given the height of the waterfall they'd plunged over. The German shepherd's rough tongue lapped at his face, somehow finding the skin beneath his partially open visor. Martin groaned, pushing himself up on one elbow. Every muscle in his body protested the movement.

"Are you okay, buddy?" he rasped, then reached up to scratch behind Cosmo's ears. The dog whined anxiously, tail wagging with relief now that his master was awake. By all indications, Cosmo was okay, miraculously.

Martin, on the other hand, felt his age, times ten. The Aegis armor had absorbed most of the impact, but the power reserves were completely drained now. Without the servos to assist his movements, the suit felt like a metal coffin. He struggled to a sitting position, assessing his surroundings.

They had washed up on a small, rocky shore at the base of another waterfall. Mist hung in the air, catching the faint moonlight that filtered down through the narrow canyon above. The roar of cascading water drowned out most other sounds, but Cosmo's keen hearing had apparently picked up something concerning—his ears were perked forward, head turning slightly as he scanned the shore.

N'joku.

Martin suddenly remembered the lieutenant through his brain fog and looked around frantically. He spotted a dark form several meters away, lying face down at the water's edge, helmet partially buried in the grit and sand.

"N'joku!" Martin called, fighting against the dead weight of his armor to get to his feet. Without power, each movement was a battle, the exoskeleton now more hindrance than help. He finally managed to stand and staggered over to the prone figure.

The lieutenant wasn't moving. Martin dropped heavily to his knees beside him and reached out with his remaining biological hand to roll N'joku onto his back. The man's face was pale beneath his visor, a nasty gash across his forehead leaking blood down the side of his face.

"Come on, Lieutenant," Martin muttered, checking for a pulse at N'joku's neck. "Don't quit on me now."

To his relief, he found a steady heartbeat. A moment later, N'joku coughed violently, water spewing from his mouth as he gasped for air. His eyes flew open. He was disoriented and panicked.

"Easy, easy," Martin soothed. "You're okay. We made it."

N'joku coughed again, struggling to sit up. "Where . . . where are we?"

"Not sure," Martin replied, helping him into a sitting position. "But that was one hell of a ride."

N'joku managed a weak laugh that turned into another cough. "Didn't think we'd survive that drop."

"Me neither." Martin checked his mission clock, the display flickering weakly before stabilizing. "Twenty-two hours and forty-five minutes left. We need to get moving."

N'joku nodded, then winced, touching the wound on his forehead. "I'm starting to think the Hollow are the least of our problems."

Martin surveyed their surroundings. The canyon had widened significantly at the base of the falls, opening into what appeared to be a broader valley. In the distance, he could make out the silhouette of artificial structures—the mining outpost, he hoped.

"We're not far," Martin said, gesturing toward the distant shapes. "We have to get to the others."

"If they're still alive," N'joku added grimly.

Martin chose not to engage with that thought. "Can you stand?"

With Martin's help, N'joku struggled to his feet but immediately grunted in pain when he put weight on his right leg.

"That bad?" Martin asked, steadying him.

N'joku nodded. "My knee was already bad from earlier, but now my ankle's fucked up. Must have twisted it in the fall." He tested it again, wincing. "I can walk, but not fast."

Martin assessed their situation. His armor was dead weight now due to loss of power, and N'joku was injured, which meant his armor was only going to make moving harder if Martin had to help carry his bulky metal ass. The trek to the outpost would be slow and difficult, but they had no choice.

"We have to lose our Aegis rigs," Martin decided. "No power means no servos, and it's going to slow us both down. We keep our helmets, but that's it."

He hated doing it, but moving slow meant death.

N'joku didn't protest, but Martin could tell he didn't like shedding his armor either.

They both sat down and began the laborious process of disengaging the emergency releases on his Aegis. The rig was designed to be removed by technicians or with the assistance of its own powered systems, not manually by the wearer. But after several minutes of struggling with clasps and seals, Martin managed to extricate himself from the exoskeleton.

Standing in just his undersuit—a formfitting garment designed to prevent chafing beneath the armor—Martin felt both lighter and more vulnerable. He salvaged what he could: his helmet; his MR-113, which still had a partial charge; emergency rations; a first aid kit; and a small water filtration system. Plus a wrist monitor that provided navigation and sensors to detect environmental threats.

N'joku had lost most everything in the river, including his rifle. All he had left was a knife and plasma pistol.

"Here," Martin said, handing the filtration device to N'joku. "Fill this and add a purifying pill. We'll need water for the hike."

While N'joku took care of the water, Martin checked Cosmo for injuries. The shepherd seemed miraculously unharmed, though his specialized tactical vest had been torn during their journey through the rapids. Martin removed it, allowing the dog to move more freely.

Martin moved to N'joku, who winced sharply, barely able to put weight on his injured leg. He grunted and then grinned.

"What's funny?" Martin asked.

"It's karma, Gunny, think about it."

"How so—oh, for making fun of me?"

"Yeah, I deserve this."

"Nah, you deserved what Frank did to ya, that humbled you. Probably saved your life."

"Probably." N'joku laughed, the sound echoing up the canyon.

"Come on, let's move," Martin said.

They set off down the shoreline, following the canyon in the direction of the outpost.

The rocky journey was grueling. N'joku's condition deteriorated with each passing kilometer, his face growing paler, his breathing more labored. Martin suspected the injuries were worse than either of them had initially thought, possibly a fracture rather than a sprain.

"Over there." N'joku pointed to what appeared to be rusted metal partially buried in the sediment near the canyon wall. "What's that?"

Martin squinted in the fading light. "Let's check it out."

With Cosmo leading the way, they made their cautious approach. As they drew closer, Martin recognized the outline of an old mining hauler—one of the massive vehicles used to transport ore during the early days of the mining operation. It had been abandoned long ago, half buried by years of rockslides and sediment buildup.

"That's a good place to dry off and rest for an hour," Martin said, examining the vehicle.

The cab was mostly intact, the reinforced structure designed to withstand minor cave-ins and rock falls. The driver's side door was jammed shut with rust and debris, but the passenger door yielded to Martin's strength after some effort.

"Home sweet home," he announced, helping N'joku climb inside.

The cab was surprisingly spacious, designed to accommodate two operators in bulky environmental suits. A layer of dust covered everything, but the seats were intact, and the compartment was sealed against the elements.

Cosmo hopped up and camped out on a seat.

"Not bad," N'joku admitted, settling next to the dog with a grimace of pain. "Better than resting on rocks."

Martin helped him elevate his injured leg on the dashboard, then conducted a more thorough examination of their shelter. The hauler's control panels were dead, the power cells long since depleted, but the vehicle offered decent protection from the elements and potential predators. More importantly, its metal frame would obscure their heat signatures from any Hollow entities that might return.

"Check this out," Martin said, discovering a storage compartment behind the seats. Inside was an emergency kit—standard issue for all mining vehicles that included a thermal blanket, climbing rope, and fire-starting kits.

"Any food?" N'joku asked hopefully.

Martin rifled through the kit. "Emergency rations. Probably taste like cardboard by now, but they're designed to last decades."

He handed N'joku a protein bar, which the lieutenant examined skeptically before taking a cautious bite. "Not bad," he admitted. "Tastes like cardboard that's been lightly seasoned."

Martin laughed, offering Cosmo a piece of his own ration, which the shepherd accepted eagerly. He then set about treating N'joku's injuries more properly, using supplies from the medical kit to create a better stabilizing brace for the damaged knee and ankle.

"This should help," he said, securing the final strap. "But you still need proper medical attention."

"And a beer," N'joku added with a weak smile. "Or twenty."

"Not me. I gave up heavy drinking a long time ago," Martin said. "I'd settle for gardening right now. Hell, I'd even settle for plucking weeds. Least they don't try and kill me."

N'joku chuckled but didn't reply. His eyelids fluttered, growing heavy as painkillers from the medical kit took effect.

Martin checked his mission clock: just over twenty-two hours remaining until bombardment. He stared out at the moonlit canyon, Cosmo resting his head on Martin's lap. He wanted to haul ass to the outpost, but with N'joku injured, they had to rest for a bit.

"Get some sleep, boy," Martin told Cosmo, scratching behind the shepherd's ears.

Martin, too, closed his eyes, exhaustion taking over and the warmth of the thermal blanket bringing him some sense of false comfort. At some point, he jerked awake.

Cosmo growled, looking to the east. Martin froze when he saw flickering patterns of silver light moving along the ridge. At least six distinct Hollow entities were up there, seemingly tracking their position.

"N'joku, wake up," Martin said.

N'joku blinked heavily, clearly out of it. "Where are we?" he moaned.

"Quiet."

Cosmo stood up on all fours, hackles raised.

"Shiiiiiiiiiit," Martin said.

The half dozen Hollow began flowing down the cliff face, moving like the waterfall, their patterns pulsing more rapidly.

"We need to move," Martin said, grabbing his MR-113 and helping N'joku steady himself. "Now."

He opened the cab door, hopped out, and then helped Cosmo and N'joku down.

"You good?" Martin asked when N'joku stumbled.

"Damn pain meds, man. I'm loopy."

"Well try to snap out of it. We have to move fast."

Together, they made their way across the rocky shore. N'joku leaned heavily on Martin, no longer in pain but moving like Frank might after a full day at the bar. Their progress was painfully slow, and the Hollow were closing the distance rapidly.

After barely fifty meters, N'joku tripped, nearly pulling them both down.

"I'm not going to make it." He gasped, his face pale with pain and exhaustion. "I'll hold them back. You and Cosmo get to the outpost."

"Like hell," Martin growled, tightening his grip on the lieutenant. "We started this together; we're finishing it together."

"Don't be stupid, Gunny. You know I'm just slowing you down. The mission—"

"The mission includes getting your ass back safely. Now shut up and keep moving. That's an order, and I have tactical command, Lieutenant."

"You might be more stubborn than Frank."

"Damn straight, I am."

They pressed on, but the Hollow were gaining ground. Two of the entities had already reached the canyon floor and were gliding toward them, while the others continued their descent.

"We can't outrun them," N'joku said, his breathing labored. "We have to make a stand."

Martin knew he was right. "Over there." He pointed to a cluster of boulders that would give them some cover. "Let's make it count."

They reached the boulders just as the first Hollow entities arrived at the shore. Martin helped N'joku into position, then raised his MR-113 and adjusted its frequency settings. Cosmo positioned himself between them, hackles raised, growling steadily.

"Remember," Martin instructed, "adjust your frequency after each shot. They adapt quickly."

N'joku nodded, raising his plasma pistol. "Nice knowing you, Gunny," he said with a grim smile. "Sorry again about what I said about your leg in training."

Martin snorted. "Don't make those be your final words. They were funny anyway, but also stupid, considering Frank was itching for a chance to prove he isn't a crippled, old asshole."

N'joku laughed. "Always wanted to go out with a joke."

"We're not going out at all if I can help it."

The Hollow moved closer, now just thirty meters away. Their patterns had shifted to the aggressive configuration Martin recognized from previous encounters, jagged and erratic.

"Back-to-back," Martin ordered. "Cosmo between us."

They positioned themselves, weapons raised, the dog standing vigilant between them. Martin's finger tightened on the trigger as the entities closed to twenty meters.

"On my mark," he said quietly. "Three . . ."

The lead Hollow entity suddenly paused, its glowing geometry stuttering briefly.

"Two . . ."

All the entities froze simultaneously, their surfaces rippling with erratic sequences.

"What the—" N'joku began.

"Wait," Martin said.

All six Hollow entities abruptly changed direction and moved away from them at startling speed. They streamed across the canyon floor, heading directly toward the distant outpost.

"They're leaving?" N'joku asked incredulously.

"Not leaving," Martin realized, lowering his weapon. "Something's calling them back. Something at the outpost."

"Frank and the others," N'joku said.

"They've either found something important or they're in serious trouble," Martin concluded. "Come on, let's move."

They set off toward the outpost with renewed determination. Cosmo led the way, nose to the ground, occasionally looking back to ensure they were following. Somewhere out there, the Hollow were responding to the Marines at the outpost. And Frank and Rex were in the middle of it all.

"I told you not to touch anything!" Frank snapped.

The chamber began to glow with pulsing silver-green light.

"I didn't touch anything," Bolesky insisted, backing away from the console. "It just . . . responded."

"You activated something," Phillips said.

The geometric patterns on every surface—walls, ceiling, floor, control panels—pulsed with increasing intensity, casting the room in a cool blue glow. The array flickered across the surfaces, creating complex sequences that reminded Frank of mathematical equations.

"It looks like this entire chamber's powering up," Fielding said, moving closer to Frank. "Like it was waiting for someone to arrive."

"Fuck, fuck, fuck, what did you do, Bolesky?" Frank asked.

"I don't know!" she wailed.

The central pedestal in the room projected a holographic display that filled the air above it—swirling points of light coalescing into a three-dimensional star map.

Frank halted, staring up in not fear but awe.

Thousands of stars hung suspended in the air, clusters and systems clearly marked with geometric symbols.

"Those are constellations," Bolesky whispered, stepping closer. "But none I recognize from any CSF charts."

Frank studied the display, noting one particular system highlighted in pulsing red light. Six planets orbited a yellow star, the third planet marked with additional geometric symbols.

"Their homeworld?" Fielding suggested.

"Maybe," Frank said.

Rex whined softly and moved to another console that remained inactive. Frank watched as the dog sniffed at it cautiously, then looked back at him expectantly.

Frank approached the console, and as he drew near, it hummed to life, projecting another holographic display. This one showed what appeared to be cities—vast, curved structures of strange geometry, soaring into cloud-studded skies of an alien world.

"This was their civilization?" Bolesky asked.

Almost as if responding to her question, the display shifted. The same cities now appeared in flames, massive ships hovering overhead. The silent destruction that played out was more terrible for the lack of sound. The structures crumbled and disintegrated into ruin. Oceans boiled away, and forests were reduced to ash. The entire planet perished in holographic detail.

"Something happened to their home," Frank said quietly. "Something drove them from their world."

The display changed again, showing the flight of thousands of ships—silver, curved vessels identical to those they'd found in the hangar. The ships scattered in all directions, fleeing something that appeared only as dark, angular shapes pursuing them.

"They were running," Phillips said. "Running and hiding, but from what?"

"Maybe an asteroid or something," Fielding said.

"No, something else did that," Bolesky replied. "This explains why there is minimal intelligent life in this system. It's not just on this world. Something must have attacked all of the planets . . ."

The theory made Frank shake his head.

The star map reappeared, now showing dots of blue light scattered across dozens of systems, each marking what Frank assumed were destinations for the fleeing ships. One of those blue dots pulsed over their current location.

"They're refugees," Bolesky said. "This isn't a base—it's a bunker."

Bolesky moved to another active console, displaying what appeared to be schematics of the facility. "This complex is huge. What we've seen is just a fraction of it."

"Can you figure out how long it's been here?" Fielding asked.

"Based on the material degradation, I'd estimate at least several centuries. Maybe longer," Phillips replied.

"So they've been hiding here all this time," Frank said. "Waiting for what?"

Rex whined again, drawing Frank's attention to a different section of the chamber. The rottweiler was fixated on a wall panel that hadn't yet activated. Frank approached, with Bolesky following close behind.

The panel illuminated in front of them, displaying rows of the same transparent tubes they'd seen in the previous chamber, revealing details of the preservation process. Frank could see intricate machinery surrounding each tube, connected to the occupants by delicate filaments.

"This isn't just stasis," Bolesky said, studying the diagrams. "It's more complex. These look like data transfers. It's like they're not just preserving bodies, but . . . scanning minds? Downloading something?"

"Information transfer," Phillips suggested. "Maybe they're learning from the preserved specimens."

"Not random victims. Selected for a reason." Frank thought of Reynolds, preserved like the others. If his team had been sent here deliberately as he claimed, not lost in the Gauntlet as Natalia had told them . . .

"The scientists specifically," Bolesky added. "People with knowledge, expertise."

"You think they've been studying us for some time?" Fielding asked, looking uneasy.

"Reynolds said his team was ambushed as soon as they landed," Frank said. His mind raced with theories that disturbed him deeply. "This is way beyond what we expected, but I know we need to get this information to Broadhurst. Someone's been lying to us."

"Wouldn't be the first time," Fielding said.

"Yeah, but this time it's personal," Frank replied.

"What if Broadhurst knew?" Bolesky asked.

Frank shook his head. "No way. I would have picked up on it by now."

"I agree," Phillips said. "Broadhurst isn't in on any conspiracy."

"Let's find a way out of this alien freak show lab," Frank said.

He waved them on deeper into the chamber, where they discovered displays showing different alien species—the same ones they'd seen preserved in the tubes. Each display included detailed anatomical information and biological data.

"I think it's a xenological database," Bolesky said.

"At this point, I don't care what it is. We need to get back to the others," Frank said. He saw the glowing form in his peripheral vision the same moment Rex growled.

Frank spun around, raising his rifle as a Hollow entity flowed toward them. But this was different— larger, more structured, with more intricate patterns flowing across its surface that was easily three times bigger than the others.

"Easy, boy," he murmured to Rex, who had positioned himself protectively.

The entity drifted closer, its surface mosaic shifting to something more regular, almost rhythmic. It seemed to be studying them, particularly the communication device on Frank's armor.

"I think it's curious," Fielding whispered.

"Try to communicate with it," Bolesky suggested.

Frank reached down and adjusted the communication device's settings to amplify its output. The geometric patterns on his armor intensified, pulsing in complex sequences that echoed the patterns on the Hollow entity.

The entity paused, hovering two meters away, its patterns shifting in response to the device. Then it moved closer, and its surface rippled with matching sequences. A moment later, the holographic display changed, showing rapid flashes of images: planets, stars, creatures, technology, all flowing together.

Frank's head suddenly exploded with fragmentary sensations. Not quite visions, not quite thoughts, but something in between: —Cities of light— —Terror, destruction— —Flight, scattering— —Sleep, watching— —Unknown beings arriving—

Frank staggered backward, the intensity of the connection breaking as suddenly as it had formed. He found himself on one knee, Bolesky supporting him by the arm.

"Cage! Are you okay?" she asked urgently.

"Yeah," he managed, his voice hoarse. "I saw . . . something. Images."

The Hollow creature had backed away five meters, its patterns now pulsing slowly, almost cautiously.

"What did you see?" Fielding asked, helping Frank back to his feet.

"Cities, then destruction—everything burning, dying. Ships fleeing. Then something about sleep and watching. New beings arriving." He shook his head. "It's all jumbled."

The Hollow entity drifted closer and extended a tendril of its fluidlike body toward the communication device on Frank's armor.

"Don't move," Bolesky whispered.

The tendril hovered just above the device. Then, to Frank's surprise, his comm unit suddenly crackled to life.

". . . repeat, does anyone copy? This is Broadhurst. Cage, Fielding, Bolesky, do you read?"

Frank's eyes widened. "Captain? This is Cage. We copy."

"Where the hell have you been?" Broadhurst's voice came through clearly. "We've been trying to reach you for the past hour."

"We got . . . sidetracked," Frank replied, watching the Hollow entity. "Found some kind of archive room. The Hollow blocked our way out, forcing us deeper."

"Well, get back here," Broadhurst ordered. "Bolesky's needed to help Ali finish with the comms array. We're getting power fluctuations."

"Copy that. And Captain? We found something important."

"Just get your asses back here," Broadhurst said. "The clock's ticking."

The Hollow entity drew back, its patterns shifting once more before it faded and vanished completely. The holographic displays dimmed but didn't shut down entirely.

"It let us communicate," Fielding said in wonder. "It wanted us to."

"Was it helping us?" Phillips asked.

Frank stared at the space where the entity had been. "Maybe. Or it got what it wanted."

"Which was?" Bolesky asked.

Frank touched the communication device. "To see this. To confirm what it is."

He turned and started out of the chamber the way they had come. Back in the corridor, the other creatures had vanished. Still, Frank kept his guard up as he moved. His mind kept circling back to Reynolds and his team. If they weren't the first Marines sent here, who else knew about this place? If Natalia had lied about the third team being lost in the Gauntlet—why? What else was she hiding?

"You don't think they're just invaders, do you, Cage?" Bolesky asked as they navigated the winding passages.

Frank shook his head. "I don't know what they are. But those weren't military installations we saw. Those were refugees, survivors of something."

"Could explain why they're collecting knowledge," Phillips suggested. "Maybe they are benevolent."

"But why target military vessels like *Squanto*?" Fielding countered. "Why appear at Titan Station? Why attack us now?"

"Who said they attacked us first? I was on *Squanto*, I was at Titan Station," Frank said. "I don't know if the crew attacked the Hollow when they discovered the ship, but my guess is they did, because I sure would have if I was on that vessel. And we know what happened at Titan . . ."

"And here, the pirates, they shot the ship down," Bolesky said.

"Damn straight," Frank said.

He wasn't trained for these types of revelations, but the pieces were starting to fit together. The fragments he'd glimpsed provided some new clues but also more questions, especially when combined with Reynolds's dying words about being ambushed.

When they finally made it back to the central hub, Frank immediately scanned the area for any sign of Martin, Cosmo, and N'joku. His heart sank when he saw only Broadhurst, Hernandez, Gillford, Ali, and Grommet huddled around a communications terminal.

"About time," Broadhurst said, looking up as they approached. "Bolesky, we need you on the comms array."

"What's the status?" she asked, moving toward the terminal.

"Almost operational," Ali replied. "Transmitter's online, but we're having trouble with signal strength."

"I can boost it," Bolesky said, examining the equipment. "Give me twenty minutes."

"What did you find down there?" Broadhurst asked, turning to Frank.

"Tubes . . . preservation chambers. Not just for the Hollow, but for multiple species—including humans." Frank took a deep breath. "We also found a CSF Marine—Lieutenant Reynolds. His team was sent here before us. Natalia lied to us about them being lost in the Gauntlet."

Broadhurst's eyes widened. "What?"

"He died before he could tell us everything, but he said they were ambushed as soon as they landed. Someone knew they were coming." Frank's jaw tightened. "Someone sent them here deliberately."

"We have to tell the *Vigilance*," Broadhurst said, turning to look at the comms array.

"How long until we can transmit?" Frank asked.

"With Bolesky's help, hopefully under thirty minutes," Ali responded.

Frank nervously checked his mission clock, finding twenty-two hours and four minutes. Time was running short, but there was still enough to get the message up before they blew this place to hell.

"Any sign of Martin?" he asked Broadhurst.

He shook his head. "Nothing yet."

Frank tried not to let his disappointment show. Martin was out there somewhere—he had to be. Rex looked toward the main entrance, his ears perked up as if expecting Cosmo and Martin to walk through at any moment. The rottweiler seemed to share Frank's concern, which only intensified his worry.

The images he'd glimpsed in that strange connection haunted him as he waited—destruction on a scale he could barely comprehend, an entire civilization in flight, seeking refuge among the stars. Combined with Reynolds's revelation about being ambushed, it painted a disturbing picture.

Twenty-two hours left. Twenty-two hours to solve a mystery that spanned centuries and light-years. Twenty-two hours to understand an alien civilization that had been hiding beneath their feet all along.

And somewhere out there, Martin was still missing.

CHAPTER TWENTY

The first rays of dawn painted the canyon walls in shades of amber and gold. Martin jerked awake, momentarily disoriented by his unfamiliar surroundings. He immediately checked his mission clock: twenty-one hours and thirteen minutes remaining.

"Fuck," he whispered, frustrated he had fallen asleep, even for a short while.

Back in the day, he could have stayed up all night, no problem, to watch for hostiles. But he wasn't a young man anymore.

They'd lost precious time, but the rest had been necessary after fleeing another Hollow patrol the previous night. Finding the cave had been Cosmo's doing—the shepherd had led them to the hidden opening just as the silver entities had nearly caught up to them.

Cosmo was already alert, standing at the cave entrance, staring intently outside. The shepherd's ears were perked forward, his body tense with anticipation.

N'joku stirred nearby and winced as consciousness brought awareness of his injured knee and ankle. "Is that the sun?" he mumbled, rubbing his face with grimy hands.

"How's the leg?" he asked, watching N'joku carefully.

The lieutenant gingerly tested his knee, moving it slightly. "Still hurts like hell, but I think I can manage."

"The brace helping?"

"Yeah. Good field medicine, Gunny."

Martin nodded, pleased. The improvised brace had been constructed from medical supplies in his emergency kit and strips torn from N'joku's undersuit. Not pretty but functional.

"Let's check our surroundings before we move out," Martin said, reaching for his MR-113. "Cosmo, stay."

The German shepherd reluctantly backed away from the entrance and sat obediently, but kept his attention fixed on whatever had caught his interest outside.

Martin eased toward the opening with his rifle shouldered. The canyon looked different in the morning light—less ominous, but no less alien. The walls rose sharply on either side, their red-tinged stone catching the early sunlight. No sign of the Hollow entities that had pursued them.

"Clear," he called back to N'joku. "Let me help you up."

With Martin's assistance, N'joku maneuvered to his feet and hissed as he put weight on his injured leg. He leaned heavily against the cave wall, taking slow, deep breaths.

"I can do this," he assured Martin, though his pale face suggested otherwise.

Martin didn't argue, instead focusing on preparing for their journey. He refilled their canteens using the last of the water purification tablets, packed the remaining emergency rations, and made a final check of their weapons.

Cosmo had moved deeper into the cave and was now investigating something at the back wall about twenty meters away, his nose to the ground, tail wagging slightly.

"What's he found?" N'joku asked, watching the dog's enthusiastic exploration.

"Let's find out," Martin replied. "Can you walk?"

With a nod, N'joku pushed himself away from the wall. Martin stayed close, ready to offer support if needed, but allowed the lieutenant to maintain his dignity. They moved slowly toward Cosmo, who looked back at them impatiently before returning to his investigation.

"Good boy," Martin murmured as they reached the shepherd. "What is it?"

The answer became apparent as they drew closer. A narrow fissure was in the back of the cave, barely visible until you were almost upon it. A cool breeze emanated from the opening, carrying a scent that was oddly metallic and unfamiliar.

"Natural cave system?" N'joku suggested, leaning closer to examine the opening.

Martin studied the fissure with professional caution. "No," he said after a moment. "Look at the edges—too clean, too precise. This was made deliberately."

Upon closer inspection, the walls of the fissure showed signs of tool marks—not the rough gouges of primitive excavation, but the smooth surfaces left by advanced boring technology. The passage angled slightly downward into darkness.

"Hollow?" N'joku asked.

"Maybe," Martin said. "Or maybe the miners found something and kept digging."

Cosmo whined, pawing at the ground near the entrance. Unlike his earlier wariness of Hollow entities, he seemed curious rather than alarmed.

"Should we check it out?" N'joku asked. "Might be another way to the outpost."

Martin hesitated. The sensible choice would be to continue toward the visible outpost, especially with N'joku's injury. But the precision of the tunnel's construction suggested it might be connected to the facility—perhaps an emergency exit or maintenance passage.

"Just a quick look," he decided. "Stay behind me. Cosmo, heel."

The German shepherd fell into position beside Martin as they approached the fissure. Martin activated his helmet light, illuminating a tunnel that extended into the rock, curving gently downward. The walls were unnaturally smooth, almost polished, with faint geometric shapes etched into the surface.

"Definitely the Hollow," N'joku observed quietly.

They advanced cautiously, Martin leading with his MR-113 at the ready. The tunnel was wide enough for them to walk side by side, the ceiling high enough to prevent claustrophobia. N'joku limped alongside. His injured leg was clearly paining him despite his efforts to hide it.

"The air's fresher in here than I expected," N'joku noted after they'd traveled about fifty meters. "Maybe there's some kind of ventilation system?"

Martin nodded, noting the slight breeze that flowed through the passage.

The tunnel continued its gentle downward slope, and the geometric patterns on the walls grew more complex, more intricate the deeper they went. Occasionally, they passed side passages or small chambers, but Martin kept them on the main path, not wanting to risk getting lost in a labyrinth.

After about ten minutes of cautious advance, they reached what appeared to be an observation platform overlooking a vast underground cavern. The platform extended several meters from the tunnel mouth, suspended over darkness.

"Hold up," Martin cautioned, approaching the edge carefully. His helmet light couldn't penetrate the full depth of the cavern, but he could make out the distant gleam of metallic structures far below.

"What is this place?" N'joku wondered, stepping forward to join Martin at the edge.

The platform beneath them suddenly shifted with an ominous creak. Before either man could react, the floor gave way completely, disintegrating beneath their feet like sand washed away by a wave.

"Shit!" Martin shouted as they plunged into darkness.

He twisted in midair, reaching desperately for anything to break his fall. His hand caught a protruding strut where the platform had connected to the cavern wall. The impact sent pain shooting up his arm, but he held on, dangling precariously over the abyss.

N'joku wasn't as fortunate. Martin watched helplessly as the lieutenant continued to fall and disappeared into the darkness below. Seconds later, a dull thud and a pained groan confirmed he'd hit bottom.

"N'joku!" Martin called down, heart pounding in his chest. "You okay?"

There was a moment of terrifying silence before N'joku's strained voice responded. "Still alive. Not sure how far that'll get me with this knee, though."

Martin's helmet light, still miraculously intact, revealed Cosmo clinging to the edge of the remaining platform, whining anxiously. "Stay, Cosmo!" he ordered, not wanting the dog to attempt to follow him.

Carefully, Martin pulled himself up onto what remained of the platform structure, his enhanced cybernetic arm making the task possible. Once secure, he directed his light downward, searching for N'joku.

The lieutenant lay about fifteen meters below on what appeared to be a smooth stone floor. He was moving, slowly pushing himself to a sitting position, his face contorted with pain.

"How bad is it?" Martin called down.

"Knee's on fire," N'joku replied through gritted teeth. "But I don't think anything's broken. Small miracle."

Martin examined the situation. The fall hadn't been enough to kill, but climbing back up would be impossible for N'joku in his condition. Martin would need to descend and help him find another way out.

"I'm going to get you out," Martin called down. "Just stay put."

N'joku looked up and nodded weakly, then frowned as he glanced around. "Wait a minute . . . there's something down here."

Martin began preparing a rappelling line from the rope they had found in the mining rig. He uncoiled it, working quickly to secure one end to the remaining platform structure. "What do you see?" he asked.

"I'm not sure," N'joku replied, his voice stronger. "It looks like I'm in some sort of ancient cave system."

Martin paused in his preparations, a cold feeling settling in his gut. "Stay put," he ordered sharply. "Don't move."

But N'joku was already hobbling toward one of the walls, drawn by whatever he'd discovered. "You need to see this, Gunny."

"N'joku, get back to the center!" Martin shouted, suddenly desperate. "That's an order!"

Too late. A brilliant blue-green light suddenly erupted from the walls around N'joku, illuminating the cavern with pulsing geometric patterns. In the new light, Martin could see that the chamber was enormous, extending far beyond the reach of his helmet lamp. The floor was inscribed with intricate circular designs that now glowed with the same eerie luminescence as the walls.

N'joku backed away from the wall, his expression shifting from wonder to alarm. He looked up at Martin, mouth opening to speak—and then his face transformed into a mask of pure terror.

A shimmering form materialized behind him, gigantic and rising with tendrils that formed what appeared almost to be wings.

"N'joku!" Martin screamed, abandoning the cable preparation and raising his MR-113. "Behind you!"

The lieutenant spun around, but there was no time to react. The Hollow surged forward, engulfing N'joku in its fluidlike form. The man didn't even have time to scream before the entity was pulling him away, dragging him toward a previously invisible tunnel entrance on the far side of the chamber.

"Help!" N'joku cried, his voice muffled.

Martin fired a desperate burst from his MR-113, adjusting the frequency settings frantically. The plasma charge passed harmlessly through the entity and splashed against the far wall in a shower of sparks.

"Gunny!" N'joku's voice was rapidly fading as the Hollow dragged him deeper into the tunnel. "Gunny, help!"

Then silence, the illumination fading until only Martin's helmet light remained to pierce the darkness.

"N'JOKU!" Martin bellowed, his voice echoing through the empty chamber.

No response came.

Cosmo whined anxiously from the platform edge, sensing Martin's distress. The shepherd paced, clearly wanting to help but unable to reach his master.

Martin swept his light back and forth across the chamber, searching for any sign of N'joku or the Hollow entity. Nothing moved in the vast space; the glowing patterns had dimmed to barely perceptible outlines on the walls and floor.

"God fucking dammit," he muttered, sinking to his knees on the platform.

What options did he have? He could continue to the outpost, find Frank and the others, and bring back reinforcements. But that would mean leaving N'joku in the hands of the Hollow for hours. By then, it would be far too late.

He tried his comm unit, desperate for any connection. "This is Gunny Martin Kelvin calling Broadhurst, Cage, anyone from Wolverine-9. Do you copy?"

Only static answered him. Either the rock was blocking transmission, or something else was interfering with the signal.

"Help!" a voice suddenly called from below—not over the comms but echoing through the cavern.

Martin scrambled to his feet, heart pounding. "N'joku?"

"Gunny, help me!" N'joku shouted again. His voice was raw, strained, but unmistakably human, not changed or altered like the other Marines.

Martin swung his light toward the source of the voice. The beam caught a glimpse of movement near the tunnel entrance where the Hollow had dragged N'joku. Was it really him? Or was it a trap? The Hollow had demonstrated capabilities far beyond what Martin had initially believed possible. Creating a false voice to lure him deeper might well be within their abilities.

"N'joku?" he called cautiously. "Where are you?"

"The tunnel," came the reply, weaker now. "I broke free but . . . I can't move. My leg . . ."

Cosmo's behavior gave Martin pause. The dog had calmed considerably, ears perked forward with interest rather than alarm. If the Hollow were still present, Cosmo would be growling, hackles raised. Instead, he seemed almost eager to descend, as if detecting a familiar scent.

Martin made his decision. He couldn't leave N'joku behind, not when there was even a small chance of rescuing him. The Hollow had taken him alive for a reason, and that gave them a window of opportunity.

"I'm coming down," he called. "Hold on."

Working quickly, Martin secured the rappelling line to the platform structure and tested it with several sharp tugs. Satisfied it would hold, he turned to Cosmo.

"We're going after him, boy," he said, attaching a harness to the shepherd that would allow Martin to lower him safely. "Ready?"

Cosmo licked his hand, tail wagging slightly. Taking that as agreement, Martin carefully lowered the dog first, controlling his descent until Cosmo reached the chamber floor. The shepherd immediately began investigating the area with his snout down and ears up.

With Cosmo safely below, Martin began his own descent, the thin cable playing out smoothly as he rappelled down the wall. His boots touched the floor with a soft thud, and he immediately detached from the line, weapon at the ready.

"N'joku?" he called again, sweeping his light across the chamber.

No answer.

Cosmo growled . . .

"Get back, boy," Martin whispered. As his dog retreated over to him, Martin couldn't help but wonder if he had just taken the bait like some stupid fish on a line, offering them both up to whatever horrors lurked in the shadows.

The central hub of the mining facility hummed with nervous energy as Bolesky and Ali continued working to establish contact with the *Vigilance*. Frank paced restlessly near the makeshift planning table, his boots echoing on the concrete floor. Rex lay nearby with his ears perked up, occasionally whining as if sensing his master's unease.

"So these tubes," Broadhurst said, his eyes narrowed in concentration as he studied the images Frank had captured in the underground chamber. "You're saying they're preserving different species?"

"Not just preserving," Bolesky replied from behind the comms array. "They're extracting something. Knowledge, memories, maybe even consciousness."

Phillips nodded in agreement. "The patterns we've documented suggest a systematic cataloging. The Hollow aren't just collecting specimens—they're creating a comprehensive archive of life-forms."

Grommet looked up from his station, his round face slick with sweat, hands trembling visibly. "Archiving? They killed half our squad, and you're calling them librarians?" His voice cracked with barely contained panic. "Those things are going to turn us all into metal zombies, and we're sitting here like we're in a damn research lab!"

"Pull yourself together, Sergeant," Broadhurst snapped, though his own tension was evident in the rigid set of his shoulders.

Phillips stepped forward. "I'm saying there's more going on here than we initially thought. The star maps, the crystal databases, the precise selection of human subjects—it all points to a larger purpose."

Bolesky nodded. "The evidence is consistent across all sections of the facility we've explored."

Broadhurst folded his arms, his expression guarded. "What purpose?"

Bolesky and Phillips exchanged glances.

"We're not sure yet," Phillips admitted. "But the ship we found in the forest wasn't an invasion craft. It was a scout or research vessel. And this facility . . . it's ancient. It's been here far longer than humans have been on this planet."

Ali, who had been quietly working on the comms array with Bolesky, spoke up. "You think they were here first? That we're the invaders?"

"The situation is more complicated than simply 'us versus them,'" Frank cut in. "The Hollow aren't just attacking randomly. They're selecting specific targets, gathering specific information. You don't have to be a big-brained scientist to understand that."

"Like the scientists in the tubes?" Ali asked. "The ones with xenobiology backgrounds?"

"Exactly." Frank nodded. "People who might understand them, communicate with them. People who study alien life."

"Or exploit it," Fielding suggested quietly.

Grommet's breathing quickened, his eyes darting toward the corridor. "Oh God, oh God . . . what if they're watching us right now? What if they're in the walls?"

"Grommet!" Broadhurst barked. "Get a grip, Marine, or I will sedate you."

"Let me do it," Hernandez said. "I'm getting sick of watching over this sorry excuse for a Marine."

Grommet glared at the lieutenant but then backed down and sulked behind a desk. A silence passed over the group for a long moment until Broadhurst broke it.

"Regardless of the Hollow's motivations," he said firmly, "our priority remains the same. We need to establish contact with the *Vigilance*."

"I've almost got it," Bolesky said. "The transmitter's working, but the signal strength is weak. Too much interference from the surrounding rock."

"What do you need?" Frank asked.

"I need to get to the surface," Bolesky replied. "Set up a signal relay at one of the exterior vents. The storm's mostly blown over, but there's still too much interference. With a direct line to orbit, we should be able to punch through."

Broadhurst nodded. "Take what you need. Ali, go with her."

"Actually," Bolesky said, "I need someone with more technical expertise. Gunny Cage would be more helpful."

Frank raised an eyebrow, surprised by the request.

"Your cybernetics," Bolesky explained. "The new ones are quantum-shielded. They can help amplify the signal without attracting . . . unwanted attention."

Frank understood immediately. The Hollow had shown unusual interest in electronic systems, particularly those connected to communication networks. His enhanced cybernetics might provide a buffer against their interference.

"Alright," Broadhurst agreed after a moment's consideration. "Cage, escort Bolesky to the surface vent we located. The rest of us will stay here and take turns on overwatch. I want everyone to take in nutrition. Make sure you're hydrated. Got it?"

"Yes, sir," came the responses in near unison.

Frank knelt beside Rex and scratched the rottweiler behind the ears. "Stay here, boy. Guard the fort." The dog whined softly but settled back down, his intelligent eyes tracking Frank as he followed Bolesky toward the exit.

The journey through the facility's upper levels was tense but uneventful. They passed through narrow maintenance corridors and service shafts, carefully avoiding the sections where Hollow signatures had been detected earlier. Bolesky moved with quiet efficiency, her specialized communications equipment packed securely in a rucksack.

"You do know what you're doing, right?" Frank asked as they climbed a rusted maintenance ladder.

Bolesky glanced down at him, a small smile playing at the corner of her mouth. "Yeah, I do."

"I know, just making conversation," Frank said. "You're smart enough to know when to shoot and when to run."

"Smart enough to know we need both," she countered, reaching the top of the ladder and pushing open a hatch. Fresh air rushed in, carrying the scent of vegetation and damp earth. "Sometimes the best shot is the one you don't take."

They emerged into what appeared to be a ventilation hub, a circular chamber with multiple ducts leading to the surface. Morning sunlight streamed through grates above and created patterns across the dusty floor. Bolesky immediately set to work, unpacking her equipment and assembling the relay unit.

"Keep watch," she instructed, connecting cables and aligning directional antennas. "This will take about ten minutes."

Frank positioned himself near the entrance, weapon ready, eyes scanning for any signs of movement. As Bolesky worked, the silence between them grew uncomfortable.

"You're worried about him, aren't you?" she finally asked, her voice soft.

Frank didn't pretend to misunderstand. "Martin's a survivor. He's gotten out of worse situations. He's out there."

"Mind if I ask what happened between you two?"

"You just did."

"Yeah, but you don't have to answer."

Frank's jaw tightened. "We've been through a lot together. Some of it good, some of it . . ." He trailed off, memories of Titan Station threatening to surface. "He saved my life once. I didn't want him to. It's as simple as that."

Bolesky kept working, not taking her eyes off the equipment. "Because of your family?"

Frank nodded, surprised at how easily the admission came. "I wanted to die with them. He didn't let me. Fucking tased me and dragged me onto the evacuation shuttle."

"And you never forgave him," Bolesky said. It wasn't a question.

"I never thanked him," Frank corrected. "There's a difference."

"Maybe you should, when we find him." She paused for a beat. "If he didn't save you, I'm guessing we would have all died on this mission. You kept a lot of us alive, including me. So, thank you, Cage."

She looked up and smiled. "He's out there with Cosmo," she said with surprising conviction. "So is N'joku. I can feel it in my gut."

Frank nodded. He wasn't good with compliments, not like these. Something about what she said and the way she said it really made him think about losing Martin for real.

Despite what happened at Titan Station, despite the bitterness that had poisoned their friendship, he couldn't imagine a world without Martin in it. They had been brothers in all but blood, sharing a bond forged in combat that even hatred couldn't completely sever. There were things left unsaid that Frank wanted to say to Martin. Now he might not get the chance.

While Bolesky continued her work, Frank activated his comm unit and switched to the private channel he and Martin had established during their first day on the mission.

"Martin, do you copy? It's Frank." He kept his voice low, not wanting to disturb Bolesky's concentration. "Where are you and Cosmo . . . and N'joku?"

Only static answered him. He adjusted the frequency and tried again.

"Martin, this is Frank. If you can hear me, respond." More static, slightly different in pitch but no more helpful. "Dammit, Martin, where are you?"

"The geological composition of these mountains contains high concentrations of minerals that interfere with comm signals," Bolesky explained without looking up from her work. "That's why we need this relay."

Frank continued trying different frequencies, and every attempt met the same wall of static. With each failure, his concern deepened into genuine worry. Martin was out there somewhere, possibly injured, possibly worse. And Frank was stuck here, unable to help.

He considered his options. He could request permission to lead a search party and track down Martin and N'joku before the bombardment. But that would divide their already depleted forces, potentially endangering the entire mission. And if the Hollow were still hunting them . . .

"I should be out there," he muttered, more to himself than to Bolesky.

"And risk the entire mission?" she replied, proving she'd been listening after all. "Martin wouldn't want that. You know he wouldn't."

She was right, and Frank knew it.

"Relay's almost ready," Bolesky announced, making final adjustments to the antenna. "Just need to calibrate the quantum frequency to match your cybernetics."

Frank moved closer, allowing her to connect a thin cable to a port in his cybernetic arm. A strange tingling sensation spread through his prosthetic as Bolesky ran the calibration sequence.

"How does it feel?" she asked.

"Weird," Frank admitted. "Like someone's playing a violin using my nerve endings as strings."

Bolesky smiled. "That's normal. Your quantum shielding is resonating with the relay. It should—" She broke off as the equipment suddenly hummed to life, displays lighting up with active signals. "There! Connection established."

Frank felt the change immediately, a subtle shift in the background noise of his cybernetics. "It's working?"

"Signal strength at eighty-seven percent," Bolesky confirmed, disconnecting the cable. "That should be enough to punch through to the *Vigilance*. Let's get back to the others."

They made their way through the facility quickly, both feeling the pressure of time. Frank checked his mission clock: twenty hours and six minutes remaining. Plenty of time, assuming the *Vigilance* stuck to the schedule.

When they entered the central hub, Rex instantly perked up, his tail wagging as he trotted over to Frank. The rottweiler circled him once, sniffing carefully as if checking for injuries, before pressing against his leg.

"All clear, boy," Frank said, briefly running his hand along the dog's broad head. "No trouble out there."

Rex seemed to understand but kept close to Frank as they approached the communications terminal where Broadhurst and the others had gathered. Excitement rippled through the group as Bolesky announced their success.

"The relay's active," she reported, moving to the terminal and initiating the connection sequence. "We should have a direct line to the *Vigilance* in moments."

Broadhurst nodded, composing himself for the upcoming transmission. "Good work, Sergeant. Let's hope they're in a listening mood."

The terminal crackled with static as Bolesky finalized the connections. Then, miraculously, the static cleared, replaced by the distinctive tone of an active military channel.

"Signal acquired," Bolesky announced. "Channel open."

Broadhurst stepped forward, his posture straightening as he addressed the microphone. "CNS *Vigilance*, this is Captain Broadhurst, Wolverine-9 ground team. Authentication code Sierra-Tango-Seven-Four-Niner. Do you copy?"

A moment of tense silence followed, then a voice responded through the speakers.

"Wolverine-9, this is CNS *Vigilance* Actual. Authentication confirmed. We read you five-by-five. Report status."

Broadhurst exhaled slowly, relief visible in his features. "*Vigilance* Actual, situation is as follows: We have encountered multiple Hollow entities at the designated coordinates. Have sustained casualties—six KIA, two MIA. Currently holding position in underground facility of unknown origin."

"Clarify 'unknown origin,' Captain," the voice requested.

"Facility predates mining operations by centuries, possibly millennia," Broadhurst replied. "Appears to be Hollow in construction. We have located multiple Hollow vessels in underground hangar and extensive data repositories."

Grommet paced near the back of the room, gnawing at his fingernails, muttering quietly to himself.

A pause from the comm. "Are you under immediate threat, Wolverine-9?"

"Negative, *Vigilance*. We have established a secure position. But request immediate extraction. We have gathered critical intelligence on Hollow operations and capabilities that must be delivered to Shield Command."

Another pause, longer this time. When the voice returned, it carried a different tone—more measured, more formal.

"Captain Broadhurst, this is Captain Hargrove, stand by for orders."

Frank and Broadhurst exchanged alarmed glances.

"Understood, *Vigilance*," Broadhurst replied.

The channel went silent.

Seconds stretched into a minute, then two.

"*Vigilance* Actual, do you copy?" Broadhurst tried again. "*Vigilance*, come in."

Nothing but static answered him.

"What happened?" Hernandez asked, looking between Broadhurst and Bolesky.

"Signal's still transmitting," Bolesky reported, checking her equipment. "They've gone silent on their end."

Broadhurst's expression darkened. "Keep trying."

Grommet's face contorted with panic. "They've abandoned us!" He grabbed his head with both hands. "Those things are going to fucking kill every single one of us—"

Frank threw a punch that silenced Grommet instantly. His body crumpled to the ground.

"Damn, guy has a tough head for such a little bitch," Frank said, shaking his real hand.

Broadhurst looked at him but seemed to be more focused on the comms. "I don't like this," he said. "Going dark like that on us. I got a bad feeling . . ."

CHAPTER TWENTY-ONE

The tunnel stretched before Martin like the throat of some ancient beast, swallowing light and sound. His tactical light mounted to his rifle cut a narrow beam through the oppressive darkness, revealing just enough of the path ahead to navigate but leaving the periphery shrouded in shadow. Cosmo padded silently at his side, the shepherd's keen senses alert and helping guide them.

With nothing but his helmet left from his Aegis armor, Martin felt naked and vulnerable, but there was no turning back now. Not until he found N'joku or confirmed he was gone.

"N'joku," Martin called, his voice bouncing back at him from the stone walls. "Can you hear me?"

Only his own echo answered, mocking his growing concern. He checked his mission clock: twenty hours and fifty-three minutes remaining until the scheduled bombardment. Time was slipping away, and with it, N'joku's chances of survival.

The tunnel jutted into a trio of very similar-looking passages. Martin hesitated, uncertain which path to follow. Cosmo provided the answer, moving confidently toward the rightmost tunnel, nose to the ground as he tracked N'joku's scent.

This new passage was different from the one they'd entered through. The walls were lined with the same strange metallic material he'd seen in the Hollow ships and etched with geometric patterns that seemed to pulse faintly as he passed. The air grew noticeably cooler, carrying the metallic tang that the creatures produced. But there was something else in the air that reminded Martin of the moments before an electrical storm.

"Artificial construction," he noted, running his hand along one wall. The surface was unnaturally smooth, almost frictionless, yet warm to the touch despite the cooling air. These definitely were not natural cave formations.

Cosmo suddenly stopped, ears pricked forward, body tense. The shepherd whined softly, pawing at a section of the floor that appeared no different from the rest. Martin knelt to examine it and found tiny variations in the geometric array—slight depressions that might once have been footprints, though whether human or Hollow was impossible to determine.

"You've got his scent," Martin said, scratching Cosmo behind the ears. "Lead on, boy."

They continued deeper, and the tunnel gradually sloped downward for as far as the beam from his rifle would penetrate.

Occasionally, Martin passed side chambers or alcoves, each containing equipment or structures whose purpose he couldn't begin to guess. He directed his light into one of the largest rooms. Inside, spherical objects roughly a meter in diameter hung suspended in midair, rotating slowly without any visible means of support.

"What the . . ." he whispered.

In the next alcove, he spotted what appeared to be liquid metal flowing upward against gravity, forming complex three-dimensional shapes before dissolving back into the pool below. Cosmo growled, and Martin stepped back.

"Yeah, I don't like this place either," Martin whispered.

After nearly twenty minutes of exploration, the tunnel opened into a gigantic, cavernous space chiseled out of the canyon rock. Unlike the previous spaces, this one appeared to serve a specific function. The walls were lined with control panels or interfaces, each covered in the now-familiar geometric symbols. The center of the room held what looked like a three-dimensional star map, projected from a pedestal on the floor.

Martin approached it cautiously, weapon ready. The map showed a spiral galaxy—the Milky Way, he presumed—with several points illuminated in different colors. One pulsed red over a planetary system he didn't recognize. Others glowed blue, scattered throughout the galactic arms, while a cluster of yellow points concentrated in another unfamiliar system.

"Is this tracking something?" he wondered, studying the display without touching it. "Monitoring systems? Colonies?"

Cosmo growled softly, drawing Martin's attention away from the map. The shepherd was staring intently at one of the tunnel exits on the far side of the chamber, hackles raised slightly. Not the aggressive posture the dog adopted when facing immediate threats, but a warning nonetheless.

"Okay, I'm coming," Martin said, giving the star map one last look before following Cosmo toward the tunnel.

This new passage was narrower than the previous ones, forcing Martin to duck his head in places. The walls here were rougher, more natural, as if this section had been carved through existing cave systems rather than constructed from scratch. Water dripped somewhere in the darkness, the sound echoing eerily.

As Martin rounded a bend, his light caught something that made him pause—scorch marks on the wall. He moved closer and examined the distinctive pattern. Plasma weapon discharge, military grade. Next to it, several small impact craters pockmarked the stone, consistent with high-velocity rounds. That ruled out it coming from the plasma pistol N'joku had when he fell.

But someone had a firefight down here. He kneeled to examine scorch marks across the floor. They were definitely from plasma rifles, which told him Frank's team had found this place, and found trouble.

Cosmo sniffed the ground, then continued down the tunnel, seemingly unperturbed by the evidence of combat. Martin followed, his unease growing. Fear burned his heart that something terrible had happened to his friend and the rest of their squad.

The temperature continued to drop during the descent. Martin's breath began to fog against his visor, his environmental readout on his wrist-monitor showing the ambient temperature approaching just above freezing.

After another ten minutes of careful progress, the tunnel widened suddenly and opened into a vast cavern that Martin's light couldn't fully illuminate. What he could see left him speechless.

Stretching before him was what could only be described as a catacomb—rows upon rows of recessed chambers cut into the walls, extending upward beyond the reach of his beam. Each niche was about two meters long and one meter high, reminiscent of ancient Earth burial sites, though these contained no human remains.

Instead, each recess held glass-like structures that caught his light and refracted it in complex patterns. Some pulsed with internal luminescence, while others remained dormant. The active ones cast eerie, shifting colors across the cavern walls, creating an otherworldly aurora.

"My God," Martin breathed, his voice barely above a whisper.

The cold was intense now, his readout showing temperatures well below freezing. Frost coated every surface, and his cybernetic joints had begun to stiffen from the extreme cold. Cosmo whined uncomfortably and lifted his paws one at a time from the frigid floor.

Martin advanced cautiously and studied the glass-like structures more closely. Each appeared unique, their geometric patterns similar to the ones on the walls but infinitely more complex, more dynamic. They reminded him of three-dimensional circuit boards, but with an organic quality that defied technological explanation.

"Data storage?" he wondered, careful not to touch any of them.

As they moved deeper into the catacombs, Martin noticed that some sections were dark, their surfaces shattered or missing entirely. The damaged areas showed signs of deliberate destruction rather than natural decay. These were done by precision cuts and surgical removals rather than random breakage.

Someone's been harvesting these or destroying them systematically, he thought.

Cosmo suddenly barked, and the sound was explosive in the tomb-like silence of the catacombs. The shepherd raced ahead, then disappeared around a corner before Martin could call him back.

"Cosmo!" Martin hurried after him, his boots slipping on the icy floor. "Cosmo, halt!"

He rounded the corner to find Cosmo standing over a dark form huddled against the wall. The shepherd whined anxiously, pawing at the figure without touching it. As Martin's light fell on the form, he recognized N'joku.

The lieutenant was barely conscious, his back propped against the wall, injured leg stretched out before him. He shivered in his undersuit, arms folded across his chest, lips blue. Blood had frozen in thin rivulets from a cut above his eyebrow, creating macabre tendrils down his face. His eyes were open but unfocused, and he blinked slowly as Martin's light hit them.

"N'joku." Martin knelt beside him and set down his weapon to check the lieutenant's pulse. It was present but sluggish, his skin cold to the touch. "Can you hear me?"

N'joku's eyes focused slowly on Martin's face. "G-gunny," he managed through chattering teeth. "T-took you l-long enough."

Relief flooded through Martin. Hypothermia was setting in, but N'joku was still lucid enough for sarcasm—a good sign. "Let's get you warmed up," he said, removing the emergency thermal blanket from his pack and wrapping it around N'joku's shoulders.

"W-won't help m-much," N'joku stammered. "T-too cold down h-here."

Martin activated a chemical heat pack from his medical supplies and broke the inner capsule to start the reaction. "Put this against your chest, under the blanket," he instructed. "It's not much, but it'll help."

"Thank . . . thank . . ." N'joku trembled as he clutched the heat pack gratefully. "Thank you."

Martin nodded and surveyed their surroundings more carefully. The section of catacomb where N'joku had been deposited was different from the rest. The niches here contained no crystals but were carved with deeper, more intricate geometric sequences. The floor before them bore what appeared to be a circular platform or dais, its surface inscribed with spiraling designs that converged at the center.

"What happened to you?" Martin asked, returning his attention to N'joku. "How did you end up here?"

N'joku shivered violently, the tremors wracking his entire body. "That H-Hollow just let me g-go," he said. "D-dragged me through t-tunnels, brought me h-here. Looked me over, then d-dropped me. Like I wasn't w-what it wanted."

"Or like they found exactly what they needed."

"W-what is this p-place?" N'joku asked, his gaze traveling over the empty niches.

"I'm not sure. Storage of some kind, or preservation chambers. The glass in those sections might be data repositories, records of some kind."

"No." N'joku shook his head weakly. "These n-niches. They're d-different."

Martin examined them more closely, noting subtle variations in the carvings. "You're right. These patterns are more complex, more—" He broke off, a realization striking him. "These aren't data storage. They're prepared chambers."

"F-for what?"

"Not what. Who." Martin's unease grew as the pieces fell into place. He remembered something from the medical checkup right before the mission, when he was looking at a CAT scan of his brain. "The patterns match human neural structures," he said. "These were prepared for human subjects."

N'joku's eyes widened with comprehension and fear. "You m-mean—"

"They're collection points. Designed specifically for humans. Or human minds, at least."

"Why didn't they p-put me in one?"

Martin shook his head. "I don't know. Maybe you weren't the right candidate. Or maybe they took what they needed without having to preserve you."

He studied N'joku more carefully, checking for any signs of the transformation they'd seen in previous Hollow victims. Nothing obvious. "Did they do anything to you? Tests? Probes?"

"N-nothing I remember," N'joku said. "Just f-felt cold. Very c-cold. And a h-humming in my h-head."

Martin checked the lieutenant's pupils, noting they reacted normally to his light. No immediate signs of neural tampering, but that didn't mean nothing had happened. The Hollow technology was beyond human understanding.

"It's like they wanted us to see this," Martin said. "Like we were meant to find it."

"Why?"

"I don't know. Maybe to show us what they're doing. Or to warn us." He helped N'joku take a sip from his canteen. "How's the leg?"

"C-can't feel it, but that m-might be the c-cold."

Martin checked the injured knee and then his ankle, finding the swelling for both had actually decreased in the extreme cold. "We need to get you out of here and back to the outpost."

"Might need a bit of assistance, Gunny."

"I got you."

Martin positioned himself under N'joku's arm, supporting most of his weight as the lieutenant struggled to his feet. N'joku grunted but remained upright, determination etched on his frost-nipped features.

"That's it," Martin encouraged. "One step at a time."

They began the slow journey out of the chamber, N'joku hobbling on his good leg while Martin bore the brunt of his weight. Cosmo led the way, retracing their path through the catacombs toward the exit tunnel. Every few meters, Martin had to pause to let N'joku rest. The lieutenant's strength was clearly fading despite his best efforts.

"Keep it up," Martin urged during one such break. "We're making good progress."

N'joku nodded weakly, his breathing labored. "S-sorry for slowing you d-down."

"We're finishing this together, remember?"

A nod. "Thanks, Gunny."

"Thank me when I get us out of here."

A sudden pulsating light illuminated the path ahead, but this was coming from behind. Martin halted and turned with N'joku. The glow increased, cobwebbing across the walls, and then right over them.

They turned again and saw the engravings on the rock flashing like a train racing down a tunnel.

"That isn't good," Martin said. It was like the facility, or whatever this place served as, was waking up.

Cosmo let out a low whine.

"We need to move faster," Martin said.

The corridors continued to glow brightly as they pushed up the incline toward the surface. They had covered perhaps half the distance to the exit when the first tremor ran through the cavern. It was subtle, just a brief vibration beneath their feet, but it sent dust sifting down from the ceiling.

"What w-was that?" N'joku asked, looking up nervously.

"Not sure," Martin replied. "Seismic activity maybe."

Another tremor followed, stronger this time. Small pebbles skittered across the floor. The engraved Hollow language, or whatever it was, burned even brighter.

"It's reacting," N'joku said.

Cosmo whined, ears flattened against his head, his body tense and alert. The shepherd's behavior confirmed Martin's growing suspicion that this was no ordinary earthquake.

They had nearly reached the exit tunnel when a deep rumbling vibrated through the cavern. Not from below, but from above, far above. It came in rhythmic pulses, like the firing of heavy artillery. Larger chunks of rock began to fall, smashing and shattering along the ground.

Realization struck with horrifying clarity.

"*Vigilance*," Martin huffed. "They're firing early."

"But we've still got twenty hours!"

"Tell that to whoever's giving the orders."

The bombardment intensified, and the impacts transmitted through kilometers of rock to reach them. The ceiling groaned ominously, spiderweb cracks appearing in the ancient stone. The engravings were reacting violently now, many pulsing with blinding intensity, while others shattered in spectacular bursts of light and energy.

"We need to find another way out." Martin half dragged N'joku away from the chamber they had descended through after N'joku fell.

Cosmo barked urgently, racing back down the way they had just come. His instincts had never failed them before, and Martin trusted the dog's judgment implicitly.

The rumbling grew deafening, and the entire catacomb shook as if gripped by a titan's hand. Complete sections of ceiling began to collapse, massive chunks of rock plummeting to the floor with bone-crushing force.

Martin spotted the alcoves ahead and pulled N'joku inside the first one, hoping for some sort of cover. Deep down, he knew the bombing would likely kill them and turn the entire canyon into dust, but he had to try.

As they entered, Martin's light swept across something that made him pause—a CSF Marine combat boot protruding from beneath a pile of rubble. Taking a precious second to investigate, he shifted some debris and revealed the remains of a Marine. It was hard to tell how long it had been here due to it being partially frozen by the cold.

"Who is it?" N'joku asked.

Martin held in a breath as he bent down to examine it, praying it wasn't Frank. When he turned the body over, he didn't recognize the face, or the insignia on the armor, some kind of classified unit designation.

"Someone was here before us," Martin realized, as more ceiling fragments rained down around them. This explained the firefight evidence—another team had been sent in ahead of them, and they hadn't made it out. But that meant Natalia hadn't told them the entire truth, if she did know about teams coming here.

Maybe she didn't . . . he thought.

Martin knew that was likely a lie. There was no time to consider this further as the ceiling cracked above them and rained down more debris.

"We have to find somewhere else!" Martin shouted, abandoning further investigation and practically carrying N'joku out of the alcove.

They descended deeper into the flashing main corridor, N'joku crying out in pain but forcing himself forward on adrenaline and sheer will. Ahead, the main chamber with the preservation nooks glowed like salvation.

Cosmo waited outside, barking frantically, urging them to hurry.

An extreme tremor shook the entire facility. Martin entered the chamber and looked up just in time to see a massive crack racing across the ceiling hundreds of meters above them, now illuminated by the flashing glass units. Tons of rock hung suspended for one impossible moment, then plunged downward in a thunderous avalanche.

"Move!" he yelled, shoving N'joku forward with all his strength.

The lieutenant stumbled away from the main collapse and fell to his hands and knees. Martin lunged to follow, but he was a split second too late. A massive slab of stone struck the ground behind him, forcing him to fall. More debris rained down, partially burying him in rubble.

"Martin!" N'joku screamed, dragging himself back toward the collapsing entrance.

"Stay back!" Martin shouted, struggling to free himself. A rock struck his helmet, cracking the visor. Another rock smashed his rifle, crushing the tac light. In the sudden darkness, he heard Cosmo's frantic barking and felt the dog trying to dig through the debris to reach him.

Then came a final, catastrophic collapse. The ceiling gave way completely, unleashing an avalanche that buried everything in its path. Martin felt the crushing weight of stone pressing down on him, driving the air from his lungs. He couldn't see, couldn't move, could barely breathe.

His last thought before consciousness faded was of Frank—wondering if his old friend had found the answers they sought, wondering if any of them would survive to tell the tale. Then darkness claimed him, and the world around Martin Kelvin went silent.

CHAPTER TWENTY-TWO

The first impact hit without warning.

Frank was in the middle of discussing evacuation routes with Hernandez when the entire facility shuddered violently, dust and fragments of concrete raining down from the ceiling. The lights flickered, plunging the central hub into momentary darkness before the emergency systems kicked in, bathing everything in an eerie red glow.

"*Vigilance* Actual, this is Captain Broadhurst! Cease fire, cease fire! There are CSF Marines still in the facility!" He waited, adjusting frequencies frantically as only static answered him. "*Vigilance*, do you copy? We have critical intelligence to report! Cease bombardment immediately!"

The next impact was close enough to crack the console beside him, sending sparks flying across the room. Broadhurst tried again, desperation edging into his voice. "This is Captain Broadhurst, authentication code Sierra-Tango-Seven-Four-Niner! We are still on site! Cease fire!"

Frank shook his head. "They aren't going to listen," he said.

Broadhurst looked to Frank, both men immediately understanding what was happening. Shield Command had decided to deal with the intel they had relayed with extreme prejudice.

"Those motherfuckers are trying to kill me again!" Frank growled.

Another impact struck, closer this time. Phillips dove under a workstation as a section of ceiling collapsed nearby.

The floor bucked beneath them like a living thing, throwing Fielding to his knees. Equipment crashed from tables, monitors shattered, and a support beam groaned ominously above them.

"Move!" Frank ordered, grabbing his pack and weapon. "Everyone out! Now!"

Rex was already at the exit, barking frantically. The rottweiler's instincts had never failed them before, and Frank trusted the dog's judgment implicitly. The squad scrambled to collect essential gear, abandoning anything noncritical.

Grommet stood frozen, his eyes wide with panic. "We're fucked!"

"Pull yourself together," Frank snapped, grabbing him by the shoulder. "Or I'll knock you out again and leave you here."

Grommet swallowed hard but managed to nod, falling into line behind Hernandez.

"Which way?" Broadhurst demanded as they reached the corridor junction.

A third impact hit, this one close enough to send a visible ripple through the facility's structure. Cracks spiderwebbed across the ceiling, and dust and debris showered down in earnest now.

"Not up," Frank decided, pointing to the passage leading deeper into the facility. "Down. The lower levels will have more structural integrity."

"But that takes us further from extraction!" Fielding protested.

"There is no extraction," Frank shot back. "We're on our own. Now move!"

They raced down the corridor. Frank took point with Rex, and Broadhurst brought up the rear. The impacts continued, each one stronger than the last, the intervals between them shortening. The *Vigilance* wasn't just firing warning shots—this was a destruction pattern designed to collapse the entire facility. But if they wanted to, they could have done that with a single nuke. This seemed more systematic, like they wanted something to survive. Perhaps evidence . . .

As they reached the junction leading to the lower levels, a massive tremor shook the corridor. The ceiling above them buckled, large chunks of concrete breaking free.

"Look out!" Frank shouted, diving forward.

Ali wasn't fast enough. A support beam snapped and caught him squarely across the shoulders. He went down hard, pinned beneath the massive weight, blood pooling beneath him.

"Ali!" Gillford rushed to his side and tried desperately to lift the beam. Her face contorted with effort, but the massive concrete slab wouldn't budge. It was immediately clear that the sergeant was beyond saving. The beam had crushed his upper torso, his eyes already glazing over as life fled his body.

"He's gone," Broadhurst said, his voice tight with controlled grief. "We have to keep moving."

"But—" Gillford began, still trying to shift the beam.

"Now, Sergeant!" Broadhurst barked, physically pulling her away from Ali's body. "Or we all die here!"

They continued their desperate flight while the facility disintegrated around them. The bombardment had settled into precision strikes designed to compromise key structural points. Whoever was targeting them knew exactly what they were doing.

"They're going to bury us alive." Fielding gasped as they rushed down a maintenance shaft, the ladder vibrating dangerously beneath their hands.

"Not if we keep moving," Frank growled, dropping the final meters to the lower level. Rex landed beside him with surprising grace for his size, and was immediately alert for new threats.

Hernandez helped Phillips down the last few rungs, both men looking grimly up at the creaking structure above them.

The lower level was glowing when they arrived. The geometric patterns on the walls pulsed with increased intensity, responding to the destruction occurring above.

"This way," Frank directed, recalling the route to the underground chambers they'd discovered earlier. "If the Hollow built this place, the deepest levels should be the most fortified."

They moved swiftly through corridors that looked increasingly alien, and the architecture shifted from human mining facility to something else entirely. The bombardment continued overhead, but the impacts seemed more muffled now, the structure around them absorbing the shock waves more effectively.

"Head to the specimen chamber," Frank replied. "It's the deepest part of the facility we've found. Our best chance."

A roaring tremor cut through the relative stability, sending a support column crashing to the floor directly in their path. As they detoured around it, Frank noticed a familiar silver-green glow at the end of the passage.

"Hollow!" he warned, raising his weapon.

But the entities—three of them now—weren't advancing toward the Marines. They were retreating, flowing through the corridor away from the bombardment above, their surface patterns conveying what Frank could only interpret as panic or alarm.

"They're running," Bolesky said. "They're afraid of the bombardment."

Frank made a split-second decision. "Follow them!"

"What?" Hernandez stared at him in disbelief. "Follow the Hollow?"

"No fucking way!" Grommet said.

"Fine, stay here then, but those things built this place," Frank explained rapidly. "If they're running, it's toward shelter."

"You think they will share it with us?" Broadhurst asked.

"It's our only shot."

Broadhurst hesitated only briefly before nodding. "Okay, follow them, but maintain distance and keep weapons ready."

They pursued the retreating entities through a maze of corridors, descending deeper into the facility than they'd explored previously. The bombardment continued above, but the sound was becoming less intense, suggesting they were putting significant distance between themselves and the surface.

The Hollow led them back to the massive specimen chamber they'd discovered earlier, passing through the walls as if they were mist. The Marines had to take the long way around, following the corridor to the main entrance.

"No, no, I won't go in there," Grommet said, his voice rising in panic.

"Fine, stay here then," Frank said.

He led the way into the preservation chamber. Everything looked different now—more active, more alive. The tubes containing countless specimens glowed with heightened energy, and Hollow entities moved purposefully between the rows, their quicksilver geometry conveying urgency.

"They're trying to save their collection," Phillips observed quietly.

A tremendous impact struck directly above. The entire chamber shuddered, and several tubes near the entrance cracked, their preservation fluid leaking onto the floor. Another impact followed immediately, stronger than the first, and more tubes fractured under the strain.

One tube shattered completely, and its inhabitant—a human male in what appeared to be mining coveralls—spilled out along with the fluid. The man lay motionless for a moment, then began to twitch and convulse, gasping like a drowning victim suddenly finding air.

"He's alive." Fielding moved toward the fallen miner.

"No time!" Frank shouted as another impact sent more tubes crashing to the floor. "We need to keep moving deeper!"

The miner's eyes opened, confusion and terror warring in his expression as he tried to comprehend what was happening. He opened his mouth, forming words they couldn't hear over the sound of destruction all around them.

Frank hesitated, torn between helping the man and ensuring the survival of his remaining squad. Before he could decide, a massive support beam broke free from the ceiling and plummeted toward them.

"Run!" he ordered, pushing Fielding ahead of him.

They sprinted with the squad toward the far side of the chamber, where another set of doors promised potential escape. Behind them, tubes continued to shatter, preservation fluid flooding the floor, turning their footing treacherous. Frank glanced back just in time to see the miner looking up, confusion giving way to pure terror as the support beam crushed him into the floor.

Another impact hit the surface. The ceiling began to collapse in sections, massive chunks of material raining down on the precious archive. The Hollow entities reappeared. Their patterns were frantic as they tried to save what specimens they could, moving some tubes deeper into the facility while abandoning others to destruction.

"Almost there!" Broadhurst called, reaching the far doors.

Frank urged Rex ahead of him, and the dog bounded toward safety. Fielding was next, then Phillips and Hernandez. Gillford and Bolesky were at the tail end, with Grommet following. Broadhurst held the doors, waving them through.

"Quickly!" he shouted over the deafening rumble of collapsing architecture.

Frank had nearly reached the doors when he heard a different sound—a high-pitched whine cutting through the chaos. He recognized it instantly: the distinctive signature of a plasma charge building to critical mass.

"Down!" he screamed, diving forward and tackling Bolesky through the doorway.

The explosion came milliseconds later—not an orbital strike but an overloading power core within the facility itself. The blast wave rushed through the chamber, vaporizing tubes and specimens, disintegrating the falling debris, and sending a wall of superheated air racing toward the escaping Marines.

Frank caught a glimpse of Rex safely inside the next chamber, of Broadhurst diving through the doorway after them. Then the wave of fire and debris hit. It slammed him against the far wall with bone-crushing force. Pain lanced through every nerve ending before merciful darkness encroached.

His last conscious thought was of Martin, wondering if his old friend had found shelter from this apocalypse, wondering if any of them would survive to tell what they'd seen. Then consciousness fled, leaving Frank adrift in the void between life and death as the world burned around him.

The darkness was absolute, but it wasn't empty. In the void, geometric patterns danced behind his closed eyelids—patterns he recognized from the Hollow entities, from the facility walls, from the mysterious artifact in his pocket. They pulsed with meaning just beyond his comprehension, like a language he almost recognized but couldn't quite understand.

Not dead, came a thought that wasn't entirely his own. *Protected.*

Frank drifted in that strange half consciousness, aware that something was happening to him but powerless to respond. The geometric array grew more intricate, more complex, conveying concepts that his human mind struggled to process. Images flashed through his awareness: stars exploding, planets forming, civilizations rising and falling, all in accelerated time.

Must understand, the alien thought-voice continued. *Must prepare.*

"For what?" Frank tried to ask, though no sound escaped his lips.

The answer came not in words but in a cascade of terrifying imagery—massive ships of angular design, planets reduced to ash, entire star systems extinguished. A relentless, consuming darkness moving through the galaxy, methodically eliminating all advanced life it encountered.

They come, the thought-voice warned. *Soon.*

The darkness began to recede, and reality bled back in around the edges of Frank's consciousness. Pain returned, sharp and insistent, along with the sensation of hands pulling at him, voices calling his name. He fought to hold on to the vision, to understand what he'd been shown, but it slipped away like water through his fingers.

"Frank! Frank, can you hear me?"

The voice was familiar but wrong somehow—the inflection strange. Frank struggled to open his eyes, to return to the world of the living. Light seeped in, blinding after the darkness. Shapes moved above him, resolving slowly into faces.

Broadhurst hovered over him, helmet gone and expression changed—too stiff, too mechanical. His eyes held an alien intelligence that Frank recognized immediately.

"You're not Broadhurst," he croaked, his voice barely audible.

"No," he agreed, his head tilting at an unnatural angle. "Not anymore."

Darkness. Then light. Then darkness again.

Martin Kelvin floated somewhere between consciousness and oblivion, the weight of the collapsed tunnel pressing down on him like the hand of God. Strange, how the mind worked when the body was broken. He should have been panicking, screaming, fighting, but instead, a peculiar calm had settled over him.

He could hear things, distant and muffled. The scrabbling of hands against rock. Cosmo's desperate barking. N'joku's strained voice calling his name. But these sounds seemed to come from another world, separate from the dreamscape he now inhabited.

"Martin!" The voice penetrated the fog momentarily. "Gunny! Can you hear me?"

Martin tried to answer, but his lips wouldn't move. Instead, his mind drifted backward, floating through the corridors of memory.

He was on Eden again, kneeling in the rich soil of his garden. The sun warmed his back as he methodically pulled weeds from between the neat rows of vegetables. This had been his salvation after Titan Station—the simple, honest work of coaxing life from the earth. Cosmo lay nearby, head on paws, watching him with those soulful eyes.

"Weeding again?"

The voice startled him. He hadn't heard that voice in years. He looked up, squinting against the sunlight, to see Lucia standing at the edge of the garden. His ex-wife, looking exactly as she had the day she'd walked out of his life.

"Someone has to do it," he heard himself answer.

"Always the dutiful one," she said, her smile sad. "That's why I left, you know. Not because I didn't love you. But because you loved the Corps more."

"That's not true," he protested, but even as the words left his mouth, he knew they were a lie. How many anniversaries and birthdays had he missed? How many promises broken because duty called?

"It is true," Lucia said gently. "It's why you've never forgiven Frank, too.

Because he wanted to abandon his duty to die with his family, and you couldn't allow that. It violated everything you believed about being a Marine."

The garden began to fade, the sunlight dimming. In its place, the sterile corridors of Titan Station materialized around him. Alarms blared. Emergency lights flashed. And Frank was there, pounding on a sealed bulkhead with bloody fists, screaming for Sarah and Lily.

"I can get through!" Frank shouted, his voice raw with desperation. "I can still save them!"

Martin felt himself move, felt his arms wrap around Frank from behind and drag him away from the door. He heard himself shout, "There's no time!" even as Frank fought against him with the strength of a madman.

The memory played out exactly as it had happened, every detail painfully clear. Frank breaking free, Martin drawing his sidearm and setting it to stun. The look of betrayal in Frank's eyes as the charge hit him, his body convulsing before collapsing to the deck.

"You should have let me die with them." Frank's voice, but not from the memory. Martin turned to see his friend standing beside him, watching the scene unfold. "Why didn't you let me die with them, Kel?"

"I couldn't," Martin whispered. "We weren't done yet."

"Weren't done?" Frank's laugh was hollow. "What was left to do? What was so damned important that I had to live while they died?"

The scene shifted again. He was back on Eden, but not in his garden. He stood at the edge of his property, looking out at the mountains in the distance. The beauty of it struck him anew: the majesty of the peaks against the sky, the sweep of forestland, the clarity of the air.

"It's why you saved him," said a voice beside him. Sarah Cage stood there, Lily's small hand clasped in hers. Mother and daughter, exactly as they'd appeared in the photo Frank had shown him just before that fateful mission to Titan. "You knew there was still beauty in the world, even if he couldn't see it anymore."

"I didn't want him to die," Martin said simply.

Lily looked up at him with eyes that seemed far too wise for her five years when the picture was taken. "Nobody wants to die, Mr. Martin. Not really."

The words hit him with unexpected force. Not really. Even Frank, in his darkest moments, hadn't truly wanted death. He'd wanted an end to pain, an end to loss. But death? No. What Frank had wanted was his family back.

What Martin wanted was to live.

The realization burned through the fog in his mind like sunlight through morning mist. He didn't want to die here, buried under tons of rock in an alien catacomb. He had things to finish. Questions to answer. A friend to save, still.

I don't want to die. The thought became a mantra, pulsing in time with his heartbeat. *I don't want to die. I don't want to die.*

"Martin!" N'joku's voice again, closer now. "Gunny, hang on! I can see you!"

Martin forced his eyes open. Darkness still surrounded him, but there was a thin shaft of light now, illuminating the dust that swirled in the air. He tried to move and found his right arm pinned beneath a slab of rock, but his left hand could wiggle slightly.

"Here," he managed to croak, his voice a ragged whisper. "I'm here."

Cosmo's excited bark echoed through the small space, followed by the sound of renewed digging. The shaft of light widened as rocks were pulled away, revealing N'joku's dust-covered face peering down at him.

"Thank God," the lieutenant breathed. "I thought you were gone."

Martin tried to smile, though he wasn't sure if his face actually moved. "Not yet."

N'joku worked with desperate efficiency, moving smaller rocks first to create space, then leveraging the larger ones away from Martin's trapped body. Cosmo helped as best he could, pawing away debris and whining anxiously whenever Martin groaned in pain.

"Almost there," N'joku encouraged, his own breathing labored as he strained against a particularly heavy slab. "Just a little more . . ."

With a final heave, the rock shifted, and Martin felt the pressure on his chest ease. He drew a deep breath, relishing the burn of oxygen in his lungs. N'joku reached down and pulled Martin upward through the narrow opening in the rubble.

The pain hit then, a wave so intense that black spots danced before Martin's eyes. His head throbbed mercilessly, and his right arm hung at an unnatural angle. Blood trickled down his face from a gash on his scalp.

"Easy, easy," N'joku murmured.

Cosmo pressed against Martin's leg, whimpering softly, his fur gray with dust. Martin reached down with his good hand to touch the shepherd's head, reassuring himself as much as the dog.

N'joku helped Martin sit with his back against a relatively smooth section of wall, then knelt to assess his injuries. "That's a nasty cut on your head," he said, opening the medical kit. "And your arm is definitely broken."

Martin looked down at his twisted arm and grunted.

N'joku worked quickly to clean the head wound and apply a pressure bandage. The lieutenant's hands were surprisingly gentle as he manipulated Martin's broken arm, aligning the bones before splinting it securely.

"Didn't know they taught field medicine so well at the Academy," Martin said through gritted teeth.

"They don't. Had a grandfather who was a doctor. He taught me a few things."

When the lieutenant finished, Martin sat wrapped in bandages, his arm immobilized against his chest, his head swathed in white gauze.

"Now I really look like an egg," he said with a weak laugh. "A cracked egg. Frank will love this."

Martin took stock of their situation. The tunnel they'd passed through was completely blocked by the cave-in. Their only option was to move deeper into the complex, hoping to find another way out. The catacomb chamber remained mostly intact, though many of the glass structures had shattered, leaving fragments scattered across the icy floor.

"Why do you think they fired early?" N'joku asked.

Martin steadied himself, testing his weight. His cybernetic leg had sustained damage but was still functional, though it whined more loudly than before. "Something must have spooked them," he said. "Maybe they detected increased Hollow activity."

"But why are we still alive? They could have glassed this entire place."

"That's what bothers me," Martin admitted. "These weren't kill shots. They were targeted strikes. Precise."

"Maybe they didn't want to destroy everything. Just certain sections."

"Which means they know more than they're telling us." Martin gestured around them. "Like the fact that Marines have already been here before us . . . It means Captain Ivan and Colonel Shafter lied to us. Shield Command knew exactly what was here."

"You think they sent us in as cannon fodder?"

"Maybe. Or maybe they just needed people with firsthand Hollow experience." Martin paused, wincing as pain lanced through his arm. "But why hide it? Unless . . ."

"Unless they wanted plausible deniability," N'joku finished his thought. "If something went wrong, they could claim they had no prior knowledge."

"Or they wanted to see how the Hollow would respond to us specifically. Frank and me. Because of our history with them." Martin shook away his questions. "How's your knee and ankle? Can you walk?"

"Yeah, I can."

"Good, let's find a way out of here."

Martin began moving toward one of the undamaged tunnels leading away from the catacombs that he hadn't seen the first time.

"Let's try that, looks like it leads up," he said.

"Up is good," N'joku said. He limped along, using a beam as a cane. They followed Cosmo's lead, moving carefully through the debris-strewn passage. The tunnel Martin had noticed was definitely sloping upward rather than down.

Along the trek, Martin found his thoughts drifting back to his half-conscious visions. Lucia. Frank. Sarah and Lily. The garden on Eden. Dreams, or something more?

About twenty minutes into their hike, Cosmo froze and turned to look back at them, then looked forward again, as if indicating something ahead.

"What is it?" Martin whispered, moving cautiously.

The tunnel opened into a small chamber different from any they'd seen before. Unlike the geometric precision of the other rooms, this one appeared almost organic, its walls flowing in curves and spirals. At its center stood what looked like a control console, though without buttons or screens as humans would understand them.

"What is this place?" N'joku asked.

Martin approached the console slowly, drawn by an instinct he couldn't explain. "I think it's a communication node."

A strange sensation washed over him as he walked toward it, a tingling that began in his cybernetic limbs and spread throughout his body. The console responded to his proximity, sections of it illuminating with a soft blue glow.

"Gunny?" N'joku's voice held a note of warning.

Martin raised his good hand. "It's okay. I think it's scanning me."

The console's light intensified, focusing on Martin's cybernetic components. With a low hum, a section of the floor began to recede, revealing a hidden chamber below. Cosmo whined and backed away slightly before returning to Martin's side, his ears flat against his head.

"What did you do?" N'joku asked.

"I'm not sure, but I think we just found something they didn't want anyone to see."

A narrow stairway spiraled down into darkness. Martin's helmet light barely penetrated the gloom below, revealing only hints of metallic surfaces.

"Stay behind me," Martin instructed, descending carefully, mindful of his broken arm. Cosmo followed, showing no signs of immediate panic.

The chamber was smaller than the catacomb, roughly circular and lined with smooth walls that seemed to absorb light. The center of the room was dominated by metallic platforms, three of which hovered above the floor with no visible means of support.

"How are they doing that?" N'joku whispered, moving closer.

"Some kind of antigravity technology," Martin suggested.

N'joku circled one of the hovering platforms. "These look operational. Not just artifacts."

Martin nodded, studying the room more carefully. Along one wall stood a control station, similar to the one they'd activated above but more complex. Blue-white energy pulsed through channels in the floor, connecting the station to each platform.

"This is a manufacturing facility," Martin said. "Or a laboratory."

Cosmo growled softly, staring at one platform in particular. Unlike the others, this one had a depression in its center, roughly the size and shape of a human torso, ringed by delicate filaments.

"Careful," Martin warned but too late.

N'joku's equipment pack had shifted, and a loose strap brushed against the filaments. They immediately flared with brilliant silver light. Cosmo barked in alarm, retreating to Martin's side.

"What did you do?" Martin demanded, blinking away the afterimage.

"Nothing! I barely touched it!"

The platform activated, its surface glowing with silvery luminescence. The filaments had risen higher, weaving an intricate pattern above the depression. Then something began to form within—a swirling mass of liquid-like metal that coalesced into an increasingly complex structure.

"Is that—" N'joku began.

"A Hollow," Martin confirmed, raising his weapon with his good arm. "It's forming a Hollow."

The entity took shape gradually, starting as a sphere before extending tendrils. Unlike the Hollow they had encountered before, this one seemed less defined, its surface rippling with unformed patterns.

A transparent barrier shimmered into existence around the platform.

"It can't get out," N'joku observed. "It's trapped."

Martin kept his weapon trained on the forming Hollow, but Cosmo's behavior changed. The shepherd no longer growled but watched with apparent curiosity.

"It's incomplete," Martin noted. "Like a prototype."

The Hollow had stabilized into a roughly humanoid form, though still flowing and shifting. It moved within its containment field, exploring the boundaries without aggression.

"Gunny," N'joku said slowly, "what if these things aren't entities? Designed, not born?"

Martin glanced at him. "You're talking above my pay grade, son."

"Hear me out. Everything we've seen—the preservation chambers, the mathematical patterns, the way they interface with technology—they don't behave like any life-form we understand."

He gestured at the partially formed Hollow. "Look at it. It's being manufactured. What if the Hollow aren't aliens at all, but advanced weapons or tools created by something else? Something that's gone now, leaving only its creations behind?"

Martin considered this, watching the silver entity. The idea would explain the strange behavior they'd observed: preservation and destruction intermingled.

"If you're right," Martin said, "then what's their purpose?"

"Protection? Preservation? Maybe both?"

The Hollow had gone still, its surface geometry changing to match those on the chamber walls. It seemed to be studying them.

A sudden tremor ran through the chamber, dislodging dust from the ceiling. The bombardment had resumed, though more distant than before. The Hollow entity reacted immediately, its patterns cycling more rapidly.

Martin turned away from the contained Hollow. "We need to find Frank and the others and get the hell out of here."

Cosmo had already moved to the exit and was looking back expectantly.

Before leaving, Martin glanced over his shoulder one last time. The partially formed Hollow pressed against its containment field, its surface geometry aligned in what almost resembled an eyeless face, watching them depart.

Not a monster. Not an alien. Something else entirely: a creation abandoned by its creators, still fulfilling its ancient purpose that Martin didn't fully understand.

CHAPTER TWENTY-THREE

Frank shot upright, and his lungs burned as he coughed up dust and blood. The world spun around him, a kaleidoscope of emergency lights and shadow. His head throbbed with each heartbeat, and something wet trickled down his face. Blood or sweat, he couldn't tell. Didn't matter.

"Rex?" he rasped, reaching out blindly.

A warm muzzle pressed against his hand, followed by a soft whine. The rottweiler was there, covered in gray dust but seemingly uninjured. Small mercies.

The explosion had thrown them clear of the main collapse, but the facility was still coming apart around them. Frank's ears rang, muffling the chaos. The orbital bombardment had begun early—much earlier than the agreed timeline. Someone aboard the *Vigilance* had decided they'd seen enough.

He forced himself to focus, to assess. Ali was dead—he'd seen that before the blast. But now Gillford lay half buried under a slab of fallen concrete nearby, her leg crushed, face contorted in silent agony. Still alive, but not for long without help.

"Hang on," he called to her, his voice barely audible even to himself. This time, he saw her eyes flutter in response.

Bolesky and Fielding were huddled behind a fallen support beam, their weapons drawn but not firing. Their armor was streaked with dust, and their eyes were wide with a mixture of shock and terror behind their visors. Grommet, Hernandez, and Phillips were nowhere to be seen—either crushed, or they had fled.

Frank saw Broadhurst standing unnaturally still in the shadows. His posture was rigid, head tilted at an unnatural angle, and when he finally shifted position, his movements were stiff, mechanical, a crude imitation of human locomotion.

"It wasn't a dream," Frank muttered. "He really has been taken over by those things."

He remembered Broadhurst's strange behavior earlier, the unnatural tilt of his head, the way he'd spoken with multiple voices layered upon each other. For a moment, he'd thought it might have been a hallucination brought on by the explosion, but the terror in Bolesky's and Fielding's eyes confirmed the truth.

"Something's wrong with Broadhurst," Bolesky said. "One minute he was giving orders, the next he was standing there with those silver eyes, talking about preservation and witnesses."

Frank struggled to his feet and grabbed his rifle from where it had fallen. The weapon was dented but operational, its charge indicator showing half power. He staggered toward Bolesky and Fielding, Rex at his heels.

"That's not Broadhurst anymore," he said. "Stay away from him."

As if sensing Frank's awareness, the figure emerged into the dim emergency lighting. Frank couldn't suppress a shudder as those inhuman eyes fixed on him—Broadhurst's irises had dissolved into swirling patterns of liquid silver, identical to the surface of a Hollow entity.

Frank raised his rifle, training it on the thing that had been the captain. "Keep back," he said.

The transformed Broadhurst stopped several meters away and regarded them with those alien eyes. The chamber fell silent except for the distant rumble of the facility crumbling around them.

"Gillford's still alive," Frank said, not taking his eyes off Broadhurst. "We need to help her."

"I'll check on her," Fielding volunteered, moving cautiously toward their trapped comrade.

Frank and Bolesky provided cover as Fielding knelt beside Gillford. The sergeant's face was ashen, lips turning blue. The concrete slab had crushed her lower body, and dark blood pooled beneath her.

"She's in bad shape," Fielding reported. "We need to get this off her."

Just as they moved to help Gillford, Hollow entities began streaming into the chamber from multiple entry points, their silver forms rippling with complex patterns. Frank, Bolesky, and Fielding backed into a defensive position around Gillford, and Rex growled at Frank's side.

"We're surrounded," Fielding said, his voice surprisingly steady now that the moment had come. "No way out."

The transformed Broadhurst took another step forward. When he spoke, his voice was that disturbing blend Frank remembered: human vocal cords producing inhuman speech and multiple tones layered upon each other, creating a dissonant chorus.

"Lower your weapons," he said. "We mean you no harm."

"Like hell," Frank snarled, keeping his rifle aimed at his head. "Let him go."

"This vessel was already damaged beyond recovery," Broadhurst's body replied, gesturing to a wound in his abdomen and chest that Frank hadn't noticed before. "We merely preserve what was being lost."

A particularly violent tremor shook the chamber, dislodging more debris from the ceiling. A chunk struck near Fielding, causing him to stumble back in alarm.

"Frank, what do we do?" Bolesky asked.

A few things went through his mind. First, that he should probably blow Broadhurst's head off, especially since Broadhurst had straight up told them he would want that end if he was ever infected. But Frank also saw the potential in communicating with the enemy in a way they hadn't been able to before. Especially if they weren't attacking.

The Hollow entities moved in, surrounding them completely. More silver forms glided toward Gillford's position.

"Stay away from her!" Frank shouted, but the entities continued their approach.

Fielding raised his rifle. "Cage, should I fire?"

"That depends on this thing," Frank said. He looked at what had been Broadhurst. "What are you?"

The transformed captain's expression shifted to something approximating sadness. "We are what remains. The final defense. The last sentinels."

He gestured around them at the facility. "We were created by a species called the Halcerites. Our purpose now is to warn, to preserve, to prepare. Our makers came, conquered all intelligent life, and left us behind."

"Created?" Frank repeated, the pieces falling into place. "You're artificial?"

"We are what you would call weapons," replied the entity. "Our creators built us to protect their investment as you might understand it, until the Halcerites return and claim these planets."

While Broadhurst spoke, Frank saw his chance. He nodded to Fielding and Bolesky, and they quickly moved to the concrete slab pinning Gillford. Together, they strained against the massive weight, muscles burning with the effort. Finally, the slab shifted enough for them to pull Gillford free. She grimaced but didn't cry out in pain, probably because she couldn't feel much, if anything.

As soon as they moved her, blood began pulsing from her crushed lower body. The dark pool spread rapidly across the floor.

"She's bleeding out," Bolesky said. She pressed her hands against the worst of the wounds, but the blood continued to flow between her fingers.

Gillford's eyes fluttered open, surprisingly clear despite her injuries. "It's okay," she whispered, her voice barely audible. "I know I'm done." Her gaze shifted to the approaching Hollow entities, then back to Frank. "Please, don't let them take me."

Frank gripped her hand, his cybernetic fingers closing gently around hers. "I won't."

But even as he made the promise, he could see the life fading from her eyes. With a final shuddering breath, Gillford went still, her hand falling limp in his grip.

"She's gone," Bolesky said softly.

The Hollow entities paused in their approach, as if acknowledging Gillford's passing. Then they resumed their advance, silver tendrils reaching toward her body.

"At first," Broadhurst continued, seemingly unmoved by Gillford's death, "we thought your species might have been the enemy returning. But you are nothing compared to what is coming. Mere insects as you might consider microbes."

"What is coming?" Frank said.

"Our creators. They consume all advanced sentient life, harvest all technology above a certain threshold. They left this system a thousand human years ago to cycle through neighboring systems. Soon, they will return to colonize and expand."

Frank's mind raced. If what he was saying was true, it would explain so much. The scarcity of advanced alien life despite the abundance of habitable planets. The strange behavior of the Hollow; not invaders but guardians, trying to wake humanity to a threat it couldn't comprehend.

"Titan Station," Frank said, realization dawning. "You weren't attacking. You were trying to warn us."

"Yes," Broadhurst confirmed. "We attempted to establish communication through your networks. Your military mistook our presence for invasion. They destroyed the station rather than risk contamination."

The tremors were increasing, and the facility continued to collapse around them.

"And now you're doing it again," Frank said bitterly. "Destroying what might save you."

Broadhurst's silver eyes fixed on him. "Time grows short. We must preserve what we can."

More entities flowed into the chamber, these different from the others—larger, more complex in their patterns. Between them, they carried what appeared to be an empty preservation tube, similar to those they'd seen in the great hall. Its transparent surface caught the emergency lights, reflecting them in prismatic geometric arrays.

To Frank's horror, he saw other entities lifting Gillford's body with surprising gentleness, then carrying it toward a second preservation tube that had materialized behind them.

"Oh god," Bolesky breathed, understanding dawning on her face. "They want to preserve us. Like those specimens we found."

A cold dread settled in Frank's stomach. "No," he said, backing away. "No!"

"You have seen," Broadhurst explained. "You understand. You must be preserved to share this knowledge when the time comes."

"Frank!" Fielding shouted as silver tendrils began wrapping around his legs. "I can't move!"

Frank tried to run, but similar tendrils wrapped around his own legs, immobilizing him. Rex charged the nearest entity but passed harmlessly through its fluid form. The dog growled in confusion and frustration, then tried again and again to protect his master.

"Let me go!" Frank shouted. He was lifted off his feet, and the entities carried him toward the waiting preservation chamber. Through the silver forms surrounding him, he could see Fielding being enveloped by entities. Gillford's body was already being lowered into a preservation tube, silver fluid rising around her still form.

Bolesky was the only one that hadn't been taken yet. She backed away, looking at Frank in horror.

"Go," he mouthed. *RUN!*

Frank fought with everything he had, his cybernetic arm tearing through one entity before two more restrained it. "We're not your test subjects!"

"No," Broadhurst agreed, following as they positioned Frank before the open tube. "You are witnesses. Messengers. When the time comes, you will tell your people what is coming. You will help them prepare."

The tube opened with a pneumatic hiss, revealing a gel-like substance within. Frank redoubled his efforts, twisting violently against the restraining tendrils. He caught a glimpse of Rex, who was pinned to the floor by two entities but unharmed and watching with desperate, confused eyes.

"Let him fucking go, you silver ass fuckers!" Frank shouted. He snarled, trying to break free, and almost accomplishing it. Another Hollow drifted over and restrained him. All at once, they worked to remove his Aegis. With ease, they removed Lucky and then stripped Frank out of his suit.

"No! No, stop!" he shouted. "Let go of my dog!"

Broadhurst tilted his head in that unnatural way. "The animal will be preserved as well. Its bond with you makes it valuable."

Frank was forced kicking and screaming backward into the tube. The cold gel rushed over his naked skin. He tried to hold his breath as the fluid rose around him, but silver tendrils pried his mouth open, the gel flooding his lungs.

The sensation was horrifying: drowning but not dying, his body fighting against the invasion while his mind remained cruelly aware. He screamed, but the sound was swallowed by the gel. His vision began to dim, consciousness fading at the edges.

His last thought was of Martin. If anyone could help, it would be him. If anyone could tell the truth about the Hollow, about what was coming, it would be his old friend.

As darkness claimed him, geometric patterns danced behind his eyes. The language of the Hollow, imprinting itself on his consciousness.

Not just preservation, he realized. Programming.

Preparing him to be a messenger when humanity would need one most.

The gunfire echoed through the labyrinthine tunnels, the distinctive whine-crack of plasma rifles reverberating off alien walls. Martin froze, his broken arm throbbing sharply at the sudden movement. Cosmo's ears perked up immediately, and his head swiveled toward the distant combat.

"That's CSF Marine weaponry," Martin said.

"Could be Frank and the others," N'joku replied.

Or it could be the Marines that were sent here first, although Martin doubted there were any survivors.

"Which way is it coming from?" Martin asked. He was all turned around in the labyrinth of tunnels they found themselves in now.

Cosmo took point without being commanded, nose to the ground. He went to a junction ahead and smelled both ways, then selected left.

"He's got a scent," N'joku observed.

"Good job, buddy!" Martin called.

Side by side with N'joku, Martin hurried down the passage toward the sound, each step sending jolts of pain through his splinted arm. N'joku winced as he limped along.

"God, I bet we look like absolute shit," he said with a chuckle.

"Good thing you're not trying to impress any ladies," Martin replied. "Only thing you got to worry about is surviving."

The gunfire grew sporadic ahead, then abruptly ceased.

"Faster," Martin said.

The architecture around them shifted as they pushed deeper, tunnels transitioning from rough-hewn mining passages to something far more alien. Occasional tremors shook the facility, dislodging dust and small fragments from the ceiling. Martin stumbled during one such tremor and barely caught himself against the wall with his good arm.

Cosmo stopped, hackles rising as he stared into the darkness ahead. A low growl rumbled from his chest.

"What is it, boy?" Martin whispered.

A wet, gurgling sound echoed from a side passage. Martin raised his weapon one-handed, and the awkward grip made accurate aim difficult. N'joku positioned himself at Martin's side, his own pistol steady despite his injured leg.

"Who's there?" Martin called out. "Identify yourself!"

The only answer was a soft scraping sound, like something dragging itself across the floor. Then a familiar voice, distorted by pain or worse.

"G-gunny? That you?"

Martin tensed. "Identify yourself, now!"

"It's me, Phillips," came a rough voice.

Movement shifted from the shadows where a figure slumped against the wall. As Martin's light fell upon it, he recognized Phillips, at least part of Phillips. The sergeant's face was partially transformed, silver veins spreading beneath his skin like frost on a windowpane. His left eye had already changed, the iris dissolved into swirling patterns of liquid metal.

"Help . . . me . . ." Phillips gasped, his human eye wide with terror and pain. A plasma rifle lay beside him, its barrel still hot from recent firing. The surrounding walls were scorched with plasma burns, evidence of a desperate last stand.

"They . . . came from the walls. Tried to . . ." He coughed, and silver-flecked spittle ran from his mouth. "Couldn't stop them all."

Martin approached cautiously, weapon still raised. Cosmo stayed close to his leg, growling softly at the transformed Marine.

"Where are the others?" Martin asked. "The rest of the squad? Frank?"

"They're . . . inside . . ." Phillips choked out. "Can't . . . fight it . . ."

N'joku moved closer, his pistol trained on Phillips's chest.

Phillips managed a jerky nod, his movements becoming less coordinated as the transformation progressed. The silver veins spread visibly across his exposed skin, pulsing with an internal light that matched the patterns on the walls.

Martin pulled out the syringe that Natalia had given him. He wasn't sure he still trusted the woman, but this might be the only chance to save Phillips.

"I'm going to help you," Martin said.

"What is that?" N'joku asked.

"Experimental medicine to reverse the infection," Martin said. He slung his rifle and bent down to Phillips. "Hold still, okay?"

"Oh . . . okay . . ." Phillips said.

Martin removed the cap from the syringe using his teeth and prepared to plunge it into Phillips, when he noticed the Marine's human eye suddenly clouded. Something in his gaze changed from fear to anger.

Phillips's hand shot out with inhuman speed and grabbed Martin's splinted arm with crushing force. Martin gasped in pain, then dropped the syringe as agony lanced through his broken bones.

"Preserve! Must preserve!" Phillips's voice changed, multiple tones layering over each other in an unsettling harmony.

Martin looked down in horror as silver tendrils flickered away from Phillips.

N'joku didn't hesitate. He fired a short, controlled burst, and the plasma discharge struck Phillips squarely in the chest. The sergeant's body jerked backward, his grip releasing Martin, who fell the opposite direction. Silver fluid erupted from the impact point before impossibly flowing back into the wound and sealing it.

Phillips rose, his movements now entirely inhuman. The transformation was accelerating, patches of his skin taking on a metallic sheen.

"Gunny, move!" N'joku shouted, firing again as Phillips lunged toward them.

Martin rolled aside, white-hot agony shooting through his broken arm as he impacted the floor. Cosmo attacked, jaws snapping at Phillips, but the shepherd's teeth passed through the partially transformed flesh as if through fog.

Phillips slammed N'joku against the wall, and the lieutenant cried out as his injured knee took the impact. His pistol clattered away across the floor. Martin drew his sidearm with his left hand, the awkward grip making aim difficult.

"Phillips, stand down!" he ordered, a final, desperate appeal to whatever humanity might remain.

The creature that had been Phillips turned toward him, its face now more Hollow than human, expression eerily serene despite the violence of its actions.

"Join . . . us . . ." it said, voice a discordant chorus. "Salvation . . . through . . . preservation . . ."

Martin fired, the plasma bolt striking the entity's shoulder. It staggered briefly before recovering, advancing on him with unnatural grace. Behind it, N'joku was struggling to regain his feet, blood running from a fresh gash on his chin.

"Get down!" N'joku said.

Martin noticed the lieutenant holding something—a grenade, that he had plucked from Phillips. He tossed it right behind the transformed Marine.

N'joku dove to the ground and Martin scrambled over to Cosmo, piling on top of the dog to shield him with his body as the grenade detonated.

The explosion filled the corridor with blinding light and superheated plasma. When Martin looked up, Phillips's transformed body lay in pieces, the silver fluid that had animated it dispersing into the air like mist.

"God rest your soul, Phillips," Martin murmured, pushing himself upright with a grimace. His arm screamed in protest, the splint now cracked and barely holding.

Cosmo pushed up, shook, then licked at Martin.

"Smart thinking," he told N'joku, helping the lieutenant to his feet.

N'joku nodded, his face pale with pain as he put weight on his injured leg. Martin picked up the plasma rifle Phillips had left behind and handed it to N'joku. Then he picked up his own rifle. Finally, he grabbed the syringe off the ground. Before he even got the cap on, Cosmo growled.

A blur of motion came from the shadows and slammed into N'joku from behind, sending the lieutenant sprawling with a cry of pain. Martin whirled, weapon raised, and found himself face-to-face with Sergeant Grommet—or what remained of him.

The transformation was further along than Phillips's had been. Grommet's skin had taken on a complete metallic sheen, geometric forms flowing across its surface like mercury. Only his basic humanoid shape and fragments of his uniform indicated he had ever been human.

"Join . . . us . . ." Grommet's voice was barely recognizable. "Preservation . . . only . . . hope . . ."

The transformed Marine attacked with blinding speed. Martin fired instinctively, but the plasma discharge passed harmlessly through Grommet's semifluid form. The entity barreled into him, knocking his weapon away and driving him to the ground. In a second, the creature was on him, tendrils of light and silver flickering down on Martin.

Cosmo leapt to his defense, teeth bared, but the shepherd's attacks were also ineffective. Grommet backhanded the dog with casual strength, sending Cosmo yelping across the chamber.

"N'joku!" Martin called, struggling to free himself from Grommet's inhuman grip. The pain in his broken arm made it nearly impossible to fight back effectively.

"Preservation . . . necessary . . ." Grommet intoned.

A plasma burst struck Grommet from the side, momentarily disrupting his form. N'joku had recovered his weapon and was firing steadily, his face set with determination.

Martin seized the opportunity and rolled away from Grommet, then scrambled toward a fallen section of machinery. After drawing his knife from the sheath with his good hand, he swung it with all his strength at the re-forming figure.

The impact was like striking water—momentarily disruptive. Grommet flowed around the obstruction, his body reconstituting faster than Phillips's had.

"We can't stop him!" Martin shouted. "Fall back!"

N'joku fired another burst, covering Martin's retreat as they backed toward the chamber's far exit. Cosmo had recovered and growled at their side, limping slightly from Grommet's strike.

Grommet advanced steadily, seemingly untroubled by the plasma fire. Each hit disrupted his form briefly before it flowed back together, the patterns adapting, changing.

Cosmo barked farther down the corridor, and Martin turned to see a door at the very far end, illuminated by a glowing interface.

"N'joku, hurry this way!" he shouted.

While N'joku continued firing, Martin rushed after Cosmo. The interface was alien, covered in a mosaic of geometry. Acting on instinct, he pressed his cybernetic hand against the panel.

The symbols flared with light, and the door slid open. Martin waved N'joku through, and the lieutenant hobbled past, his injured leg dragging noticeably. Cosmo followed without prompting.

"Close it!" N'joku shouted.

Grommet surged toward them, his form almost completely reconstituted.

Martin pressed his hand against the panel, and the door began to close. Grommet's arm elongated, stretching toward the narrowing gap. Martin fired his rifle, and the plasma bolt severed it from the main body. The door sealed shut, the severed portion dissolving into silver mist.

"That won't hold him for long," Martin said. He leaned against the wall, his body trembling with pain and exhaustion.

A familiar sound echoed from deeper in the facility that made him perk up. The deep, resonant bark was a noise that Martin would recognize anywhere.

"Rex," he said with a smile. "That's got to be him!"

The shepherd's ears perked up at the sound of his canine companion. Cosmo surged ahead, leading them down a corridor that sloped downward.

"Wait," Martin called. He hurried after the dog, his rifle slung over his back.

N'joku followed, limping heavily and grimacing with each step. The corridor curved to the right ahead. As much as Martin wanted to call out for Frank, he knew they could be walking into a trap.

Cosmo slowed, his ears flattened against his skull. A low whine escaped his throat at the corner.

"Quiet," Martin whispered.

N'joku nodded. With their weapons raised, they cautiously rounded the corner and found a vast chamber that stopped them both mid-step.

"What in God's name is this?" N'joku whispered between pained breaths.

Rows of transparent tubes stretched before them, each occupied by a suspended figure—humans, some in CSF Marine uniforms. And there, inside one of those tubes, was Frank.

Even from this distance, Martin could see his friend struggling against the silver tendrils that restrained him. Rex was similarly restrained nearby, fighting against entities that flowed around his body.

Dozens of Hollow hovered around the tubes, their surfaces rippling with patterns that shifted. Martin caught glimpses of other squad members already sealed in tubes, although he couldn't make out individual features.

Martin went to move, but N'joku pulled him back behind the corner.

"Hold on," N'joku said. "We need a plan. If we rush in, we're all dead."

Mind spinning, Martin realized he was right. But what kind of plan could they come up with? Between his broken arm, their depleted weapons, and N'joku's deteriorating condition, their tactical options were severely limited.

A shriek suddenly came from the door they had closed.

Grommet was breaking through.

They were trapped, cornered between the enemy.

"Gunny," N'joku said. "Plan?"

Martin considered their options, which were very few at this point. The situation had gone beyond FUBAR. "Shoot the pods," Martin said. "Free them, and fight like hell, that's our only chance."

N'joku nodded.

Martin burst around the corner with his rifle.

The Hollow entities suddenly shifted around the pods, preventing a clean shot when Martin moved into view.

A figure emerged from their ranks, walking with unnatural precision.

Captain Broadhurst. But not Captain Broadhurst.

His body moved mechanically, each step measured. His head tilted at an impossible angle, and when he looked up, his eyes had transformed completely—featureless pools of liquid silver.

"Martin Kelvin," he said, his voice a chilling harmony. "You have come."

Martin raised his weapon one-handed, the pain in his broken arm making it almost impossible to aim steadily. "Let them go," he demanded.

"They are being preserved," Broadhurst replied. "As you must be."

"Preserved for what?"

"For what comes," he answered. "For the return of our creators."

Martin's finger tightened on the trigger, but he hesitated. There was something in his words, something that resonated with their theories about the Hollow's purpose.

His hesitation cost him. Broadhurst flew forward, crossing the remaining distance in the blink of an eye. Before Martin could fire, Broadhurst's hand passed directly through his chest as if he were made of fog.

The pain was indescribable; not physical agony, but something deeper. Martin dropped to his knees, weapon clattering uselessly to the floor. He tried to scream, but no sound escaped his constricted throat.

Through dimming vision, he saw N'joku backing away in horror, dragging a reluctant Cosmo with him. The lieutenant's face was pale with shock, his weapon half raised at Martin.

"Do it," Martin managed to choke out.

"Now you will understand," Broadhurst said. His silver eyes met Martin's as darkness began to claim him.

The last thing Martin saw was Frank's face, contorted in anguish as he watched helplessly from the partially sealed tube. Then consciousness fled, leaving only the geometric patterns of the Hollow dancing behind his closed eyelids; patterns that, for the first time, Martin was beginning to understand.

CHAPTER TWENTY-FOUR

Frank floated in a twilight realm between consciousness and nothingness. His last clear memory was of Broadhurst, or the thing wearing Broadhurst's face, approaching him, silver tendrils extending from his fingertips. Then a sensation like being simultaneously frozen and liquefied, his body suddenly weightless, moving without his control.

Now he was suspended in something thick, viscous, neither air nor water but a composition in between. It filled his lungs, pressed against his eyelids, and invaded every part of him. He should have been terrified, should have been fighting, but a strange lethargy had settled over him, dulling his panic to a distant concern.

Where . . . ?

He forced his eyes open against the pressure of the fluid. Distorted shapes swam beyond curved glass—a preservation tube, he realized dimly. Like the ones they'd discovered in the lower levels. They'd put him in one of the preservation tanks, just like the miners, just like the other specimens.

The thought should have horrified him, but the preservative fluid was affecting his mind as well as his body, smoothing the jagged edges of fear into something more manageable, more distant.

Don't fight it, whispered a voice that wasn't entirely his own. *Surrender. Remember.*

And suddenly he was remembering.

Sarah on their wedding day, sunlight catching in her hair as she turned toward him, smile radiant. Not the posed photos they'd taken later, but a private moment when she'd thought no one was watching, adjusting her veil with quiet joy.

Lily's first steps, tiny hands reaching for him, face alight with triumph and wonder. The way she'd laughed when she fell, then promptly climbed back to her feet to try again.

The memories came with perfect clarity, as if he were reliving them rather than merely recalling. He could smell Sarah's perfume, feel Lily's small hand in his. For fifteen years, he'd tried to numb these memories with alcohol, to drown them until they couldn't hurt him anymore. Now they surrounded him, as real and immediate as the preservation fluid itself.

I could join them, he thought, temptation washing over him. *Just let go. Stop fighting.*

The alien presence in his mind encouraged this line of thought, offering glimpses of what could be: an eternity with his lost family, a life where Titan Station had never happened, where the Hollow had never entered their lives.

Frank felt himself sinking deeper into the temptation, the preservation fluid seeming to thicken around him, cradling him in its embrace. His resistance ebbed away like a receding tide.

Then the memories shifted, flowing backward to a time before Sarah and Lily died.

His Aegis armor, the one he'd nicknamed "Lucky" after it had saved him during an ambush in the jungles of the planet Zonova. A plasma bolt had struck him directly in the chest and should have killed him instantly, but instead it had somehow been deflected by a manufacturing anomaly in the chest plate. The techs couldn't explain it; by all rights, he should have been dead. After that, the name stuck.

"You're getting superstitious in your old age," Martin had teased him when Frank refused to use any other suit, even when newer models became available.

"It's not superstition if it works," Frank had replied, patting the armored shoulder with genuine affection. "Lucky's saved my ass seventeen times. I'm keeping count."

By the end of his career that number had tripled.

The memory shifted to another firefight—Lucky's leg servos locking up just as Frank was about to step onto a hidden mine. The malfunction had saved his life, even as he cursed the suit's temperamental systems.

Another shift, another memory.

After Titan, after losing Sarah and Lily, and during the first few months of retirement, Frank had hit rock bottom. Drinking himself unconscious every night, picking fights with anyone who looked at him wrong. One particularly bad night, he'd found himself in an alleyway behind several bars in Eden, so drunk he could barely stand.

The black and tan rottweiler had been in the shadows, watching Frank with intelligent eyes that somehow seemed to understand everything.

"Don't get too close," said a man smoking outside. "That dog has aggression issues."

Frank had laughed bitterly. "We'll get along just fine then."

Rex had followed him home with a little enticing of the half-eaten cheeseburger Frank had snagged off a plate and stuffed in his pocket. The dog was standoffish for the first few weeks, watching Frank's drinking binges with silent judgment. But gradually, a bond had formed. When Frank had nightmares about Titan Station, Rex would somehow sense it and climb onto the bed to lie across his legs, grounding him back to reality.

For almost a decade, when Frank had lost everything else, Rex had kept him from eating his pistol on more than one night. The dog never judged his drinking, his anger, his slow descent into self-destruction. Just stayed by his side, a silent witness and companion.

Where's Rex? The thought cut through the numbing effect of the preservation fluid. *Where's my dog?*

Panic began to set in, his heart rate accelerating despite the fluid's calming influence. Rex had been with him in the chamber. Had the Hollow captured him too? Preserved him? Or worse?

Be calm, the alien presence soothed. *Your companion is safe. He awaits your return to the memories.*

Fuck you, I don't want to be calm, motherfucker! Frank thought.

The warmth of the alien presence flowed through him again, attempting to guide him back to the comforting unreality of perfect recollection. It would be so easy to surrender, to retreat into a past where everything was still whole, still right.

But something else intruded on the perfect surrender—a sound. Distant, muffled by the liquid surrounding him, but unmistakable. A voice calling a name he knew.

Martin?

Frank's awareness sharpened, cutting through the preservation fluid's numbing effects. Through the distortion of the curved tube wall, he saw figures moving in the chamber beyond. Fighting. And there, charging across the room with reckless determination despite his visibly broken arm, was Martin Kelvin.

Martin came for me. Again.

The realization struck Frank like a physical blow. After fifteen years of bitterness and drinking and pushing everyone away, Martin was still coming for him. Still refusing to leave him behind.

Just as he had at Titan Station.

Understanding bloomed in Frank's oxygen-deprived brain. Martin hadn't saved him from Titan out of duty or protocol. He'd saved Frank because he couldn't bear to lose him. Just as Frank now found he couldn't bear to lose Martin, couldn't bear to retreat into false memories while his friend faced death in the real world.

Frank pushed against the numbing comfort of the preservation fluid, fighting his way back to full awareness. The chamber came into sharper focus beyond the glass. Through the translucent fluid, he saw the transformed Broadhurst leaning over Martin.

He watched in helpless horror as Broadhurst's hand passed impossibly through his chest. Martin's face contorted in agony as he collapsed to his knees, N'joku backing away with Cosmo, uncertain how to help.

No! Frank slammed his fist against the tube wall. The impact was absorbed by the thick fluid and reduced to a gentle tap that no one would hear.

Movement across the chamber caught his eye. Through the distortion of the glass and fluid, Frank could make out a figure moving cautiously between the tubes. Tall. Female.

Bolesky. The sergeant was free of Hollow control, with two plasma pistols in hand and a rifle slung over her back. How she had escaped capture or transformation, he couldn't guess, but she was heading toward him.

Bolesky raised her pistols directly at his tube.

Oh shit. Frank tried to shout, the words emerging as nothing more than bubbles in the preservation fluid. She was going to kill him. After everything, he was going to die at the hands of his own squad member.

But then Bolesky made a signal he recognized from countless combat missions. Stand by for extraction. She wasn't aiming to kill him—she was planning to free him.

Frank braced himself as best he could, pressing his back against the far side of the tube, away from where she would fire.

Bolesky took aim. Frank closed his eyes and turned his head. A muffled blast, then the sound of cracking glass. The preservation fluid's pressure shifted suddenly, the liquid level dropping as it began to pour through a growing fracture in the tube's surface.

A second blast finished the job. The tube's entire front section shattered, preservation fluid cascading onto the chamber floor in a rushing torrent that carried Frank with it. He crashed onto the hard surface, choking and gasping as his lungs expelled the alien substance, dragging in precious oxygen with desperate, burning breaths.

"Sergeant!"

Bolesky was at his side, steadying him as he struggled to his feet. Frank realized belatedly that the preservation process had stripped him of his uniform and gear—he was completely naked, covered in the slimy residue of the warm fluid.

"Rex . . ." he managed to choke out, his first concern for his loyal companion.

Bolesky thrust the rifle into Frank's hands.

"Time to move, Gunny," she said.

He nodded.

Frank's vision was clearing, strength returning to his limbs as he recovered from the warm preservation process, but the cold of the chamber was quickly setting in. Broadhurst had noticed the commotion now, his silver eyes turning toward them. The tendrils connecting him to Martin pulsed, causing him to cry out in pain.

Frank didn't hesitate. He aimed the plasma rifle directly at Broadhurst's head, his stance wide and balanced despite his nakedness and the slick fluid still coating his skin. His finger tensed on the trigger, all his training focused into this moment.

"Let him go, you silver alien fucker," he growled.

Martin fought against the invasion, against the silver tendrils spreading beneath his skin. He could feel himself changing, being rewritten, preserved in a way he didn't want or understand.

Movement nearby caught his attention. Through pain-blurred vision, he saw Frank—naked—aiming a plasma rifle at Broadhurst. Relief and terror warred within him; relief that his friend was free, terror that Broadhurst would kill him instantly.

"I said let him the fuck go!" Frank shouted, his voice hoarse.

The silver tendrils in Martin's chest paused their advance, frozen but still present. Broadhurst turned slightly toward Frank, his movements unnaturally precise.

"This one understands," he said, indicating Martin with a tilt of his head. "He is being prepared to serve as messenger. To warn humanity of what comes."

"What comes?" Frank demanded, never lowering his weapon. "What the hell are you talking about?"

"Our creators," Broadhurst replied. "An advanced race that views all intelligent life as a threat to their expansion. They cleansed this system once before. They will return soon to begin colonization."

Frank's expression didn't change, but Martin could see the subtle shift in his stance—the slight tensing that indicated he was processing this information, evaluating it as a tactical concern rather than dismissing it outright.

"And you're what? Their messengers?" Frank asked, skepticism evident in his tone.

"We are weapons," Broadhurst confirmed. "Designed by the Halcerites to eradicate any intelligent life once again. We have now determined you to be intelligent, and also a threat to our creators due to your violent nature. We opted to warn humanity and offer a chance to return to your homeworld, an anomaly in our protocols, perhaps a flaw."

Or perhaps a trap to lead your creators to our homeworld, Martin thought.

"Well, I'm glad we passed your alien overlords exam for intelligence," Frank said, his grip on the rifle never wavering. "But it's your funeral. If these Halcerturds want a war, the Marine Corps will make them wish they were never conceived."

The silver tendrils in Martin's chest, which had paused momentarily, suddenly surged forward again, resuming their inexorable spread. Pain lanced through him, sharper than before, as if Broadhurst were punishing him for Frank's defiance. He couldn't suppress the scream that tore from his throat.

Broadhurst emitted a harmonic tone that seemed to resonate at multiple frequencies simultaneously. The other Hollow entities in the chamber responded, their silver forms rippling with increased activity.

"Your fellow human, or what you believe to be your brother," Broadhurst clarified in that alien voice, "will pay for your threatening words. You will now witness his death."

The silver spread rapidly now, branching outward from Martin's chest toward his throat, his face, his brain. He could feel his consciousness being systematically overwritten and replaced with something alien. The sensation was worse than death, worse than torture. It was erasure, the ultimate violation of selfhood.

Through dimming vision, he saw Frank scream something unintelligible, trying to surge forward, only to be pinned down by silver tendrils that erupted from the floor. Bolesky and Fielding, whom she had freed, were similarly restrained, their weapons useless in their immobilized hands.

This is it, Martin thought as darkness crept in from the edges of his awareness. *This is how it all ends.*

The silver was at his throat now, cold tendrils slithering beneath his skin toward his brain. In seconds, whatever made him Martin Kelvin would be gone, replaced by a Hollow consciousness wearing his body like a suit.

Then came a deep, resonant growl, followed by a higher-pitched bark. Through the haze of pain and transformation, Martin saw two blurs of movement converging on Broadhurst from opposite sides.

Cosmo and Rex, acting with uncanny coordination, leapt simultaneously at the transformed captain. Cosmo went for his legs while Rex, the heavier of the two, slammed into his upper body with the full force of his weight.

Broadhurst staggered, his concentration broken. The silver tendrils connecting him to Martin wavered, their advance halting momentarily.

It was enough. Frank broke free from his restraints, rolled sideways, and came up firing. The plasma discharge caught the nearest Hollow entity square in its center mass, disrupting its form long enough for Fielding to wrench free as well. Within seconds, Bolesky was also loose, grabbing her fallen weapon and joining the fight.

N'joku limped out of a corridor where he had been hiding. "Over here, you Hollow assholes!" he shouted while firing a plasma rifle.

The chamber erupted into chaos. Plasma fire crisscrossed the space, temporarily disrupting Hollow entities wherever it struck. The dogs continued their assault on Broadhurst, keeping him off-balance and separated from Martin.

Frank came up behind the captain. "Sorry, Broadhurst," he said.

An explosion of bone and brains erupted from the transformed Marine's head. The corpse slumped, releasing the Hollow from within.

Martin remained on his knees, the silver contamination still spreading through his body, albeit more slowly now without Broadhurst's direct control. He could feel it moving inside him, cold and alien, rewriting him bit by bit.

Suddenly, Frank was there, kneeling beside him, one hand on Martin's shoulder.

"Hold on," Frank said, reaching for something at Martin's belt—the syringe from Natalia. "I can save you."

Martin shook his head weakly. The silver had reached his vocal cords, making speech difficult. "No . . . too late . . ."

"I know why you did what you did now," Frank said, his voice cracking slightly. "Time for me to do the same for you. You need me, brother, and I need you." His lips quivered. "I'm sorry, Kel."

"I'm sorry too, Cage."

"And I'm also sorry for this, cause it's going to hurt like a motherfucker."

Frank plunged the needle directly into his chest, right where the silver tendrils were thickest, and depressed the plunger.

Fire erupted in Martin's veins. The injector must have also contained a combat stimulant: adrenaline, synthetic endorphins, and a cocktail of other compounds designed to keep a wounded Marine fighting even with catastrophic injuries. It wasn't designed for this purpose, had never been tested against whatever the Hollow were doing to him, but it was Frank's only option.

Martin's heart rate skyrocketed, pounding against his ribs like it might explode from his chest. The silver tendrils beneath his skin seemed to recoil from the chemical invasion, withdrawing slightly before surging forward again, as if two forces were now battling for dominance over his body.

"Hang on, Kel," Frank urged, gripping Martin's shoulders hard enough to bruise. "Fight it, goddammit!"

Cosmo and Rex circled them protectively, occasionally darting forward to drive back approaching Hollow entities before returning to lick at Martin's face, whining anxiously. The taste of dog slobber was absurdly mundane amid such alien horror, and Martin almost laughed despite the agony consuming him.

His vision swam red, blood vessels straining from the stimulant's effects. He could feel his veins hardening, or at least that's what it felt like. The silver material was solidifying, changing from fluid to something more crystalline.

"We have to get out of here!" Bolesky shouted from somewhere nearby.

"Can you stand?" Frank asked, already knowing the answer as Martin slumped further toward the floor.

Without waiting for a response, Frank slung his weapon and bent down, then lifted Martin in a fireman's carry despite his own exhaustion and injuries. The movement sent waves of fresh agony through Martin's transforming body.

"N'joku!" Frank called out. "Take point! Bolesky, Fielding, cover our retreat!"

Martin's consciousness wavered as they moved, the world fading in and out of focus. The stimulant was keeping him alive, but only barely, his system overwhelmed by the combined assault of the drugs and the Hollow transformation.

"Worst rescue ever," he managed to croak against Frank's shoulder.

"Shut up," Frank replied.

Despite everything, Martin felt a weak laugh bubble up from his chest. The absurdity of it all—Frank carrying him through an alien facility, nude and covered in preservation fluid, while silver tendrils rewrote his biology and orbital strikes rained down from above—was almost too much to process.

"Your dog is . . . drooling on my face," Martin said, feeling Rex's tongue lap at his cheek again.

"He likes the taste of silver, apparently," Frank replied, adjusting his grip to better support Martin's weight. "Always knew that mutt was weird."

They were moving through corridors now, following N'joku and Cosmo as the shepherd led them unerringly through the labyrinthine facility. Bolesky and Fielding brought up the rear, firing occasional bursts at pursuing entities.

"They're not following," Fielding reported, checking over his shoulder. "Just . . . watching us leave."

"Don't question our good luck," Bolesky replied tersely.

Martin's world narrowed to the rhythm of Frank's footsteps, and each movement sent jolting pain through his transforming body. The silver material had stopped spreading, halted by the stimulant, but it hadn't retreated either. They were at a stalemate, neither fully human nor fully Hollow.

"Hold on," Frank kept saying, a constant litany of encouragement. "Just hold on, Kel."

Martin wanted to tell him he was trying, that he was fighting with everything he had left, but speech was becoming more difficult. The patterns behind his eyes had returned, the alien data transfer continuing even without Broadhurst's direct connection.

He understood now. The Hollow weren't turning him into one of them—at least, not exactly. They were making him a conduit, a translator, someone who could comprehend their complex geometric language and convey it to humanity. A messenger, as Broadhurst had said.

But the process was imperfect, rushed, possibly damaged by Frank's intervention with the stimulant. The knowledge poured into him was fragmented, incomplete. Vital information about the Halcerites: their weaknesses, their patterns—all corrupted by the aborted transformation.

A particularly violent tremor shook the facility.

"This whole place is coming down!" N'joku shouted.

Then it happened. Martin felt a familiar sensation that he'd experienced once before while gardening on Eden. A sudden, crushing pressure in his chest, as if someone had placed a boulder on his sternum. Pain shot down his left arm, and his jaw tightened involuntarily.

Cardiac arrest.

He remembered that day in the garden vividly—the sun beating down, the peaceful rhythm of weeding interrupted by that same crushing pressure. He'd barely managed to call for Cosmo before collapsing. The VA doctors later told him he'd been clinically dead for nearly two minutes before the emergency responders restarted his heart.

This was worse. Much worse. The stimulant had pushed his already compromised system beyond its limits, and the Hollow transformation was fighting back, creating a perfect storm in his cardiovascular system.

"Frank," he tried to say, but no sound emerged. His vision tunneled rapidly, darkness encroaching from all sides. His heartbeat, previously racing like a runaway train, stumbled, stuttered, then simply . . . stopped.

CHAPTER TWENTY-FIVE

The facility shuddered around them, a deep, resonant groan emanating from somewhere in its core. Frank had been in enough collapsing structures to recognize imminent structural failure when he felt it. The orbital bombardment had stopped, but the damage was done. The facility was coming apart at the seams.

"Move!" Frank shouted, adjusting his grip on Martin's arm as they hurried down the corridor.

Frank ran, wearing only a pair of undershorts he had grabbed from the pile of what was his Lucky armor, stripped off by the Hollow. The effort of half carrying Martin taxed his stamina. Despite being cold, sweat dripped down his scarred muscles.

Martin's feet dragged, his energy failing as the silver contamination spread beneath his skin, pulsing with every labored breath. They had gotten his heart working again, but he was in bad shape and slipping in and out of consciousness.

"I got you, Kel, don't you give up," Frank said. "We have that cigar you promised me."

Rex and Cosmo led the way, the dogs' instincts somehow more reliable than any tactical training in this alien environment. N'joku and Fielding brought up the rear, plasma rifles at the ready, while Bolesky scouted side passages, her weapon raised.

An explosion suddenly threw them all to the ground. Coughing and groans echoed through a cloud of dust.

"Everyone okay?" Frank asked. He helped Martin, who was still breathing but had a weak pulse.

"That isn't from the bombardment," Bolesky said. "I think the Hollow have started a self-destruct sequence."

Frank shot her a questioning look. "How do you know?"

"She's right," Martin hissed weakly. "The knowledge is . . . leaking into me. They're overloading the power systems."

"They don't want their technology to fall into human hands," N'joku said.

Martin nodded, his gaze distant.

"Hang on, brother," Frank said.

A section of ceiling collapsed behind them, forcing them to move faster.

"Two more levels to reach the surface," Fielding reported, checking his tactical display. "Main shaft should be just ahead."

The corridor before them warped and rippled, the metal seeming to liquefy. A Hollow entity emerged, and its silvery form coalesced into something vaguely humanoid.

"Contact front!" N'joku barked, raising his weapon.

The entity flowed across their path, apparently fleeing rather than attacking. It disappeared through the wall, leaving behind a strange distortion in the metal surface.

"They're running," Bolesky said. "Abandoning the facility before it all comes down."

Another violent tremor shook the corridor, dislodging more debris. Frank stumbled and nearly lost his grip on Martin.

"We need to find that main shaft now," Fielding said.

They pushed forward, following Cosmo and Rex's lead as the dogs navigated the increasingly unstable corridors. The maintenance shaft curved upward and grew narrower as they ascended. The walls hummed with energy, strange patterns of light pulsing through what had initially appeared to be solid metal.

"Movement behind us!" Bolesky called sharply.

Frank glanced back to see silvery tendrils probing up the shaft.

"Double time!" he ordered, shifting his grip to practically drag Martin up the incline.

A violent tremor shook the shaft, knocking them against the walls. Martin cried out as his shoulder impacted hard, the silver contamination flaring in response. Frank steadied him, ignoring the fresh cuts opening across his own bare torso from the jagged metal.

"Almost there," N'joku called from ahead. "I can see a junction point."

Another tremor, stronger than before. The facility's systems were cascading toward critical failure. Frank could feel it in his bones, that familiar sense of impending collapse that every veteran developed after enough close calls.

They reached the junction N'joku had spotted, a circular chamber where multiple shafts converged. The lieutenant was already scanning for the best route as he limped forward, his rifle tracking across potential threats.

Martin, who had been drifting in and out of consciousness, suddenly snapped fully awake. His eyes cleared, and the silver patterns beneath them pulsed with renewed intensity.

"That one," Martin said with unexpected clarity, pointing to a shaft that angled sharply upward. "It leads to the surface access hub."

N'joku hesitated, looking to Frank for confirmation.

"You heard the man," Frank said, nodding. "His silver brain upgrade seems to know the layout."

They entered the indicated shaft, which proved steeper than the previous one. Frank's muscles screamed as he hauled Martin up the incline, every step a battle against exhaustion and gravity.

"Almost there," N'joku called back. "I can see the hub!"

Frank looked up to see the harsh glow of emergency systems. Just one more level after that, and they'd reach the actual surface. So close to freedom, to safety.

N'joku emerged into the hub first and helped pull Cosmo and Rex through. Frank maneuvered Martin through the opening next, the effort nearly causing them both to collapse. Fielding and Bolesky followed, weapons trained back down the shaft they'd ascended.

The hub was a vast circular chamber, with tunnels branching out in all directions like spokes from a wheel. One massive central shaft led upward, clearly the main access to the surface. Emergency lights flashed along its length and illuminated the path to salvation.

Frank's momentary relief died as he looked more closely. The main shaft had collapsed, massive sections of metal and rock sealing it completely about twenty meters up.

"Fuck," he breathed.

"We're trapped?" Fielding asked, his composure finally cracking.

"There," Martin said, pointing to one of the smaller tunnels. "Maintenance access. It's narrow, but it should reach the surface."

They moved toward it, hope rekindling, only to halt as silver tendrils began to seep through the metal floor around the tunnel entrance. More appeared from other shafts, flowing like quicksilver to block potential escape routes.

"We're being corralled," N'joku said.

Frank made a quick tactical assessment. The hub was defensible, with clear lines of fire and limited approach vectors. But they were exhausted and low on ammunition, and Martin's condition was deteriorating by the minute. A prolonged stand would only end one way.

"New plan," he said, pointing to the collapsed main shaft. "Bolesky, you're with me. We're going to dig through that blockage."

Without waiting for acknowledgment, Frank moved to the collapsed shaft, Bolesky following close behind. Rex and Cosmo bounded ahead to the rubble and began to dig with their paws.

Frank spotted a void space near the left edge. It was partly obscured by twisted metal paneling. A potential path. "There," he said. "Help me clear that section."

They set to work, pulling away debris and forcing bent metal aside. The dogs assisted, somehow knowing exactly where to dig for maximum effect. Behind them, the first plasma shots rang out as N'joku engaged approaching Hollow entities.

"Multiple contacts!" the lieutenant called. "They're coming from all tunnels now!"

Frank redoubled his efforts, ignoring the fresh cuts opening across his hands and arms as he tore at the jagged metal. Blood slicked his grip, but he pushed through the pain, driven by desperation and the need to get Martin to safety.

"Almost through," Bolesky reported, excitement edging her voice as they cleared enough debris to reveal the void space Frank had spotted.

"It's clear!" he called back to the others. "Let's move!"

Another tremor shook the facility, more violent than any of the previous ones. The hub's structure groaned ominously, support beams visibly bending under unsustainable stress.

"We've got a problem," Fielding shouted over the rumble. "They're everywhere now!"

Frank turned to see Hollow entities flowing in from every tunnel, their silver forms merging and separating like mercury. N'joku fired continuously. Plasma rounds temporarily disrupted the approaching entities, but they re-formed almost immediately and adapted to the weapon's frequency.

"Get Martin through first!" Frank ordered, returning to the defensive line. "I'll hold them here!"

"Negative," Martin rasped, pushing himself upright with visible effort. "No one gets left behind."

He raised his sidearm, the silver patterns beneath his skin pulsing rapidly as he fired. His shots were precise, targeting points where the geometric arrangements were most concentrated. Each hit caused the affected entity to destabilize more thoroughly than N'joku's plasma fire.

"He knows where to aim," Frank realized. "The contamination is showing him their weak points."

"Still not enough," Fielding said.

Frank looked with dread at the ever-increasing number of entities flowing into the hub. It was like an entire swarm of the artificial creatures had broken out of a nest.

"Bolesky, get back to that opening. Take Martin and the dogs through," Frank ordered. "N'joku, Fielding, we'll cover your retreat, then follow."

Bolesky nodded, moving to Martin's side. The injured man resisted briefly, but his strength was failing, the silver contamination sapping his reserves.

"Covering fire!" Frank yelled over a barrage of fire from his rifle. The hub filled with the acrid smell of ionized air, and the coppery stink of the disrupted Hollow entities.

One by one, the Marines made it through the narrow opening Frank and Bolesky had cleared. Frank was last, squeezing through with Rex's help after a Hollow entity nearly pulled him back.

"Good boy." Frank gasped, patting the dog's flank.

Beyond the blockage, the shaft continued upward for another thirty meters before opening to what appeared to be a surface access point. Bolesky and N'joku had taken defensive positions midway up, while Martin leaned heavily against the wall, Cosmo at his side.

"Almost free," Frank said, forcing himself upright despite the burning in his muscles.

A deafening crash sounded from the hub they'd just escaped, followed by the screech of tearing metal. The facility's death throes were accelerating. They needed to reach the surface immediately.

"Move!" Frank ordered, supporting Martin once more as they hurried up the shaft.

They'd covered half the remaining distance, when a powerful quake shook the facility. "This whole place is coming down!" N'joku shouted.

A deep rumbling sound came from above them—not the groaning of failing metal, but something different. Methodical. Deliberate. The surface access point above them began to glow cherry red, the metal heating rapidly.

"Get down!" Frank shouted, pulling Martin to the floor as the others dropped for cover.

The access point exploded inward in a shower of molten metal and debris. Through the newly created opening, intense beams of coherent light sliced down, catching the nearest Hollow entities in their paths. Where the beams struck, the silver forms didn't just temporarily destabilize—they disintegrated completely.

Armored figures dropped through the opening, their specialized weapons firing continuously. CSF Marines in full tactical gear were wielding equipment Frank had never seen before—weapons that emitted not the familiar blue-white of standard plasma rifles, but an ultraviolet frequency that proved devastatingly effective against the Hollow.

The entities retreated, flowing back through the walls in a desperate bid to escape the lethal beams. Within seconds, the shaft was clear of silver threats.

"Area secure," one of the Marines announced, voice modulated through their helmet speakers.

Frank should have felt relief. Instead, wariness prickled along his spine as he noted the Marines' unmarked armor, the lack of unit insignia, the nonstandard weapons. This wasn't a normal rescue op.

His suspicion was confirmed when the lead figure stepped forward, helmet retracting to reveal Natalia's face. Her expression was unreadable as she surveyed them, gaze lingering on Martin's silver-veined features.

"Captain Ivan," N'joku acknowledged, his tone wary.

"Lieutenant," she replied coolly. "Sergeant Cage. I see you found what we were looking for."

"Like you didn't know it was here," Frank shot back, positioning himself protectively in front of Martin.

"We had theories," she replied. "This complex is . . . more extensive than anticipated."

"Bullshit," Frank spat. "Reynolds told us everything before he died."

"Reynolds?" Martin questioned weakly.

"The Marine from the third team she sent here," Frank explained. "The one she claimed was lost in the Gauntlet. They were ambushed as soon as they landed."

Natalia's expression hardened. "Reynolds was part of a classified operation."

"Like the two teams before him?" Frank pressed. "How many Marines have you sacrificed, Captain?"

"The mission parameters required—"

"Shut up," Frank growled. "I'm not interested in your classified bullshit. You knew about the Halcerites and the Hollow, didn't you?"

"We've pieced together fragments," Natalia admitted. "The Halcerites came to this system approximately two thousand years ago and eradicated all life. This was revealed by archeological teams, and the information was classified. We believe they left the Hollow behind, buried on these planets to protect them until their eventual return."

She forced a smile. "Thanks to your work, we have filled in the gaps. Now we have all the information we need to test a weapon that will be imperative to destroying the Hollow and the Halcerites."

"You fucking used us," Frank said.

"I knew you'd get the job done. Trust me, it took some convincing of Shield Command. Most everyone thinks you two are idiots. But I knew better."

Her smile vanished. "Put your hands up, Cage, and step away from Kelvin."

"Like hell," Frank growled, positioning himself more firmly in front of his friend.

"Captain, Martin and Frank helped us survive down here," Fielding said.

Natalia ignored him, her focus entirely on Frank and Martin. "The facility is about to undergo complete structural collapse. We need to extract Master Gunnery Sergeant Kelvin immediately for his own safety."

"Something tells me you don't care about my personal safety but what's contained inside of me," Martin murmured.

"Smart as always, Martin," Natalia acknowledged. "The extraction is specifically for you. The Hollow contamination you've experienced represents critical intelligence about both alien species that Shield Command requires."

She looked Martin up and down.

"We needed a human who could interface with the Hollow network without being completely transformed," she said. "You're our first success, Martin."

"So we were lab rats," Bolesky said in disgust.

"You were Marines following orders," Natalia corrected. "Orders that helped us develop countermeasures against the greatest threats humanity has ever faced—the Halcerites who want to reclaim their system and destroy humanity."

"And now you want to dissect him to learn more about this enemy," Frank concluded, his voice hard.

"Not dissect. Study. The knowledge Martin now carries could save billions of lives. He knows the weaknesses of both the Hollow and their creators: their technologies, their battle plans."

"So we're all expendable?" N'joku asked.

Natalia shrugged slightly. "Strategic concessions to buy time for developing effective countermeasures against an alien species that views humanity as either vermin or lunch."

She took a step forward, looking at the other Marines in turn.

"You'll each receive appropriate medical care at the Department of Strategic Intelligence and Analysis facility. Once you've recovered, you'll be reassigned with commendations."

"What she means," Bolesky cut in, her voice cold, "is they'll erase our memories. DSIA has neural scrubbing technology. Nothing quite like forgetting the last week of your life while they draft up a cover story."

"A necessary security protocol," Natalia replied, not bothering to deny it. "What we're dealing with is beyond standard military classification."

"You're not taking him," Frank stated flatly.

"This isn't a negotiation," Natalia replied, signaling her Marines to advance. "We have extraction orders and the means to carry them out."

The Marines moved forward in practiced formation, weapons ready but not yet aimed directly at the survivors.

A final, massive tremor shook the facility, the strongest yet. The shaft walls buckled, support struts snapping like twigs. Everyone staggered and fought to maintain footing on the suddenly unstable surface.

"This place is coming down now," Natalia said urgently. "Last chance to cooperate."

Frank looked around at what remained of Wolverine-9—N'joku, Bolesky, Fielding, all exhausted and injured but standing firm. He glanced next at Martin, his oldest friend, silver veins pulsing beneath his skin, yet still undeniably himself. Then he looked at Rex and Cosmo, loyal companions who'd fought alongside them through this nightmare.

Something in him hardened, a resolve he hadn't felt since Titan Station.

"Natalia," he said, his voice steady despite the crumbling facility around them, "if you want silver egghead here, you're going to have to kill us all. And somehow, I don't think that's in your orders."

"I figured you'd say that," Natalia said with a frown. She raised a hand, and the special forces stormed forward, firing at Frank and his comrades. He recognized the electrical charge that tore into his body. The same type that Martin had used on him at Titan Station.

Not again, god fucking dammit!

Frank fought the surge, and convulsions, managing to throw his cybernetic fist into the helmet of one of the Marines. The man crumpled from the blow, but two more slammed against Frank and pinned his jerking body against the ground.

Natalia leaned down. "Sorry it had to come to this, Cage. Truly."

"Fuck off, you lying bitch." He grunted.

She shook her head wearily with disappointment. Then she nodded up to the Marine Frank had punched, who was now up on his feet. He lifted and brought a boot down on Frank's face.

The world went dark yet again.

CHAPTER TWENTY-SIX

The world flickered in and out of focus. Martin Kelvin drifted through layers of consciousness, silver patterns pulsing beneath his skin like lightning through storm clouds. He was being carried—that much registered through the haze of pain and transformation. Armored hands gripped him roughly, his body nothing more than cargo to be transported.

Hollow. Halcerites. Warning. Messenger.

The concepts bombarded him in flashes, geometric formations searing themselves behind his eyelids. Not his thoughts, but not entirely alien either. The silver contamination had integrated with his cybernetics, creating something unprecedented: not Hollow, not human, but a bridge between worlds.

Martin forced his eyes open. Sunlight assaulted him, blindingly bright after the darkness of the facility. The silver substance reacted, contracting painfully beneath his skin to shield his enhanced senses. He was outside, he realized. They'd made it to the surface.

But not to safety.

Through silver-tinged vision, Martin took in the scene. A canyon stretched before him, an ancient riverbed cutting through red stone. The facility entrance gaped behind them like an open wound, emergency lights still flickering weakly from its depths. Outside, black armored trucks formed a perimeter, their DSIA insignias reflecting the afternoon sun.

His bearers were Natalia's special forces team. Four of them carried him on a portable stretcher. At least twenty more Marines in full combat gear secured the area, weapons ready. Martin tried to move, but his limbs refused to respond. Some kind of paralytic, he guessed, administered while he'd been unconscious.

Nearby, a cluster of scientists in white environmental suits hovered around portable equipment stations. One crew was pulling sealed body bags out of the facility, accompanied by more Marines in Aegis suits.

One woman in environmental gear approached, her face hidden behind a protective mask. She aimed a scanning wand at him to document the silver propagation through his system.

"Remarkable integration with the cybernetic components," she observed clinically. "The contamination has followed the neural pathways rather than consuming tissue indiscriminately."

"How long until transport can remove him?" Natalia's voice came from somewhere beyond Martin's field of vision.

"Twenty minutes, minimum," the scientist replied. "We need baseline readings before we risk movement to the lab. The contamination appears unstable."

Not unstable. Evolving. Adapting. Learning you.

The alien thought-pattern surfaced and submerged again, leaving Martin gasping. The silver wasn't just changing him physically, it was altering how he perceived reality. Time seemed to stretch and compress in irregular pulses. His senses sharpened to painful clarity, then dulled to near nothingness.

With effort, he turned his head enough to locate Frank and the others. His heart sank. Frank was being restrained by two Marines, his bare torso covered in cuts and bruises, face contorted in fury as he struggled against his captors. Beyond him, Bolesky, N'joku, and Fielding were similarly subdued, being marched toward one of the waiting trucks. Even the dogs were captured; they'd been muzzled and caged in a separate transport.

"Frank," Martin tried to call, but his voice emerged as little more than a hoarse whisper.

A male scientist appeared above him, adjusting what looked like a cranial scanner. "Subject is regaining speech capability," he noted dispassionately. "Increasing sedative levels."

Martin felt a cold sensation of an injector pressing against his skin. With a supreme effort of will, he focused on his cybernetic arm, channeling what remained of his strength. The silver contamination responded, liquefying the metal joints momentarily. His hand shot up and grabbed the scientist's wrist before the sedative could be administered.

"No," he snarled, saliva bursting from his mouth.

The man recoiled in shock, dropping the injector. "The subject has motor control! Containment team, respond!"

Martin's victory was short-lived. Two Marines appeared instantly and pinned his arms while a third prepared another injector. He struggled weakly, the silver contamination flaring beneath his skin in response to his distress.

Not yet. Too soon. Must remain conscious.

Through his struggling, Martin caught sight of Natalia approaching. She observed him with clinical detachment, as if he were a particularly interesting laboratory specimen rather than a man she'd served alongside.

"You're fighting the inevitable, Martin," she said. "The process has already begun. Your consciousness is fragmenting. Soon, what remains of you will be secondary to what you're becoming. That shot Frank gave you can only hold back the infection for so long."

"I still got fight in me," Martin said through clenched teeth.

A flicker of interest crossed her face. "Can you distinguish between your thoughts and the Hollow patterns?"

"Some," he admitted, sensing an opportunity to keep her talking, to delay whatever they had planned.

"That's precisely why you're so valuable. The knowledge you've acquired needs to be extracted, analyzed, processed."

"You mean I need to be dissected," Martin countered, watching her reaction carefully. Even through the silver haze, he could read the truth in her expression. "You don't care about saving everyone. Just the core worlds of the Lort System. The places that matter to Shield Command."

Natalia didn't deny it. "Strategic sacrifices for the greater good. Your military career was built on that principle, Master Guns."

"Never sacrificed civilians," Martin ground out. "Never abandoned our own."

"Really? Did you forget about Titan Station?" Her eyes hardened. "You forced Frank to abandon—"

Martin snarled again, his lips frothing like a wild animal. "That was different."

"Maybe, but relevant. Now prepare for transport. The lab facility is standing by."

Martin's gaze shifted again to Frank, who was still fighting his captors despite the futility. His oldest friend, who'd fought beside him for decades and now faced termination as an inconvenient loose end. Beyond him, N'joku, Bolesky, and Fielding—young Marines who'd survived horrors only to be betrayed by their own. They deserved better. All of them.

The silver patterns pulsed in Martin's brain, bringing fresh pain and a surge of alien knowledge. Fragmented coordinates, weapons capabilities, strategic assessments. The Hollow had been gathering intelligence on humanity for decades, learning their weaknesses.

"Take him away," Natalia said.

A distant crack answered her order. The noise echoed across the canyon, distinctive and familiar to any veteran.

Sniper fire.

One of Natalia's Marines jerked backward, a neat hole appearing in his helmet visor. He dropped to the ground, motionless.

Confusion erupted. A second crack, and another Marine fell. The remaining troops scrambled for cover, weapons raised but with no clear target. Scientists scattered, some ducking behind equipment, others making a panicked dash for the trucks.

"Sniper!" someone shouted. "Multiple positions!"

Three more shots in rapid succession dropped Marines at the perimeter. Precise, professional fire that spoke of military training and high-end equipment.

Natalia drew her sidearm and barked orders as she positioned herself behind a transport vehicle. "Secure the package! Defensive formation!"

Her Marines moved with practiced efficiency and formed a protective cordon around Martin's stretcher. But they were exposed, caught in the open with minimal cover.

Martin felt the paralytic beginning to wear off. Sensation was returning to his limbs, the silver contamination accelerating his metabolism, burning through the chemical restraint. He saw his opportunity.

With a surge of effort, Martin rolled off the stretcher and crashed to the ground in a painful heap. The sudden movement startled the Marines guarding him, creating a momentary distraction.

Frank seized the chance. He drove his head backward into the face of one captor, then twisted violently, breaking the grip of the second. His movements were instinctive from decades of combat experience condensed into seconds of precise violence.

"Bolesky, N'joku, now!" Frank shouted, diving for a fallen Marine's weapon.

The younger Marines reacted instantly. Bolesky executed a perfect sweep kick that toppled her guard, while N'joku, despite his injuries, managed to wrench free and tackle another Marine. Fielding joined the fray, slamming into a Marine who was firing at the canyon ridge.

The dogs added to the chaos. Rex somehow slipped his muzzle and was tearing at the cage door, metal bending under the force of his determined assault. Cosmo barked frantically, spurring his companion on.

A voice boomed across the canyon, amplified and distorted through what sounded like a tactical communications system:

"DSIA operatives! Lay down your weapons immediately or you will all die!"

Armored figures appeared along the canyon ridge, at least thirty of them, all in specialized tactical gear. Their weapons were trained on Natalia's forces with unwavering precision.

Natalia wasn't intimidated. "This is a classified DSIA operation!" she shouted back. "You have no jurisdiction here! Stand down or I will call in an air strike that will wipe you from existence."

Her bluff was called by a hail of precision shots that kicked up dust inches from the feet of her remaining Marines. A warning demonstration of overwhelming firepower.

Frank had seized a plasma rifle and was now crouched behind a transport vehicle's wheel, aiming directly at Natalia. "It's over," he called to her. "You're outnumbered and outgunned."

"You don't understand what's at stake, Cage," she spat back, her weapon still raised. "What's in Martin's head could save billions."

"Not your way," Frank replied. "Not by keeping this all a secret and sacrificing more Marines or civilians."

She shifted her aim toward Martin, who was still struggling to regain full mobility. "Then I'll take what we need right now."

Frank didn't hesitate. His shot caught Natalia in the leg, spinning her around, and she fell with a cry of pain. Her weapon clattered away across the stone.

"Next one's in your head," Frank said coldly.

For several tense seconds, no one moved. Then Natalia raised her hand, grimacing through the pain.

"Goddammit, you are a stupid asshole, Cage," she said.

"Damn straight I am," Frank replied. "Now tell your forces to stand down."

Natalia nodded. "Do it."

They complied reluctantly, placing their weapons on the ground and raising their hands. Almost immediately, black-clad figures began rappelling down the canyon walls. Their armor was nonstandard, clearly custom-built for specialized operations, faces hidden behind tactical masks with enhanced vision systems. They secured Natalia's team methodically, applying restraints and corralling them into separate groups.

Martin managed to push himself to his knees, the silver contamination flaring beneath his skin as he fought for control of his body. Someone approached through the chaos—a tall figure whose confident stride spoke of authority.

The tactical mask retracted, revealing a face Martin hadn't seen in years, a face he'd given up hope of ever seeing again.

"Thomas," he whispered, emotion thickening his voice.

"Hey, Pops, you don't look so good." Thomas Kelvin's expression was a complex mixture of relief, concern, and barely contained rage as he took in Martin's condition. "You really got yourself in some trouble this time."

"Thomas," Martin repeated, still not quite believing. "How . . ."

"Long story," his son replied. "Let's get you stable first."

Another of Thomas's team approached, carrying advanced medical equipment. "Preliminary scan shows the contamination has integrated with his cybernetics. It's not consuming tissue, but it's rewiring neural pathways."

"Can we move him?" Thomas asked.

"Sure can, boss, but carefully."

Boss? Martin thought. Was his son really in charge of this entire merc crew?

Thomas nodded. "We're getting you out of here," he said, looking at Frank and the others. "All of you."

Cosmo bounded over, having been freed from his cage during the confusion. He whined anxiously, licking Martin's face before circling protectively around him.

"Good boy," Martin murmured, finding comfort in the familiar presence.

Across the clearing, Frank approached, now armed with both a recovered plasma rifle and a sidearm. Rex limped faithfully at his side, his hackles still raised at the DSIA Marines.

Thomas straightened as Frank neared, two men sizing each other up with wary recognition.

"Cage," Thomas acknowledged.

"Damn, you grew up, kid," Frank replied.

"Yeah . . . not a kid anymore."

"Right, you're a—"

"Boss," Martin said with a grunt.

Thomas extended his hand. "Thank you for keeping my old man alive down here."

"He did the same for me, kid—Thomas," Frank corrected. His expression softened slightly as he clasped Thomas's hand. "Your timing could've been better, but your entrance was impressive."

Thomas's expression turned grim. "I've been monitoring this operation from the beginning. Dad's involvement raised red flags immediately. We moved as quickly as we could once we figured out what was happening. DSIA's communications are heavily encrypted, but we intercepted chatter about the extraction."

A muscular soldier rushed over to Thomas, whispering, "Marine teams are already inbound from orbit, boss."

Thomas whistled. "Let's pack it up and get to the *Sparrow*," he said.

Frank turned to check on Bolesky, N'joku, and Fielding, who were helping secure the DSIA personnel.

Thomas's medic team helped Martin onto a stretcher. As they prepared to move him, he gasped, back arching as geometric patterns flashed behind his eyes—star charts, tactical assessments, weapons capabilities. He saw images of strange-looking aliens that reminded him of featherless birds, humanoid in some ways, almost like a demon. More information flooded through him, threatening to overwhelm his human mind.

"Information overload," he managed through gritted teeth. "Too much . . . can't process . . ."

Another medic hurried over and scanned Martin with sophisticated equipment. "The contamination is accelerating its integration with his neural network. We need to stabilize him now."

Martin felt a cool sensation at his neck—not a sedative this time, but something else. The pain receded slightly, and the flood of alien data slowed to a more manageable trickle.

"Neural buffer," the medic explained. "It won't stop the contamination, but it should moderate the information transfer rate."

Thomas helped Martin sit up on the stretcher and supported him as the world spun and steadied. "Can you walk with assistance?"

Martin assessed his condition honestly. "I don't think so, and we're in a hurry." A matter of pride, of showing whatever might be watching—human or otherwise—that he wasn't defeated but he didn't want his ego to affect lives.

Thomas nodded, understanding without further explanation. He and Frank helped pick Martin up and carried him.

"I actually kind of like this treatment," Martin said.

"Don't get used to it," Frank replied. "At least not until you lose that gut."

"Man, you two are just like you were when I was a kid," Thomas said.

"Yup, Frank's a dick," Martin said.

"And Martin's an idiot, but he's my idiot." Frank chuckled.

They hauled Martin toward a sleek black ship, predatory in design, clearly built for speed and stealth rather than regulation conformity. It perched on a nearby mesa like a bird of prey, engines humming at ready status.

"*Ghost Sparrow*," Thomas said. "Fastest merc vessel out there. And completely untraceable."

Martin looked over his shoulder and caught sight of Natalia, who was now secured between two of Thomas's operatives. Her leg had been treated with a field dressing sufficient to prevent blood loss, nothing more. The look she gave Martin was one of cold fury mixed with calculation.

"She's behind it all," he said, voice strengthening. "She knew about the Hollow and the Halcerites. She's been preparing for their arrival."

"We'll explain once we're on board," Frank said to Thomas, who looked perplexed.

They carried Martin up the ramp into a cargo bay. The *Ghost Sparrow*'s interior was as impressive as its exterior, with cutting-edge technology seamlessly integrated with combat functionality. Martin was transferred to a specialized medical bay, the containment unit already configured to monitor the silver contamination.

"Where did you get all this?" he asked as Thomas helped settle him into the unit.

"Hard work pays off," Thomas replied. "I'm good at what I do."

"Yeah, you were a good Marine too."

"That again?"

Martin thought back to their last conversation, the one that had caused their falling out. Frank glanced at him but said nothing.

"What I mean to say is you were a good Marine, and you're clearly good at what you do now." Martin nodded. "I'm proud of you, son, and I appreciate you risking your neck for my old ass. I sure as hell don't deserve it."

"You'd do the same for me, Dad."

The ship growled as the engines prepared to launch.

Thomas leaned down. "Tell me what this is all about. I know fragments. Intelligence that didn't add up. Ships disappearing near the outer boundaries. We intercepted a classified communication about enhanced scanning protocols for quantum distortions characteristic of nonhuman vessels, the Hollow."

"The Hollow were trying to warn humanity," Martin said. "At *Squanto*. At Titan Station. Here."

"And Shield Command chose to silence those warnings rather than listen," Frank said. "Certain elements decided it was easier to keep the colonies in the dark about the threats."

The ship hummed to life around them, inertial dampeners engaging as they prepared for departure. Through a nearby viewport, Martin could see the rest of their group being brought aboard—N'joku helping Fielding, whose injuries appeared worse than initially evident; Bolesky already in deep conversation with one of Thomas's team, comparing tactical notes; Cosmo reunited with Rex, the dogs unusually subdued after their ordeal.

Thomas squeezed his shoulder. "Rest now. We'll figure it all out once we're safely away."

Martin nodded, suddenly overwhelmed by exhaustion. The neural buffer was working, containing the worst of the information overload, but his body had been through profound trauma. He needed time to recover, to adapt, to understand what he was becoming.

As the medical bay door slid closed, leaving him in peaceful semidarkness, Martin heard the engines power up to full capacity. The *Ghost Sparrow* lifted off, artificial gravity compensating so smoothly he barely felt the transition.

Through the viewport, he caught a final glimpse of the facility entrance far below, still disgorging smoke and debris as internal systems continued to collapse. Whatever secrets remained down there—Hollow technology, evidence of the Halcerites, proof of Shield Command's betrayal—would soon be buried beneath tons of rubble.

Not just buried. Preserved. Protected until needed again.

The ship banked sharply and accelerated into the clouds. Martin closed his eyes, the alien thought pattern surfaced and submerged again, leaving him wondering how much of it was the Hollow contamination and how much was his own intuition. The line between them was blurring, the silver integration creating something new, something neither fully human nor alien.

"Kel," came a voice. Frank appeared at the doorway, looking in on Martin with concern, a far cry from the resentment and anger from just days ago during their forced reunion.

"You good?" Frank asked.

"Egg head intact but now alien infested," Martin said.

Frank laughed.

"How about you, brother?" Martin asked.

All sense of jocularity passed over Frank; his face hardened at the use of the word.

"Frank?" Martin entreated. "You okay?"

"Yeah, yeah . . ." He reached up to his mouth. "I lost a tooth, but nothing that can't be replaced. I'm more worried about where we go from here."

"And what we do with Natalia . . ."

Frank's response was firm, decisive. "She was going to use us. Now we use her. To explain to brass that will listen what we're up against, what needs to happen to protect this system from the Hollow and the Halcerites."

"Who's going to listen?"

"I know just the person." Frank moved closer, concern evident in his expression. "Rest, Kel. We'll figure it out."

Martin nodded weakly, his consciousness fading to somewhere else—a place of geometric patterns and ancient knowledge, a realm where the Hollow's memories and his own began to intertwine.

His last thought before surrendering to the silver dreams was of Frank and Thomas standing side by side, the two people he trusted most in the universe now working together to save him—and perhaps, through him, to save humanity itself.

The messenger becomes the message. The vessel becomes the content. The warning becomes the weapon.

And then he was drifting through silver-tinged darkness, carried away on currents of alien knowledge flowing like mercury through the recesses of his mind.

CHAPTER TWENTY-SEVEN

Frank shifted uncomfortably in the new Aegis armor. It wasn't Lucky—nothing would ever replace that suit—but the Mark VII had the same reassuring heft, the same whisper of servos as he moved. Thomas had somehow procured it along with the rest of their gear before they landed on Zonova.

The jungle planet sprawled beneath them as Thomas's ship began its descent, accelerating to the top-safe speed and staying low to avoid orbital detection systems. Through the viewport, Frank could see the terrain giving way to familiar mountain ranges that housed the resort city of Elysium. Eighteen years earlier, he and Martin had been here clearing out insurgents who'd been attacking shipping lanes from bases hidden deep in the jungle. Now the area was a playground for the wealthy elite: retired military brass, corporate executives, and government officials who wanted luxury combined with the proximity to what had once been the most dangerous region in the sector.

"Approaching drop zone," announced the pilot.

Frank glanced at the medical pod where Martin lay, silver contamination visible beneath his skin even through the transparent canopy. He had been in an induced coma since their escape from Galean, the neural buffer they'd cobbled together barely containing the flood of alien knowledge overwhelming his system.

"Status?" Frank asked Bolesky, who monitored Martin's vitals.

"Stable, for now," she replied, not looking up from her instruments. "But we're running out of time."

Frank nodded. They were all running out of time—Martin, most immediately, but humanity wasn't far behind if what they'd learned about the Halcerites was true. They were coming back to claim their stake, and they had a new species in their crosshairs to exterminate.

"How's our other guest?" Frank asked.

"Secure," N'joku reported from near the ship's brig.

Captain Natalia Ivan had been surprisingly quiet since their escape from Galean, despite Frank trying his damn best to get her to talk more. Frank wasn't sure if that was a good sign or not. She knew more about Shield Command's plans than she'd shared so far, and he intended to get those answers, one way or another.

"Landing gear deployed," the pilot announced.

Thomas approached, clad in tactical gear that made him look far older than Frank was comfortable acknowledging.

"My team will secure the perimeter," Thomas reported. "Volker's compound is half a kilometer north along the ridge. Heavy security, but mostly automated systems. Tech officer Dilouie will create a blind spot in the sensor grid that should get us to the main terrace undetected."

"Just like the Marines taught you," Frank said with a hint of pride.

Thomas's expression tightened. "Dad taught me that one, actually."

Frank absorbed the correction without comment. Now wasn't the time to dwell on the complex dynamics between father and son. Martin's condition was deteriorating, and they were fugitives with a risky strategy to convince Shield Command of the true Halcerite threat.

"What's your plan once we get to Volker?" Thomas asked.

"Simple approach," Frank decided. "You and I make contact first. We assess his position, then bring in Martin and Natalia if necessary."

"And if Volker doesn't cooperate?"

"We move to Plan B."

"Which is?"

"Haven't figured that out yet," Frank admitted. "Let's hope Plan A works."

They disembarked, Rex following close behind. Frank had wanted to leave him aboard ship, but Rex had nearly torn through a bulkhead at the suggestion. Some battles weren't worth fighting.

The jungle air hit Frank like a physical force—hot, humid, and heavy with oxygen and the scent of vegetation. It triggered memories of his previous time here: the insurgent camps hidden beneath dense canopy, Martin's tactical precision as they cleared compound after compound, the shipping lanes finally secured after months of brutal fighting. They had lost a lot of young Marines out here, some of their bodies still trapped in the tunnels underground.

Frank shook away the memories. He pushed through the underbrush, following Thomas's lead. His Marine training showed in every movement—precise, economical, aware. Frank felt a strange combination of pride and sadness watching Martin's son. The boy had become a formidable man in his father's image, and now his father was dying.

At the crest of a ridge, Volker's compound came into view. It was exactly what Frank expected from a man of his rank and history: elegant but defensible, luxury tempered with tactical considerations.

The main structure was built into the mountain itself, with terraced gardens and a sprawling stone deck that overlooked the jungle canopy below. Solar shields provided protection from Zonova's harsh afternoon sun while allowing unobstructed views of the spectacular landscape.

And there, standing alone on the stone deck, was retired Admiral Don Volker. The man who had ordered the strike on Titan Station—the man who had erased Sarah, Lily, and countless other innocent lives with a single whisper of breath.

Even from this distance, Frank recognized the rigid posture, the military bearing that never quite leaves those who've spent decades in command. Volker was facing away from them, looking out over the jungle, a glass of what was probably expensive whiskey or vodka in his hand. He appeared smaller somehow, diminished by retirement and perhaps by the weight of his decisions.

Thomas signaled his team to secure their position, then glanced at Frank. "You good to go?"

Fuck yeah, I am. Been waiting fifteen years for this.

"If you're asking if I'm going to break his neck, no, don't worry," Frank said.

"Just making sure I still understand plan A," Thomas said with a grin.

With a nod, Frank moved forward, emerging from the jungle's edge onto the immaculately landscaped grounds. He approached the deck silently, weapon holstered but ready. Frank could feel his heart rate accelerating, adrenaline flooding his system. This wasn't from tactical concerns, but from the emotional weight of confronting the man who had taken everything from him.

Frank pulled himself up onto the deck silently.

"You're slipping, Don," he called out. "Your security grid has holes."

Volker didn't turn, didn't even tense. He took another sip of his drink before responding.

"The holes are intentional, Frank. I've been expecting you."

Thomas hurried over, his rifle pointed at Volker.

"You knew we'd come here?" he asked. "Frank, if he knows—"

"I knew Frank would come," Volker replied, finally turning to face them.

His features were more lined than Frank remembered, hair completely silver now, but his eyes remained sharp and calculating.

"Relax, I don't have a team hiding to take you down," Volker said. "It's just me."

Frank stepped up, muscles tensing, part of him wanting to break his promise to Thomas and snap this fucker's neck right where he stood. But that wouldn't help Martin or anyone else.

"After what happened on Galean, there aren't many places a fugitive can go," Volker said. "Especially one with your particular vendetta."

A flicker of anger surged through Frank. "A vendetta I've earned."

"Yes," Volker agreed simply. "You have."

For a moment, they regarded each other in silence—two old warriors with too much history between them, too much pain and betrayal to pretend at easy reunion.

Volker broke first. "A lot of people are looking for you. CSF Intelligence, DSIA, even some private contractors. You're a fugitive with a considerable bounty on your head."

"I'm aware," Frank said. "Good thing I'm smarter than those assholes."

A smile creased on Volker's face, but it vanished as fast as it had formed.

"Did you come to kill me for what I did at Titan Station?" he asked, setting his glass down on the stone railing. There was no fear in his voice, just resignation. "I've been half expecting it for fifteen years."

Frank hesitated a moment. That was good, make him wait.

"No," he said after two long beats. "I came so you can make up for it."

"Oh?"

"I need your help," Frank said through gritted teeth.

Surprise flickered across Volker's face, quickly masked by professional composure. "My help?"

"Shield Command has every gritwipe in the system looking for my old ass because we discovered something on Galean. Something more significant than you, me, or what happened at Titan Station and *Squanto*."

Volker's eyes narrowed, assessing. "The Hollow."

"And their creators," Thomas added. "The Halcerites."

A shadow passed over Volker's face at the mention of the alien species. "Come inside," he said after a moment's consideration. "Whatever you have to say shouldn't be discussed in the open."

He led them through sliding glass doors into a spacious living area that continued the theme of elegant functionality. The furniture was expensive but comfortable, the decor minimal, with subtle defensive features Frank's experienced eye immediately identified: reinforced walls, multiple egress points, concealed weapons caches.

"Who's the muscle?" Volker asked, nodding toward Thomas as he moved to a cabinet and retrieved a bottle of amber liquid.

"Martin's son," Frank corrected. "Thomas Kelvin. Special operations turned private security."

"Mercenary," Thomas clarified, no apology in his tone.

"He's a Marine too."

Thomas nodded.

Volker didn't comment on either as he poured himself another drink. "Where is Martin, by the way? I expected you both."

"That's the other reason I need your help," Frank replied while watching Volker tip back the glass. He resisted the urge to ask for a glass himself, but right now he was sober enough, and smart enough to know that would be a really bad idea.

"He's alive but in bad shape," he said after the brief pause.

Volker's hand paused with the drink halfway back to his mouth. "Sorry to hear that."

"On second thought, I think you should see for yourself." Frank activated his comm. "Bolesky, bring Martin up. And our other guest too."

"Other guest?" Volker questioned.

"Someone who can fill in the gaps in a story that I don't think you're going to believe from my mouth."

Several tense minutes passed before the door slid open again. Bolesky entered first, weapon ready, followed by N'joku pushing Martin's hover chair. Frank heard Volker's sharp intake of breath at the sight of Martin—the silver contamination now visibly pulsing beneath his skin, geometric patterns shifting across his face and arms with each heartbeat.

"My God," Volker whispered, moving closer despite himself. "He's been infected by the Hollow?"

Martin's eyes opened, the irises shot through with silver filaments. When he spoke, his voice had an unsettling harmonic quality but was still formal. "Hello, Admiral."

"Gunny," Volker acknowledged, clearly shaken by his condition.

The door opened once more, and two of Thomas's mercenaries escorted Natalia in. Her hands were bound, her expression a mixture of defiance and resignation.

"Captain Ivan," Volker said, clearly surprised. "This just keeps getting stranger by the minute."

"She sent us to Galean, knowing exactly what we'd find there," Frank said. "A Hollow nest buried deep in the mountains."

Natalia's eyes fixed on Martin, widening at the sight of the silver contamination pulsing beneath his skin.

"Don't worry, I won't touch you," Martin said dryly.

"Actually, that depends on you, *Captain*," Frank said.

"The hell does that mean?" Natalia asked.

Frank moved to stand between them. "Tell Volker everything you know, and you won't find out."

Natalia pressed her lips together, her expression hardening.

"The hard way?" Frank asked. "Okay then."

He glanced at Martin, who nodded almost imperceptibly. As fast as he could manage, Frank grabbed Natalia by the throat and slammed her against the wall, his cybernetic hand tightening just enough to make breathing difficult but not impossible.

"I'm not in a patient mood," Frank growled, his face inches from hers. "We can do this the easy way, or we can get creative."

Volker moved forward. "Frank—"

"Stay out of this, Don," Frank snapped without looking away from Natalia. "You lost the right to object to my methods when you gave the order at Titan Station."

Natalia's eyes were defiant despite her predicament. "Do your worst, Cage. I've been trained to resist interrogation."

"Not like this," Martin said, nudging his hover chair closer. The silver patterns beneath his skin pulsed faster, more intensely, as if responding to his emotions. He raised a hand, silver tendrils beginning to extend from his fingertips toward Natalia's face.

"The Hollow can extract information directly from neural tissue," Martin hissed in a harmonic tone. "Trust me, it's not pleasant. Worse than dying."

"They were going to do that to me too, 'cause of you, Natalia," Frank said. "Even stuffed my naked ass in one of their fish tanks. Trust me, you do *not* want to test me right now."

Fear flickered across Natalia's face as silver tendrils came within centimeters of her skin.

"Want to know what it feels like?" Martin continued, his voice taking on that unsettling harmonic quality. "To have your thoughts, your memories, your very identity pulled apart and examined. To be unmade, piece by piece, until nothing remains but the information we need."

"You're bluffing," Natalia whispered, but uncertainty had crept into her voice. "You don't have that kind of control over it."

"Want to bet your sanity on that?" Frank asked, relaxing his grip just enough for her to speak. "Last chance. Tell us everything."

Natalia looked from Frank to Martin to the silver tendrils hovering before her face. Something in her broke.

"Alright." She gasped. "I'll tell you what I know."

Frank released her and stepped back, but Martin kept his hand raised, the silver tendrils still extended. A reminder of the consequences of further resistance.

Natalia rubbed her throat, her composure cracked. Then she relented, and her shoulders sulked in defeat. Over the next five minutes, she explained everything about the Hollow being a weapon built by the Halcerites, who arrived at the Lort System 2,000 years earlier. After erasing the advanced life, they moved on, leaving the Hollow to guard it until their main forces could arrive to colonize.

Volker shook his head, not from lack of belief, but clearly from dread. Frank had felt the same way when he first began to understand the true intent of the Hollow.

"This is all confirmed?" Volker asked.

"Yes, we know for certain now," Natalia said. "Thanks to Wolverine-9, the fourth squad we deployed to the region on Galean where the Hollow structure was buried."

"But that didn't go as planned, did it?" His eyes shot down to her cuffs.

"No, Admiral, it did not."

Volker looked to Frank, then Martin, and gave them a nod in turn.

"What else?" Frank said. "Tell us *every* detail. If you know their buttholes are their weakness, we want to know. If they have three dicks, we want to know—"

"I get it," Natalia said. She sighed. "God, you haven't changed one bit, Cage . . ."

"Nope, never will."

Natalia was quiet a moment, then raised her chin, almost in pride.

"Shield Command has been developing a weapon," she announced. "The Quantum Disruption Array is the official name. They are going to use it to destroy the Hollow before the Halcerites can arrive."

"Based on what technology?" Volker asked.

"Reverse-engineered from artifacts recovered through the system," she replied, her voice still shaky. "The Array targets the quantum entanglement that allows both Hollow and Halcerite technology to function. One strike could theoretically neutralize both threats permanently."

"Like the rifles your Marines used when they found us at the mining outpost?" Frank said.

"Yeah, but on a massive scale," Natalia said.

"You had that technology available and you sent us in with plasma rifles and grenades, you fuckin—"

"Frank," Martin said.

Frank clenched his jaw and started counting just like his mom told him as a kid. On three, he exhaled and forced a fake smile.

"I'm fine, Kel," Frank said.

"How is brass planning on targeting the Hollow with this weapon?" Volker asked. "And what are the side effects to us? To humanity?"

Natalia's eyes darted to Martin's silver-veined hand that was still hovering near her face. "Potential side effects on our own quantum-based systems," she said. "And possibly on neural activity in sentient beings within the blast radius."

"And deployment?"

Natalia swallowed hard. "We have targeted several Hollow structures across the system and are still searching for more. We will deploy the array at each one."

"Civilian populations in proximity?" Thomas asked.

"All efforts will be made to evacuate."

"You know how that will go," Frank said. "How many colonists gave up everything to move to the System from the slums on Mars, Earth, Europa? They came here for a better life like my own family. They aren't going to give up their homes."

"Unless you tell them about the Hollow," Martin said. "If they see what the Hollow can do . . ."

The tendrils shot out closer toward her face, but she remained firm.

"Shield Command wants this bottled up. Anyone that stays despite evacuation orders is an acceptable loss," Natalia replied, some of her clinical detachment returning despite her fear. "We will destroy the Hollow and the Halcerites. Whatever the cost."

"Just like Titan Station," Frank said, looking pointedly at Volker. "One more sacrifice for the greater good."

"The greater good is to protect our species, Frank," Natalia said. "When are you going to understand that?"

Martin finally withdrew his hand, the silver tendrils receding beneath his skin. Natalia visibly sagged with relief, though she maintained her rigid posture.

Volker set his glass down carefully. "Not exactly the same. Titan Station was an emergency response to an immediate threat. This is . . . premeditated."

"It's mass murder," Thomas said bluntly. "There has to be another way."

Volker turned to Martin. "Can you confirm this? Does the Hollow knowledge support her claims? Are the Halcerites coming back to destroy humanity?"

Martin nodded, the silver patterns beneath his skin pulsing more rapidly. "The Halcerites will return—when, I don't know."

"Do you know the timeline?" Frank asked, his attention back on Natalia.

She hesitated again. Martin raised his hand slightly, silver filaments shifting.

"Not exactly," she answered. "It could be tomorrow, or it could be ten years, or even one hundred."

"When does Shield Command plan on using the array?" Volker asked.

"It will be operational in two weeks, and we will strike the Hollow then."

"What about the Halcerites? What is your plan for them?" Thomas asked.

"Same they have for us," Natalia said. "Eradication."

"Do you even know what they look like? What their capabilities are?" Martin asked. His hand twitched, quicksilver flowing rapidly beneath his skin. "The Hollow integration gives me access to their knowledge. Including vital information about Halcerite physiology and technology. Their weaknesses, their vulnerabilities. There might be a way to repel them without sacrificing anyone."

"We know how to repel them," Natalia said. "The Hollow are their weapons, and if we destroy them, then Shield Command believes the same weapon will work on their creators."

"Big fucking gamble," Frank said. "You're risking everything on this array."

"I'm following orders to save humanity in what we believe is the best and most logical path forward," Natalia countered.

"Killing innocent people on a theory," Frank said, anger rising in his voice. "Families. Children. Just like on Titan Station."

The reference hung heavy in the air as Frank and Volker locked eyes.

"There will always be people like you," Frank continued bitterly. "People who choose the greater good over saving the few, even if the few are tens of thousands. Even if the few include families like mine. Now you have a chance to help us make up for your decision."

"How?" Volker asked.

"Give me time to figure out another way to fight back," Martin said.

"You think the enemy will allow that?" Natalia asked. "The silver contamination has compromised your mind. There's no way to know if what you're seeing is real or what the enemy wants you to see."

"I want to hear what Martin knows," Volker intervened. "If there's even a chance of an alternative . . ."

Natalia shook her head. "Admiral, with all due respect, you know better than anyone how big this threat is and what we must do to respond. Shield Command has committed to this course. They won't change direction because a few rogue Marines, one of them infected by the enemy, and a retired admiral ask nicely."

"Then we'll have to be more persuasive," Frank replied coldly. He turned to Martin. "But first we need to get more information from you. Can you do that?"

"Each time it spreads further, but yes, I will try," Martin said.

He closed his eyes, concentrating. The silver patterns beneath his skin intensified as he accessed the alien knowledge. When he opened his eyes again, the filaments had spread further, nearly consuming his natural iris color.

"I see their fleet, I see them . . . demons," he said. "They look like demons."

There was silence for a long moment.

Martin began to shake, and Frank reached out to him, fingers just shy of touching his friend, who pulled back. "Stay away, Cage."

Frank hesitated, heart pounding.

"He needs specialized medical care," he said. "Someone that can help him process what he's seeing."

"No one can help with that," Natalia said. "I know—"

"You don't know jack shit," Frank said.

Natalia raised her chin, defiant but quiet.

Frank glared at Volker, waiting for his answer.

"I say it's worth a shot," said the admiral. "I'll make arrangements. I know a research physician on DaVinci Station who might be able to help stabilize his condition."

"We'll need secure transit," Thomas interjected. "My ship is likely being tracked by now."

"I have resources. Old patterns never completely fade away in our line of work."

"Thank you," Thomas said.

Frank felt the words form on his tongue, but he couldn't speak them. Not yet, not to this man who had taken Frank's family from him. He would never forgive him, but he would give him the chance to right his wrongs.

As the admiral busied himself with preparations, Frank moved to Martin's side, aware of Natalia watching them with calculating eyes even as Thomas's men returned her to restraints.

"You holding up?" Frank asked quietly.

Martin managed a weak smile. "I'll last long enough to see this through."

"You are too stubborn to die properly," Frank said, forcing lightness into his tone.

"Like you're one to talk. How many times have I saved your ass now?"

"I've lost count. But who's keeping score?"

They shared a brief moment of familiarity amid the chaos—two grumpy old Marines facing one more impossible mission together.

"Think we can trust him?" Thomas asked, nodding toward Volker.

Martin's expression turned thoughtful. "I think he's carried Titan Station with him every day since. Whether that's redemption enough . . ."

"It isn't," Frank said flatly. "No peace until I know Sarah and Lily's sacrifice helped save humanity, and wasn't just a callous command decision."

"It's a start, and it's the only option we've got if we want to save innocent lives."

Frank nodded, accepting the reality of their situation if not entirely at peace with it. Titan Station—Sarah and Lily—remained an open wound that would never fully heal. But right now, humanity's survival took precedence over personal vendettas, even ones as justified as his.

Frank turned his gaze to the jungle stretching to the horizon that was lush and vibrant. This planet had survived insurgencies, wars, and colonial exploitation. It had endured and adapted, just as humanity would need to in the face of what was coming.

The Halcerites were returning to claim what they saw as theirs. But they would find that humanity wasn't so easily displaced. Not while Frank had breath in his body. Not while Martin still carried the knowledge they needed. Not while there was even a chance to stop Shield Command from unleashing a weapon that could kill hundreds of thousands of innocents if there was another way.

"One more battle," Frank said, more to himself than to Martin.

"The biggest one yet," Martin agreed, silver light pulsing beneath his skin.

Behind them, Volker coordinated their departure, his voice carrying the authority of a man who had made the hardest decisions and lived with their consequences. Natalia watched them all with wary calculation, her belief in Shield Command's solution unshaken despite everything.

And perhaps, Frank thought as he watched the complex interplay of allies and adversaries around him, *this would be the one that finally brought closure—one way or another.*

CHAPTER TWENTY-EIGHT

The medical bay on DaVinci Station gleamed with cold efficiency, its sterile white walls and constant hum of monitoring equipment creating an artificial cocoon of calm. Frank shifted uncomfortably in his bed and winced as the movement pulled at the medi-patches covering the worst of his wounds. They'd insisted on treating him for multiple lacerations, two bruised ribs, and what the doctor had called "severe systemic exhaustion." As if not sleeping for three days while fighting alien technology was something they had a proper medical term for.

What he really wanted was a drink, mostly due to boredom. But if Martin could resist the Hollow infection, Frank could resist drinking.

In the adjacent bed, Martin's condition had deteriorated in the hours since their arrival. The silver contamination had spread visibly, geometric patterns pulsing beneath his skin in complex rhythms that sometimes synchronized with the medical monitors. His breathing was labored. Seeing him like this was almost harder than Frank could manage to bear. Especially without any alcohol to numb himself.

If he's going to suffer, fuck it, so will I.

"Looking good, egghead. No alien is going to be able to conquer that dome of yours," Frank said, breaking the silence.

Martin's eyes fluttered open, the irises clouded with silver filaments that caught the light in unnatural ways. "You always were a terrible liar, Cage." His eyes focused on the bandages. "Those from the ceiling that kicked your ass?"

"It was a very aggressive ceiling," Frank defended himself. "Came right at me."

"Right, next you'll tell me the floor was out to get you too."

"Don't get me started on the floor. Sneaky bastard."

They shared a laugh that turned into a grimace for Martin as a wave of pain hit him. The silver patterns beneath his skin flared in response, geometric shapes briefly visible before subsiding again.

"Looks like your new tattoos don't appreciate humor," Frank said.

"Just jealous they don't have your sparkling wit," Martin replied, closing his eyes briefly as the pain subsided. "Though I gotta say, these things are handy for impressing the ladies. Built-in light show."

"Yeah? How many ladies you planning on impressing from that bed, Romeo?"

"More than you will with those ugly-ass medi-patches."

Frank snorted. "Thomas says I'm rocking the wounded warrior look."

"Thomas is being kind. You look like something Rex dragged in after it died twice."

Speaking of the dogs, Rex and Cosmo lay between their beds, the rottweiler and German shepherd maintaining a vigilant watch despite the secure surroundings. Somehow, they'd managed to convince the station security that separating the Marines from their canine companions would cause more problems than it solved.

"Remember that time on Helios?" Frank asked, settling back against his pillows. "When you fell in that pit of what we thought was mud?"

Martin groaned. "Don't remind me."

"Turned out to be the local equivalent of a sewage treatment facility. You smelled so bad the squad made you walk ten meters behind us for the entire trek home."

"Yeah, and who was the genius who said, 'Looks solid enough to me, Kel, go on ahead?'"

Frank grinned. "I was encouraging initiative in your troops and supporting your lead by example strategy."

"There you go again with the lying. Just admit it, you were being an asshole."

"Some things are consistent in this universe."

They fell into a comfortable silence, the years of camaraderie—interrupted by the bitterness after Titan Station—somehow restored in the face of their current crisis. Frank studied his friend, noting how the quicksilver ebbed and flowed beneath his skin, sometimes forming complex geometries before dissolving back into seemingly random movement.

"It's accelerating," Martin said after a while, as if reading Frank's thoughts. "The integration. Information coming faster now. Harder to process."

Frank's smile faded. "What's it like? Having all that alien crap in your head?"

Martin considered the question, the gleaming array shifting beneath his skin as he focused. "Like . . . trying to understand a language you've never heard before, but it's being downloaded directly into your brain. Fragments of knowledge, tactical data, star charts, biological information . . . but none of it organized in a way that makes sense to human cognition."

"Are you getting any better at controlling it? Accessing specific information?"

"Sometimes. Other times, it's like . . . like trying to drink from a fire hose. Everything comes at once, and I can't separate what's useful from what's just noise."

The medical bay door hissed open, interrupting their conversation. Thomas entered, his expression tight with worry that he tried to mask when he saw them both conscious. Behind him came a woman in a white medical coat, her bearing precise and military despite her civilian attire.

"Good to see you both awake," Thomas said, approaching Martin's bed first. "You had us worried for a while there, Dad."

"Takes more than some alien goo to shut me up," Martin replied, though the effort of maintaining his humor was visibly taxing.

Rex and Cosmo perked up at Thomas's entrance but remained in their protective positions between the beds.

"Gunnies," the woman greeted them, moving directly to check Martin's monitors. "I'm Dr. Eliza Malzhan, xenobiology division. Admiral Volker brought me in to help."

"Have you treated this before?" Frank asked.

"Nothing exactly like this," Malzhan admitted, running a specialized scanner over Martin's chest and head. "But I've studied Hollow contamination for the past eight years. The integration patterns forming in Master Gunny Kelvin's neural pathways are . . . extraordinary."

"That's one word for it," Martin said dryly.

Malzhan leaned down for a closer look. "Your cybernetic enhancements created an interface rather than allowing complete replacement. The alien elements are following those pathways, creating a bridge between your human neural network and the Hollow communication matrix."

"Can you help him?" Thomas asked.

"I believe so," Malzhan replied, though her cautious tone suggested limitations. "I'm not sure if I can reverse this fully, but we can stabilize the integration, help him maintain control rather than being overwhelmed."

The door slid open again, and Admiral Volker entered. Unlike the doctor, he made no attempt to examine the patients, instead moving to stand at the foot of their beds with his hands clasped behind his back.

"Doctor, your assessment?" he asked without preamble.

"The contamination is advanced but potentially manageable," Malzhan reported. "Master Gunny Kelvin's cybernetic enhancements have created a unique integration pattern that I haven't seen in previous cases. With the right approach, we might be able to help him control and direct the flow of information."

"Good," Volker said with a nod. "Because we need that information now. I'm heading to Shield Command with whatever intelligence we can gather to convince them to cancel the Quantum Disruption Array deployment."

Frank exchanged a glance with Martin, whose silver-traced eyes narrowed at the news.

"You're going to meet with them directly?" Thomas asked.

"I've called in every favor I have," Volker replied. "Several admirals who still respect my opinion have agreed to hear me out, but I need more than just my word and your testimony. I need concrete intelligence about the Halcerites: their weaknesses, their capabilities, their intentions. Without that, I can't convince them to abandon their current plan and consider something else."

Malzhan frowned. "Admiral, Gunny Kelvin needs stabilization treatment before we attempt any significant information extraction. His neural pathways are already under extreme stress."

"We don't have that luxury, Doctor," Volker countered. "Shield Command is committed to the Array. I need something concrete to show them why this is the wrong approach, something only Martin can provide."

"There is a procedure," Malzhan said reluctantly. "A neural interface that could potentially allow direct access to the Hollow information matrix through Gunny Kelvin's cybernetic pathways. But it's experimental, and the strain could kill him—"

Frank sat up straighter despite the pain from his ribs.

"Kill him?" he asked.

Malzhan hesitated, then nodded. "Yes. The neural load could overwhelm his human consciousness entirely. There's no way to predict how stable the connection will be or what forcing such an interface might do to his remaining organic neural tissue."

"No," Thomas said immediately, stepping between the doctor and Martin's bed. "No way. We'll find another approach."

"There isn't time," Volker insisted. "Once the Array is deployed, Shield Command will proceed regardless of consequences."

"Do it," Martin said, his voice stronger than it had been all day.

All eyes turned to him. The silver patterns beneath his skin had intensified, pulsing with a steady rhythm that seemed almost deliberate.

"Dad, you can't be serious," Thomas protested. "This could kill you—or worse, turn you into . . . into something else entirely."

"It's already doing that," Martin replied calmly. "Might as well make it useful before I forget which memories are mine and which belong to an alien weapon system."

Frank studied his friend, seeing the determination in those silver-streaked eyes. The same stubborn resolve that had kept them both alive through decades of impossible situations.

"Martin," he said quietly, "you don't have to do this."

"Actually, I do," Martin corrected him. "You'd do the same if our positions were reversed."

Frank couldn't argue with that. He would have made the same choice, the same sacrifice.

"Thomas," Martin continued, turning to his son, "I need you to trust me on this. The information I'm carrying could save millions of lives—maybe billions. But it's coming in fragments, pieces I can't put together fast enough on my own."

Thomas's expression was anguished, caught between respect for his father's decision and desperate fear of losing him. The complex history between them—the years of estrangement after Thomas left the Marines, the reconciliation that had come so late—all of it visible in the tension in his features and posture.

"There has to be another way," he insisted, though with less conviction.

"There isn't," Volker said. "Not in the time we have left."

Malzhan looked between them all, then sighed. "If we're doing this, we need to prepare immediately. The neural interface system takes time to calibrate, and Gunny Kelvin will need preliminary stabilization at the very least."

"How long?" Volker asked.

"Four hours minimum," she replied. "And I'll need specialized equipment from the research lab on Level 6."

Volker nodded. "You'll have whatever you need, Doctor." He turned to Frank. "And you should be resting, Gunny Cage. We'll need you at full strength for what's coming."

"I'm staying with him," Frank said in a tone that brooked no argument.

The admiral didn't waste time trying to change his mind. "As you wish. I'll be in the command center coordinating our response. Dr. Malzhan will keep me updated on your progress."

After he left, an uncomfortable silence fell over the medical bay. Malzhan moved to a terminal, already beginning preparations for the procedure. Thomas remained by Martin's bedside, his expression still troubled.

"It'll be okay, son," Martin said, reaching out to grasp Thomas's wrist with his silver-streaked hand. "I'm tougher than I look."

Thomas managed a weak smile. "I've always seen you as strong. When you were out on all those missions, I wasn't worried, and I would tell Mom you were a superhero, that you couldn't die out there."

A look of regret passed on Martin's face.

"I always wanted to believe him, because I couldn't help but worry," came a female voice from the doorway.

They all turned to see a tall, elegant woman with steel-gray hair enter the medical bay. Despite her civilian clothes, she carried herself with rigid military bearing from years of being married to a Marine like Martin.

"Mom?" Thomas said in surprise.

Lucia Kelvin slowly approached Martin's bed, her expression unreadable as she took in the silver contamination visible beneath his skin. Frank hadn't seen her in over fifteen years, not since she left Martin. She looked older, of course, but still formidable—the same sharp intelligence in her eyes, the same no-nonsense demeanor.

"What are you doing here, Lucia?" Martin asked, genuine confusion in his voice.

"Admiral Volker contacted me," she replied simply. "Said you were injured. Again." Despite her words, there was no real bite to her tone. "Thought I'd come and see you just in case I never got the chance again."

Martin's mouth quirked up at one corner. "You came all this way just to say hello?"

"Old habits," she replied, but the ghost of a smile played at her lips. She turned to Frank. "You look terrible, Cage. I figured you'd be here."

"Nice to see you too, Lucia."

She nodded to him, then back to Martin. "Thomas explained what happened to you. I'm sorry, Martin."

"Life I chose," Martin said. "I knew the risks."

Lucia studied him for a long moment, then nodded. "Always the hero," she said, but there was something in her voice Frank couldn't quite place; not quite pride, not quite resignation, but some complex mixture of both.

"Hero is an understatement," Frank said. "Crazy part is, I never thought that egghead would have the knowledge to potentially save humanity."

There were a few chuckles, interrupted by Dr. Malzhan, who cleared her throat. "I need to begin preparations," she said. "If you could all give us some space for the preliminary treatments . . ."

"I'm staying," Frank, Thomas, and Lucia said in near-perfect unison.

Malzhan looked like she might argue, then thought better of it. "Very well, but stay clear of the equipment. And the dogs will have to leave, I'm afraid. This is precision work."

As the doctor began setting up various devices around Martin's bed, Frank caught his friend's eye.

"You sure about this, Kel?" he asked quietly.

Martin raised a hand, looking at the silver patterns beneath his skin pulsing steadily. Then he lowered it and looked at Frank. "No one else can do it, and someone has to."

Frank held his gaze for a long moment, then nodded. "Alright. But if you die during this thing, I'm going to be seriously pissed off."

"Wouldn't want to inconvenience you," Martin replied dryly.

"Damn right. I've got plans that require you alive."

"Such as?"

"Retirement," Frank said with a straight face. "Two old Marines on a beach somewhere. I'll buy you a sombrero to protect your bald head from the rays."

Martin actually laughed at that, a genuine sound that momentarily pushed back the tension in the room. "You'd last about three days before starting a bar fight."

"Three and a half, at least," Frank corrected. "I'm mellowing in my old age."

"You two haven't changed a bit," Lucia said.

She stepped back as Dr. Malzhan began attaching neural monitors to Martin's temples and chest. Thomas and his mother watched from the foot of the bed, united in their concern despite whatever complicated history lay between them.

Frank settled back in his bed, watching as the preparations continued. Through the observation window, he could see Volker conferring with station officers, the admiral's bearing that of a man who'd carried the weight of impossible decisions. In a few hours, they would either have what they needed to change humanity's course, or Martin would be gone.

CHAPTER TWENTY-NINE

Frank sat in the copilot's chair of the *Ghost Sparrow*, his feet propped up on the console as he stared out at the vast emptiness of space beyond the viewport. DaVinci Station loomed just off their starboard side, its clinical white structures a stark contrast to the *Sparrow*'s sleek, predatory lines. The docking clamps held them secure to the station's outer ring—close enough for necessary access but positioned for a quick departure if things went south.

Frank couldn't argue with the logic. They were fugitives now, after all.

Lucia had remained at the station with Martin for the procedure. That helped Frank relax some, knowing his friend wasn't by himself.

Frank rolled Martin's unlit cigar between his fingers, occasionally bringing it to his nose to savor the rich tobacco scent. He was saving it to smoke later, after Martin got better.

Behind him, Rex and Cosmo lay curled up next to each other by the hatch. Frank envied their simplicity sometimes.

"You gonna light that thing, or just fondle it all day?" Thomas asked, dropping into the pilot's seat beside him.

"Waiting for your old man to wake up," Frank replied, tucking the cigar back into his breast pocket. "He promised to smoke one with me."

Thomas nodded, the gesture so reminiscent of Martin that Frank had to look away.

"Going to be a long four hours," Frank said, holding up his watch for the tenth time since they had arrived in the cockpit.

"Something else to pass the time then?" Thomas asked.

He reached beneath the console and pulled out a bottle of whiskey and two glasses. He poured a generous measure into one and slid it toward Frank, then recapped the bottle without serving himself.

"Don't drink?" Frank asked, lifting the glass.

"Dad's influence. Haven't touched the stuff in years," Thomas replied. "Keep it for guests and negotiations. In my line of work, sometimes you need to get the other guy loose-lipped."

Frank nodded appreciatively. Martin's sobriety had been hard-won, and it made sense the man would have impressed that upon his son after his own struggles. Frank sniffed the whiskey, inhaling the almost intoxicating aroma. "Good stuff."

A week ago, he would have easily given in to the temptation without a thought. But things had changed dramatically over that time. He had a mission, a purpose—lives were on the line. More lives than perhaps ever before.

Sure as hell seemed like a good time to give up drinking.

Frank passed the glass back. "Maybe another time."

"Fair enough." Thomas poured the whiskey back in the bottle.

The ship's proximity alert pinged softly. Through the viewport, Frank could see a patrol skiff making its rounds, scanning docked vessels. Thomas reached over and dimmed the external running lights, the gesture automatic, practiced.

"Third patrol in two hours," Thomas noted. "Station security's been doubled since we arrived."

"Volker must be pulling some serious strings to keep us hidden," Frank said. "Shield Command doesn't usually miss fugitives parked at their back door."

Thomas snorted. "They're not missing us. They're just pretending to while Volker makes his case to the admiralty." He tapped a display on the console, bringing up the CSF Security Network. "Look at this."

Frank leaned forward and grimaced at his own face staring back from a wanted bulletin. The bounty figure beneath his name had increased substantially since the last time he'd checked.

"Five million credits?" Frank let out a low whistle. "That's a lot of beer."

"It's not just you." Thomas swiped across the display. Martin's face appeared, followed by Bolesky, N'joku, and the rest of the survivors from Galean. "Shield Command has designated everyone who made it off that planet as 'high-risk security threats.' How long before Volker decides we're more valuable handed over than protected?" Thomas's tone was pragmatic, not accusatory. "You sure you trust him?"

"Hell no, I don't trust him." Frank shrugged. "That's why you're keeping the engines warm, isn't it?"

Thomas's lips quirked in a half smile. "Always have an exit strategy. First rule of survival." He gestured toward several alerts blinking on secondary displays. "I've got the crew running continuous scans for approaching vessels, and Dilouie's monitoring Shield Command frequencies. Any whisper of an incoming strike force, and we're gone."

"And Martin?"

"Dad's portable enough. The medical pod is self-contained, and we've got the doctors' protocols stored. We can manage his care until we reach sanctuary."

Frank raised an eyebrow. "You have a sanctuary lined up already?"

"I have several," Thomas replied with a hint of pride. "Mercenary work has its perks. Corporate interests who'd love to get their hands on Hollow intelligence before Shield Command does. Plus some old contacts in the Outer Colonies who owe me favors."

"Clever kid." Frank gave him a respectful nod.

Thomas tapped another display, checking something, then relaxed slightly. Frank didn't even ask him what it was that had captured his attention. The kid knew what he was doing, that was for damn sure. Especially after he had saved their asses on Galean.

"He talked about you, you know," Thomas said after a moment. "Even after all that bad blood."

"That so?" Frank asked.

"Yeah." Thomas leaned back in his chair, studying Frank with a gaze that was analytical, professional. It was the look of a man who'd seen enough combat to know how to read people. "Said you were the stubbornest bastard he'd ever met. Said that's why you were so hard to kill."

Frank chuckled despite himself. "Pot calling the kettle black."

"He also said you were the best Marine he ever served with."

Frank said nothing, just stared out at the stars. The cigar in his pocket felt heavier somehow.

"I've read the reports from Titan Station," Thomas continued. "The unredacted ones."

Frank's jaw tightened. "Classified. How'd you get those?"

Thomas shrugged. "I have my ways. Mercenary work opens certain doors."

"Right. The job that broke your father's heart." There was no judgment in Frank's tone, just statement of fact.

Thomas's eyes hardened slightly. "He ever tell you why I left the Corps?"

Frank shook his head.

"My first deployment was to Sig-4AV during an uprising of locals. Shield Command told us we were putting down violent insurgents." Thomas's voice was eerily steady. "Truth was, they were civilians protesting mining conditions. Toxic exposure had killed thousands already."

Frank watched as Thomas's hands clenched into fists on the armrests.

"I followed orders," Thomas continued. "We all did. Found out later we'd been sent in to make an example, discourage other colonies from similar 'disruptions to productivity.'" His jaw tightened. "Dad couldn't understand why I wouldn't re-up after that. Said the Corps needed good Marines to prevent those kinds of mistakes."

"He wasn't wrong," Frank said quietly.

"Maybe not. But I couldn't wear the uniform anymore." Thomas looked Frank directly in the eye. "At least as a mercenary, I can choose which orders to follow."

Frank nodded slowly. He couldn't argue with that logic, not after everything he'd seen. "Your father always believed in the system. Even when it failed him."

"Yeah, well, we can't all be war heroes. Some of us have to be practical." Thomas's voice carried an edge of old resentment. "Not that it matters now. If those Halcerites are really coming—"

"They're coming," Frank said quietly. "Trust me on that."

A soft beep from Thomas's wrist device interrupted them. He checked it quickly. "Natalia's being moved by Volker's people."

Frank knew it was happening soon, but suddenly he wasn't sure this was the best option. Natalia was leverage, and evidence for them to prove what they knew. But Volker had insisted on taking her with him when he went to his allies.

"You think this is going to work?" Thomas asked.

"Nope, and I hate counting on those two, but like I said, our options are slim to . . . we don't have any."

Thomas agreed with a nod. "Strange times, strange allies."

The cockpit fell silent. The distant hum of the station's docking mechanisms and the soft purr of the *Sparrow*'s systems created a cocoon of white noise around them. Outside, stars glittered against the void.

"You think he'll make it?" Thomas asked.

Frank met his gaze. "If anyone can survive, it's your old man. He's a committed bastard when he has a plan. That garden of his—you ever see it?"

"Once, about three years ago. The last time we talked . . ."

"So then you know he put everything into that place. Same way he used to approach missions back in the day. Total commitment."

"That's why you two worked so well together. Different approaches, same intensity."

"We balanced each other out," Frank admitted. "He was the measured one. I was the crazy bastard willing to try anything."

"What happened? Between you two, I mean. After Titan."

Frank looked at the bottle of whiskey, fighting the urge to burn the memories. Then he looked away and sighed. "He made a choice for me. Saved my life when I wanted to die with my family. Took me fifteen years to realize he did exactly what I would have done in his place."

Thomas studied him for a long moment.

The proximity alert sounded again, more urgently this time. Thomas checked the display, his brow furrowing. "Military transport just docked on the opposite side of the station."

"Strike team?" Frank asked.

"Too small. Looks like a courier vessel." Thomas's fingers flew across the controls, bringing up enhanced sensor readings. "Two personnel, minimal armament. Probably just delivering orders or personnel."

Frank relaxed slightly, but his hand still drifted toward the sidearm strapped under the console. Thomas had insisted on weapons being within reach at all times since they'd arrived. Old merc habits, he'd explained, but Frank approved.

The comms unit suddenly crackled to life. "Captain? You need to get down here." One of Thomas's crew said, voice tense.

Thomas straightened immediately. "What is it, Dilouie?"

"We're picking up something strange," replied the technician.

Thomas and Frank exchanged a look.

"Show me," Thomas ordered.

Not a minute later, the tall and muscular technician with wavy brown hair rushed into the cockpit. He took a seat at the main display.

"Stand by," he said.

The main display illuminated with a complex waveform pattern, oscillating rhythmically across multiple bands. Even to Frank's untrained eye, the mathematical precision was obvious.

"What am I looking at?" Frank asked, leaning forward.

"Quantum distortions across multiple frequencies, but . . . they're synchronized somehow," Dilouie said. "It's similar to Hollow signatures, but more structured, more powerful. And here's the weird part: I'm detecting it from multiple sources simultaneously."

"Multiple sources?" Thomas's brow furrowed. "Like what, ships?"

"No, sir. Planets."

Frank felt his heart flip. "Planets? Which ones?"

Dilouie's voice held a note of disbelief. "That's what's crazy. We're picking this up from at least four different bodies in the system. Galean, in the vicinity of the mining outpost where you found the Hollow. On Illior, deep under the western oceans. Dorn, on the vast golden plains, and on Zonova, in the Proxi Mountains."

"All four, at the same time?" Thomas said.

"Yes, the signal is identical on all of them," Dilouie insisted. "Same frequency, same modulation, same pattern. It started exactly seventeen minutes ago, all at once."

Frank stood abruptly and moved closer to the display. "Can you isolate the pattern?"

"Working on it. Hang on."

The screen shifted, displaying the isolated waveform. Frank stared at it, recognition dawning. The geometric shapes matched what he'd seen on the Hollow's surface—the complex mathematics that seemed to be their language.

"I've seen this before," he said quietly. "These patterns—they're communication."

Thomas's eyes narrowed. "Communication to whom?"

"I'm tracking the signal trajectory now," Dilouie reported. "It's . . . it's being broadcast outward. Beyond the system. Beyond the range of our sensors."

Frank's gaze locked with Thomas's, understanding dawning simultaneously.

"It has to be a beacon," Frank said, the realization settling like a stone in his gut. "Or a message. They're calling their creators."

"The Halcerites," Thomas said.

"Warning them about something, or summoning them."

"About us."

Frank couldn't help but feel partly responsible. The timing told him the Hollow were responding to what had happened at the mining outpost. He thought back to what the Hollow had said through Broadhurst when he threatened them.

"Maybe I should have been nicer down there," Frank mused. "Chosen my words more carefully."

"What did you say, exactly?" Thomas asked.

"Something like if they come, it's their funeral. And if these Halcerturds want a war, the Marine Corps will make them wish they were never conceived."

"Jesus, Cage," Thomas said.

Dilouie chuckled but then stopped when Thomas looked up.

"Are you picking up any other signatures?" Thomas asked. "Anything incoming?"

A pause. "Nothing yet, boss, but our range is limited."

Thomas turned to Frank. "If they're calling the Halcerites—"

"Then they're already on their way," Frank finished. "This isn't a warning. It's a dinner bell."

The implications settled over the cockpit like a shroud. Four planets, all signaling in perfect synchronization. The Hollow hadn't just been on Galean—they had structures buried on multiple planets. That aligned with what Natalia had said, but now Frank wondered if there were even more.

"How long do we have?" Thomas asked.

"Not long enough." Frank pulled out the cigar and turned it over in his hands. "And the only person who might have the knowledge to stop them is your father."

Thomas stared at the medical bay through the viewport. "I hope he wakes up soon."

"Yeah. Me too."

Something flashed across Thomas's face—pain, regret, determination. "If that knowledge dies with him . . ."

"Don't think like that," Frank said. "He'll pull through."

Thomas reached across to another console and brought up the ship's defense systems. Status indicators flashed green across the board—weapons charged, shields at full capacity, engines ready for immediate departure. They were fugitives with the highest bounty in CSF-controlled space, docked at a military installation with only one admiral's word keeping them from being swarmed by security forces. And now, with the Halcerites being summoned by the Hollow, they were sitting on possibly the only human with knowledge that might save them all.

Both dogs were alert now, sensing the shift in mood and watching Dilouie as he continued to scan the monitors.

Frank looked down at the massive rottweiler beside him, then to Cosmo, who watched them with intelligent eyes. It was as if they knew something horrible was about to happen. For some reason, all Frank could think about was Titan Station and losing his family. He had blamed Martin for so long, and now he regretted that. Fifteen years he could have spent forgiving him and living with him.

"Whatever happened between you and your old man, I know he's proud of you and loves you," Frank said quietly. "I spent too long being mad. I hope you can bury the hatchet."

Thomas raised an eyebrow.

"When he pulls through, we both should strive for that," Frank said. "Still going to make fun of him, but I'll lay off the egghead jokes."

Thomas smiled. "Let's go check on him. I want to be there if anything changes."

"Ship's on standby alert." He rose from the pilot's chair, activating several automated protocols. "Dilouie."

The technician looked up from his station across the cockpit, brushing long brown hair out of his eyes.

"Let me know the second you learn anything new about that signal," Thomas ordered. "Or if any military vessel approaches."

"You got it, boss."

Frank grabbed his rifle and cast one last glance at the stars beyond the viewport. Somewhere out there, an advanced alien enemy was stirring—beings that had cleansed entire worlds of life, that viewed humanity as nothing more than vermin to be exterminated. And all that stood between them and annihilation when they returned was a retired drunk trying to get sober, a mercenary captain with a conscience, and a half-transformed old Marine with alien knowledge in his brain.

And two dogs who proved they'd follow their masters through the gates of hell and back.

It wasn't much. But it would have to be enough.

THE GAUNTLET

AN OLD GUNS PREQUEL NOVELLA

J.N. CHANEY
AND
NICHOLAS SANSBURY SMITH

CHAPTER ONE

March, 2165

The CSF Heavy Cruiser *Armistice* hung in high orbit over Mars, its massive hull reflecting the dim sunlight. Sergeant Frank Cage slouched against a stack of supply crates in one of the vessel's crowded launch bays, watching Staff Sergeant Martin Kelvin spin a combat knife on a finger.

In front of them, a makeshift table of empty munitions boxes was already ringed with casualties from their drinking game. Three of their fellow squad mates sat around them, all on their way to getting blitzed before their much-deserved leave that had just kicked in.

Four hours from now, 2nd Squad of Terminator Platoon would be lounging in one of the biodomes of Mars's largest city, Olympus, enjoying the artificial beach environment in the advanced structure. Some of his teammates were no doubt looking forward to real beer and the locals in bikinis, but not Frank. He was looking forward to seeing his wife, Sarah, and their one-and-a-half-year-old daughter, Lily. He even had a plan to take them to a wildlife biodome for a new nature display.

"Your turn, Frank," said Corporal Will Popovich.

"Never have I ever"—Frank paused, letting the alcohol fuel his creativity—"lost a firefight to a Chitin."

Martin's dark features twisted into a scowl. Even at thirty-two, the barrel-chested Marine already had the weathered look of someone who had spent too much time in low gravity and combat armor. The ops tempo was high for a Space Marine, and double for the Exo Special Operations Teams. His broad shoulders hunched forward slightly as he studied Frank.

"How could you win a firefight with something that doesn't shoot back?" Martin asked. "I seem to remember you retreating, which in my book is *losing*."

"Nah, that wasn't losing," Frank protested, running a hand through his perpetually messy regulation-cut brown hair. "It was a tactical repositioning."

"You ran away, Cage."

"After you shot it and pissed it off, *Kelvin*!"

Frank smirked, knowing Martin hated being called by his last name. Frank, on the other hand, wore "Cage" like a badge of honor—it was far superior to Kelvin, which sounded like some ancient comic strip character.

"Details." Martin waved his knife dismissively. "Tell them about the TacRec."

"Oh no." Frank grunted. "You don't get to turn this around. Tell them what happened first. The *full* story. I still have the footage so you can't lie."

"Fine, but hold up a minute." Martin stabbed a hole in a beer can, tipped it back, and shotgunned it down. He let out a belch, then dragged his tattooed wrist across his mouth. "Frank and I were deployed to some shithole mining colony on Europa to clear out a Chitin nest. Don't even remember the name of that outpost. But the beetles were picking off miners left and right. Pulling 'em underground and eating 'em like snacks. We tracked the alpha into an ice cave, where we found the corpses of about twenty-two people."

"Not that many."

"Twenty-two, exactly."

"Whatever," Frank said.

"Hold up, amigos," Corporal Ron Torres said in his richly Mexican-accented voice. He leaned forward, his dark eyes bright with interest under the bay's harsh lighting. At twenty-five, he was the newest addition to Terminator Platoon and the youngest of 2nd Squad, but he'd already proven himself over the previous three missions. "How big was the alpha?"

"Biggest one I've ever seen," Martin said. "This was a goddamn dinosaur. Easy to track through the cave . . ." He paused and gestured with his knife. "Frank here says we should wait for backup—"

"Which was the correct call—"

"But I figure, hey, we'll find it easily." Martin's grin widened. "Turns out, not so much. The thing had made the whole cave its hunting ground. Covered the walls in some kind of bioluminescent gel that interfered with our motion trackers."

"Wait, was this the Proxima-4 mining incident?" asked Lance Corporal Dominga Rodriguez. She was twenty-eight years old and new to their unit, but she was already showing promise, both in combat and in keeping up with their drinking sessions.

"Nah, that was worse," Popovich said without looking up from his datapad that reflected on his pale features. "This was T-11. I have the exact date if you—"

"Nobody needs the exact date, Popovich," Martin cut him off. "Anyway, we did have it cornered, but it wasn't alone." He made an obscene gesture. "This thing was humping some beetle half its size. Turns out it was the queen."

"Tell them about your 'brilliant' next move." Frank shifted his weight, feeling the familiar ache in his shoulder from their last deployment. At thirty-one, he was already collecting scars along with medals that sat in a box. Came with the ESOT territory. For Exo Special Operations Teams, every mission was top secret.

Least we can talk about it here, he thought.

"I was getting to that." Martin grabbed another beer. "So I figure, well, two birds, one stone, and I opened fire."

"Wait." Popovich raised a thin eyebrow, suddenly very interested. "You fired at a mating alpha? That wasn't in the file I read. You do realize they are extremely aggressive when the queen is in heat."

"Yeah, we figured it out," Frank said. "Kelvin royally pissed her off by going pew pew. Too bad she came right at *me* in response like a bat out of hell. I had no other option but to retreat."

"She came at you because you were closer." Martin laughed. "My pew pew was still better than you throwing your TacRec at it."

"I deployed a tactical distraction device while documenting a historical encounter."

"You were trying to take a selfie with it!"

"Hold up, yo, what the fuck is taking a selfie?" Torres asked.

"Something only Martin, Frank, and Earth teenagers from one hundred years ago like to do," Popovich said, already looking back at his screen.

"It would have been an amazing shot," Frank said.

Rodriguez burst out laughing, her short hair falling over her dark eyes. She swept it back and then cracked open another beer. "Jesus, this story keeps getting better."

"It was a good throw, I'll give Cage that," Martin said. "Went straight into the queen's mouth."

"Wait, but you said earlier you still have the footage," Rodriguez said.

"That's the best part." Frank grinned, the expression making the fresh scrape on his jaw pull tight. "Three days later, we're tracking the same alpha with reinforcements. And right when we corner it in another ice cave, it starts making this weird noise. Like it's choking."

"Oh god." Martin covered his face.

"The thing regurgitated my TacRec. Completely intact. And you know what? That beautiful piece of engineering was still recording." Frank raised his beer in triumph. "Got the best combat selfie of my career. Me diving for cover while Martin blasted the alpha and queen. And that, kids, is why in combat you learn to improvise."

Frank wagged a finger. "You don't always have to shoot to win."

"Tell them about the smell."

"The smell wasn't *that* bad—"

"That thing reeked like burnt circuits mixed with alien bile. You should have turned it over for quarantine."

"Never have I ever," Popovich said loudly, "had my equipment quarantined as a biological hazard."

Frank drank, then pointed at Popovich. "Hey, that targeting system of yours got quarantined on our first trip into the Gauntlet."

"That was different," Popovich protested, his thin face flushing. "The quantum field sensors were merely exhibiting unexpected temporal displacement effects that resembled biological growth patterns—"

"It was growing tentacles, Popovich."

"Technically, they were temporal appendages manifesting in our dimension due to a cascading quantum—"

"Tentacles."

Torres raised his bottle. "Never have I ever built something that grew tentacles."

Popovich sighed and took a drink. "They weren't tentacles. And I've since corrected that design flaw. Mostly."

"Mostly?" Rodriguez asked, leaning forward with interest.

"Eighty-seven-point-six percent chance of no temporal appendage manifestation in the current model."

Frank was about to demand an explanation of the other 12.4 percent when the emergency klaxon resonated across the launch bay, its piercing wail drowning out all conversation. Red warning lights began strobing across the steel walls. The sound sent a familiar surge of adrenaline through his system, cutting the alcohol haze.

"What'd you do now, Frank?" Martin asked.

"Nothing . . . yet."

Their CO, Captain Rivera, burst through the open pressure doors, his face flushed either from running or anger—probably both. "Sober up, shitheads, briefing in ten!"

Popovich stood with his datapad. "Sir, I'm in the middle of a recalibration. Can you give me a few minutes?"

"Negative. Pack it up, Popovich. That's an order." Rivera's tone left no room for argument. "And somebody get Cage vertical."

"I am vertical," Frank protested, then walked straight into a support beam. "That's new."

"The beam?" Martin said, steering his friend toward the exit with the ease of long practice.

"No, the tentacles."

Popovich stopped wrapping his screen in a static-free cloth. "What, where?"

"Haha, you're such a nerd, Popovich," Frank said as he broke out laughing.

With a frown, Popovich finished tucking his pad into a small bag.

The young Field Science Marine handled his equipment like it was made of glass—typical FSM behavior. They were supposed to extend the team's situational awareness, but half the time they just made easy targets for the trigger pullers to mock.

"Nobody likes a know-it-all, Popovich," Frank called back, letting Martin guide him around another support beam.

"Except when he's saving your ass with precise targeting data," Popovich replied, falling in behind them. He carried his bag like it was a newborn. "Remember the uprising on Station X-8?"

"That was different. We needed those calculations to determine whether our firepower would blast a hole in the station shielding."

"You need all my calculations. You just don't appreciate them until something's shooting at you."

"True," Frank admitted quietly.

They reached the corridor with the briefing room just as Colonel Daugherty strode past, not even sparing them a glance. But Frank caught a look at the datapad in Daugherty's hands and saw the classified markings and the single word at the top: GAUNTLET. The sight of it sent an ice-cold tendril of sobriety down his spine.

"Well," Frank muttered. "There goes leave."

CHAPTER TWO

"Frank, Martin, hold up," Popovich said. Once outside the briefing room, he pulled out a small pill case from his vest. "This should help with the alcohol."

"I don't need help," Frank protested as he staggered.

"Actually, you do, Sarge, and this metabolic accelerator will—"

"I've taken them before, I know what they do." Frank grunted.

"Me too," Martin said. "Not a big fan of the side effects of nausea, plus the last time it gave me the runs."

"Something we agree on."

"Take the damn pills," said Rivera. He stood in the corridor outside the open hatch of the briefing room. "That's an order. We need you two sober."

"The nausea passes in approximately a minute," Popovich assured him. "Usually."

"Fine," Frank said with a grunt. He took a pill, and Martin took another.

The Marines of 2nd Squad were filing toward the briefing room, all looking equally annoyed about their interrupted leave. Frank saw the familiar faces of 4th Squad, but the rest of Terminator Platoon was either still on mission or enjoying their own leave.

Frank felt the near-instantaneous effects of the metabolic accelerator clearing his mind but also attempting to clear his digestive system. "Son of a bitch," he whispered.

But it wasn't just the pill, nor was it the presence of his company and battalion commanders that helped him regain clarity.

Through a viewport, Mars hung like a red jewel against the black, its surface dotted with the lights of CSF outposts that were starting to green. For ten years now, the terraformers had been working night and day, but it was an extremely slow process.

Frank paused when he laid eyes on what he thought was Olympus Colony, the largest city on the planet. Sarah and Lily were waiting for him in their modest apartment that was packed in the slums.

"Promised I'd take Sarah and Lily out to a wildlife display this weekend," he said. "Got any plans with Lucia or your kids?"

Martin shook his head but didn't say anything beyond that. The silence was everything Frank needed to know. Things between Martin and his wife had been rocky for a while now. The deployments, training, and grind of being a CSF Marine had caused a divide between them—a divide Frank understood. Marriage was hard enough when you were at home, but being away made everything harder—especially being a good partner and parent.

"I'll try to get back to the surface when we return," Martin said. "I want to take Thomas to a ballgame."

"That would be awesome," Frank said, glad to hear Martin speaking up.

"Cut the chitchat," Rivera said as he followed them into the briefing room. "I want your eyes and ears inside, got it?"

"Yes, sir," Frank said.

Martin nodded.

"And sit in the back," Rivera said.

Frank took a seat next to Martin in the last row of the packed briefing room.

Colonel Daugherty took his position at the front and activated a holographic display of the Gauntlet—that twisted corridor of space-time that had swallowed far more ships than were ever officially documented.

The display highlighted a particular section in red, and Frank felt his stomach drop. This wasn't from Popovich's pill.

"Seventy-two hours ago, we lost contact with Scout Team Seven," Daugherty began without preamble. "They were operating in an unmapped section of the Gauntlet under classified orders."

"Like figuring out what species your first wife was?" Frank whispered.

"Still a mystery," Martin replied, a bit too loud. "I hardly knew her."

Rivera glared at them angrily, but Daugherty didn't seem to notice. Frank stiffened in his chair as the colonel continued.

"*Squanto* wasn't just another probe mission," he said. "They were testing new quantum mapping technology, attempting to find a stable route through to the Lort System."

Popovich's hand shot up. "Sir, previous attempts to map quantum signatures in the Gauntlet have all failed due to temporal interference patterns. How did they account for—"

"The details are classified, Corporal. What matters is they found something. Their last transmission was scrambled, but our techs translated enough."

Daugherty clicked the remote for the presentation.

Audio crackled.

"This is Captain Reeve, reporting from *Squanto*." The stern voice was enthusiastic, excited. "We found it. The path—"

White noise rushed through the speakers, followed by some noise that sounded almost like a whale communicating under the ocean.

The transmission came back online. "There's something out there," Reeve said.

"My God, what is that? I've never seen . . ." asked someone in the background.

Daugherty let that hang in the air before the speakers shut off. He faced the Marines, setting his square jaw and raising his eyes.

"Three rescue teams have already been dispatched to find *Squanto*, but none have returned," he said. "We believe Captain Reeve and his crew located a way through the Gauntlet to the Lort System but have encountered some sort of anomaly, preventing their return."

The room went completely quiet. Even Frank sat up even straighter, the last effects of the alcohol burning away under a surge of adrenaline.

"A little over one hour ago, we received this." Daugherty played an audio file. Static again crackled, then three clear beeps—*Squanto*'s emergency beacon.

Daugherty advanced the holographic display, showing a more detailed map of the target area where the beacon had activated. "This section of the Gauntlet has unique properties," he said. "Standard navigation systems often fail. Quantum sensors give false readings. The laws of physics become . . . suggestions."

"My favorite kind of laws," Frank quipped a bit too loud.

"Do you think this is funny, Cage?" Daugherty glared angrily at Frank. "The Gauntlet's taken more ships than pirates and rebels combined."

"No, you're right, sir. My apologies."

Daugherty raised his chin and glanced back at the display. "Now that we have a general idea of where *Squanto* is, I am deploying 2nd Squad to do some reconnaissance. 4th Squad will provide backup."

Of course you are, Frank thought.

"Your mission is simple: locate *Squanto*, recover their data, and get back here safely," Daugherty said. "The quantum mapping data they collected could be our key to finally establishing a stable route through the Gauntlet and into the Lort System."

"Sir, permission to speak," Rivera said.

Daugherty glanced over. "Go ahead, Captain."

"2nd Squad is not exactly in tip-top shape."

"I can see that, but I presume they are ready for what's out there," Daugherty replied. His gaze swept over Frank, Martin, and their comrades. "Your track record in impossible situations is . . . unique, and I trust you are ready for this mission?"

"He means we're expendable," Frank stage-whispered.

Rivera glared at them.

"Sir, yes, sir," Martin said.

"Good. Seeing how Lieutenant Sanders is still occupied with 1st Squad of Predator Platoon . . . Gunnery Sergeant Kelvin, you are in tactical command of 2nd Squad."

Frank thoroughly enjoyed the angst in Rivera's face when the captain realized he wasn't coming along for the ride.

"The success of this mission is imperative to establishing a bright future for CSF," Daugherty said. "The Lort System is crucial to expansion. Without a stable route through the Gauntlet, we're stuck here. *Squanto*'s data could change everything."

Rivera took a deep breath, clearly frustrated.

"We're counting on you," Daugherty said. "Any questions?"

"What about the other rescue teams?" Martin pressed. "Any signs of what happened to them?"

Daugherty's expression darkened. "Nothing. No wreckage, no bodies, no distress calls. They just . . . vanished."

"Like my mother-in-law after the wedding," Frank mused. "Maybe they're related."

"Cage," Daugherty warned.

"Sorry, sir."

Popovich raised a hand.

"Yes?" Daugherty said in an annoyed tone.

"Sir, the quantum instability readings from that sector of the Gauntlet suggest possible temporal displacement effects. If *Squanto* encountered a time dilation field—"

"In English, Popovich," Rivera interrupted.

"Time gets weird."

"Which is another reason why I am sending 2nd Squad." Daugherty raised the remote again, bringing up mission parameters on the display. "You deploy in one hour. Full combat load-out. Corporal Popovich will brief you on special equipment requirements during prep. Dismissed."

As they filed out, Martin caught Frank's arm. "You thinking what I'm thinking?" he whispered.

"Since when do you think?"

"Since my eleventh beer. Makes me philosophical."

"Whatever, you going to tell me what you're thinking? Or do I have to guess?"

"I think *Squanto* isn't *Squanto* anymore."

"Huh?"

"I mean, it's their ship, but, wherever they went, they came back . . . different."

Popovich rushed up next to them. "I believe you may be onto something," he said. "I have my own theory . . ."

Before he could go into detail, Rivera cleared his throat down the corridor.

"Frank, Martin, a word," he said in his deep voice.

"This doesn't sound good," Martin replied.

"Yeah, better keep your mouth shut for real," Frank muttered.

"Me?" Martin scoffed. "I'm not taking that bait."

Rivera stroked his mustache as they approached. "I'm sure your heads just got even bigger for being selected for this mission, and for being issued tactical command, Martin." Rivera grunted. "But what everyone in *my* platoon knows is you two idiots somehow manage to survive crazy shit, like the Chitin alpha and that classified mess on NL-19. Though God knows how."

"Skill," Frank said.

"Luck," Martin countered.

"Math," Popovich added as he passed by.

Rivera shook his head and left.

Frank grinned, but his eyes strayed to the viewport, to Mars hanging below them, thoughts of his wife and their young daughter in his mind.

Back in the day, before a mission like this, he had no fears. Things had changed when Lily was born. Now when he stepped into his power armor he always worried about not coming home to see her grow up.

"You got that worried look again, Cage," Martin said, reading him like a book.

Frank shrugged. "Just thinking about what happened to *Squanto* and the rescue teams."

"Don't focus on that, brother. Focus on succeeding where they failed. If we do, we're going to go down in history as the two greatest Space Marines of the Colonial Shield Federation."

CHAPTER THREE

The *Armistice* blasted away from Mars toward the classified coordinates of the Gauntlet beyond the solar system. Martin stood in the corridor as the heavy cruiser picked up speed, the sparkling stars racing by out the portholes.

Whispering came from the comm hub where Frank had jumped inside to send a quick message to his wife. Martin had tried his wife, Lucia, but she didn't answer. Not surprising. He was in the doghouse again. It wasn't the first time, nor would it be the last.

As always, it was his fault. He had promised her he would be home for his daughter's concert. But duty had called, and Martin had missed that, like he missed so many other things. Normally Lucia understood, but the list had racked up on so many occasions it had built a mountain of resentment. Especially because some of those occasions were from him simply forgetting to do family stuff.

He sighed with guilt as he leaned against the corridor wall, giving his friend some privacy while keeping an eye on the time. Deep down, he hoped Frank didn't make the same mistakes he had as a husband and a father.

Right now though, Martin had to get his head in the game for this mission. Only thirty minutes remained until they needed to be suited up, and thirty minutes more for their Compactified Access Tunnel, or CAT drive, to jump to the edge of the Gauntlet.

Martin didn't want to push Frank, but he decided to step inside and tap his wrist, indicating they were on a crunch.

Frank was still trying to get a connection on the display. He didn't even turn when Martin cleared his throat.

"Yeah, I know, but as soon as we jump, I'll lose my chance to send a message," Frank said. As if in answer, the display flared to life with the youthful face of his wife, Sarah.

"Babe," Frank said. He held up a hand to Martin, but not to shoo him away. "Hold up, say hi to Sarah and Lily."

"Frank?" Sarah asked in an exhausted, confused tone.

Her tired features came into focus, eyes baggy, hair disheveled.

Martin had seen the look of fatigue many times before. Back on Earth, at the refugee colony in Montana where his mother worked as a nurse and his father had served as a mechanic. He spent more nights at the local watering hole than at home, leaving all of the work raising Martin and his younger sister to their mother. When Martin was older, he had stepped in to help take care of his sister when their mother was at work.

Sometimes Martin wondered if that was part of the reason he wasn't a good dad himself. Because he had essentially already raised kids when he was a kid. But it was more than that. He wasn't a great dad because he was always gone, and when he was home, he drank too much.

"Hey, Sarah," Martin said after the brief pause.

Sarah smiled at the screen. "Martin, good to see you."

"You look good."

She scoffed. "You're a bad liar."

Crying echoed in the background, crackling slightly over the feed.

"One second," Sarah said. She got up and returned a few moments later, cradling Lily in front of the screen. "Look who just woke up early from her nap."

Martin chuckled as he watched Lily. The squirming, crying one-and-a-half-year-old looked just so much like her dad. "She's a cutie," he said. "Good thing she has your looks, Sarah."

"You're a *really* bad liar," Sarah said playfully. "Everyone agrees she looks like her dad."

"My little angel," Frank said. He smiled and whispered, "Dee, dee, dee."

His playful voice instantly got his daughter's attention. She stopped squirming and grinned, revealing two square teeth on the bottom and top of her mouth.

"Dee, dee, dee," Frank said.

It had taken a long time for Martin to adjust to his warrior friend transforming into a googling dad, but the kid was cute, despite looking like her father. Made him miss his own kids, who were now nearing their teenage years. Martin regretted that he had hardly seen them when they were this young.

"Sarah, listen—" Frank pressed closer to the comm screen, lowering his voice. "I know I promised, but—"

"How long will you be gone?" Sarah interrupted.

Martin hung back as her smile faded.

"Quick mission. A day or two tops. Nothing crazy."

"You said that last time."

"This is different. I'll be back before Lily even notices I'm gone." Frank reached out, his fingers brushing the screen where his daughter's hand pressed. "Hey, princess, you be good for Mommy, okay?"

Lily babbled something that might have been "dada."

"Frank." Sarah's voice dropped. "Does this have to do with the Gauntlet . . . They're saying two ships already—"

"Don't believe the rumors." Frank glanced at Martin, a silent request for support.

Martin leaned into view of the screen. "Sarah, you have my word we'll bring him back in one piece."

Sarah's expression softened slightly. "Keep him out of trouble, Martin."

"Always do."

"You really need to work on your lying," she said, but there was affection in it. "Both of you come back safe."

"Will do. I love you, babe," Frank said.

"Love you too."

"Bye, sweet Lily."

The screen went dark.

Frank stayed there for a moment, his hand still raised where Lily's had been. Martin watched his friend's shoulders tense, then relax with practiced control.

"You good?" Martin asked quietly.

"Yeah, did you get ahold of your family?"

"No."

Frank looked him in the eyes to get a read on Martin if he was really okay.

"Come on," Martin said. "Let's go suit up."

The armory was organized chaos when they entered. The familiar smell of gun oil and power armor lubricant filled the air as 2nd Squad prepped for deployment. Rodriguez was already in her black Aegis power armor, making her look twice her normal size as she methodically checked the squad's demolition load-out. Torres worked nearby at the weapons bench, field-stripping two of the squad's X-15 heavy plasma cannons. Popovich looked up from his corner workspace, surrounded by delicate instruments that Martin had no idea how to work, or their purpose.

"Good morning, Staff Sergeant Kelvin."

The calm, feminine voice of Eva distracted Martin as he approached his power armor station. The bipedal medical AI robot encased in combat armor strode over, firing a beam of light at Martin.

"I see you're maintaining your perfect record of premission inebriation," said the AI.

"Morning, Eva," Martin groaned. "Still a smartass, I see."

"I prefer the term 'tactically honest,' sir."

"Don't worry, I gave him and Sergeant Cage metabolic accelerators," Popovich said.

"I'm aware, but I've been tasked with ensuring both sergeants are combat ready."

"We are," Martin and Frank said at the same time.

Martin pushed over to his station, where his Aegis power armor waited in its maintenance cradle like a silent carcass of the beast it was named after. The dark surface bore the scars of countless missions: plasma scoring along the left pauldron from a firefight with insurrectionists when they raided a military outpost on Mars, acid burns on the chest plate from the Chitin nest, and that weird temporal distortion from their fifth Gauntlet run that had somehow left a perfect spiral pattern in the armor.

"Back into the fray," he said as he ran a finger down the dented armor.

The chest piece came first, heavy plates settling onto his shoulders as servomotors whined to life. Then the arm segments, each one clicking into place with pneumatic hisses.

After he was suited up, Martin began his premission ritual, checking every seal and connection with practiced precision.

Frank stumbled into his own station next door, cursing as he nearly tripped over a power cable. "Who the hell reorganized the maintenance bay?"

"Nobody," Martin said. "You're still drunk."

"Wrong. Popovich's magic pills are working." Frank paused. "Though Torres does look like a bird . . . Never mind, that's just his beak."

"I'm hearing this, pendejo," Torres called from the weapons bench.

Popovich looked up from his workspace. "Would you like another pill, Cage?"

"Negative, Popovich. But I will take a beer."

Martin watched Frank struggle with his armor seals, noting how his friend's hands shook slightly. Different from his usual premission jitters. The call home had hit him hard.

"Need help with that?"

"I got it." Frank forced the chest piece into place with more strength than necessary.

"You sure you're good?" Martin asked in a moment of pure seriousness.

"Yeah." Frank's voice was quiet.

Martin felt the tension—and now he was starting to worry.

"In and out, Cage, just like I told Sarah," he said.

Frank scoffed. "Since when do our missions go according to plan?"

"First time for everything."

"Attention, 2nd Squad." The crisp voice of Eva, the AI, resonated through the room. "Preflight checks are complete. My quantum navigation systems are calibrated for Gauntlet conditions. Please report to Hangar Bay Three in fifteen minutes."

"How's the interference looking, Eva?" Martin asked.

"Significant temporal distortions in the target sector. I've plotted sixteen potential approach vectors, but be advised—standard navigation protocols may become problematic."

Eva paused. "The Gauntlet appears to be exhibiting unusual energy signatures in the target sector. My analysis suggests—"

"Save the details for Popovich," Martin cut in. "Just get us there in one piece."

"Acknowledged, Sergeant. Though I feel compelled to note that—"

"How about you don't note anything," Frank cut in.

"Very well," Eva replied.

The squad fell into step together, headed for the hangar bay. Their heavy footsteps echoed off the steel deck, the sound of five sets of power armor moving in formation. The sleek frame of the dropship *Hyperion* waited in the hangar. Three times longer than a standard corvette but with half the radar signature, the ship represented the perfect fusion of military might and infiltration capability. But it was also armed to the teeth across the dark hull with retractable weapon pods and sensor arrays. Beneath the hood was an extraordinarily powerful CAT drive. The revolutionary propulsion system that could tear holes in space-time for faster-than-light jumps across millions of kilometers.

Captain Rivera stood in front of an open hatch on the port side of the dropship, his face showing the resentment of Daugherty's orders.

"Gunny," Rivera addressed Martin directly.

"Yes, sir." Martin gave a sharp nod.

Rivera sized him up as he approached, perhaps checking to see if he was fully sober.

"No heroics out there," said the captain. "Just get that data back."

"Understood, sir."

"And Kelvin?" Rivera lowered his voice. "Keep Cage from doing anything too stupid."

"Copy that, sir."

The squad boarded efficiently, each member performing final equipment checks before heading to their assigned crash seats. Martin took his position near the front, noticing Frank staring at a holo-pic of Lily that he'd somehow smuggled into his suit's HUD display.

"Comms check." Rivera's voice came through clear over the comms. "I'll be monitoring your progress. Eva has full autonomy for flight operations. Kelvin, tactical control is yours out there, but don't forget who's in charge of this platoon. Is that clear?"

"Crystal, sir," Martin replied, already running through combat scenarios in his head.

"Good hunting, Marines."

Eva's voice filled the cabin. "Launch sequence initiated. ION drive activating. Stand by for insertion."

The advanced drive hummed to life, its massive electromagnetic field generators creating the controlled plasma stream that would punch them through normal space. The hangar doors opened silently outside.

Martin watched Mars fall away below them, its red surface dotted with outposts and biodomes. Somewhere down there, a little girl was wondering where her father was, and a wife was wondering if that father would return.

He will, Martin thought. *I promise.*

That wasn't the only promise Martin made. He thought of his wife, Lucia, and better times. Before the bickering, fighting, and resentment. Every time he left, he told himself he would do better when he got back.

This time, he would.

"I promise, Lucia," he whispered. "I promise, Thomas and Terecia."

Once they were a safe distance from *Armistice*, they blasted away with a jolt. The ion stream painted everything in a soft blue glow as they accelerated. Martin tried to relax during the journey.

It wasn't long before Eva announced, "Approaching Gauntlet entry point. ION drive shifting to stabilization mode. The Gauntlet's quantum tunneling effect will handle the real acceleration from here."

Martin understood why. The Gauntlet might be unstable and dangerous, but it beat the hell out of conventional space travel. An ION drive would take twenty years to reach the Lort System. The Gauntlet could get them there in hours if they could just find a way through.

The twisted corridor of space-time waited ahead, already swallowing the light from their engines in ways that hurt to look at. Time to find out what was waiting for them in that quantum shortcut through reality.

CHAPTER FOUR

The *Hyperion* shuddered as it entered the Gauntlet, the barrier between normal space and whatever lay beyond rippling like heat waves over hot metal. Frank gripped his harness tighter, trying to focus on anything except how the laws of physics seemed to bend around them.

Through the viewport, the Gauntlet stretched ahead like a twisted corridor of energy. Bands of colors pulsed along its length, forming what looked like walls that somehow contained this broken piece of reality. The whole thing reminded Frank of an old lava lamp he'd had as a kid, if that lava lamp had been designed by someone having a nightmare.

"Eva, status report," Martin called from his command position.

"We have crossed the threshold and are maintaining optimal transit velocity," the AI responded. "Compensating for temporal shear. Warning—local space-time distortions increasing by twenty-three percent compared to predicted models. Quantum stabilizers are holding at sixty percent efficiency."

The *Hyperion* glided through the quantum tunnel with an eerie steadiness that belied the chaos around them as they punched through the warped space-time.

Frank watched streams of energy flowing past the ship in ribbons of blue and violet. Some seemed to move forward, while others flowed backward, like rivers running in opposite directions. "I think I need another one of those magic pills, Popovich," he said. "'Cause this is some trippy shit."

"The Gauntlet's quantum field is particularly active in this sector," Popovich said. "These energy patterns . . . It's as if—" He stopped suddenly, his face pale behind his face shield, illuminated by the glow of his instruments in front of him.

"As if what?" Martin prompted.

"Multiple contacts ahead," Eva announced before Popovich could answer. "I'm detecting debris consistent with CSF naval vessels."

The *Hyperion*'s engines pulsed as Eva automatically reduced their quantum velocity, bringing them to a relative drift through the Gauntlet's swirling energies. The searchlights activated, cutting through the strange luminescence.

Frank leaned forward against his straps for a better view. The beams captured a CSF rescue ship that hung suspended in the void, the hull warped and stretched as if it had been pulled like taffy. The ship's markings were also warped, making it impossible to read the entire name.

"Stand by for scans," Eva said, maintaining their reduced speed as the sensor arrays swept the wreckage. "Maintaining safe distance from temporal distortion field."

"That's the *Concordia*," Eva confirmed. "The second rescue vessel sent out."

"Look at the hull composition," Popovich said.

Frank had just noticed large sections of dull exterior, like the vessel had been sitting in a junkyard for a century.

"The molecular structure shows signs of extreme aging," Popovich explained. "According to these readings, that metal has experienced several decades of decay."

"That's impossible," Rodriguez said. "The *Concordia* launched two days ago, right, Eva?"

"That is correct," replied the AI.

"Time behaves . . . differently here," Popovich said. "These energy patterns we're seeing are not just distorting space, but rather time itself. The *Concordia* could have been here for forty years from its own perspective, even though it left Mars just days ago."

"What about the crew?" Torres asked.

"No life signs detected," Eva reported. "Hull integrity is compromised in multiple sections."

A chirping cut through the tension.

"The hell is that?" Frank asked.

"Quantum disturbance detected," Eva accounted. "Anomaly forming at bearing zero-three-five."

The Gauntlet's swirling wall seemed to bulge inward, energy patterns writhing like a living entity. A massive shape tore through the barrier, trailing ribbons of temporal energy.

"Evasive maneuvers," Eva said. "Prepare for turbulence."

The *Hyperion*'s engines flared as she executed a rapid defensive roll. The ship's hull groaned under the strain as they narrowly avoided the object that had just materialized in their path. Frank clenched his jaw, feeling bile rising up his throat from the sharp maneuver.

"Oh god," he muttered.

As the *Hyperion* stabilized, the searchlights illuminated a vessel that matched nothing Frank had seen in his career. The bulky hull was a patchwork of plates and repairs, like someone had tried to keep it flying after a brutal battle and long past its intended lifespan.

"Eva, can you identify that vessel?" Martin asked.

"Accessing historical records . . ." A two-second pause passed before she added, "Match found. The vessel appears to be the *Stellar Horizon*, a deep space research vessel. Last known contact: 2146."

"That's nineteen years ago," Frank muttered, watching as temporal energy continued to cascade off the ancient ship's hull.

"The *Stellar Horizon* was one of the first vessels outfitted with an ION drive," Eva added. "And yet, molecular dating of the hull suggests the damage is recent."

"Like I said, time isn't flowing linearly here," Popovich explained. "These ships . . . they could all exist in the same moment from the Gauntlet's perspective, even though they entered decades apart. The rescue ships might have aged considerably while *Squanto* could still be experiencing their first moments after arrival."

"Which means what for us?" Martin asked. "Give me the short version."

"It means we need to be fast," Popovich replied. "Very fast. The longer we stay here, the more temporal displacement we risk experiencing—"

"We end up looking like the monster that's about to come out of my ass," Frank said.

Martin looked over but didn't laugh.

"Sorry," Frank said. "I blame those pills."

Popovich snorted. "Maybe blame the dozen beers."

"Maybe shut your nerdy—"

"Everyone cut the shit," Martin said. "Eva, resume course. Maximum safe velocity through the Gauntlet."

"Acknowledged," Eva responded. "Increasing quantum velocity."

The *Hyperion* pushed deeper into the twisting tunnel of light making up one of countless corridors of the Gauntlet. Each Marine watched from their crash seat in silence; no joking, no discussion of what they were seeing. Frank thought of Sarah and Lily, longing to be with them. Never had he felt so far away—so separated. Normally he could bury those thoughts, but something about coming out here was different this time, especially after what they had just seen.

His sour gut warned him things were not as they seemed.

"Contact," Eva reported.

Hyperion slowed, the thrusters burning down as they came up on a debris field that drifted across the passage. Unlike the first two ships, there wasn't much left of this one: a hatch, a partial wing, and some plates of hull. All of it in a cloud of flotsam.

"Confirming this was the *Viper*," Eva said.

"The third rescue ship," Martin said.

"Correct."

"What the hell happened to it?" Torres asked. "Looks like it was blasted to pieces."

"Could this have been pirates?" Rodriguez asked.

"Unlikely," Popovich cut in. "I'm not seeing any sign of conventional weapons. Something else did this."

"Was it the Gauntlet?" Frank asked. He had seen ships come apart before in the dangerous stretch of uncharted space, but nothing like what was in front of them now.

"Perhaps," Popovich said after a pause.

Frank picked up a sense of hesitation in the young tech's voice. Uncharacteristic hesitation that indicated Popovich had another theory.

"Be advised, I'm detecting another contact," Eva announced suddenly.

There was a long pause, but Frank could already see something through the cockpit viewport—a vessel that appeared to be in one piece. A 3-D image transferred to his HUD, confirming it was a scout vessel.

"Configuration matches *Squanto*," Eva said.

"Bring us in . . . *slowly*," Martin said.

"Understood, stand by."

Hyperion blasted away from the remains of *Viper*.

Frank tensed as they did a wide curve toward their target. The scout ship appeared through the cockpit viewports, floating dead in space. Unlike the *Concordia*, its hull showed no signs of the temporal aging. Nor was there any major damage from what Frank could see. But there was something wrong about it.

When they were 3,000 meters away, Martin said, "Eva, stop here."

Thrusters fired, reversing course and bringing *Hyperion* back a few hundred meters.

Frank narrowed his gaze on *Squanto*. There was damage on the hull after all. Along the aft section, the surface was bent, and the cockpit had been crushed inward.

"Shit, looks like they ran into something," Rodriguez said.

"Confirming hull damage in multiple sectors," Eva confirmed. "Transferring to squad view."

Frank's HUD fired up, showing zoomed-in images along the hull. Several of the dents were the size of a man, like someone outside had been slamming against it in an attempt to get inside. The worst of the damage was along the cockpit, where both of the main viewports were shattered inward.

"Damn," said Martin. "Eva, you picking up any life signals?"

"Negative, but there appears to be some interference."

"Clarify."

"Anomalous energy readings."

"Don't need readings to know there ain't no way anyone survived," Torres said. "Unless they were fully suited up, I guess."

"But they'd be out of air by now . . ." Rodriguez replied quietly.

Frank looked to Martin, who seemed to be considering their next move. "Eva, are these anomalous energy readings a risk to us?"

"Hard to say, Sergeant, but I would proceed cautiously," replied the AI.

"Okay, bring us in and prepare for docking."

"Stand by."

The *Hyperion* rotated and came up along the portside hatch of *Squanto*.

"Be advised, I am detecting unusual energy signatures emanating from the ship," Popovich said. "Power readings are inconsistent with standard CSF technology."

He looked up from his scanner. "I've never seen anything like this—not in person at least."

"Eva, have you?" Martin asked.

"That's classified, Sergeant."

"What? We need to know what you know."

"I am authorized to tell you there are traces of radiation in different parts of the ship," Eva said. "In other areas, they are more concentrated. Your suits will protect you from those."

"Uh, but what about those energy signatures?" Torres asked. "Could they like, age us? Or turn us into jelly?"

"Inconclusive," Eva said.

Frank and the other Marines rotated toward Martin, waiting for orders.

"Our orders are to retrieve that data, and that's what we're going to do," he said. "Get ready to board. Eva, bridge us over."

"Copy that."

A thud sounded, followed by clanking as the *Hyperion*'s docking collar extended. The metal groaned when it made contact with *Squanto*'s airlock. The sound echoed through their ship like a death knell.

"Alright, Marines," Martin announced, unstrapping from his harness. "Standard boarding protocol. Rodriguez, Torres, you're on point. Popovich, find us that data. Frank, watch our six."

"You got it," Frank replied.

Their seats released the levers, and the squad fell into formation to the hatch. Frank charged his Gauss rifle with a satisfying click. This was the part he knew, straight military operation, no quantum physics required.

The airlock cycled, and they entered *Squanto*'s dark corridors.

"Artificial gravity is active, but life support systems are offline," Eva said. "Multiple hull breaches, currently contained by emergency seals."

Frank stepped onto the deck of the ship. 2nd Squad's lights cut through the shadows, revealing bulkheads covered in strange patterns. They advanced slowly but halted almost immediately.

"Check this out." Torres played his light over the bulkhead. "What is it?"

Frank spotted markings that were drawn in what looked suspiciously like blood.

"I think I know what they are," Popovich said.

"Enlighten us," Martin replied. "And hurry."

Popovich held up his scanner over the hull, then turned, the interior of his helmet illuminating his surprised features. "These look like navigation coordinates to me."

He continued down the hull, his sensors whirring.

"These patterns . . . they're not random. This is the route through the Gauntlet."

"What the fuck do you mean? Why would the crew draw them on the hull?" Torres asked.

"Maybe they ran out of paper," Frank suggested, but his attempt at humor fell flat. Something about those markings sent a chill down his spine.

"So where is the crew?" Rodriguez asked. She swept her X-15 plasma cannon down another empty corridor.

As if in answer, a clanking sound echoed through the ship.

Frank shouldered his Gauss rifle, trying to track the sound.

"We found the way . . ." came a disembodied voice.

The Marines all stiffened around Frank.

"Please tell me that was one of you doing a really bad impression," he said.

"That wasn't any of us," Martin replied.

Popovich held up his scanner, the pings coming back negative. "Maybe someone's still alive on this vessel."

"Then find them, and hurry," Frank said. "I got a bad fucking feeling about this."

CHAPTER FIVE

Martin held his Gauss rifle ready as his helmet lights swept *Squanto*'s main corridor. Through his helmet's filtration system, he picked up the distinct scent of copper and burned dirt.

The hell is that smell? he wondered.

The Marines moved forward into the passage. Emergency power was barely functioning, red warning lights pulsing dimly in the darkness like a dying heartbeat. Their boots echoed on the deck plates, the sound hollow in the dead ship.

"Eva, status report," he said into his helmet comm.

"Still negative on biological signatures according to my scanners," the AI responded. "However, I am detecting a greater concentration of unusual radiation patterns throughout the vessel. These emissions are interfering with standard bioscanners."

"How bad?"

"Severe enough to compromise some of the standard scanning frequencies. The patterns do not match any known weapons discharge or reactor leak."

"Maybe that's the source of the scent? Anyone else picking it up?"

"Yeah, smells like if you stuck earthworms in a microwave," Popovich said.

Frank snorted. "You'd know."

"I'm getting more of a copper smell." Rodriguez wrinkled his nose. "Like pennies left in a gym sock."

"Great, maybe they found some metal worms in the Gauntlet," Frank said. "Space's newest delicacy. Coming to a Marine mess hall near you."

Martin considered their options. *Squanto* wasn't large, but with compromised sensors, every shadowy corner became a potential threat. And something about those strange markings they'd seen on the bulkhead made his skin crawl.

"Sensors are compromised, so we're flying blind," he said. "Rodriguez, take point. Rest of you, five-meter spread. Check your corners and keep it tight."

They made their way forward, passing walls covered in the same navigational markings. Up close, they looked like precise geometric patterns. Some had been carved deep into the metal; others appeared to have been drawn in dried blood.

"This is giving me the creeps," Rodriguez whispered as she traced her light over the hull.

Martin considered making a joke about it looking like something a kid might fingerpaint, perhaps what Frank had in his future with Lily, but this was too chilling for jokes. Plus, he was starting to get spooked himself. For the second time since launch, he thought of his own kids and his wife, Lucia, opening up the floodgates for years of built-up regret and guilt.

Don't do that, Kelvin. Not here, not now, Martin thought. *When you get home, you be a better man.*

If *you get home,* almost entered his mind, but he stomped that bullshit down like a prairie dog sticking its head out of a hole in Montana.

They moved forward until they reached a junction. The medical bay access was to their left, bridge access to the right. Martin noted scorch marks around the medbay door.

"Those look like plasma rounds," Popovich said. "But what were they shooting at?"

The sight of the damage gave Martin pause. None of this made any sense. All he could think of was that the crew went crazy and started killing each other. Maybe there would be some more evidence in Medical.

"Let's clear that hatch," Martin said. "Rodriguez, with me. Frank, take Popovich and Torres to watch our six."

Frank fell into a defensive position as the squad advanced. The medbay doors were partially open, jammed with what looked like a crowbar. Martin's helmet lights caught dried blood on the metal grip. He signaled Rodriguez forward, and both of them moved in smoothly, weapons ready.

The smell of rot hit them first, even through their suit filters. Martin swept his rifle across the room, the beam catching movement. He nearly fired before realizing it was just their reflection in the glass display cabinets.

"Clear left," Rodriguez reported.

"Clear right," Martin responded, then froze as his lights hit a body *under* a surgical table. "Mother of God . . ."

What remained of a Marine lay spread out like a museum specimen. The male body had been systematically dissected, but not with any medical tools Martin recognized. The cuts were impossibly precise, and the flesh around them showed the geometric burn patterns.

"What could have done that?" Torres asked.

"I don't know," Popovich said. "But my rad sensors are going crazy. Whatever made these marks, it's changed the tissue somehow. Still changing it."

Martin bent down as the geometric burns seemed to shift slightly under their lights, like circuitry coming alive. His filters picked up the same metallic, coppery scent mixed with burned dirt.

"Sarge," Rodriguez called from deeper in the bay. "Got two more. Same thing."

Martin approached the second body. This one's armor had been peeled away in layers, each piece laid out with methodical care. The chest cavity was open, organs removed with surgical precision. But it was the face that hit him hardest—frozen in an expression of absolute terror.

"These aren't combat injuries," he said.

Frank moved closer, his experienced eye scanning the methodical arrangement. "Look at how they focused on the nervous system. The spine. Brain tissue. Whatever did this . . . they were looking for something specific."

"A weakness?" Torres suggested.

"Information," Popovich corrected, still taking readings. "This was a systematic examination of human biology."

"Research . . ." Martin said.

The word seemed to echo through the room.

"These radiation readings and patterns suggest technological origin, but far beyond anything in our database," Popovich said.

"Eva, what about you?"

"Classified, Sergeant," replied the AI.

"What the fuck," Frank chimed in with an angry snort. "Classified tells me Shield Command has seen this before, and if they have, we need to know everything—"

"Cage, hold on," Martin ordered. He turned to Popovich. "Corporal, give me a theory here."

"My theory?" He shrugged. "Whoever did this was using tech we don't know about, or . . . it wasn't human."

Martin's tactical training kicked in. "Alright, Marines, combat intervals, we're heading to get that data. Torres, six. Frank, Popovich, center mass. Watch the shadows, whatever did this could still be here."

They advanced toward the bridge, every shadow now a potential threat. The access corridor was blocked by a sealed pressure door with scorch marks around its edges.

"I'll blast through," Rodriguez said, already pulling demo charges. "Give me two minutes."

"Make it one," Martin replied. "Rest of you, defensive perimeter. Nothing sneaks up on us."

The charges blew with a controlled thump. The bridge beyond was a wreck: panels torn open, screens shattered, seats ripped. A gaping hole in the main viewport offered a view of the Gauntlet's twisted energy patterns outside.

"Jesus," Frank muttered, sweeping his sector. "Looks like they were trying to keep something out. Or in."

"Hold security here," Martin said. He strode inside, while Frank moved down the corridor to hold sentry.

"Sarge," Rodriguez called from the nav station. "Nav terminal's destroyed, but look at this." She pointed to a comm panel still functioning. A light blinked steadily from a recorded message.

The voice that emerged through static turned Martin's blood cold: "We found the way . . . through the Gauntlet . . ."

The message cut off.

"Popovich, see if you can get all of it," Martin said.

Popovich stepped up and worked the settings for a few moments. "Okay, I think I got it."

He pushed the screen, and the same voice crackled from the speakers.

"They showed us . . . the paths between . . . you have to see . . ."

Martin had heard enough. "Popovich, I want that data extracted, asap."

"I wish I could tell you that was possible, but everything's broke dick, Sarge," Popovich said from the nav terminal. "We're going to have to find the backup drive."

"Where?"

"Probably in engineering."

A scream erupted from somewhere deep in the ship—raw and terrified.

"Contact!" Frank snapped. "Port emergency airlock!"

Martin was already moving. "Form up! Tactical advance!"

Their rad sensors began chirping as they approached the airlock section. The same frequencies they had detected in the medical bay but stronger now.

"Those readings again," Popovich warned. "But the source . . . it's moving."

"Moving where?" Martin demanded.

A long pause. "I can't track it . . . but it appears to be inside and outside of the vessel."

They found the airlock two minutes later, and Martin raised a hand. The squad slowed to a halt. Through the reinforced viewport, a figure wearing a shredded CSF naval uniform pressed tightly against the far hull.

"He's alive," Frank said quickly. "But not sure he has all his marbles."

The man inside rocked slightly, arms wrapped around his knees. Blood streaked his face from a gash across his forehead, but it was his eyes that made Martin tense. He had seen the wild look before of someone who had broken from the horrors of combat and space travel.

"Corporal Hayes," Popovich read from his partially functioning scanner. "*Squanto*'s navigation specialist."

Martin tapped the comm button to communicate. "Corporal, my name is Sergeant Kelvin with Terminator Platoon, 2nd Squad. We're here to help you and retrieve data you transmitted."

Hayes continued to rock, not even looking up.

"Who's still here, Corporal?" Martin kept his voice steady, like he was talking to a spooked animal. "What happened to your team?"

"The Hollow," Hayes whispered back, his gaze still on the deck. "They came through the walls. Not solid . . . like shadows but not shadows. We found it. The stable route." He laughed a broken laugh that turned into a cackle. "But they were waiting."

Martin flashed quick hand motions that put the squad on defensive positions. Frank was already on guard, scanning the darkness with the beam from his rifle.

"What are the Hollow?" Martin pressed. "Why did they attack you?"

"Didn't attack at first . . ." Hayes pressed closer to the viewport, his bloodshot eyes desperate. "They tried to communicate, I think—"

"Communicate what?"

No response. Martin began to get frustrated. "You need to start talking, Corporal. Your fellow crewmates were torn to shit—and I, *we*, need to know what by if you want us to help you."

"Help me?" Hayes stared at Martin in a sudden look of awareness. "You don't get it, do you?"

"I want to understand. Who or what are the Hollow?"

"Gods—"

Hayes's blank stare returned, and he went back to rocking.

"Son of a bitch," Martin whispered. With a grunt, he turned to Popovich. "We need to get him out of there, safely. Prepare a suit."

"Understood, Sarge," Popovich said.

Martin tightened his grip on his rifle. "Rest of you, stay frosty. I'd say our pal here is nuts, but something diced up the rest of the crew, and I don't think it was him."

"I'd say that's a good guess," Frank said. "Not sure I want to meet what did it either."

Popovich stepped up to the hatch. "I'm going to cycle the airlock and get you out of there, okay? We have an extra EV suit—"

"No!" Hayes scrambled back. "Can't let them take me. Can't let them make me see again . . ." His hands found the emergency release. "The shadows . . . the empty places between spaces . . . I can't . . ."

"Hayes, you have to calm down," Martin said. "You're a Marine, for God's sake. Whatever's out there, we can protect you."

The corporal's bloody fingers tightened on the emergency lever. "You don't understand. The Hollow . . ." His voice dropped to a whisper. "I'm sorry . . ."

"Hayes, don't—"

The airlock's explosive bolts fired with a dull thud. Martin watched helplessly as Hayes was sucked out into the Gauntlet's twisted void and his body cartwheeled through the streams of bizarre energy.

For a long moment, no one spoke.

Then Eva's voice cut through their stunned silence: "Alert. Multiple radiation signatures detected. Moving patterns consistent with biological entities."

"Where?" Martin demanded.

"Outside the hull," Eva replied. "They appear to be . . . approaching."

"Outside?" Frank asked, disbelief clear in his voice. "How is that possible?"

"In the Gauntlet?" Rodriguez added. "Nothing can survive out there."

"Nothing we know of," Popovich corrected quietly, his sensors whirring.

The deck plates beneath their feet began to vibrate with a frequency that set Martin's teeth on edge. And in the viewport where Hayes had just vanished, shadows began to move against the Gauntlet's twisted light—shadows that shouldn't exist in the void of space.

CHAPTER SIX

"Multiple contacts," Eva reported. "Unable to determine size or mass. Radiation signatures increasing."

"Sarge, what do we do?" Torres asked.

"Weapons free. If they attack, we open fire," Martin ordered. "Form up on—"

Frank flinched as the shadows took form down the corridor.

The coppery, burned scent suddenly exploded into his helmet. Not a second later, a glowing figure flowed out of the deck, another through a bulkhead, and a third down from the overhead. Each one was roughly four meters tall and composed of geometric shapes that shouldn't have been able to connect yet somehow formed coherent wholes. Their surfaces caught and bent light like crystal, trimmed with that same otherworldly energy that filled the Gauntlet. But these things, whatever they were, didn't match the kaleidoscope of colors out there—these beings were translucent yellow and green.

Through a viewport, Frank saw a fourth being outside of the ship. This one had taken on a diaphanous shape, like a cloak that he could see through, the surface refracting violet and electric blue light like liquid prisms.

The creature suddenly shifted into what might have been considered a humanoid shape, with a featureless face that twisted toward Frank.

"Open fire!" Martin shouted.

Frank turned back to where the three aliens ahead of them had solidified into writhing masses of what appeared to be liquid mercury with an oily black sheen. Each one moved like living quicksilver, their fluid forms stretching and contracting as they surged forward.

He pulled the trigger, firing a burst at the nearest entity. Every round passed straight through as its metallic surface rippled and parted, the holes closing instantly like disturbed water. The being didn't even seem to notice.

The Hollow.

Hayes's words echoed in Frank's mind as he squeezed off calculated bursts, sending chunks of the liquid metal splattering across the hull. Those chunks re-formed, surging back into the creature.

"Fall back!" Martin yelled.

The squad put down covering fire, but the creatures didn't seem affected as the kinetic rounds punched through their forms and slammed into the armored hulls.

"Still no effect!" Frank shouted, already slapping in a fresh mag.

Popovich's sensors beeped. "Their molecular structure . . . It's shifting! We need to—"

One of the Hollow flashed right for Torres. Its flowing form extended what might have been a limb. The appendage passed straight through Torres's armor and into his chest. His scream over the comm made Frank's blood run cold.

"Get back!" Rodriguez opened up with her X-15 plasma cannon, the superheated matter illuminating the corridor. Where the plasma hit, the Hollow's fluid surface bubbled and steamed, then droplets of its metallic form scattered before flowing back together.

"The plasma!" Popovich shouted. "It's affecting them! Rodriguez, keep firing!"

She adjusted her X-15 cannon's settings, increasing the plasma density. The Hollow withdrew from Torres, its mercury-like mass contracting as it retreated.

Torres collapsed against the bulkhead as Frank moved to help him, expecting to find him dead—but as he reached down to grab Torres, the Marine pushed Frank back.

"Don't!" he shouted. "It did something inside of me . . ."

There was terror in the younger Marine's eyes as Frank tried again to help him.

"Felt like liquid ice inside my chest," Torres said, stammering. "Like it was searching . . ."

More of the Hollow emerged through the walls. Frank counted six now, but it was hard to track due to their speed. They moved like time-lapse waves.

"Torres, get up!" Martin ordered. "We're falling back. Rodriguez, cover our six! Popovich, find me a way to hurt these things!"

The squad retreated down the corridor, Rodriguez's plasma fire keeping the Hollow at bay. But only barely. Every time the superheated matter forced them back, they simply flowed through another bulkhead and emerged in new geometric formations of glass.

Frank had fought pirates, rebels, even Chitins, but this . . . this was something else entirely. Nothing in his training had prepared him for enemies that could ignore solid matter. He thought of Sarah and Lily waiting on Mars, and for the first time in his career, the real fear of not making it home gripped him.

Through the torn hull of *Squanto*, the Gauntlet's twisted energies cast strange reflections off the Hollow's liquid metal surfaces.

"I'm running low!" Rodriguez shouted.

"The radiation signatures are changing," Popovich reported. "They're reacting to something."

"Less science, more shooting," Martin snapped. "We need to get to engineering."

Torres stumbled, and Frank reached out to help him.

"Wait." Rodriguez held up a hand, studying her weapon's readout. "Popovich, what frequency are you picking up from them?"

"Multiple bands, but the strongest is in the quantum range that—"

"The plasma." She adjusted her X-15's settings. "If I match the frequency . . ."

The next Hollow that flowed through the bulkhead met a precisely tuned plasma burst. Instead of dispersing, the superheated matter clung to its mercury-like surface. The entity's fluid form contracted violently, droplets of its substance scattering before it retreated through the wall.

The burned scent grew more intense.

"That hurt it!" Frank couldn't keep the excitement from his voice.

"Rodriguez, show me those settings." Popovich's fingers flew over his instruments. "If we can match the—"

"Later," Martin cut in. "Engineering deck, now. Before more show up."

They moved in tight formation through *Squanto*'s twisted corridors, Rodriguez's modified plasma fire keeping the Hollow from overtaking 2nd Squad. But Frank could see her power cells depleting with each shot. They weren't going to have enough juice to fight their way to engineering and back to the *Hyperion* with the data.

Another entity materialized ahead, its black-silver mass flowing across the ceiling like liquid mercury in reverse. Rodriguez fired, but this time the Hollow didn't retreat. More emerged through the walls, their fluid forms merging and separating like drops of oil in water.

"They're herding us," Popovich said. "They don't want us to get the data."

"We have to," Martin said. "Whatever *Squanto* found, it's the key to finding the way through the Gauntlet and understanding what these creatures are."

"Sarge, get them to engineering." Rodriguez squared her shoulders. "I'll hold this junction."

"That's not happening." Martin's voice was steel.

"With respect, Sarge, it is." She was already advancing toward the intersection, plasma cannon at the ready. "Someone has to keep them off your backs, and I've got the only thing that hurts them."

Frank saw the resolution in her stance. Saw her checking her power cells—maybe enough for two minutes of sustained fire. She had already made her choice.

"Rodriguez . . ." Martin started.

"I'm right behind you." She managed a grin. "Now move your asses and make it worth it—you can name a route through the Gauntlet after me if I don't make it."

The first Hollow flowed through the deck at her feet, its metallic mass rising up like a tide of living mercury.

"GO!" Rodriguez shouted, her back pressed against the corridor bulkhead.

The first wave of Hollow surged toward her, their liquid metal forms merging into a tide of writhing silver-black. Her X-15 barked, the superheated matter catching one entity mid-flow. The alien's surface boiled, scattering into a thousand metallic droplets that rained against the walls.

Martin turned with Torres and Popovich, but Frank hesitated.

"You drunk still? I said move it, Sarge!" she yelled. "I got this!"

Her cannon's power cell indicator was already flashing red. Maybe ninety seconds left. They both knew it.

Two more entities flowed through the ceiling, their fluid forms stretching down like mercury waterfalls. Rodriguez adjusted her aim upward and sent the plasma cutting through them. The superheated matter made their surfaces splatter and steam, pieces of their liquid forms exploding outward, only to begin re-forming a moment later.

Frank nodded his respect, then ran with the others. Rodriguez's voice came through their comms, a string of curses in Spanish punctuated by plasma fire. Then a scream of defiance that made Frank's chest tight.

"Come on, you liquid metal bastards! Come get some!"

More plasma fire. The ship's superstructure vibrated with each blast. Another flurry of shots, then . . . silence.

Frank halted with the squad as they reached the engineering deck's main access. Torres nearly collapsed as they sealed the pressure doors. Frank could feel the deep thrumming of his heart firing like an automatic weapon.

"Eva," Martin called as they reached the core housing, his voice rough. "Status of Lance Corporal Rodriguez?"

The AI's pause seemed to stretch forever. "No life signs detected in that section."

Torres lowered his helmet and cursed. The young Marine had been closest to Rodriguez, the two of them always sharing jokes in Spanish that drove Martin and Frank crazy. Now Torres looked lost, but his grip on his weapon remained steady. Ready to make the Hollow pay.

"Popovich." Martin's voice had gone cold. "Get that data. Fast."

"Working on it." The tech specialist's hands dove into the backup systems, fingers flying over connections.

But they were already out of time.

Through the viewport, Frank watched more of the liquid metal forms begin flowing through the ship's structure like beads of sweat from flesh. Ten of them now, their fluid bodies merging and separating as they moved. The Hollow were no longer trying to herd them away.

They were coming to finish what they had started.

Frank raised his useless rifle, thinking of Rodriguez going down fighting. "Let's make sure she didn't buy it for nothing."

CHAPTER SEVEN

Martin stood behind Popovich as he continued to work on retrieving the data from the backup core. The creatures kept to the outer edges of the engineering chamber, dancing around the equipment cautiously. By now, Martin had gotten used to their stink. It was bad enough that he might have shut off his helmet filters, but the smell was also a good warning when these entities were around.

"Popovich, I need options here," Martin said. "Any way to slow these mercury bastards down?"

"I don't know, I don't know, fuck—" Popovich's voice filled with panic.

"Sergeant," Eva said over the comms. "*Squanto*'s environmental systems are failing. Coolant lines are rupturing due to quantum interference."

"Not helping, Eva." Martin grunted.

"Actually, Sergeant, it might be. The liquid nitrogen in the coolant system is currently at minus two hundred degrees Celsius. I would advise trying to freeze the hostiles."

"Excellent idea," Popovich said.

"Where's the nearest feed line?" Martin asked.

"Over here." Frank slammed his rifle butt into a marked panel, exposing the pressurized line. "Hey, Martin, you got your TacRec handy?"

"Now is not the time for—"

Frank grinned and fired into the nitrogen line, his recorder flashing as it documented the blast. The pressurized gas exploded outward in a white cloud just as the first Hollow flashed toward him. The liquid metal entity hit the supercooled air and froze mid-motion, its mercury-like surface crystallizing into a twisted sculpture.

"Say cheese, motherfucker!" Frank said. He turned for a selfie, then pulled his handgun and fired it into the dome of the frozen creature. Pieces of debris exploded away.

"Cage!" Martin shouted. "Get your ass over here!"

Frank rushed back to the squad as the frozen Hollow began to vibrate.

"Get out of the way!" Torres yelled.

Hunching down, Frank got below the burst of bullets as Torres opened fire. Chunks of the creature shattered off in all directions.

"Got it!" Popovich yanked the data core free just as a Hollow flowed through the engineering deck behind them.

Martin grabbed Popovich and yanked him away from the liquid metal entity that whipped two solid metal limbs right at the Field Science Marine. This time not to explore his insides like Torres, but to cut him apart like the other Marines from *Squanto*.

"Move!" Martin fired a burst that shattered both of the limbs off. They plopped to the deck and squirmed, then made a slithering return to the creature.

"Back to the *Hyperion*!" Martin ordered.

Frank fired into another nitrogen line, sending out clouds of the mist.

They almost made it to the hatch, when Torres stumbled. Martin caught him as his legs buckled, feeling an unnatural cold radiating through both their armor. Torres's breathing came in sharp, painful gasps over the comm.

"Oh god," Torres choked out. He grabbed his chest. "Something's inside of me."

Martin tried to steady him, but Torres's body locked up.

Through the younger Marine's visor, Martin could see frost crystallizing across the inside of his helmet. Torres's eyes were wide with terror.

"My legs," Torres whispered. "I can't feel my legs anymore."

"Popovich!" Martin called. "Something's happening to him!"

The tech specialist rushed over with his scanner. "His core temperature is dropping rapidly. Cellular structure is changing. Whatever the Hollow did when it touched him, it's not just affecting his nervous system anymore. It's rewriting him at a molecular level."

Torres tried to move, but his arms were going rigid now too. Ice crackled across his armored joints. "It's like needles in my blood. Moving through me . . ."

"What the fuck's the hold up?" Frank yelled between blasting apart new lines.

Martin flinched as he turned back to Torres, noticing silvery lines spreading beneath his skin. The veins in his neck took on a metallic sheen, bulging outward.

"Open the hatch, Popovich," Martin barked.

Popovich did as instructed, swinging it open to the connecting corridor. Martin grabbed Torres as Frank caught up.

"Help me carry him," Martin said.

Frank got on one side and Martin on the other, and they hauled Torres down the passage.

Behind them, two of the Hollow burst through deck plates with liquid grace. Their mercury-like forms merged and split, creating an ever-shifting barrier between the Marines and their escape route. Martin could hear them now—a strange harmonic vibration.

"Eva," Martin said into his headset. "Status of the *Hyperion*?"

"All systems operational, Sergeant. But I am detecting multiple contacts attempting to breach the hull. Quantum readings are off the scale. These hostiles appear to be coordinating."

"Pull back and wait until we get to the hatch."

"Understood, retracting *Hyperion*."

Clanking echoed through the ship, and a vibration rumbled under their boots as the bridge disconnected.

Torres convulsed suddenly, his armor creaking as whatever was inside him spread. A sound escaped him: half scream, half metallic resonance.

"Leave me, I won't make it." He gasped, his voice distorting. "No . . . *Kill* me."

He collapsed to the deck with Martin and Frank both exchanging a glance. But neither of them were willing to give up on him yet.

"Not happening." Martin tried to lift him again, but Torres's armor was completely locked now, frozen solid from the inside out. The younger Marine's skin had taken on the texture of brushed steel, spreading across his face.

"I can feel them . . ." Torres's voice cracked into something that sounded almost robotic. "I know what . . . what they want."

Behind his visor, Torres's left eye transformed, the brown iris bleeding into liquid silver. Tears of mercury ran down his cheek as the other eye began to change.

"The data," Torres managed, though his throat was more metal than flesh now. "Has to get back. Has to warn . . . everyone. They're not what we think. Not attacking. Trying to . . . con—"

"Popovich, how far to the *Hyperion*?" Frank asked.

"Two hundred meters . . . oh shit."

As Martin and Frank dragged Torres around the corner, they saw what had stopped Popvich. He backed up as two more Hollow dropped out of the overhead. The liquid metal forms gathered and blocked their path to the hatch. Another entity flowed behind them. They were herding them into a kill box.

Torres's armor began to ripple, taking on the same fluid properties as the Hollow. Where his hands gripped Frank's arm, the metal seemed to flow between them.

"So cold . . ." Torres stammered, his voice now a chorus of harmonics. "I can't . . . hold . . . leave—"

Another convulsion cut off his words. His remaining human eye met Martin's.

"We're not leaving you," Martin insisted, but he knew it was too late now for Torres. Whatever was happening to him was too fast to stop without medical intervention. He wasn't even sure if it was possible to save him at the best facilities back home.

Torres broke free from Martin's grip and reached down to his hip.

"No!" Frank shouted.

Martin also tried to stop him, but Torres was too fast, drawing his pistol and pointing it at the side of his helmet. A crack sounded, and blood burst against the interior visor.

His body spasmed. As more of him transformed, his armor melted into his changing flesh. Popovich and Frank both backed away, staring at their fallen comrade just like Martin. He finally snapped out of it, remembering he was in charge of their lives.

Martin looked for the hatch behind the two Hollow creatures drifting toward them. There was no way they could make it there. But there was another way off the vessel.

"Button up, we're going for a space walk," he said. "Eva, port side, get ready for extraction, pronto!"

"On my way, Sergeant."

Martin pushed Popovich and Frank back the way they had come toward the closer hatch. When they rounded the corner, Martin froze at a guttural human scream that didn't seem possible.

It was Torres, screeching in an ethereal, otherworldly resonance.

But how could that be after he had put a bullet in his head?

"He's still alive," Frank said.

"No, that's not Torres anymore," Martin said. "Move it, Cage."

They ran. Behind them, the sounds of combat echoed through *Squanto*'s corridors. Not weapons fire, but the clash of liquid metal forces tearing into each other. Martin tried not to think about what was left of Torres back there, tried not to hear the alien song that had replaced Torres's voice.

Martin focused on the airlock not ten meters ahead—their way back home. But more of the alien creatures flowed through the bulkhead farther down the passage, mercury-like forms creating an ever-tightening noose.

Cornered, Martin decided to improvise.

"Popovich, you got an M412?" he asked.

Popovich pulled a cylindrical device from his tactical vest. "This isn't going to stop them, and the blast will cause massive damage to the ship—"

"That's the point," Martin said. "We need a clean exit."

"Configuring for three-meter dispersion." Popovich twisted the charge controls. "Setting for five seconds."

Martin ducked behind a bulkhead with Frank as Popovich slapped the charge to the hull.

"Hope you know what you're doing," Frank said.

"Here we go!" Popovich shouted.

Behind them, Hollow closed in, three of the beasts drifting toward them in translucent form. They were seconds away from being able to attack with solid slate arms.

Seconds too late.

The M412 detonated with a fierce blast. Hull plating disintegrated in a perfect circle. Atmosphere howled outward. The Marine's suits instantly sealed for complete vacuum, polarized visors snapping shut as emergency systems engaged, magnetic boots clamping down to the deck.

The force hit like a hammer and tugged on their armored rigs.

Martin watched in fascination as the Hollow reacted—their liquid metal forms stretching into impossibly thin streams, trying to anchor themselves against the pull of space. Some of them fragmented into clouds of metallic droplets before re-forming, their fluid nature even more apparent without gravity's constraints.

"Eva!" Martin shouted over the roar of escaping air. "Emergency evac on my mark!"

"Warning: hull breach has compromised *Squanto*'s structural integrity. Detecting cascading failures in multiple sections. You have approximately forty seconds before total structural collapse, but first you must submit containment protocols."

"Fuck containment protocols," Frank cursed.

"Override containment protocols!" Martin shouted. "Now!"

Popovich stood ready to jump. But Frank pulled back, eyes locked on Torres's writhing form that scrambled over the deck not twenty meters away from their position.

"Cage!" Martin grabbed him. "Ship's coming apart!"

The hull groaned, stress fractures spreading like dark spiderwebs through the corridor. Torres's transformed body stood, jerking, his helmet ripped away, his face no longer even remotely human, nor the scream.

Martin didn't wait any longer. He yanked Frank toward the breach and into the void.

CHAPTER EIGHT

The harsh lights of the decontamination chamber on *Armistice* made every scrape and bruise on Frank's body stand out like a map of their escape. His hands wouldn't stop shaking as he watched silvery decon mist coat his skin.

He could still smell the coppery, scorched stench.

Next to him, Popovich methodically scrubbed his arms for the third time, muttering equations under his breath like a prayer. The corporal's eyes were wide, haunted. He'd stopped talking after they were pulled aboard the *Hyperion*, after watching Torres's transformed body fade into the darkness of space.

Martin just stared straight ahead, letting the automated systems do their work.

None of them had spoken since returning to the *Armistice*. The silence hung heavy, broken only by the hiss of decon sprays and the soft whir of scanning equipment.

"Commencing deep tissue scan," the medical AI announced. "Please remain still."

Frank closed his eyes as purple light washed over him. Behind his eyelids, he saw Torres's face again—watched that liquid silver creep through his veins, watched his friend dissolve into something inhuman.

"They knew," Popovich said suddenly, his voice barely audible over the machinery. "Shield Command. They had to know something was out there."

"No shit. Eva even knew with her classified bullshit." Martin's words came out flat.

"The quantum readings I took . . ." Popovich continued, scrubbing harder at his arms.

"I don't want to hear it now."

"Then when?" Popovich's voice cracked. "They're going to bury this. Everything we saw. Everything that happened to Torres. All they care about is that map showing safe passage through the Gauntlet."

"Let them try." Frank's voice was harsh. "Two Marines died to a hostile alien species. That doesn't get buried."

"First contact," Popovich whispered.

The decon cycle ended with a harsh buzz, but Frank could still smell the lingering scent of the Hollow. He pulled on his fresh uniform, catching his reflection in the chamber's polished wall. He barely recognized himself. The man staring back had aged years in hours.

"Molecular scan complete," the AI announced. "No sign of contamination. Though further observation is recommended."

"Observe this," Frank muttered, flipping a security camera the bird.

They finished getting ready, went to the hatch, and waited for fifteen minutes before the AI finally cleared them. The hatch cycled open to reveal a junior officer waiting with a tablet. Her eyes widened slightly at their appearance, then quickly smoothed into practiced neutrality.

"Colonel Daugherty will see you now," she said.

They followed in silence, their boots echoing through the *Armistice*'s corridors. Crew members stepped aside as they passed, averting their eyes. Some whispered behind their hands. Frank caught fragments: ". . . only three survived . . ." ". . . something in the Gauntlet . . ." ". . . classified . . ."

Rumors traveled fast on a ship.

A pair of Marines from 4th Squad saw them coming and leaned against the bulkheads to make room for them.

"Sarge," said a private named Tate. "We heard about . . ."

Martin cut him off with a sharp gesture. The Marine fell silent, but his eyes said everything. They'd all lost friends before. But this was different. This felt wrong.

The closer they got to the briefing room, the colder Frank felt. He could see it in his squad mates too—the way Popovich's hands kept moving like he was still taking readings, the rigid set of Martin's shoulders. They all knew what was coming. The questions. The lies. The official story that would bury the truth along with their friends.

The junior officer stopped at the hatch to the briefing room. She opened it, then stepped back. Martin glanced over at Frank but let his eyes do the talking. *Don't say anything stupid.*

Frank snorted.

The briefing room felt smaller than Frank remembered. Daugherty stood at a porthole, watching Mars below. The data core 2nd Squad had retrieved from *Squanto* sat on his desk like a black box of secrets.

"Welcome back." Daugherty didn't turn around. "I've reviewed the preliminary data. Along with the . . . incomplete mission logs."

"Incomplete, sir?" Martin's tone was carefully neutral.

Now Daugherty did turn, his face unreadable. "Quantum interference corrupted most of the visual records. Convenient, some might say."

"Nothing convenient about it, sir." Frank couldn't keep the edge from his voice. "We lost two Marines out there. Good Marines."

"Three rescue teams before you," Daugherty added. "All good Marines. More than likely to the same hostile alien species you encountered. Which is why what happened out there needs to be handled . . . carefully."

"You mean buried," Popovich said.

Daugherty's eyes narrowed. "I mean classified, Corporal. There's a difference. We can't risk panic throughout the colonies."

"What about Torres's family?" Martin demanded. "Rodriguez's parents? They deserve to know how their brave children died."

"They will know their children died heroes." Daugherty picked up the data core. "The official record will show they were killed in action defending CSF interests against hostile forces. Which is the truth."

"Just not all of it," Frank muttered.

In a regular unit, mouthing off to a colonel would mean serious trouble. But ESOTs were different—their brutal selection process and classified ops created a tight-knit community where rank mattered less than trust.

Rather than issue a reprimand, Colonel Daugherty narrowed his eyes. "Something to add, Sergeant Cage?"

Frank straightened. The cold in his chest had turned to ice. "Both Hayes and Torres were saying something about the Hollow warning us—"

"Of course they were. We invaded the territory of an intelligent life-form that does not want us there. This isn't the first time, nor will it be the last. The galaxy is a big place, Sergeant."

Frank scoffed. "We have also underestimated new species before, and this one, sir, is the most advanced I've ever encountered on any mission." He cleared his voice, taking a second to calm himself after Martin shot him a glare.

"Sir, I recommend looking into what they were saying—this warning," Frank finished.

"Our experts have reviewed the footage," Daugherty said smoothly. "The medical report has already been filed. Two Marines suffering from extreme trauma, hallucinating as their bodies shut down."

"Bullshit." The word was out before Frank could stop it.

That pushed the limits on Colonel Daugherty's tolerance. The temperature in the room seemed to drop as he walked over with his steely gaze on Frank.

"Watch yourself, Sergeant. I understand you've been through an ordeal, but—"

"You don't understand anything," Frank cut in. "You weren't there. You didn't see what happened to Torres. What those things did to him. They didn't just kill him—they *changed* him."

"Why didn't it change you then?" Daugherty asked. "You all passed decon."

"Cause we were lucky as fuck."

"Frank," Martin warned, but Frank was past caring.

"We need to know what the Hollow were warning us about."

"How is it not obvious to you?" Daugherty asked. "They don't want us to invade their territory. Simple, but guess what, they haven't seen the strength of the CSF Marine Corps, now have they?"

Daugherty's expression didn't change, but something flickered in his eyes. Recognition? Fear that he was wrong?

Before Frank could be sure, it was gone.

"What if it's something else?" Frank pushed. "What if there is something else out there worse than the Hollow?"

"An interesting theory, Sergeant." Daugherty's voice was ice. "One that won't appear in any official record. Am I clear?"

Frank's jaw clenched. He gave a single sharp nod, feeling like he was betraying Torres and Rodriguez with the gesture.

"Good." Daugherty's smile didn't reach his eyes. "You're dismissed. And gentlemen? Take a few weeks of leave. You've earned it."

Frank turned to go, Popovich at his heels, but Martin halted when he heard his name.

"Staff Sergeant Kelvin," Daugherty said. "A moment."

"Sir," Martin said.

Frank looked back as the hatch started to close. Through the narrowing gap, Frank caught Martin's eyes. In that brief look, he saw everything—the weight of command, the burden of keeping secrets. Martin wasn't staying for a deeper briefing.

He was staying to make sure his men kept their mouths shut.

The hatch sealed with a final click.

CHAPTER NINE

"Da-da-da!" Lily bounced in her stroller, pointing at a holographic display of an arid African desert. Frank smiled, crouching down beside her. A week had passed since the mission to *Squanto*, since Torres and Rodriguez, but his one-and-a-half-year-old daughter's excitement still cut through the darkness that followed him home.

"That's right, princess. Those are elephants." Frank made a trumpeting sound that sent her into fits of giggles. "They used to roam all over Earth."

Sarah smiled but then frowned. "I can't believe they are extinct."

"I'm sure we can bring 'em back if we want, using 'science,'" Frank said. "Maybe someday."

"Yeah, maybe someday."

They continued down the path between the displays.

The wildlife biodome stretched around them, a perfect replica of Earth's lost rainforests, along with real plants. Bright morning sunlight, artificial but still very warm, filtered through the dense canopy above. Mist systems kept the humidity high, and somewhere hidden in the foliage, speakers played the calls of extinct birds.

Frank pushed the stroller along the winding path, listening to Lily's running commentary of babbles and half-formed words. She was talking more each day. He'd missed so much while deployed in the past, but she still lit up every time she saw him.

He heaved a discreet sigh, grateful that he had returned from *Squanto* with his life.

Memories surfaced from the mission: Finding the dissected Marines. Rodriguez sacrificing herself. Torres changing into a monster . . .

Sarah looked back at Frank, but he managed to break free from the grip of his thoughts.

Lily pointed. "Bird, bird!"

"Those are butterflies, sweetie," Sarah said as they approached a new viewing area. In this display, iridescent butterflies fluttered between exotic flowers. "Lily, look at all the colors!"

Their daughter squealed, straining against her stroller straps. Frank unclipped her and lifted her into his arms, then carried her closer to the display. The butterflies' wings caught the light, scattering it into impossible patterns that reminded him of . . .

No. Not here. Not now.

"You went away again. You sure you're okay?" Sarah asked softly.

"Sorry." Frank bounced Lily gently. "Just tired."

She didn't push, but he saw the worry in her eyes. The same look she'd given him when he'd woken up shouting three nights ago, clothes soaked in cold sweat.

"Ba!" Lily pointed at a small reptile darting between plants. "Ba-ba!"

"That's a gecko, sweetie," Sarah said. "Can you say gecko?"

"Ba!"

Frank laughed. The sound surprised him—it felt rusty but real. They continued down the path, past more holographic displays showing Earth's vanished majestic big game. Lions. Tigers. Wolves. Creatures that now existed only in labs and as holograms.

The path opened into a wide plaza with a water feature at its center. Other families sat on benches or spread picnic blankets on the artificial grass. Children played while their parents watched. All of them safe behind the biodome's thick walls, protected from the harsh Martian reality outside.

On the horizon, Frank could see the giant pyramid-shaped terraformers working silently. It would still be years before they transformed the planet into anything habitable enough to bring back any of the animals in the displays around them.

"Want to take a break?" Sarah asked. "I packed those muffins you like."

They found a spot under a real tree. Frank set Lily on a blanket with his daughter's favorite toys—soft blocks printed with animals and numbers. She immediately began sorting them by color, her small face scrunched in concentration.

"She's so smart," Frank said. "Takes after her mother."

"Thanks, but she takes after you too."

"That's a scary thought. God help us if it's true." Frank grinned playfully at Sarah, who knew he was kidding.

She pulled out a wrapped muffin from her bag and handed it over to him.

"Oh man, I love these things," he said.

A metallic chime from an environmental system cycling rang out as he unwrapped the plastic over the moist muffin. He instantly stiffened at the silver rods that sprayed mist into the canopy across the plaza, appearing in the light like liquid metal. A coppery scent hit his nostrils.

Frank clenched the muffin, squishing it.

"Frank?" Sarah's voice pulled him back. She'd taken his hand without him noticing.

"I'm okay." He squeezed her fingers with his other hand. "Really. Just tired."

Lily chose that moment to toddle over and present him with a blue block. "Da!"

"Thank you, princess." He pulled her into his lap, breathing in the sweet smell of the baby lotion Sarah was diligent about applying.

"Which block is an elephant?" he asked. "Point."

She searched the toys with intense concentration. Then she pointed at the block displaying an elephant while babbling seriously as if explaining its significance. Frank let her little voice wash over him, anchoring him in the present. In this moment with his family.

Sarah leaned against his shoulder, and for a while they just sat together, watching their daughter explore her small world. Other families came and went. The artificial sun tracked across the biodome's ceiling. It was almost possible to forget they were on Mars. Almost possible to forget what waited out there in the darkness between stars.

The peaceful moment shattered from a familiar voice calling out.

"There's my favorite little Marine!"

Martin approached from a path, looking strange in civilian clothes instead of combat armor. He wrapped Sarah in a warm hug, then crouched by the blanket.

"Hey there, General Lily." He tickled her behind an ear, earning a delighted giggle. "Getting bigger every time I see you."

Lily grabbed his finger, studying it with the same intensity as her blocks earlier. Then she reached down and grabbed the elephant block.

"El-fuhnt," she babbled as she held it up.

"For me? I'm honored." Martin accepted it solemnly. "She's so smart, unlike—"

Frank snorted. "Go ahead, say it, 'unlike her old man.'"

But Martin just smiled, not in one of his usual a-hole moods, it seemed. Quiet Martin meant he was nervous, and that made Frank nervous.

Sarah laughed. "You should see what Frank tried to dress her in yesterday."

"The dress I got her?" Martin asked.

"Yeah, with tights, and a scarf." She shook her head.

"That was tactical camouflage," Frank protested. "Got to prep her for her first date."

"She's a year and a half old, Frank."

"Can't start too young."

Martin chuckled. "I'd hate to be the guy that meets you for the first time . . . I'm still waiting for Terecia to tell me she has a boyfriend."

"She's twelve now?" Sarah asked.

Martin had to think about it. "Not yet, June twelfth."

"How are your kids and Lucia?"

"Doing okay."

There it was again, the hesitation and relative silence Frank continued to notice when Martin was asked about his family. Things must have been worse than Frank thought.

"You still taking Thomas to that game?" he asked.

"Yeah," Martin said with a nod.

"Good, that will be fun."

"Looking forward to it."

The banter still felt normal. Almost too normal after everything they'd been through. Martin must have felt it too, for his smile didn't quite reach his eyes.

"Mind if I borrow your husband for a minute?" he asked Sarah. "Marine stuff."

"Of course." She gathered Lily into her arms. "We'll go see if we can find those butterflies again. Wave bye-bye to Uncle Martin, sweetie."

Lily waved, still clutching her blocks. Frank watched them head toward the butterfly garden, Sarah pointing out colorful flowers as they went.

"You look like shit," Martin said once they were out of earshot.

"Thanks. You're not exactly calendar material yourself."

"You sleeping?"

Frank shrugged. They both knew the answer.

"I can still smell those things, and Torres," Frank said.

"Maybe you should talk to someone about it."

"Fuck that, I'd rather stick my dick in a blender than go to a shrink."

Martin chuckled but then grew serious.

"You obviously haven't heard the news, have you?" he asked, voice dropping.

"What news?" Frank asked.

"Shield Command just announced they are deploying the first vessels through the Gauntlet."

"You got to be fucking kidding me."

"Nope. Full push—three colony barges packed full of supplies, people, animals, plus support research vessels, and a third of the armada to defend them. The works. Just announced an hour ago."

Frank watched his wife and daughter standing in front of the butterfly display, both of them smiling, oblivious to what was out there—just like the people on those ships would be.

"Shield Command's going to establish a permanent CSF naval station in the Lort System. Biggest ever built, been in the works a while, I guess." Martin paused. "We don't have orders yet, but I expect we'll be on a security detail."

Frank's stomach twisted. The image of Torres's silver-threaded veins flashed through his mind. Shield Command was pushing right through, completely ignoring the threat out there, and bringing along a lot of innocent souls that had the right to know.

"We got to stop them," Frank insisted.

"That's why I'm here, brother."

Frank raised a brow.

"You can't stop them," Martin said firmly. "Shield Command knows what they are doing. They will be cautious—"

"Cautious? They are sending—"

"Everything that is needed, Cage," he said even firmer. After glancing around, Martin lowered his voice and added, "Our experience didn't just help find a route through—it helped prepare weapons that can defeat those things."

"Those *things* nearly killed us all, after slaughtering almost the entire crew of *Squanto*, not to mention countless other vessels. And Shield Command thinks it's a good idea to send out thousands of souls."

"Twenty-five thousand," Martin said coldly. "This has all been planned since the first probe came back after discovering the Lort System."

"I should have known."

"Look, I'm not saying I agree with it, but our job isn't to agree or disagree, it's to follow orders. And I wanted you to be prepared that we're going to be getting new ones soon." Martin sighed. "Best way to protect people is to be ready to fight."

Before Frank could respond, he heard Lily babbling. Sarah approached with their daughter in her arms.

"Sorry, but I just heard someone talking about the Lort System and some big colonization mission that was announced," she said.

Frank nodded.

"Oh . . . that's why you're here, isn't it?"

"Yeah," Martin confirmed.

"Wow." Sarah shifted Lily's weight to her other arm, smiling in the process. She looked at Frank with excitement. "Maybe we could go. A whole new system, a new future for us and Lily. They'll need medical staff . . ."

Frank froze, completely blindsided by her enthusiasm. But then again, it made sense. She had talked about leaving Mars for a long time. They both had.

Their small, cramped apartment, the bad schools and poor sanitation. Olympus Colony wasn't a good place to raise a child. Neither were most colonies on Mars, and Earth . . . Earth was a hellhole.

"What do you think?" Sarah asked.

Frank saw the hope in his wife's eyes that were unaware of the vast darkness that lay between here and there. Unaware of the Hollow that waited in that darkness.

"Maybe someday," Frank said.

"Yeah, best to see what they find first," Martin said. "Make sure it's safe."

Sarah looked at them in turn, curiosity, and perhaps realization in her features. She knew Frank well enough to know something was up.

"I need to get going," Martin said. "Good to see you, Sarah. Bye, Lily."

Lily smiled but then put her head on her mother's shoulder, letting out a sigh of exhaustion.

"We better get back to the apartment," Sarah said.

Frank picked up their things and then put Lily into her stroller. She fell asleep before they even got out of the biodome. On the train ride home, he watched his daughter's sleeping face and thought about Torres's final warning. About the things that flowed like liquid metal through solid walls. About what was waiting out there.

And suddenly, he started to worry not just about what the aliens would do to the fleet, but what they would do if they somehow found their way here, to Mars.

If that meant Frank heading out to fight them again, then so be it.

Some things were worth dying for.

Some things were worth keeping secrets for.

And some things—like the silver tears that had run down Torres's face as he changed—were worth remembering. Because Frank knew now: the Hollow were waiting, and humanity was about to charge right into their domain.

J.N. Chaney is a *USA Today*–bestselling author with an MFA in creative writing. He fancies himself quite the *Super Mario Bros.* fan. Chaney migrates often but was last seen in Las Vegas, Nevada. Any sightings should be reported, as they are rare.

Nicholas Sansbury Smith is the *New York Times*– and *USA Today*–bestselling author of more than forty novels with two million copies sold. Prior to his writing career, he served at Iowa Homeland Security and Emergency Management, an experience that inspired many of his story concepts. A two-time Ironman triathlete, he enjoys running, biking, and hiking. He also loves traveling, especially to his cabin in Northern Minnesota, where he weaves many of his tales. Sansbury Smith lives in Iowa with his wonderful wife and their son and daughter.